Lynsdale Ray

Lynsdale Ray

Hugh and
Colleen Gantzer

NIYOGI
BOOKS

Published by

NIYOGI BOOKS

D-78, Okhla Industrial Area, Phase-I
New Delhi-110 020, INDIA
Tel: 91-11-26816301, 49327000
Fax: 91-11-26810483, 26813830
email: niyogibooks@gmail.com
website: www.niyogibooksindia.com

Editor: Gita Rajan
Cover Design: Nabanita Das
Layout: Sarojini Gosain

ISBN: 978-93-83098-58-3
Year of Publication: 2015

This is a work of fiction. The names, characters and incidents portrayed in it are the work of the authors' imagination. Any resemblance to actual persons, living or dead, events or localities, is entirely coincidental.

Printed at: Niyogi Offset Pvt. Ltd., New Delhi, India

OVERTURE 7

- The Prince of Wales 9
- Lucia 21
- London 32
- Portsmouth 46
- Captain Hamish McGregor 59
- Barney Gun 69
- Adam's Bridge 81
- Elihu Yale Sahib 91
- Major Stringer Lawrence 103
- Coja Petrus Uscan 112
- The Blooding 121
- Thomas Didymus 127
- Ann Hawkenian 138
- The March 151
- Arcot 160
- Aga Shawmier Sultan 175
- The Camphor-wood Chest 187
- The Portrait 197
- The Bait 207
- Convergence 223
- Pre-nuptials 232
- The Wedding 243
- The Hooghly Pirates 253
- The Himalayan Offer 268

CODA 285

OVERTURE

This is a historical novel about John Lynsdale of Bath, Madras and Calcutta set largely in India in the turbulent 18th century. We have used historical events and personalities as inspirations for the incidents and characters in this book. We have, then, fleshed out this skeleton of facts with our imaginations. We have tried to ensure that there is no resemblance between our characters and any person living or dead. As for the events, they, too, are largely, figments of our imaginations.

There could, however, be unintended convergences.

Mankind has not changed much since the 18th century. In fact there has, clearly, not been much change since writing began. The Bible is still a very relevant international bestseller and Shakespeare's characters still behave in a startlingly 21st century way. As the old song puts it

It's still the same old story
The fight for love and glory.
A case of do or die.
The fundamental things of life,
As time goes by.

Having said that, however, we must emphasise that any apparent connection between the British Royal family and John Lynsdale's wife, Ann *nee* Hawkenian, is purely coincidental.

We created Ann's lineage long before genealogists revealed that the infant Prince George had an Indian Armenian ancestor.

Hugh & Colleen Gantzer

The Prince of Wales

I stand looking out over my kingdom.

Dawn-light has begun to glitter off the thermal springs bubbling in the blue valley below me. Steam rises from them, merging with the mists blowing down from the high snow-fields.

Snow never falls on the valley though it settles on the glaciers behind me. Those great, slow, rivers of ice descend from a mysterious smoking mountain, melt into the braided streams that water the valley and also create the two great rivers cutting deep gorges that moat the valley.

On the far side of the gorges rise the soaring cliffs from which huge birds fly, quartering the sky. The sun, appearing above the rimrock, touches their wide wings, glitters off the streams and village ponds, shimmers on the green paddy fields.

Now farmers have begun to appear, trudging out of their shingle-roofed villages. A few are already at work: some ploughing behind their heavy, black, plodding buffaloes; others planting; a small group of men and women harvesting their golden grain: rice, wheat, barley. And fruit: apples, pears, plums, peaches, apricots; and grapes grown on trellises behind every home.

Crops flourish all round the year because there are only two seasons in this hidden place: a balmy spring flows into an early summer and back again. The protecting cliffs and the hot springs create this gentle climate. The web of glacier-fed streams and rivers irrigate the fields and orchards all round the year. This is why everyone in my dream valley glows with quiet contentment accepting the price that this hidden valley levies on them.

There's always a price for a glimpse of Paradise.

But I don't know the price, or the name of my valley, or its location in the high mountains. All I know is that it lies behind a grove of wild alders concealing the pass they call Sangali La.

And though I see it all, I hear no sound: it is a vision living in my mind, beautiful, moving, but eerily silent.

This is the dream that has haunted me, over and over again, from as far back as I can remember. I know now that all children have to dream: dreams are as important to them as the air they breathe. Dreams cushion them from the realities of life. I needed the comfort of my dream because, though I was christened John David Albert George Yale-Lynsdale, I had been given my grandfather's surname, not my father's. That worried me.

When I was six or seven I asked Canker Nair, 'Canker-chan, who is my father?'

Canker was a slim, golden-skinned Indian who lived with us because he was my grandfather's comprador, the person who advised him on his business affairs in India. More importantly Canker was my friend because he always answered my questions, if he could. And if he couldn't he would say so, he wouldn't be evasive. And so I asked him. He looked at me for a long moment. 'He is a very important man.'

'Why doesn't he stay with us as other fathers do?'

'Because he's very busy. But he does come to Bath sometimes.'

'Have I ever met him?'

'Sorry, Johnny. I can't give you an answer to that just now.'

Then, one horrible day, when I was eight, I found out.

It was a grey, rainy, morning and I was playing indoors with William Cowper. We were the same age and my grandfather often had him brought down from the Westminster School in London to stay with us. William and I were in the hall when I heard the clip-clop of horses' hooves and the 'Whoa-whoa!' of a coach stopping. There was a blast of damp air as the door was flung open and a man in a wet cloak and a hood bounded in. My grandfather shouted, 'What the …' then his eyes widened and he bowed. Two men in livery entered and the cloaked man threw his cloak at them and said, '*Vere can ve talk*?'

His accent was strong and, from that day, I am revolted by a German accent. I will not try to imitate it.

My grandfather asked, 'What is there to talk about?'

'Much …' the man turned to his servants and barked 'Get out …' They backed out of the front door, closing it softly behind them. The room suddenly seemed very still, tingling like the air before a thunderstorm. 'Sit down, please …' the man said. He flopped into a chair and looked at me intently with slightly bulging eyes under almost invisible brows. Maureen O'Sullivan, grandfather's housekeeper, bustled in, curtsied, caught William and me by the arms, and tried to hustle us out. I shook her hand off and the man said, 'John will stay. You and the other child may leave.' I heard the door close behind them.

I looked at the man. He had a round, womanly face, a long nose, petulant lips and a soft and fleshy chin. He wore a powdered wig and smelt strongly of horses, leather, sweat and something I could not identify at first. Sour. It was fear.

The frightened man said, 'I have a son.'

'We all know that,' my grandfather growled.

The man flushed with anger and then he shook his head till his curled wig bobbed, as if to flick off his rage. 'You don't understand, Herr … Mr Lynsdale. Today, Augusta has given birth to a baby boy.' My grandfather started to rise from his chair, breathing hard. The man hurried on. 'It is my duty. I had to do it. The sheets of the bridal chamber have to be examined by the physicians. I have deferred it as long as possible but my rivals in the court have used that as a weapon against me to convince my father that I am impotent … let the child hear, he will understand in time, let him stay … that I am unfit to be my father's successor. The baby was made then. But let me tell you something … listen to me, please.' He stood up. 'Today I say, "John is my rightful heir and I will restore the Catholic faith and I shall get the Church to annul this farce of a marriage to Augusta."'

They say that a child of eight cannot understand many things. Perhaps they're right. Or perhaps I did understand most of it but my mind could not accept what the man was saying. I began to feel sick with fear and anger.

'Are you …' I heard myself asking in a quavering voice, '… are you … my father?'

I remember the man's eyes when he looked at me. They shone as if they were filled with tears. He bit his lip and nodded, 'Yes, John. I am. I am your father.'

'Then … why aren't you staying with us?'

'Because …' his voice choked and he sniffed and swallowed. He looked over his shoulder. 'Beau! Beau! You have heard?'

I remember all this. Or, rather, it is so clear in my mind that I must have remembered it but perhaps, as a child, I heard snatches of conversation and tales not meant for me and they were so important that I made them a part of my memory.

I remember the blast of cold, damp, air that swept in when the front door banged open again and Beau Nash barged in. He was the flamboyant Master of Ceremonies of Bath who had converted our town into the glittering social capital of England. He smelt of some strong oriental perfume but his clothes were drenched so he must have been standing outside all the time. 'I have heard, sire. Everything. And I shall remember every word.' He had a fruity voice.

'Is good. And to make sure that your memory remains clear, Beau Nash, I command you to erect before St. John's Court, the house we know which belongs to Mr Yale-Lynsdale … to erect a monument, a pillar, an obelisk. So all of us will remember that I keep my word.' He looked down at me and said, softly, 'I am Frederick Louis, the Prince of Wales, your father. One day, my son, you will be king.'

I didn't know what he meant. I only knew that if he could not give me the comfort of being a real father then I did not want anything else from him. So I shouted the first thing that came into my head. 'I want nothing from you.' I felt like crying with shame but I couldn't cry now. 'I don't want you to make me a king!'

The man … my father … stepped back as if he had been slapped. He looked at Beau Nash and at my grandfather. Out of the corner of my eye I saw Canker-chan step out from behind a curtain. Beau Nash and my grandfather were frozen, looking disbelievingly at me.

The blood rushed back into Beau Nash's face and he stepped forward, grimacing with rage. He raised his hand to strike me but before he could Canker-chan stood between us. He said, 'Do not touch the child, Mr Nash.'

The man … I found it difficult to think of him as my father … spun on his heel and, barking 'Come, Beau,' threw open the door and stepped out. It slammed behind Beau Nash and I heard the coach gallop away. Beau Nash strode in again. He sat down, thumped the table, and boomed, 'Listen to me, listen to me, I have a message from Mr Anver …' he looked around, savouring the impression he had made. 'Mr Anver loves the child even though the child does not love him. He has sent down his trusted men to guard the child, secretly. But beware of people with the accents of Saxe-Gotha. Augusta has learnt about the child and she wants him out of the way. Mr Anver feels that it would be best if the child left for some unknown place. But if he stays in Bath he must be confined to the house; the child must stay at home as much as possible. That is all I have been asked to say.'

Canker-chan shook his head in disagreement. 'That would be dangerous,' he said, softly. 'Hiding the child would attract attention. We have to be more subtle. Less obvious,' he advised. 'John should stay in Bath. And you should remove all restrictions on his movements. Let him meet as many people as he can. He is Bernie-chan's grandchild, his father was a distant cousin, lost in the East. No one will ask any more questions. And the more people he knows, and who know him, the easier will it be to spot strangers making enquiries about the lad. And I will teach him how to defend himself.'

Grandfather frowned. 'Will you make him a pugilist at such a tender age?'

'Fighting with the fists, Bernie-chan, is savage. It is not a skill, it is brute force. No, John's attackers will be defeated by their own strength. It is what we teach our children in my land to protect themselves.'

They all looked disbelievingly at him, then Beau Nash pushed back his chair, glowering. He sprang to his feet, fists balled, and shouted, 'Protect yourself, then, Canker!' and he swung at the slim Indian. No one saw Canker move, but he must have. Beau Nash flew off his feet and landed with a thud in the centre of the rosewood table. Canker-chan leant forward, extending his hand: 'I hope, I most sincerely hope, that I have not, in any way, hurt you.'

But Beau Nash's pride had been wounded more than his back. He growled, grabbed Canker-chan's hand and tried to wrench it. And then he screamed so loudly that Maureen O'Sullivan and William Cowper rushed into the room. Nash was sitting up in the centre of the table, surrounded by the others. His right arm hung at a strange angle and he was groaning, his airs and graces forgotten, his native Welsh cadence rising and falling in his voice. 'Oh my! Oh my! The heathen's broken my shoulder. What'll I do now … Ooooooh!'

My grandfather's face was purple with rage and he began to fill his lungs when Canker-chan said, very softly, 'It's not broken. Only dislocated …' and he reached forward, grabbed Nash's shoulder with his right hand, pressed his left against the collar-bone, and twisted. There was a click! And the shoulder was back in place.

William Cowper was so disturbed by all this that he began to shiver uncontrollably and had to be put to bed, and then sent back to London. He never returned to Shawclose.

The next day, I was admitted to the Rev. and Mrs Greenwood's Academy for Gentlefolk where I made many friends and led the life of a normal English child. I cannot forget that classes always started with the Rev. Greenwood intoning *Psalm 23*.

The Lord is my shepherd; I shall not want.
He maketh me to lie down in green pastures;

He had a strange, monotonous, way of reciting from the scriptures. I fell asleep during one of these sessions and was humiliated in front of the class. After that I kept my mind busy thinking about the girls and the things we might do on a lonely lane. Or I tried to build fantastic pictures of a dark valley filled with gibbering hob-goblins all feasting with me around a dinner table while my head dripped with oil and a large cup of tea kept overflowing. All this was triggered by the words:

Yea though I walk through the valley of the shadow of death
I will fear no evil;
For thou art with me; thy rod and thy staff they comfort me.
Thou preparest a table before me in the presence of mine enemies;
Thou anointest my head with oil; my cup runneth over.

We knew the words; we had memorised them; they sounded very reassuring even though we didn't really know what they meant. Biblical English rolls wonderfully across the tongue but it's not easily understood, particularly by children.

But in spite of what the psalm said, I did fear evil from the man who said he was my father though I never mentioned it to anyone. I wanted to forget about him. Canker helped.

Every weekday, from four to six, I entered our basement, now converted into an earth-floored gymnasium which Canker-chan called a *kalari*. Here, after I had massaged my body with herbal-oil, I learnt the callisthenics and lightning-swift responses of *kalarippayat*. Canker told me, 'You have started at the right age, when your bones and joints are soft and flexible. We shall take it slowly, allowing you to take long rests so your body learns to cope, to adjust.' And it was while I rested between bouts of training that Canker told me, over many years, about my origins and that of the Jacobite movement. Both arose, in a way, out of the great hatred that Catholics and Protestants felt for each other in Britain.

Canker told me that I was a Catholic like my grandfather and my mother. My father was a Protestant. Both the Catholics and the Protestants were Christians and yet they were fighting with each other to put their own king on the throne. The Protestants had beheaded the last Catholic king and installed a distant Protestant relative, from Germany's Hanover, on the throne. But the Catholics were still trying to change this.

And then Canker told me about my mother, Leo Anver, and my *genesis*, as he called it.

'Your grandfather worships blue blood,' Canker said. 'It is his one blind spot. And, I think, even then, he knew that the man they referred to, as "Leo Anver" was the Prince of Wales: the Protestant son of the Protestant king.'

About two years before I was born, grandfather got Beau Nash to invite him to the Lynsdale mansion, Shawclose. Here, something quite unexpected happened: Leo Anver and my mother fell in love.

Grandfather was furious, but he couldn't say why he was angry. In desperation he bellowed, 'He's not a Catholic and I will not have Protestant grandchildren!' He would probably have put mother in a convent in France but there were problems in India and the Company wanted him to sail for the East immediately.

He did the best he could. He extracted a promise from my mother that she would not see 'that man' in his absence, and he charged Maureen O'Sullivan with the task of chaperoning her very closely.

Maureen was true to her duty. She never let mother walk on the streets of Bath: she was always confined to a sedan chair. But my father was clever. He bribed the sedan chair-men and they carried love letters, of increasing passion, between the two. When my grandfather returned, after 18 months, the first question he asked was, 'Have you kept your promise to me, girl?'

'Yes, father.'

'Ah! So you've got over your folly …'

'No, father. I still intend to marry him and he still intends to marry me.'

'I will not permit it! The law will not permit you to defy your father!'

'There are some who are above the law. He will become a Catholic.'

There was not very much my grandfather could do after that. Besides, he probably felt that he was helping to put a Catholic on the throne.

They were married in a secret Catholic ceremony and began to live together, in a viner's cottage near Shawclose, whenever he visited Bath. A year after their secret marriage, I was born. And then, my father struck the blow that broke my mother's heart: the Palace announced that Frederick Louis, Prince of Wales, was marrying Princess Augusta of Saxe-Gotha, a Protestant and a German. My cowardly father had been too scared to mention his secret Catholic marriage to the king.

'Your mother never got over it,' Canker continued. He paused and looked at me. 'Now that you know who you are, how do you feel?' he asked.

'Angry. Helpless.'

'Anger is an emotion. Don't feel helpless. If you want to be a king, focus on your desire, drive it with your anger. And you will be king …'

As always, he convinced me. Why should I mope when everyone around me in Bath was enjoying themselves? There were buskers and jugglers in the Abbey Square, there were men and women frolicking together in the Baths, and Beau Nash openly kept a mistress in St. John's Court. We discovered that quite a few girls in the Academy welcomed our experienced ministrations and were prepared to give as good as they received, though it all had to be crowded into ten fleeting minutes of snuggle, quick fondle, a burst of relief if one was lucky, and depart. But it was far better than nothing at all.

Bath was blossoming like a girl on the verge of womanhood. Huge carts, creaking behind great dray horses, brought the soft, grey, Bath stone from the mountains. These were dressed and chipped and carved by armies of workmen from all over the land, many speaking an English which others found difficult to understand. They fought, called each other 'Dirty Papist' and 'Filthy Protestant', worked, and got drunk every night. Any one of them could have been an assassin, paid to kill me. But that didn't worry me. I was alert, brimming with confidence and energy thanks to my exercises in the *kalari* with Canker-chan. I was enjoying every minute of my new-found freedom.

Then, one day in '45, a liveried messenger from the Pump House … the place where the visitors 'took the waters' … delivered a letter to my grandfather. He still had it in his hand when I walked in. He spoke curtly as if he found it difficult to say the words, 'Before I could read this message about your father's imminent arrival, he came. He is waiting in the dining room along with your mother and Maureen O'Sullivan. Come on.'

They had drawn the curtains across the windows and lit only two candles. The room was full of deep shadows and flickering highlights. From the wall, portraits of my grandfather and the grandmother I had never met looked down. They had been painted by Joshua Reynolds and Thomas Gainsborough as grandfather had told me very often, adding with pride, 'They paint portraits of royalty and nobility.' But *Leo Anver*, sitting at the head of the table, under the portraits, looked neither royal nor noble. He seemed shrunk and frail in the huge, carved, ebony chair. The flame of a candle was reflected in his eyes and they looked like the eyes of an animal trapped in a cage.

My grandfather coughed and the Prince of Wales, my despised father, began to speak. His words came out flat and rasping and I had to strain to catch his words.

'The Catholics in the north have risen … against … against the King. They have started to march … they are marching … they are gathering people … gathering sympathisers … as they march. They are … I understand … that there are many und … I am sorry … and … and the King's advisers are … are very confused. Some say "Do this" and others say "Do that" and … and my father does not know … he knows not what to do …'

He seemed to run out of words. There were deep shadows on my grandfather's face but the golden light touched the faces of Maureen O'Sullivan and my mother: one filled with a scarcely suppressed elation, the other, my mother, looking at the Prince with so much compassion that I knew she still loved him. Her hand reached across the table but stopped short of touching his, and then my grandfather's voice rumbled out of the darkness.

'Thank you for telling us what is happening in the kingdom, sire; but what have we got to do with all this?'

The Prince of Wales … I found it difficult to think of him as my father … turned his head slowly to look at the old man. The flickering candlelight played on the bones and planes of his face: the roundness and femininity that had once weakened it had gone leaving a sharp gauntness. He looked like a cornered ferret: his bright eyes glistening every time he turned his head.

His gaze shifted to my mother. Very deliberately he stretched out his hand and touched hers, held it. 'Aquila …' he whispered, 'Aquila please make them believe … that I … that I love you and … and the boy. But … but I can no longer protect the two … the two of you … My men … the men who watched over you … have crossed over … they have joined the Catholic rebels …'

Again his voice faded away. He continued to gaze at my mother and their hands were locked together. Thoughts flurried in my mind. *Aquila the Eagle ... not really ... Aquilegia, the Columbine ... he had given her this flower plucked from our garden. My mother had pressed it in her prayer book. From then on he had called her Aquila. He must have loved her... then. This weak man must have loved her.*

Grandfather growled, 'Have you anything further to say … sire?'

The Prince looked up. 'Ja … yes … yes, I have this to say … I want your daughter … my wife … and my son … I want for you, John, and your mother … I want for both of you to go … now … to go to Catholic France. And I want for you to stay there till this matter is … is settled … once and for all … You will do it, Aquila?' On a rare occasion, after I had learnt that the Prince of Wales was my father, my mother had spoken of him. She had said that he always called her Aquila, the eagle, he was Leo, the lion; and I was the griffon, half eagle, half lion.

My mother continued to hold his hand but her eyes were downcast. The silence dragged on and on and I could hear the candles spluttering. I couldn't understand why the Catholics would want to kill us. I was a Catholic even though I had been sired by a Protestant.

I stood up. I did not trust this man, my weak father. 'My mother will stay here,' I said, firmly 'I will stay here. We don't need your protection.'

The Prince rose slowly and he almost looked like a king. He said, 'So be it …' He bent down and kissed my mother's hand long and lingeringly. Then he bowed and walked out of the room. My mother stood staring at the door, her eyes bright with tears. I looked away, very confused, heard the rustle of the ladies' skirts as Maureen O'Sullivan and my mother rose and left. Canker put a hand on my shoulder and whispered, 'I have had supper sent up to your room.'

When we reached the door, I looked back. Grandfather was holding the brandy decanter but it tinkled against the glass in his other hand because both his hands were shaking.

Lucia

News of the rebellion reached Bath two days later.

Suddenly, all festivities stopped and the Londoners were like bats scurrying and twittering in the light. Coaches crowded with people and luggage began to race out of the town. My mother, Canker-chan and I should have known better than to try and cross the street at that time. I heard the crack of a whip and the clatter of hooves on the cobbles and the huge, black, horses were upon us. I cried out 'Mother!' and raised my arm protectively. And then I was hurled across the street, thudded into a bath-chair, my mother sprawling beside me. Canker-chan helped us up and stared at the coach galloping helter-skelter towards London.

All Canker-chan said when we got home was, 'You'd have been run over by a coach. You and your mother would have been killed. You must be more alert, Johnny.'

Must I? Now even Canker-chan wanted to fetter me.

I was fourteen years old, bursting with energy. I wanted to do what my companions were doing all the time: throwing snowballs at fat men waddling in winter; skating with pretty girls; sneaking away for furtive encounters in the woods and the vineyard. My friends were exploring the world and their feelings towards it. But, suddenly, just when I had found my freedom, it had been snatched from me. I had to look over my shoulder, guard my mother. I did not know who my enemies were, but they were all around me, I was told. I had to escape or else I'd become like the other mean-spirited people of this small town. What use was reading, writing, and arithmetic if they didn't teach me to spread my wings? I had a vision of myself standing on a peak in a tropical land, wrapped in a cloak of silk and satin, swathed in a turban, throwing handfuls of gems to my subjects, prostrate and chanting at my feet.

The vision was so exciting that I rushed out of my room, down the stairs, and into the little room, before the *kalari*, where Canker-chan spent most of his spare hours.

It was strangely warm in here, possibly because it was directly below the kitchen where the fire never went out. It was a strange room in other ways too. Its floor, walls, and ceiling were made of inlaid wood. There was a low bed, he called it a divan, in the centre. It was covered with a spotless white sheet of pashmina: the soft, woolly, undercoat of shaggy Himalayan goats, he had once said. Beside the bed was a brass table with an earthenware flask covered by a brass beaker. At one corner of the room was a low, straight-backed, chair with a very broad seat. Canker-chan, dressed in a white shirt, a white sarong-lungi and a white waistcoat was sitting, cross-legged, on the chair, reading from strips of palm-leaf documents. Above him, bathing him with a soft light, was a brass oil-lamp. There was the faint, acrid-sweet, odour of burning coconut-oil from the many-wicked lamp.

He looked up as I entered, the light glistening off his high cheekbones and the smooth planes of his face. He didn't say anything.

'Canker-chan, I want to ask you something.'

He nodded his head very slightly.

'I want to be a trader in India. I want to learn all I can about India. I want to start now.'

He gazed unblinkingly at me, then, very slowly, he brought the hard strips of dried palm-leaf together along their retaining threads.

They clicked as they touched each other. He wrapped a length of red cloth around them, pressed on one of the wall panels near his elbow, placed the palm documents into the alcove that opened, and shut it. The panel seemed unbroken again.

'What is your dream, John? What is the vision you have of yourself as a trader? Describe it to me.'

I sat on the edge of the divan and told him how I had seen myself robed like an oriental prince distributing largesse to my subjects.

He waited till I had finished, then a little while more, nodded again.

'I have been waiting for this, John. So first, you must always keep in mind one single and most important thing.' He smiled slightly and shook his head. 'The people of the East are not savages. They do not need to trade with the people of the West. Your first duty is to convince them that you, and your people, and your country, are not savages. And to do this you must know something about their ways, their customs and traditions, their religions, their history, their language … You look worried, John.'

'How can I learn so much?'

'Because I can teach you. Because you have the black fire, sometimes called the coiled serpent, we call it the *Kundalini*. And because you are you. No, you don't understand. You must open your mind.' He rose in the effortless movement of the *kalarippayat* guru and flowed across the room to me: that is the only way I can describe his walk on that occasion. He put his hand on my shoulder and said, 'If you give people what they need, they will pay you for it; they will feel happier and stronger and so will you. Never be ashamed of trade, John. It is a sin not to trade with your talents. Avatar Jesus said so. Trade is the pumping heart of society and money is its lifeblood.'

I was confused. What had Jesus to do with all this? All I wanted was to escape from the centre of a storm but Canker was creating more storms within me. My head began to throb.

'Is money the only reason to live?' I cried out.

'No. But it gives you food, clothing, and shelter which are things all humans need.'

'And what of truth and beauty and honesty and justice?'

'Words for the disciplines which bind people together. But that is a little too much for you now. I shall teach you how to be a good trader, but traders are not made in classrooms. Learn all you can from the Rev. Greenwood, and all the *kalarippayat* I can teach you. Then I will take you to your grandfather's Company, and to the East India Docks in London. And out of these things you will become a good trader. That, I promise you.'

I believed him then but after a few months came the news that the French had taken Madras and trade with India almost ceased. The atmosphere in our house was one of oppressive gloom, every meal resembled a wake and Maureen O'Sullivan took to wearing black clothes which rustled like a widow's weeds.

But the capture of Madras also brought a new influence into our lives; or rather, into my life.

Among the services offered by the House of Lynsdale was the recruiting of artisans and craftsmen for the Princes of India. In '46 grandfather sent out to India, the famed gunsmiths Antonio and Carmen Parson-Verroneo. Not wishing to expose their only child, the seventeen-year-old Lucia, to the uncertainties of India, they had placed her in the care of a spinster aunt in Plymouth. In the Spring of '47 the aunt died. A distraught neighbour, to whom the girl had fled, had obtained grandfather's name from her and sent a messenger down asking him to take her in.

Grandfather had wanted to put her on the first ship to India, but that was quite out of the question. 'You wouldn't leave her to the tender mercies of the Froggies, would you?' asked Maureen O'Sullivan. She saw my grandfather looking thoughtfully at me; I had just turned sixteen. 'She can sleep in the room between Katherine's and mine: two good chaperones in a Catholic household. Besides …' certain that this would cap the argument, 'Katie's been looking poorly of late. A young girl around the house would cheer her up no end.'

That's how the 18-year-old Lucia Verroneo who called herself Lucia Parson, became a member of our household. She had dark hair, skin with a faint glow of gold under the surface, soft brown eyes, high breasts that seemed to have a life of their own the way they moved, and a throaty voice with a faint lisp in it. And I fell hopelessly in love with her from the moment I saw her even though I was told to call her 'Cousin Lucy.'

It was clear that she had warmed my grandfather's heart as well. He got a young painter named George Romney to come over every day and do a portrait of 'Parson's Daughter.' For me, however, Lucia's arrival changed my life. My studies in the Academy became interesting. I would do anything to win her, even if it meant working extra hard.

The Greenwoods remarked on the fact that '*John's application has improved remarkably having completed in a week tasks which take other pupils a month.*' All I really wanted to do was impress Lucia but, apart from a few pleasantries exchanged at the dining table, I couldn't get near her. Both my mother and Maureen O'Sullivan kept such a close watch on us that we were never alone. And then, quite unexpectedly, it happened.

One particularly warm day in summer, when the Academy was closed because the Greenwoods had gone to London, Maureen O'Sullivan called me. She seemed quite distraught. 'That silly girl, Lucia, has gone out without her bonnet. She'll be smitten by the sun. Here it is. Please take it to her.'

I was overjoyed, but I feigned reluctance. 'Can't you send one of the maids? I don't want to be seen walking down the road carrying a girl's frilly bonnet!'

'Stuff and nonsense! No more arguments. Run along now. She's gone to get flowers from the parsonage: we're expecting some of your grandfather's friends down from London. They're coming to dinner and there's so much to be done: I can't spare a maid. Off you go, John. And don't dawdle.'

I had no intention of dawdling: it was all I could do was not to run! The Parsonage was at the far end of the town, tucked away behind the Protestant St. Mary's Church. I was sweating when I came in sight of it and saw Lucia stepping out of the garden. She held a huge bunch of roses clasped to her bosom and, as I came near, she turned and said, 'Thank you very much. Ah! There's John with my bonnet.' She closed the gate behind her, and walked towards me, smiling radiantly. And then she said, very softly, 'Ah! My ruse worked. How difficult it is to get a moment alone with you, Johnny. Now, if you will put the bonnet on my head … Good. Reach out now, and take the flowers.' As I did so, she stumbled forward and my hands were full of her breasts. I stepped back, clutching the flowers. 'They are very beautiful, are they not, Johnny? And I don't mean the flowers! … But, yes, they are very beautiful red roses … Good morning, Mrs Carlyle … and it is possible we shall grow them in the Lynsdale house … that is enough for her to overhear. Do you know what the French say about roses? You don't?'

She nodded at the crusty old Mr Coleman hurrying by, a perpetual frown on his face. Then Lucia said, almost as if she was repeating a litany:

A white rose for virginity, a pink
rose for fidelity.
A red rose for passion.

She took a deep breath and I was fascinated watching her breasts rise and fall.

She resumed her normal tone. 'I have asked you to hold a bunch of red roses. You know what that means, Gian? May I call you Gian? I like you very much, verry, verry, much. You like me? Yes? You are blushing. That is so macho. To see a big man blush. You are a big man, Giano? A really big man? Ah! I see you get my meaning. Why do you wear your breeches so tight, Giano? I am all wet for you.

You know what it means when a woman gets wet? Men get hard, women get wet; it means we are ready to come together. Shawclose is in sight, Gian. Now we must hurry if this is to be done. I will ask questions. Nod your head for "Yes", shake it for "No." You wish me to come to your bed tonight, Giano? Good. You are worried that I have the French itch or that we will make babies? Don't worry: I am still a virgin but when I cast eyes on you it became a sore burden for me. You will get rid of it for me, won't you, my big Giano? And as for the other: I, too. don't wish to be trapped. I have plenty of the cordial my mother takes at the right time every month. She calls it her cordial but I know what it does. She got the recipe from her former classmate in the convent who was the mistress of the King of Abyssinia. Or it may be Austria. I forget … Good morning Mr and Mrs Brown. What a beautiful day … Poor Mrs Brown doesn't need the cordial. Look at her face. She hasn't had a real man for many years! So, here is my plan. Between your room and Uncle Bernard's room there are two spare bedrooms. All rooms have connecting doors. Tonight, we will leave early after dinner. Your grandfather and his friends will drink and smoke and then the guests will return to the Inn, your grandfather will return to his room and fall into a deep sleep. When everyone is asleep I shall go to the bathroom opposite the spare room next to uncle Bernard's and then I shall walk into the spare room, and through the two connecting doors, into your bedroom. Those connecting doors are always unbolted but I shall make double sure this evening. And tomorrow it will be the same thing, and tomorrow and tomorrow till you are tired of me. But I don't think you tire easily, my bull. We have arrived. You will open the door for me and smile and lift your hat and then enter the house behind me and hold your hat low in front of you, and I shall thank you.'

'Why should I hold my hat low?'

'You will see. Now smile and open the door.'

I smiled and opened the door and lifted my hat to the lady. And as the lady lowered her parasol, she touched my hard member and squeezed it, licked her lips slowly, smiled, and floated gracefully into the house. I had to keep my hat low till I was able to rush, awkwardly, up the steps, aching and throbbing.

It happened exactly as she had planned. And the first time was so bad that I can't bring myself to even think of it. She was a virgin, and she bled slightly, and gasped, but she was also very skilled, very patient and I burst out all over her, I was so excited and scared. But the next time was better. And the third time I was able to last and last till she was shuddering and moaning so loudly that I thought everyone would wake up. But the walls of Shawclose were thick and the curtains were heavy.

I don't know how often we made love that first year. We were very discreet and since I continued to do extremely well in all my lessons, everyone was very happy. There were other reasons to be happy, too.

In my seventeenth year the Treaty of Aix-la-Chapelle was signed and the French agreed to return Madras to us. There were celebrations in the streets of Bath and the whole family went out to see them: fireworks and mummers and happy crowds including people down from London. My royal father could have been in Bath on that day, but I doubt it; he certainly would not have been out on the streets.

We had just walked out of our front door, Lucy pressed closer to my side than the crowd warranted, when I felt an odd tingling sensation rising up my spine. I swung around and, without thinking, threw my mother onto the front steps and dropped, covering her with my body. I was a split second too late. The pistol must have gone off as she was falling. A bullet nicked my ear and lodged itself in the grey stone of Shawclose. The other grazed my mother's upper arm, and she screamed. But her scream and the shots were lost in the boom and roar of the fireworks blossoming in the sky. And so no one saw Canker-chan moving. One attacker had time to grunt, the other swore in German before his neck broke. Both lay at our feet, pistols still clutched in their hands.

The fireworks were still exploding in the sky when Canker-chan hustled us in, uttered a hurried explanation to my grandfather, told Lucia to bring hot water and Maureen to fetch some cloth and brandy. My grandfather just sat slumped in a chair, gasping, 'Good God! Good God!'

My mother's wound was superficial and the bleeding was soon staunched. We wended our way up the staircase, Canker-chan to his Comprador's Chambers on the next floor. On the way up Lucia said, 'John, can you get me a glass of water, please?'

When I brought a carafe and a glass of water and we were alone, she said, 'I want you tonight …'

'Tonight, Lucia? But …'

'I want you, I want you, I want you. My father's ship is due in tomorrow. And I want you to love me the whole night, all through the night. And you will come to my room because I want you to love me in my bed, on my Italian sheets, so that when I get to India, and when I get married, I can remember …'

She moaned and shouted and bit me and scratched and if it wasn't for the fireworks and the carousing in the streets, the whole house would have been awake. She was insatiable: a lithe, acrobatic, voracious animal …

The darkness was draining from the sky when I left her room. My grandfather was standing at his door, looking the other way down the corridor. I stood still. After a while he turned and went back in. I tiptoed past, touched my scratches and abrasions with Friar's Balsam from the medicine chest, waited for it to dry, then fell into an uneasy sleep.

Lucia was right. Her father came at midday, had lunch with us, thanked us all very effusively for looking after his little Lucia, and left with her.

After they had gone, my grandfather summoned me to the dining room, closed the door behind him. The only other person in the room was Canker-chan. Grandfather came straight to the point.

'John, you and Lucia have been doing what only a husband and wife are permitted to do. Do you deny it?'

I felt a hot flush spread over me. 'No,' I said.

'She is older than you, so you cannot be held solely to blame. Nevertheless, I must explain something to you. Or, perhaps, it would be better if you tell him, Canker.'

Canker-chan nodded and launched into a strange tale which, even today, I find it difficult to believe: except that I cannot disbelieve Canker-chan.

He said, 'This morning, sometime after ten, after they had removed the corpses, whom they believed had died in a drunken brawl … sometime after that, say about half an hour after, I was walking in the street when a sedan chair came near, and a tall and elegant man in a cape, a tall hat, and a scarf wrapped around the lower part of his face, got out and approached me. He stopped some distance away and said, "I know what you can do even to armed men, Mr Nair. My Lord and I have considerable respect for you …" his accent was cultured, French. "I am unarmed and I have a message for you. Can I come closer?"

'I permitted him to do so. He smelt of a strong perfume. "My Lord realises that he can never, never, ascend the throne of England. But he, and we, would like to see a Catholic monarch reinstalled. When such a move is bruited abroad, there will be a wave of support for the young king: English born, English bred, of the royal blood, and a Catholic. The Irish, the Scots, the Welsh, even the Catholic English … all will support his claim. So will France, Austria and all the other Catholic nations of Europe … What do you say Monsieur Nair: *Oui ou Non*?" "Yes or no to what, sir?" I asked.

'The man seemed annoyed. "Very well. I shall express it in so many words though such forthrightness goes against my training. Will you, Mr Nair, ask the 17-year-old son of Frederick, Prince of Wales, if he is prepared to become King John II, King of Great Britain?"'

Canker stopped talking and both he and my grandfather looked at me. I had been standing all along. I now drew up a chair and sat down, very slowly. I had difficulty finding my voice. 'I … I have not been trained to be King.' I shook my head. 'I do not want to be King … of England …'

There was silence for a moment, then grandfather rumbled, 'Very well. But I must also tell you this. There will be people who will try to kill you and there will be others who will try to crown you. It's not only your life that will be in danger. The lives of everyone associated with you will be under threat.' He paused. 'If Lucia, if the girl, is pregnant, if she is expecting your child, then she will be marked. You will have condemned her to death. Do you realise that your seed is fatal?'

I almost cried out then. Now even my love was poisonous. The dark fire stirred restlessly within and so I spoke out, rashly perhaps.

'Then there is only one thing I can do, grandfather. I must go away. I must leave England and go to another land,' I said. Thoughts swirled in my head: of both my grandfathers and the fortunes they had made; of Canker who was closer to me than my own father and who had spoken so lovingly of his native land and its wonders; and … yes I had to admit it to myself … of Lucia who had been dragged away from me. My mind was made up … I had to get away from England and its jealousies and hatreds and people who could discover my shameful origins. I cleared my throat, 'I must go to the land carved out by great-grandfather Elihu Yale, the land that has enriched you, grandfather; the land of Canker-chan.'

I took a deep breath as, suddenly, thoughts of Lucia swirled through my mind again. I blurted out, 'I must go to India …'

London

Leaving home was not as difficult as I thought it would be. But then it had taken me six months preparing for my voyage to India, so I had plenty of time to get used to the idea. We didn't tell anyone that I was going away. When Maureen O'Sullivan suggested that my grandfather should throw a 'going away' party, Canker advised against it.

'Why should we alert the Saxe-Gothas? Johnny will be far more vulnerable in London than he is here, even though many locals suspect that the Prince is his father.'

'Do they really?' I asked.

He nodded. 'You were brought into this world by the midwife, Mother Warfield. And since the Prince's own physician, Wolfgang Biergartener, was in attendance, she guessed who your father was. She was killed a few days ago because of a little rhyme she repeated about your birth, Johnny, and of about how the throne would fall if it became common knowledge. The Saxe-Gothas were furious.'

'A poem? About me?'

'Yes, it goes:

Rock a-bye baby
On the tree top

When the wind blows,
The cradle will rock.
When the bough bends,
The cradle will fall.
Down will come baby, cradle and all.

'You are at the top of the Hanoverian tree, but when the wind of rumour blows, the cradle … that's your secret right to the throne … will rock. If, however, the Jacobites bend the bough to get to you, then you and your claims to the crown of Great Britain will fall.'

I looked at Canker-chan disbelievingly. He and I knew that Mother Warfield had been a drink-sodden old hag. She couldn't, possibly, have made up something so subtle.

'She didn't make it up, Johnny. She was just stupid enough to sing it. The people who composed it wanted to send a warning to you and your more impatient supporters. If they shake the established order of things, you and your claims will be destroyed!'

I shrugged. Since I had no intention of stepping into that nest of vipers, their warning meant nothing to me.

Mother spent long hours in our little chapel praying, her face mottled by the light streaming in through the stained glass window. She had never talked much but she grew even more withdrawn now.

My grandfather became even more gruff and taciturn than he had been. But he was very generous about outfitting me for the voyage to India. He gave me cedar-wood chests, brass-bound and with enormous Chinese locks. Tradesmen came and I heard Maureen O'Sullivan's gentle Irish voice intoning as the maids packed my clothes.

I was too excited to sleep that last night at home. Grandfather had decided to accompany us to London: he said he had some work there but I felt certain that he wanted to see me safely on board the Indiaman. I saw the chests being loaded on the small diligence. This four-wheeled carriage had been ordered for the three of us with Patrick

Murphy and Ben Hackman sitting as armed guards and the burly Billy Forbes riding on a spirited grey Arab stallion which showed the whites of its eyes when anyone other than Billy approached.

Mother was asleep when we boarded the diligence at half-past three on a foggy, damp, morning. Or rather, Maureen O'Sullivan said she was asleep but when I looked up at her window, hazed by the fog, I thought I saw a pale face peeping out of the corner of the lace curtains, and a small hand waving. I waved back but, by that time, the face had vanished and my grandfather was growling his impatience and the black horses were snorting vapour in the chill morning air, their harnesses clanking and creaking. I never saw my mother again.

It was a long, foggy, lonely road to London and my heart pounded, expecting to be waylaid by highwaymen and footpads at any moment. But the rocking of the coach and my own tiredness caught up with me and, today, I don't remember much of the journey except that it was dangerous. Most of the roads between towns were unsafe, haunted by bands of brigands, tinkers, gypsies and people crippled by war and disease so we travelled by night when most of these miserable wretches were too cold to venture out. Even so, we were careful all through the long journey to London.

London shocked me. It was a dirty city full of dark alleys, choking yellow fog that left a trail of slime on the cobbled streets as if a fat slug had passed. The river, Old Father Thames, was an oily, grey-brown slither, bobbing with offal and other unmentionable things. But, in spite of all this, the week we spent with the Hogarths in Leicester Fields was exciting. William Hogarth was as brilliant as a sparkler on Guy Fawkes day.

Canker-chan must have asked him to take us round the grimier parts of this skulking city because, the second day we were there, Hogarth came bustling in, exploding words all around him.

'Mr Yale-Lynsdale is busy preparing for tomorrow. For the rest of us … the Stews. I'll show you the Stews. The viscera. That's the real London. Gin Lane and Beer Street. And I'll take Canker's advice.

I'll sketch and cut crude wooden blocks, and sell the prints cheap and coarse so that everyone can own a bit of the real London. What an idea! Canker, you old heathen, you're a genius! Where's Trump? Trump! Trump! Here, boy: we're off to see the gin-sodden harridans and the bloated beer guzzlers in the wilds of London …' and he stuck his head out of a window and whistled to a growler clopping past.

William Hogarth spoke in short, sharp, bursts, his snub nose and baby face bright and alert.

We tumbled out of the house, through the cold, grey, rain and into the growler, Hogarth's dog, Trump, yapping at our heels.

The cabbie cast a jaundiced eye on the dog. 'I don't take no hounds in my veh-i-cle, beggin' your pardon, sorr …'

'Don't beg. Never beg. And he is not a hound. He's a self-respecting pug. Aren't you Trump? We want to see the Stews. Take us to the Stews. You are familiar with the Stews, aren't you? I thought so. Get on with it, my good man, get on with it. That's a good chap!'

But the 'good chap' didn't drive fast enough for the painter. Hogarth rapped smartly on the roof of the cab and, when we stopped, swung out and onto the seat near the driver. We began to hurtle down the cobbled streets, swaying dangerously.

'What are the Stews, Canker?'

'Patience, Johnny. You'll find out.'

'But why are you taking me there?'

In the flickering lights of the street-lamps I saw Canker close his eyes. He breathed deeply and regularly. He was far away. Then the growler stopped and William Hogarth threw open the door.

'Get out gentlemen. Watch your step. Hold your breath. Stop barking, Trump, and stop sniffing. You'll choke!'

The stench was sickening: vomit and cheap alcohol and open sewers. The fog coiled through the smell, wreathed the street in a bilious haze. And the sounds poured out of it as if the gates of Hell had been opened: women cackling with wild laughter, men groaning and grunting. Every time a door was opened, shafts of light lanced out onto the slime-covered streets. Men and women, many half clothed, were lying in the wet roads and the gutters, many still clutching bottles. And even as I looked, a couple lurched out of a gin mill and filled the street with raucous laughter and shrill screams, as they tore at each other, ripping clothes, falling to the pavement, entangling themselves like bloated, copulating, swine. Trump barked and a drunk, sprawled on the road, swore and raised his cudgel. Hogarth stepped forward and kicked it out of his hand and then, for a good measure, kicked him on the jaw. The man belched and erupted yellow filth from his mouth. Hogarth leapt back in time and hustled us into the growler.

'Home, driver, home!' he gasped. The cab lurched, throwing us back in our seats, and went clattering over the cobbles.

'Why do they do it?' I asked. 'Why do they drink like that?'

Hogarth leant towards me and said, very softly, 'There are too many people on this little island, Johnny. They have no jobs, no hope of getting jobs. They seek forgetfulness from their misery. They would love to escape to a warm, sunny, land where they can vent their spleens on lesser creatures. It's the lure of the sun, pillage and dominance! But it's necessary! Ha! It's essential!'

'Why is it essential? How can misery be necessary?' I asked.

Hogarth stroked his dog for a while before replying. The fog had become viscid and sluggish, clinging to us in thick, sticky, tentacles, reluctant to let us go. Canker seemed to have been lulled to sleep by the rocking motion of the growler over the slippery cobbles.

'Because,' Hogarth said after a while, 'it is this misery that sends people away. It sent the Yales to Boston. Yes! Yes! I know all about them. Your grandfather told me. Then they came back because the natives resented their avaricious ways. Then Elihu fled to India where he made a fortune. To India. To America. Anywhere. Everywhere. They're so miserable here that other places must be better. Or so they think. They're willing to risk everything for a chance, only a chance, to lead better lives. The Power of British

Misery. I think I'll do a print about that.' He turned to me, grinning. 'Tomorrow, your grandfather wants to show you his London. But remember, John, his London makes a better living on misery than I do. I hold up a mirror in which we can see ourselves. The traders, however, trade on misery. Do you know that there are people who make fortunes trading on the prospects of misfortune!' Canker-chan had woken and was looking at us. 'Are you taking him to the underwriters, Mr Canker?'

'That is Bernard-chan's intention, I think.'

'Good. And when you go up there, Johnny, don't forget to take a deep breath. You have smelt the dregs of London's misery. Now smell the percolated essence of its wealth. You'll never forget it.'

I haven't.

The morning after we had visited the Stews, Grandfather took us to the rich, traders' area, of London. But our first stop was in a very strange place; more like an eating house than an inn. Portly, prosperous, men stepped out of carriages, waddled in as other, equally rotund men, waddled out. Many greeted my grandfather as he ushered us into a large, warm, room. The aroma of coffee lay like a coarse, brown, blanket over everything. Shafts of sunlight streamed in through the thick panes of glass, touched groups of men around scrubbed tables. They sipped steaming cups of coffee, smoked, talked in undertones, rustled sheets of paper, wrote, sanded documents, pocketed them, left. Other men entered and took their places.

'This is Edward Lloyd's Coffee House, Johnny,' Canker explained. 'The men at the tables are underwriters; they insure merchant vessels against loss or damage. Your grandfather has just visited one of the underwriters and is striking a deal.'

'Is there any risk to our ship, Canker-chan?'

'The sea is always hazardous, always dangerous. Storms and the corsairs of Algeria and Malabar, the pirates of the Konkan, the French. We're carrying a valuable cargo, Johnny. Bernard-chan wants to make sure that he won't lose everything if there's a shipwreck.'

'He'll lose you and me.'

Canker smiled and, for a moment, his face looked like a skull, grinning. 'The underwriters don't insure lives, Johnny. People are replaceable; cargo isn't. You must start thinking like a merchant. The Company runs on profit; nothing else matters.'

Grandfather joined us and said, 'I'd like you to come to the Company's headquarters in Leadenhall Street. It's a beautiful wooden structure but now it's become too small for us, so we'll have to pull it down. The world's largest company of traders is growing even larger. We have to make room for more writers … more Directors, I suppose.'

He was, obviously very proud of the Company's Headquarters but, to me, it was a number of large rooms filled with clerks sitting at high desks, and corpulent men with port-rich voices puffing at pipes or snorting large pinches of snuff. The heavy smell of stale tobacco, like over-ripe peaches, was oppressive. I had just turned around to leave when I caught a glimpse of my grandfather's face. It had that expressionless, bland, look that he assumes when he wants to conceal something that troubles him deeply.

I asked, 'Is something wrong?'

His lips smiled but his eyes were very serious. 'I've received some disturbing news. But let's behave as if nothing has happened. I'll tell you more about it when we're in a cab.' He waved one down when we stepped out onto the street, but Canker waved it away and asked us to get into the second one. He said, 'Leicester Fields, as fast as you can!' The driver whipped his horse into a gallop. Canker turned to my grandfather. 'The first cab was waiting for us. He refused to take a fare as we left the office and yet he trotted up to us when you raised your hand, Bernard-chan. Is someone laying a trap for us?'

'I'm afraid so. This morning, two foreigners came to the headquarters asking about the sailing programmes of my ships. But something about their manner and their accents alerted the porter. He asked them if they wanted the programmes of the ships belonging to the Mr Lynsdale with the moustache, Mr Vincent Lynsdale; or the white haired Mr Farrington Lynsdale. They seemed bewildered, spoke amongst themselves in a foreign tongue, and then said they'd return in the evening. I'm afraid that our hunters have found out that you, John, are due to sail out from Blackwall tomorrow. I'll leave you at Bill's and take the cab on to Blackwall. Be ready to leave for a fairly long coach trip at ten o'clock tonight …'

I was worried. We were supposed to sail for India on one of my grandfather's ships tonight but, obviously, he had had second thoughts about that. But where were we going on a 'fairly long coach trip tonight'? And wouldn't a coach trip be more dangerous than sailing? Canker-chan had sunk into a brown study. Hogarth had vanished on one of his mysterious trips leaving only his manservant Murray to look after us. He brought us tea and buttered toasts and left us alone.

After a while Canker opened his eyes and said, 'We will go by coach to Portsmouth and board an Indiaman from there. Portsmouth's a huge naval port and a lot of Indiamen pick up cargo, troops, bullion and some passengers from there. And it's not very far from London.'

'But he said it'll be a fairly long coach trip.'

Canker closed his eyes, said, 'We'll know soon enough,' and relapsed into a brown study.

The grandfather clock in the hall had just struck the half hour after eight when Murray entered, put his finger on his lips and, quickly, snuffed all but a single candle near the curtained window. A little later my grandfather came in, treading very softly, drew up a chair between us, and began to whisper. 'In a little while, three men will come in from the back door, carrying chests and cases. Murray will assist them to load it all, out of the front door, into a growler, and he'll return when they leave. A few minutes later we'll carry out our luggage by the back door, load it into another growler as quietly as possible, and be on our way to the Black Horse Coaching Inn where we will change into a post chaise. I'll tell you why we're doing all this when we get to the Black Horse.'

It all went exactly as he had described it and we didn't look at the three men who talked and laughed loudly as they carried their luggage out. We were not half as light-hearted because it wasn't easy carrying our chests out of the narrow back door and into the growler. The driver had his face muffled in a scarf and he neither glanced at us nor spoke a word all through the plodding ride to the Coaching Inn. When I started to ask a question, grandfather frowned at me so I kept quiet. He hurried us out of the growler when we reached the yard of the Inn as burly men materialised out of the misty darkness and started loading our chests into a yellow public post chaise. It was only when we were sitting in a low-raftered room in front of a blazing fire, and drinking steaming-hot tea laced with brandy, that grandfather spoke again.

'The Saxe-Gothas left you alone for many years because they thought that you were not a threat to them anymore. Now that they have learnt that you are leaving England they feel that you are going to France to revive the Jacobite movement and proclaim yourself the rightful heir to the British throne. They have suborned a man aboard my frigate the *Rajpoot Warrior,* on which you were supposed to sail at daybreak tomorrow. He has been ordered to assassinate both of you. The three men who came here, masquerading as us, will seize, blindfold, gag, render the assassin unconscious, bundle him into a sack, and leave him on the jetty at Blackwall with a label saying *Perishable Goods for Princess Augusta of Saxe-Gotha*. The sack will be covered under a pile of straw. Long before the assassin recovers and starts to struggle, the *Rajpoot Warrior* will be at sea …'

I saw the flaw in the scheme immediately. 'But if you planned to get rid of the assassin then why couldn't we have sailed in the frigate anyway?'

My grandfather sighed. 'Because sailors believe that there is a dangerous area just beyond the mouth of the Thames. They call it The Downs. There, suddenly and quite unpredictably according to them, ships become becalmed and they could lie for a week waiting for the winds to fill their sails again. This is where they are most vulnerable to being boarded by pirates and rapscallions from marauding ships waiting in the mist-banks.' He nodded his head. 'But you won't be on it!'

Canker spoke for the first time since we had boarded the growler. 'Where are we going now, Bernard-chan?'

'To an inn in Guildford. It's a little off the main coaching road so the journey will not be as rough. It's preferred by people who are not in a hurry and by many of the post-riders. We'll spend the night there. Tomorrow morning three heavily armed coaches will arrive in Guildford. One of them will be carrying bullion for Fort St. George, Madras. They were supposed to leave the day after tomorrow but I had their journey advanced by a day. By the time the Saxe-Gothas realise that their plan has gone awry, we'll be in the safety of the great Naval Dockyard of Portsmouth waiting to board the newest and best of my Indiamen.'

I looked at my grandfather with new respect. I had always tended to regard him as a rather slow-thinking, slightly pompous, old man: a good trader but not a quick-witted tactician capable of turning the tables on his enemies and mocking them in their defeat! I imagined the look on Augusta's face when she learnt of the return of her *Perishable Goods*! I burst out laughing. Grandfather looked at me, surprised. And then a slow smile spread over his face, a delighted smile, and he reached across and poured more laced tea into our mugs.

Grandfather and I had a substantial dinner of a rich broth, ox-tail stew with baked potatoes, and rhubarb pie. Canker had only the baked potatoes with a dollop of butter and the rhubarb pie. I remembered then that he never ate beef because of his religion. There were a lot of things that I would have to remember when I reached India. But that was many months ahead and I put the thought aside.

Next morning, out of the window of the post chaise, everything was new and exciting. I had never seen this part of England before and the jouncing of the carriage stimulated me unusually. Vivid images of Lucia returned and I felt her moving and groaning under me. Every clip-clop of the horses' hooves, every creak of the coach reminded me of the sounds of our passion. On a field, outside, a milkmaid flounced her skirts to straddle a milking stool. I got a brief glimpse of her legs and I stirred. She'd probably smell of cows and byres but she'd squeal and yelp vigorously when we coupled. I closed my eyes trying to still my raging thoughts, ashamed that my grandfather and Canker would wake and notice my flushed face. But the thoughts would not go way till I began, very deliberately, to breathe slowly and deeply. I noticed that Canker had opened his eyes and was looking at me. The mad rush of my thoughts subsided but they still flickered at the edges of my mind. The turmoil inside me could account for what happened when we reached Guildford.

From the moment I stepped out of the coach in the yard of *The Cinnamon Barque Inn*, I shivered though the inn seemed cheery enough: warm and brightly lit. The short, muscular, inn-keeper, Fred Ryder, was everything a welcoming host should be: apple-red cheeks accentuated by a mop of snow-white hair and a thick moustache and eyebrows framing eyes that twinkled as if sparklers were alight in them. His voice boomed and seemed to be on the verge of breaking out into uncontrollable mirth. He was also a compulsive talker as he laid out bread, ham, butter and cheese, a jug of pear perry, mugs and knives.

For a while the sound of his voice suppressed my inexplicable feeling of unease.

'My great-grandfather bought this Tudor inn. He called it the *Barque Inn* but my father added the word *Cinnamon* seeing as how most of the spice trade from India passes through here. I mean, it should really have been called the Cinnamon Bark … ha! ha! …' I heard his cheerful voice, and yet, I had this feeling of unease as if everything was not quite what it appeared to be.

I walked across the stone-flagged floor to the bar. It was shuttered and dark but, between it and a closed door, was a portrait of a woman in a white frame. I stepped closer and peered. She was dark haired, clothed in a white robe moulded to her body by the wind. Behind her was a landscape of broad-leafed trees and distant buildings with domes and minarets. It was too dark to make out her features and then the door opened and someone stepped out carrying a lamp. The light touched the eyes of the portrait: they were like glittering chips of amber. Then I saw the person standing in the door and my breath caught: it was as if the portrait had come alive: the same raven black hair, alabaster skin, the amazing amber eyes. My disturbing sense of unease increased and I began to shiver again. The vision reached out her hand and touched me and she said, in an oddly soft, deep, voice, 'You're cold, John. Let me lead you to the fire …'

I heard Fred Ryder saying that his late wife was Romany; that she died after giving birth to identical twin daughters, Megan and Gwyneth; that he allowed his childless brother, Al, to adopt Gwyneth. Then he said a very strange thing. 'Though Gwyneth is in Portsmouth, in my brother's *Pepper Pot Inn,* and Megan is here, in Guildford, they are still very close. very, very, close. Ain't that right, my pet?' Megan smiled and looked at me and I shivered again.

Grandfather asked, 'Do you have a particularly warm room in the house, Mr. Ryder? My grandson is cold.'

'I've made up his bed in the Cubby Hole,' said Megan, softly. 'I'll mix him one of Mama's sherbets.'

Fred Ryder boomed in explanation. 'The Cubby Hole is a cubicle bed behind the hearth. It's always warm and they say that's where Elizabeth slept when she was fleeing from Mary. When you slide the door shut, it merges with the oak wainscoting. And I certainly recommend Megan's sherbets: the recipes are in an old book which belonged to her mother's family. Megan grows her own herbs.'

The sherbet looked like pale green whey, and it had a spicy taste. I drank it, wished the others goodnight, allowed Megan to lead me to the Cubby Hole, took off my shoes and tumbled in. The goose-down bed was soft and warm and I fell asleep immediately.

I still don't know if what follows was a dream born of my lust for Lucia, or was real.

I hear the Cubby Hole door opening and then I am being undressed swiftly, confidently. Soft lips close on mine, a warm and naked body is pressed against me. Hands touch me skilfully awaking me to painful hardness and then I am enclosed in soft, pulsating, flesh.

'I need your maleness, John, to fill me, awaken me. Now ... now ... now ...' Silence. 'Again, John. I will see for you. A woman wants you dead John. Charge, charge, charge, meeeeeee. I am filled with power, almost to the brim, almost to the brim. Fill me again! I shall breathe life into you, John.' Soft lips move down, engulf me, moving, sliding, 'Ah-ah-ah-ah. I hurl pain at her. She writhes. Tomorrow John, you will meet Gwyneth. She and I are one, twins, created from the same egg. She knows whatever I know, feels whatever I feel. She has shared you with me, as, with me you have shared her. But she has pledged herself to another so she is reluctant to be with you though she, too, wants to tap the force of your passion. It's a very strong force, John, and people like us can sense it ....

It ends. I sleep deeply.
The three coaches with the bullion and armed guards came a little after the sun had dispersed the mist that had lain on the road. The Escort Sergeant strode up, saluted grandfather and said, 'Mr Lynsdale, sir, I have been asked to tell you that the cargo has been packed and delivered and the recipient was surprised to receive it. That is all, sir. And as soon as we have changed the horses we will be ready to leave at your pleasure, sir.'

My grandfather nodded as the sergeant saluted and marched away. The would-be assassin had been taken care of. I wondered when the Saxe-Gothas would make their next attempt.

The changing of the horses took longer than I had expected because each of the new mounts had to be inspected by the sergeant and his coachmen. Grandad and Canker went up to their rooms. I wandered around and found Megan sitting in a sunlit bay-window, hunched over a table. She held up a pack of cards and said, 'Touch them, John.' I did. She fanned them out quickly in a curious pattern, muttering something under her breath all the time. I had never seen cards quite like them: they had pictures of strange humans and grotesque creatures. She peered at them intently and then, when she heard footsteps in the hall she scooped them together and dropped them into a small drawer, covering them with a red cloth.

Canker walked up and said, 'We're ready to go.'

I was about to follow him when Megan put her hand on my arm and said softly, 'There's a shorter way through the garden.' I followed her out into a beautiful cottage garden with three hives of bees and an orange arbour. She paused in the arbour and pulled aside her neck handkerchief: her breasts were full and deep. She reached between them, drew out a small leather bag on a chain around her neck. She took something out of the bag and handed it to me. It was a gold ring with a small, spiralled, object on it. 'It's a fossil tooth of the horned whale. Wear it and your power will never leave you. It goes on the third finger of your right hand.' She blew into it, took my hand and slipped the ring onto my finger. It was a little loose. She blew on it again. The ring closed in and fitted snugly. Megan's amber eyes looked into mine, and then she laughed and was gone.

The hairs on the back of my neck were still erect when I got into the post chaise and we joined the other three carriages trotting down the road to Portsmouth.

At the end of the journey I saw her again. Except that it wasn't her.

Portsmouth

We spent most of the journey to Portsmouth in silence, lost in thought. The Escort Sergeant set a brisk pace, the horses were fresh, but the road was bumpy and so it was rather uncomfortable in the coach. We bounced along, looking out of the windows. I must have dozed for much of the journey with unreal and disturbing pictures of Megan flickering through my mind. But before I could pin them down, we were clattering through Portsmouth.

It was a strange and beautiful place. Clouds of smoke hung low and grey in the sky giving everything … the marshes, the river, the distant sea … the appearance of being covered in a thin film of quicksilver. This was, clearly, a sailors' town but though there were many of them about, they did not behave in the sort of unruly way I had noticed in London. They walked briskly, as if they each had a purpose. And even the brick and stone houses, though they did have a layer of grime on them, even they looked cared for. And then I realised that this was the biggest port, for His Majesty's navy, in all England. Things just had to be ship-shape!

We rumbled into the yard of the *Pepper Pot Inn.* There were many carriages of various types lined up in a neat row, ostlers were currying horses in the stables, a farmer was removing vegetables and milk pails from his cart. Two men hurried out of the inn, touched their caps to my grandfather, and asked, 'Mr Yale-Lynsdale and party, sir?' My grandfather nodded. 'Ah, sir, your coachman should have stopped at the front door. Mr Ryder has been expecting you.' They had hardly said that when a man who looked like a larger, stouter, version of Fred Ryder came hurrying out, wiping his hands on his apron which he then handed to one of the men who had greeted us.

'Mr Bernard Yale-Lynsdale! This is a great honour, sir. The Captains of many of your ships stay with us, sir.' He tended to boom, like his brother, but he didn't have the other's white thatch and white moustache. 'Al Ryder at your service, sir.' My grandfather was not in the habit of shaking hands with tradesmen and people of that ilk but I saw him look over Ryder's shoulder and then, absentmindedly, he extended his hand, his eyes still fixed beyond. I followed his gaze.

They had just stepped out of the back door of the inn and into the yard: one was a tall, striking, woman dressed in black and with her fiery red hair worn loose about her shoulders; the other was a buxom girl in a strawberry-coloured sack dress which emphasised her full breasts. I had no doubt that the girl was Gwyneth, Megan's sister.

Together, the woman and the girl had a magnetic presence, riveting our attention. And then they stepped apart and the spell was broken. The red-haired woman strode up to us with long, purposeful, strides, her dress moulded to her firm thighs with every step she took. She reached us, curtsied slightly and Al Ryder said, 'My missus, Branwen.' The girl came up, gave us such a deep curtsy that I saw half her breasts. She said, 'Mr Yale-Lynsdale, Mr Canker Nair, Mr John Yale-Lynsdale.' Men in leather aprons bustled up and began to remove our luggage from the post chaise. Ryder and the women led us in with Ryder saying, 'Mr Yale-Lynsdale and Mr Canker Nair we have given you the Admiral and Commodore rooms … we prefer naming our rooms rather than giving them impersonal numbers. They are at the end of a corridor and have their own small garden. The noise of the bar will not reach you, good sirs. For you, Mr John, there is The Bridge on the second floor with the best views of the harbour, Spithead and the Isle of Wight.' We stepped into the warm bar: all dark oak, copper and gleaming brass. Senior seafarers, with mutton-chop whiskers and wind-burnt faces, sat nursing their drinks. The room smelt of rum and tobacco. Ryder turned around and said, 'The Agent, Mr George Huish junior, Attorney and Town Clerk, has held himself in readiness to meet your honours. If you would like to receive him in say, half an hour, I shall send a boy to summon him.' My grandfather grunted his assent and then said,

'Mr Ryder!'

'Sir?'

'How did you recognise us?'

Ryder frowned. 'We've been expecting you, good sirs.'

'How so, Mr Ryder? We had not given prior intimation of our intention to seek accommodations in your establishment.' When grandfather was suppressing his anger he spoke in a stilted, formal, manner.

Ryder looked at his wife and daughter. Gwyneth said, 'I told father and mother.'

'Really! And who told you, young lady?'

'The post rider brought a message from Megan last evening. He probably passed you, on the way back, as you were driving in …'

I said, 'I saw a post rider galloping past.' Canker nodded.

When we were alone in Grandad's room, he admitted, 'I was worried about that. I thought the Saxe-Gothas had made enquiries about us.' He sounded relieved but when I stood at the window of my room, looking out at a superb view of the sea, I remembered that Fred Ryder had said, 'Even the post rider didn't stop.' Very odd! Certainly very odd indeed.

I decided to keep far away from Gwyneth and messages read in cards and in the flights of birds as the fairy tales said of witches. I had had enough of Romany spells to last me for a long time.

George Huish was a very interesting man. There wasn't anything he didn't know about Portsmouth, having succeeded his father who had been the company's Agent, Attorney, and Town Clerk from '31 to '46. He was soft spoken, excruciatingly polite, and a fastidious dresser. I never saw him in anything but a wig, a three-piece suit of coat, waistcoat, and knee breeches of wool worn over a linen shirt, and buckled leather shoes with a mirror-bright polish. And, for the week we were in Portsmouth, he never wore the same suit twice.

I spent a lot of time with him. Though at first sight Portsmouth had seemed to be a very disciplined naval town, on closer acquaintance I found that many of the people who infested the harbour were boors. I wasn't easy in the presence of Malays, rough-mannered Hessians, Swiss soldiers, Highlanders and the painted women from the notorious Spice Island who were their transient companions.

George Huish taught me much about the Company: its policies, the goods it dealt with, the passengers its ships carried.

I was leafing idly through his passenger manifests when a name caught my eye and my heart thumped. A little more than six months earlier two people had taken passage on the *Sussex* bound for Tellicherry on the Malabar coast. Their names were *Antonio Parson-Verroneo, Gunsmith and Lucia Antonia Carmen Parson-Verroneo, Spinster, Daughter of the above*. I tried to still the trembling in my hands and then took the book over to George.

'Do you remember these passengers?' I asked.

He thought a while and then said, 'Yes. They came with a letter of recommendation from your grandfather. They were supposed to sail from Blackwall but then they decided to embark from Portsmouth.'

'Do you know why?'

'Er … yes. They wanted to be on the same ship as Mr Gabriel Goldsmith, virtual owner of the famous GG South Indian and Himalayan Products Company.' He looked up and smiled. 'What a coincidence. Klaas Jansz has just come in. He knows something about them …' A blonde giant with a Viking beard and steel-blue eyes came striding up. When he sat on the Indian cane chair it creaked and I thought it would collapse under him. 'Klaas, John is interested in your story about Lucia Verroneo and Goldsmith …'

The giant turned his cold eyes on me. 'You are related to him or her? Yes?'

'Neither. Her parents left her with her aunt in England. When the aunt died they asked my grandfather to look after her till they could take her to India where they are working.'

'Ah! So you want to tell your grandfather that she is safe. No?'

I nodded. I was feeling sick because I knew how the story would end but I didn't realise quite how bad it would be.

Klaas threw back his head and bellowed with laughter. 'Ho! Ho! She is not only safe. She is rich … so I'll tell you and you can reassure your grandfather. It's like this …' He settled back in his chair and pulled out a clay pipe which he proceeded to fill with shag tobacco; tamped it down; lit it from a candle Huish had been using to seal some letters. When it was puffing to his satisfaction and the room was filled with clouds of harsh smoke he said, 'I was sailing my ship back from Tranquebar: it is a Danish colony on the east coast of India, not far from our trading posts of Pulicat, Sadras and Nagapatnam. I am Dutch, ja! So I had anchored in Kapstaad and was waiting to pick up some supplies and this other ship, the *Sussex*, was also anchored in the Bay. I have known Thomas Wallace, the Captain of the *Sussex* for many years, so I invited him over to dinner. Generally he's a quiet person …'

George interrupted. 'Very quiet. In fact his nickname is Sphinx Wallace.'

'Correct. But this time the Sphinx was bursting with news. He said that this girl, Lucia, had come on board with her father in Portsmouth and they had, specifically, asked for the cabin next to Goldsmith's. Yes, like that … Anyway, who are we to ask questions? But the whole thing became very entertaining for the crew. This girl, say 18-19, and this widower, say 55 maybe more, they couldn't keep their hands off each other …' I felt a knife twist into my guts but I kept a straight face. 'They started a lottery betting that this … how you say it? June-December? Ja! This June-December wedding would be celebrated on board with Wallace marrying them at sea. He didn't bet but he said he should have. Sure enough, before the *Sussex* reached Kapstaad he married them. Things became worse, or perhaps better, after that. Now they made love at all times and she was very noisy. She screamed and sighed and urged him on. And he grunted and groaned. Whenever Wallace's crew heard those noises they said "Gabriel's playing his strumpet!" Ha! Ha! …' I wasn't in a laughing mood, but I managed a smile. That bitch, Lucia. Wanting me to make love to her on her Italian sheets so that she could remember us. But before my sperm was dry she had seduced this old fogie, for his money. And that whore-master of her father had urged her on! I was beginning to seethe with rage and humiliation. And to think that I had wanted to search all across India for her. But more was to come.

'The next evening,' Klaas continued, 'the old bridegroom threw a party, buying up all the champagne in Kapstaad. And what a party! The food was great, but I don't drink, so I noticed things that other's didn't. Every time that little vixen thought no one was looking she touched her stomach as only an expectant mother would. And yes, she was expecting. She was probably pregnant when she came on board. So they must have known each other, like Adam knew Eve. Ha! Ha! … for some time. You sure, John, Gabriel did not fly in through her window in your grandfather's house? Eh? Ha! Ha!'

I stayed on for ten minutes or so after that and then I walked back to the Inn. If Lucia was expecting a child before she embarked then only I could have made her pregnant. She had been a virgin before we made love that first time. Was that why she had trapped Goldsmith into marriage, with the connivance of her father? It seemed likely; it seemed very likely. And would my illegitimate child … though, technically, he would not be illegitimate because he would be born in wedlock … also attract the wrath of the Saxe-Gothas? So it was without any tug that I wished Gwyneth and her uncle and aunt goodbye and went with my grandfather and Canker to board the ship that would take us to India.

It was as if I had turned the page and started a new chapter in my life.

We drove in a cab to the famous India Wharf, also known as the T&S Wharf because it had been specially built by the Company for its tea and spice trade. Here, grandfather's ship, the *Coromandel Trader* had been berthed, I had just begun to admire her when Captain Hamish McGregor, master of the Indiaman, came rolling towards us. He looked like a red tar barrel covered in bristling fur out of which two ice-blue eyes peered, as swift and sharp as gimlets. His serge uniform was faded but spotlessly clean and he smelt of strong soap. I liked him from the moment I saw him.

'Morning Mr Yale-Lynsdale, Mr Canker,' his voice emerged out of his russet beard and whiskers like a muffled roar, as if he was used to bellowing above a nor'wester. His stubby forefinger made a token attempt to touch his forehead but did not succeed. 'So this is the young man who'll take passage with me!' he boomed. 'It's a six month voyage but we'll do it in five if the winds are fair, as I'm sure they will be. You need just a whisper of wind to send her skimming like a flying-fish. You've not seen a flying-fish Master John? Never mind. You'll have enough time to have your fill of flying-fish, whales, dolphins and the like. No mermaids, though. But what would you do with a mermaid, if you take my meaning? Har-har …' He guffawed, coughed, cleared his throat and my grandfather frowned like a thundercloud, but it didn't deter Captain McGregor for long. 'Look at her, Master John. Just look at her!' He waved a gnarled hand at the *Coromandel Trader*. 'The most beautiful thing ever to sail the seas, or my name's not Hamish McGregor …'

The clouds parted and the English sun touched the great ship. It seemed to stretch on and on, rising high into the blue sky, its white sails neatly furled. Sailors were busy scrubbing and washing down its decks. Drovers herded livestock up its gangway. 'We're carrying two milch cows and their calves,' said the Captain. 'Also pigs, sheep, geese, ducks and hens … I believe in fresh meat, vegetables and fruit. Plenty of each. Keeps one fit and vigorous.' Heavily built men smelling of sweat and beer swore and exchanged coarse jokes as they carried laden baskets on their heads or plodded up, bowed under the weight of huge chests. Gulls mewed plaintively, swooping and floating on the slight swell like fat, white, ducks. Hawsers creaked and strained at the black bollards as the great ship rose and fell on the water as if it was impatient for the challenge of the wind buffeting its prow, the sea breaking on its stem. I felt the call of India tugging at me.

There was the crisp cadence of booted feet and a line of uniformed soldiers marched up another gangway, carrying their weapons, barked at by a Sergeant-Major with handle-bar moustaches.

'Are we carrying the army?' I asked.

'I'm afraid so, Master John. Though the Company is not as generous as other passengers are; still, we've got to be ready for the Froggies. But here I am talking when we can be settled in the comfort of our cabin.' He turned to my grandfather. 'I've given him the Owner's Cabin, seeing as how he's your grandson and all,' and he bounded away in his curious rolling gait. It was only then that I saw that his right leg was a stump of wood.

Grandfather followed the departing Captain with his eyes, a curious mixture of admiration and puzzlement on his face. 'I'll have to go now, John and Canker-chan. I have some work with the Agent. I'll be back tomorrow morning before you sail out with the tide.' And he turned on his heel and hurried away to his hansom as if he was reluctant to linger.

The Captain was waiting for us at the head of the gangway. He didn't ask after my grandfather: he'd probably seen him leaving. He picked his way through a mass of cordage and canvas and sailors and porters. He opened a door and we walked down a small passageway with polished cedar walls. At the end was a door marked OWNER. We entered.

My cabin was huge. It was on the upper deck, in the stern of the ship: a living room half-circled by windows, a bedroom with a four-poster bed, and a bathroom with a bath and a commode. McGregor pointed to it. 'Makrana marble from India, Master John. I picked up the idea from the castle of Padmanabha in the kingdom of Travancore. You pour a bucket of water and its all washed out to sea. Ingenious, isn't it? Those Indians are nothing if not ingenious. Make yourself at home. Your chests are in this foot-locker. Your steward is an Italian named Gregorio: not related to the McGregors. Har!-Har! Canker's cabin is the first on the starboard side of the ....' he hesitated, searching for the right word, 'right-hand side of the corridor, going out. On the port side, the left-hand side, is the cabin of the Rev. Brandell Scythe and Mrs Joanna Scythe. I'll introduce them to you at supper at half-past six this evening. And now, if you'll excuse me, I must get about my business.' He trundled away.

Canker-chan had an amused expression on his face. 'He talks a lot, Johnny. Too much, perhaps. But that is to cover up his uneasiness when he's here. I sailed with him when he brought this ship from the shipbuilders in Bombay. He had spent more than a year in India, supervising every detail of the construction of the *Coromandel Trader*. He's a different man when he's out at sea.'

'We have five months ahead of us, Canker-chan. What are we going to do?'

'We are going to prepare you for India. You will not find the voyage long, I assure you. But beware of distractions, Johnny. Be very careful of them.'

It was much later that I realised what he had meant.

A little after the Captain left, the noise started. Carpenters began to hammer shelves in the cabins, nail furniture to the deck. Two came to my cabin, followed by the slim, clean-shaven, dark-visaged, Gregorio. He wore a white, buttoned-up, jacket with brass buttons, white trousers and white shoes. He was quick, efficient, carried a faint fragrance of scented powder, and spoke in a soft, deep, voice with only the faintest of Italian accents. He supervised the carpenters, unpacked and laid out my clothes, and vanished, saying that he had to attend to the Captain.

The noise increased,

To the incessant hammering was added the noise of the cattle, sheep, pigs and poultry, two buglers blowing for two hours every day, morning and evening, the choir of the Welsh Battalion of the Madras Artillery practising with full-throated harmony, and the pumps thump-thump-thumping at odd hours like an erratic heart.

'You'll get used to it Johnny,' Canker said, with a smile. 'You'll miss it when it stops. And now, if you're ready, let's go to the Captain's Cabin for supper. We'll meet the only other gentry on board: the Scythe couple who have, so far, been as quiet as church mice.'

They also looked like church-mice. He was a small man with a round, florid face and mouse brown whiskers which tended to twitch long before he said anything as if his words were mustering the courage to venture out. He also had a habit of extending his neck and peering, adding to his mouse-like appearance. She, in contrast, was a buxom woman with chubby features and brown hair drawn back into a severe bun. She had a disconcerting habit of addressing all conversation to her fat little hands folded, primly, on her lap and resting below her tightly laced waist and her rigidly corseted torso. Her clothes were black and ash-grey, his were brown corduroy. Both spoke so softly that we had to lean forward to hear what they were saying which, at the best of times, was innocuous. They were both as dull as ditch water.

Captain Hamish bubbled like a kettle on the hob, steering us unerringly through the entrée, soup, fish, meat and pudding while holding forth on his favourite topic: his ship.

'Twenty-six sails set on her, 1,200 tons of sleek beauty is my *Coromandel,* built by the greatest ship-builder in the world: the inimitable Lowji Lassaramjee. He is a Parsee: a pure Persian whose people fled to India because they were being persecuted. Wonderful people. More salmon, Mrs Scythe? But though Lowji built her, I chose everything myself. The teak is from the royal estates of the Zamorin in the deep south-west of India, felled under my personal supervision. Another helping of roast beef, Reverend? Nothing like a full belly to ward off *mal-de-mer*. And she has a copper bottom. Ever seen a bottom clad in copper, madam?' The Reverend Scythe choked over his pudding. His wife looked mildly concerned and tapped him lightly on the back. 'My apologies,' said the Captain. 'Yes, Gregorio, you may clear. Do we all wish to retire early? Excellent. We have plenty of time, plenty of time to get acquainted. We sail with the tide at the half hour after ten, tomorrow morning. Goodnight Reverend, madam. Goodnight Master John, Canker.'

The ship rolled gently under my large bed, lulling me to sleep. That night, the dream returned but it had changed a bit. I heard the sound of water cascading off the cliffs, and it roared in the unseen rivers. From high above, the call of the great birds were a shrill, piping, whistle. But the chimeras no longer gibbered and I felt more at peace with myself. The only irritant was that the third finger of my right hand, where the ring fitted snugly, was a little sore. I remembered what Gwyneth had done and I breathed on it. The soreness vanished. After that, I slept soundly on my first night aboard the *Coromandel*.

Grandfather strode out of the grey drizzle at nine the next morning. He nodded to the Captain and walked down to my cabin. He sat for a moment in silence, sipping the coffee served by Gregorio. When the steward left, Grandfather cleared his throat. The drizzle had starred his beard and the cold must have made his eyes water. He probably had a cold coming on because his voice was hoarse.

'Are you happy to go, John?'

'I'm not sure, Grandfather. I think I am.'

'It's still not too late to change your mind.'

I thought of the events that had brought this about. Lucia was out in India, possibly with my child. India was a big country, but then surely Canker would be able to find her.

'I have to go, Grandfather.'

'Very well.' He reached into the pocket of his coat. 'I have written to the governor of Fort St. George in Madras. The letter was sent a week ago through the captain of one of the frigates. It should be delivered at least a fortnight before you land. Present this copy to the governor. I had him appointed and he will do all that is necessary without making it obvious. He's discreet when he wants to be.' He stood up, and so did we. For a long while he looked out of the window. 'Your father's people and the savages of Saxe-Gotha have never forgiven you for being born. They have a long reach. We are doing everything to mislead them and they're furious about what we did to their would-be assassin. That may make them act in haste and concentrate on France. And I hope that when they discover that you are in India, they will give up their attempts to assassinate you. But you can never be too careful.'

He handed me a letter closed with his seal. Then he put out his hand and shook mine but, suddenly, he reached out and embraced me in a bear hug. I felt a sob rise in his great chest but he suppressed it before it could emerge. All he did was whisper in my ear, 'John, John, my son, my son. Carry my blood into the future. Our blood is our honour …'

He pushed me away then, shook Canker-chan's hand hurriedly; and strode down the gangway without wishing the Captain goodbye. I stood at the window, looking at him walking out in the grey rain. He never looked back and I never waved to him. I heard Canker-chan leave my cabin.

I was still standing at the window when I heard the orders being barked and the sharp toots of the bosun's pipe. Above me the great sails unfurled and filled with wind. Slowly, the *Coromandel* moved out of the harbour. George Huish had told me that ships that sail out from Portsmouth are guarded by naval ships all the way to Land's End and even beyond. Such convoying protects merchant ships from the corsairs of Tripoli, Algeria, and Tunis. Or rather, that is the theory. But when I came out on deck, and looked around, I couldn't see any of our chaperones. In fact there were no other ships in sight so, presumably, both our navy and our predators had taken a holiday!

The drizzle had stopped, England was a yellow-grey smear blurring into the distance and the *Coromandel* was digging her nose into the sea, starting her five month voyage to Madras … which Great-Grandfather Yale had governed … and to India.

Captain Hamish McGregor

I was standing on the deck, looking at England vanishing into the distance, when Canker came and stood beside me. The last of the English gulls cried overhead and then wheeled away, returning to a shore I would never see again.

After a while Canker said, 'We have very little time, Johnny.'

There was nothing ahead of me but endless sea: five months of it. 'We have five months, Canker!'

'Yes, Johnny.' His voice was calm, unhurried, 'We have only five months to prepare you for the rest of your life. You will spend it in a strange land, among strange people, with strange customs. How will you live with them if you can't even speak their language? Have you thought about all this Johnny? Have you given it any thought at all?'

My breath caught in my throat. I looked at Canker and, for the first time, the enormity of my decision struck me. I got a sinking feeling in the pit of my stomach. I had condemned myself to spend the rest of my life as an exile. I'd be assassinated if I returned to England or to any European country which the hateful Germans could reach. But would my life be any better, any safer, in India? I began to feel very sorry for myself.

'What do you want me to do, Canker-chan?' I tried to suppress the sob in my voice.

'You must forget the past. Get ready for the future, Johnny. You are Bernard Yale-Lynsdale's grandson, the great Elihu Yale's great-grandson. You're starting with a greater advantage than any of your future colleagues ever had. If they can make a success of India, then so can you: a brighter, greater, success. Besides …' He smiled slightly and looked into my eyes, 'you're a man who would be king. Or have you forgotten that, Johnny-chan?'

The black mood left me as suddenly as it had come. Yes, by Gad, I would be king; and not with my hateful father's help.

I turned to Canker. 'You're right. I have no time to lose.' England had vanished behind our long wake. Ahead, the *Coromandel's* stern sliced through the sea, racing into an uncertain but glorious future. I basked in that image for a while: intrepid young adventurer facing unseen perils with courage and indomitable will! Then reality caught up with my heroic vision. I turned and followed Canker into my sunlit quarters. My mentor was right, as usual. There was so much to do before the shores of my strange new home appeared.

I settled into the ship's routine easily. At daybreak, the pumps thudded and water gushed as the decks were scrubbed, the livestock fed and their pens cleaned out. I had thought that the ship would reek like a farmyard but, in fact, it smelt refreshingly like a pine forest: all woodwork, including the decks, were wiped down with an extract of juniper berries. Sea-sickness touched me only briefly during the first two days of the voyage and then it left me alone, even when the weather was foul and the sea rough. Canker, too, seemed to be unaffected.

And so I was able to spend long hours, in my cabin, learning Persian, the language of the Mughal Empire of India and Portuguese, the language of trade. For centuries the Portuguese had dominated the commerce between India and the rest of the world. And then there was the lingua franca of the Hindus of northern India: Hindi. Also Tamil, the language of Madras and the areas around it. This language also had its own script and, at first, Canker said that there was no need for me to learn its alphabet; but when he found how easily languages came to me, he changed his mind.

Languages, however, were only part of the instructions I received in my five months at sea. Early into the voyage, Captain Hamish looked into my cabin and saw me hard at work with Canker. That evening, at dinner, he asked, 'If you'll take no offence at what I say, Mr Canker-chan, and if there's any time to spare and, of course, if Master Johnny is so inclined, then could I, too, instruct him in the ways of the sea? What say you?'

Canker-chan smiled and looked at me. I said, 'I would be most interested, Captain Hamish.'

'Good!' bellowed the Captain, thumping the table so hard that the crockery jumped and the Scythe couple looked at him owlishly. 'Begging your pardon!' the old seafarer boomed. 'Gregorio will wake you, Master John, an hour before dawn, starting tomorrow, and I'll show you some of the new-fangled devices which, by the grace of Lord Neptune, tell us exactly where we are in the wide, and seemingly … I say *seemingly* … trackless ocean.'

And so I learnt how to recognise the constellations and to use the 'new fangled' sextant. Barney Gun, the Chief Steersman, even let me handle the wheel. 'Just to let you get the feel of this beauty as she moves under you, sorr. She's as sensitive as a passionate woman, if you get my meaning!' The *Coromandel*'s wheel twitched and trembled under my hands and, for a moment, I was in Lucia's bed with her moaning and writhing under me. Barney Gun's eyes slid slyly over my face and he said, 'I see you understand, Master John,' and he giggled like a mischievous child.

Then there were my times with Bosun Adam Stitch. He was a tall, almost emaciated, man whose deep-set eyes peered out from under white eyebrows, a startling contrast with his glistening, black, hair drawn into a pigtail and tied with a black ribbon. His voice was curiously soft and yet it carried with remarkable clarity even when the sea had howled up a gale. Those who disliked him, and there were many who did, said he never slept because he was scared of the Devil appearing to him in a dream and snatching away his soul. Others, who had great respect for his ship-husbanding knowledge, said that the soul of the ship had replaced his human one and that he slept only when the ship did: at anchor!

I never heard him walk up to me but, every so often, he would appear at my side when I was on the upper deck and point out fascinating things that I had not noticed. 'That's a basking turtle, John Yale-Lynsdale. He's sleeping in the sun, but if you try to get anywhere near him his senses will come awake and he'll dive to the bottom of the sea.' Or, 'You see that shark, swimming like a wraith just under the surface? There's a remora … some people call it a pilot fish, but that's nonsense … stuck to it by the suckers it has on its head. That way it doesn't have to swim on its own, searching for its next meal: it picks up the scraps that float past from the shark's dinner. If sharks stop swimming, they'll drown. They were created too early and the Good Lord hadn't had enough practice in making gills. S'truth!' And once he whispered, 'You see them? You see those Portuguese-Men-o-War? They look like gentle, drifting, silken umbrellas, don't they? Opening and closing, opening and closing. But look carefully, look at them swimming after that school of little fish. You see those tentacles trailing below? Two fathoms long, these ones have, but I've seen longer, much longer. One time, when we were becalmed, a shipmate jumped overboard to swim and cool himself. And before he could say "Davy Jones" they had embraced him like lovers. He screamed and screamed and screamed and when we lowered a boat and hauled him in he was whimpering and asking me to kill him. His body was a mass of raw, red, blisters. I put a ball through his head: it was the kindest thing I could do.' Stitch spat over the side and wiped the flecks off his lips with the back of his hand. 'Evil creatures, these …' Then he grinned, and, for a moment, his cadaverous mask slipped, 'But don't you worry your head about them creatures, John Lynsdale.' He had dropped the 'Yale' and I learnt, later, that double-barrel surnames reeked of snobbishness, so I decided not to make an issue of it. Stitch continued, 'Our Cap'n'll make sure they never get anywhere near you. He's a great mariner, is our Cap'n. Not another like him on the Seven Seas; not another one …'

The Captain certainly knew his job. We touched the lesser-known ports, rather than the more popular ones which might have closer ties with England, and the German princes. And at every port we took on huge baskets of citrus fruit. 'It keeps away the scurvy, according to the Captain,' said Gregorio.

The winds were favourable and we made good time sailing around the west coast of Africa … not too close to attract marauders and yet always with the Dark Continent a reassuring blur on the horizon.

We started swinging into land when we approached the Cape of Good Hope. Though it was cold and there were white horses on the crests of the waves, it wasn't as rough as we had expected. The evening before we put into Table Bay I wondered if I should try and track Lucia's movements again. And then I realised that she had got married at sea just about where we were sailing now. She and her husband had celebrated their wedding reception on board a ship anchored in the Bay which we would enter tomorrow. I felt a churning beginning in my stomach again.

A bank of clouds was rolling off Table Mountain when we entered. I was standing behind the captain as he conned his ship skilfully into the harbour. 'They call that cloud the Table Cloth, John. It rolls off the mountain then curls up again. Very curious.' He raised his right hand, then dropped it. The heavy anchor clattered down, there was a slight tug, and then we were still. Seamen scrambled up the rigging, furling the sails, and Stitch's deceptively soft voice issued orders to secure the ship.

A little settlement of iron-roofed houses rose at the foot of Table Mountain. Below was an untidy scatter of ramshackle huts where the blacks lived. Cape Town didn't seem to be a very interesting place, but I wanted to feel solid ground under my feet again: I had been very relieved to touch the earth in St. Helena even though that trip had had a rather disturbing ending. Besides, it was a beautiful day in spite of the white, rolling, 'Table Cloth.'

'Are you going ashore, Master John?'

I turned around, recognising Mrs Scythe's voice, though it seemed to be throatier than it had been; and it certainly had a deeper timbre. But the woman before me wasn't Mrs Scythe. This was no timorous mouse in grey and black with her hair tied tightly in a bun. This was someone else. She was a full-bodied woman in a lemon-green sacque showing the deep separation of her breasts. Most remarkable, however, was her hair. It was thick and a rich nut brown with auburn tints, swept up and vanishing under a large straw hat which threw a shadow over her laughing eyes. And there were tiny, very tiny, freckles on her nose.

'Mrs Scythe?' I asked, 'Mrs Joanna Scythe?'

She laughed merrily and said, 'Why Master John Lynsdale, you look as if you'd seen a ghost. And you, too, Captain.'

'And a very pretty ghost, at that,' rumbled Hamish McGregor. 'Were you asking a question, madam?'

'I was. I asked Master John if he was going ashore. Because, if he was, I would like to accompany him. If you have no objection, Master John …'

'And the Reverend?' asked the Captain.

'No … no. He's feeling a trifle tired after the voyage. I had wanted us to go ashore and stretch our legs in St. Helena but he had some … er … *spiritual* duties to perform.' I got the strangest feeling that she had deliberately emphasised 'spiritual'. 'He suffers terribly from *mal-de-mer* and so he took a sleeping draught and … and now he's asleep. Will be for the next four or five hours, I should imagine.'

Stitch floated silently up the ladder and touched his cap. 'Mr Jan van der Staal to see you. He's the leading stevedore and ship chandler, so he informs me,' the bosun said in his soft voice.

Mr van der Staal came clomping up the stairs with great deliberation. He was a burly man with snuff stains on his grey waistcoat, sweat stains under his armpits, puffing and panting and fanning himself with a large black hat.

'Good morning, Captain …' he pronounced it *gut morgen kapitan.* 'I am Jan van der Staal at your service. What can I have the pleasure of doing for you?'

I felt my hackles rising at his accent, even though it was not German. He mopped his brow with a large, red, spotted handkerchief, scattering clouds of snuff. Joanna Scythe stepped back and put a tiny square of lace to her nose. Then she said, 'Oh Captain, could you ask the charming Mr van der Staal if he could let us have two riding horses. Side-saddle for me, of course. You do ride, Master John. Of course you do. Quite tirelessly …'

Something about the way she said it made me flush.

The stevedore leant over the guard rail and rattled something in a guttural tongue to a black sitting in a boat near the accommodation ladder of the ship. The black said, 'Ja baas …' and rowed away.

'It is done, beautiful lady,' said Mr van der Staal with as much gallantry as he could muster. He turned to me. 'You are very lucky to have such a … companion.'

I returned to my cabin to get a hat and found Canker-chan waiting at his door. He let me go in without a word. When I returned he said, 'The woman's husband is in a drunken stupor. Do you remember my words about diversions, Johnny? Some diversions are much more dangerous than others.' Then he went into his cabin and shut the door behind him.

It was too late to back out now, but his words had a sobering effect on me. While the black rowed, his muscles rippling with the effort, Joanna Scythe sat close to me and looked at the approaching shore. She said, 'I love Kapstaad. My father came out here as a missionary and worked among the natives for many years. I went to school here, learnt riding and swimming. I had friends. It was a wonderful life for a growing girl.'

She looked at me thoughtfully, the bright sun lighting up her face through her hat. 'All right, Johnny,' she said. 'I'll tell you something that even my husband doesn't know. When I was fourteen, I fell in love with a farmer's son. He was twenty-one. We used to meet in a secret place.' She smiled at me. 'He looked very much like you and we often went riding to our secret place at the base of the Table. I think I'll show it to you, today.'

I didn't know what to make of all this, but I didn't have much time to think because the boat grounded on the beach. Our boatman leapt out and helped Joanna ashore. Another black was holding two horses: a roan mare with a side saddle and a black gelding. Joanna Scythe swung herself easily onto the mare, placing her foot in the cupped hands of the groom.

'I come?' the groom asked.

'No,' she said. 'It won't be necessary. We will be back here in three hours. Come Master John. Or may I call you John? You may call me Joanna when we're alone. Let's ride to the rough lands at the foot of the Table. Race you there!' and she was off.

She rode superbly, and the feel of the wind on my face and the horse moving effortlessly under me made my blood pound. We rode out of the settlement, into the base of the mountain, and up a narrow, winding, mountain track. She stopped where a clear stream gushed off the Table. We were in a small, green, terrace backed against a sheer cliff. A dense curtain of trees surrounded us, leaving only the bay side open. The stream trickled across the terrace, fell over the bay end. The only trail that led up to this was the one we had followed. She took off her hat, flicked her head, and her hair cascaded loose, all around her shoulders, half concealing her face.

'Help me down, John.'

I dismounted and went to her. 'No, not like a black. Open your arms and I'll jump into them.'

I did and she was in my arms and a warm, womanly, smell rose from her. She looked into my eyes, her hair felt soft and thick against my face, and we were both breathing hard. She began to tremble so uncontrollably that she nearly threw me off my feet. I kept holding on to her, to steady her at first, and then because I liked the feel of a woman in my arms. Her skin was covered in a faint film of sweat and mingled with its feminine aroma was a perfume that was disturbingly like the one that Lucia had used. Pictures of Lucia flashed across my mind and I felt myself stirring. Joanna … I had suddenly begun to think of her as Joanna … noticed it too because she opened her eyes wide and held me close, her hips and groin moving slowly against me. Her hand went up to her bodice and began to unfasten the bows. My breath was thick in my throat and I lowered my open mouth to hers. Her neckerchief had slipped to the ground and much of her bosom had been bared. Her hand crept up to the back of my neck and pulled down my head.

And then she screamed, 'A snake! A snake!' I turned round and looked over my shoulder and saw it. It was slithering down one of the trees. It was about nine feet long and its scales were greenish-black and large. Its beady, unblinking, eyes seemed to be fixed on us. The horses raised their dripping muzzles from the stream, whinnied loudly. The snake slid off the tree and started wriggling towards us. Joanna screamed again and again and again. I pushed her behind me, searching for a stick. The horses stepped forward, reared up on their hind legs, and slammed their fore-hooves down on the snake. They worked like a single, insane, animal, rising and thudding, rising and thudding, breaking the creature's back, crushing it into a gory mess, mashing it into the soft, damp, soil. Then they stood, flecked with foam, their coats varnished with sweat, trembling. Joanna Scythe staggered across, stroked them, talking softly till their trembling stopped. She went to the stream, washed her hands, splashed water on her face and on the back of her neck. She picked up her neckerchief and, turning her back to me, adjusted her bodice and draped the neckerchief again. She turned to me and said, 'I've recovered. I think we should return now.' We mounted our horses and, slowly, rode back to the harbour. The black groom and boatman were still waiting for us.

We were silent on the way back. There was nothing I could say. But just before we reached the ship, Joanna said, 'It was a sign, John. The serpent had caused Adam and Eve to sin. But this time it was sent to stop them from sinning again.' She hurried up the ladder ahead of me and vanished into their cabin.

Canker-chan did not ask me what had happened. All he said was, 'You've learnt your lesson, Johnny. European women behave very strangely out of their own continent. Let's go back to learning the other lessons.'

But, for all his foresight, not even he could predict who would teach us, all of us, the next terrifying lesson before we reached the distant shores of India …

Barney Gun

When we sailed out of Kapstaad, I had no premonition of what was going to happen. The repetitive routine on board had begun to pall and I longed for a change.

We touched a few African ports and islands off the coast, but they looked unattractive. Besides, Canker-chan had increased the pace of my studies. The changeable Joanna Scythe had decided to revert to her role as the self-effacing Mrs Scythe, demure spouse of 'a man of the cloth': eyes downcast whenever we met, ever the dutiful wife looking after an ailing husband.

I began to spend as much time as I could on the upper deck with the strange Bosun Stitch and the chief helmsman Barney Gun.

I was with him when he said. 'Ah! Isn't that strange?'

'What is?'

'Flying fish. Too many flying fish. Look there and there … and even there!' he pointed.

I followed his stubby brown finger, and saw them. They came leaping out of the water like silver arrows, flew over the sea, then plunged in again. I counted at least five schools of them, some with as much as fifty or sixty fish.

'They're all flying in the same direction, Master John, across our bows from starboard to port. From right to left. But I see no sharks or dolphins chasing them. And I don't like it.' His face was wrinkled with worry and the knuckles of his hands were white as he fought to keep the ship on course. 'There's a new current building up beneath. The *Coromandel* feels it: she's getting nervous. Hey Watson!' he called out to one of the watch, 'my compliments to the Captain and Mr Stitch. Something strange is happening.'

I could feel his unease. 'What could it be, Barney?'

'Something's happening deep in Davy Jones's Locker, Master John.' He shoved a quid of tobacco into his mouth and chewed rapidly.

Stitch came up first; followed by the Captain. They spoke to Barney and then to each other in low voices. The bosun hurried below decks and I heard the shrill toots of his pipe and men poured out like ants. They battened down the hatches, scrambled up the rigging and reefed the sails. I heard a lot of activity below decks and knew that they must be securing the cargo, luggage, and the animal pens, and rolling up the few hammocks that were still stretched. They had done all this when we had anticipated the usual rough weather as we approached the Cape. But there had been a relaxed, routine pace to it then: the men had laughed and joked as they worked. This time they were tense and hurried about their tasks as swiftly as they could. I picked up some of their tension.

Then I heard a strange sizzling and hissing above me, and looked up. The tips of some of the masts and spars were sparking as if they were alive with fireworks. And yet, the wood was not alight.

Barney's eyes followed my surprised gaze and he exclaimed, 'Holy Mother of God! St. Elmo's Fire!'

The Captain's voice was taut, 'A thunderstorm's coming, John. St. Elmo's Fire is "sitting lightning," a warning of what is to come. We're heading into Neptune's Guy Fawkes Day. It'll be loud and bright and terrifying!'

But the storm took its time building up. At first it was just a dimming of the sun as if someone had held a smoked glass against the sky. The clouds started appearing, quite rapidly now. They seemed to rise out of the ocean like steam from a cauldron, spreading in a grey sheet. It began to clot and curdle and swirl like cream being churned, slowly, at first, then faster and faster. Fat, warm, drops of rain splattered down and the *Coramandel* shivered and bucked like a fractious mare. The sky and the sea became frighteningly dark as if a starless dusk had descended. Barney gritted his teeth, his muscles bulging as he strained to control the wheel. The Captain stood straddling the deck, his face raised to the rain and the sky as if defying them to do their worst. Only Bosun Stitch seemed impassive but once, when he looked up at the spluttering St. Elmo's fire on the spars, his eyes glittered like those of a wild animal in the dark. I shivered and found myself breathing hard as if I had been running.

The first thunderclap was deafening and the sea and the sky blazed with a brilliant white light, searing my eyes. The ship shuddered like a horse when huge crackers explode on the Fifth of November. I felt the hairs on my arms and the back of my neck rising, but it wasn't fear, it was as if something in that storm-tormented sky was drawing them up. And there was a distinct metallic taste in my mouth a bit like the taste of blood but sharper. The ship bounced and heaved and bobbed like a cork in a mill-race. Water broke over the bows and flooded across the deck. A sailor was swept off his feet and was almost washed overboard but he managed to grab onto a cleat on the deck, scrambled to his feet and, after struggling with a door, opened it, and vanished below decks. Waves buffeted us from all sides, their crests and troughs increasing every minute. The wind howled and hit me with a force that took my breath away. The storm seemed to be a living creature hell-bent on destroying us.

The Captain stood four-square on the rolling, pitching, corkscrewing, deck, with the wind tearing at his red hair, his face raised to the sky as if he were sniffing something. Lightning lanced out of dark, scudding, clouds, shaft after jagged shaft, and the roar of the wind and sea clashed with the continuous thunder till it seemed as if we were in the heart of a titanic tympanic cacophony. Curiously, I was not scared at all. Uncertainty breeds fear. If you aren't sure if you'll live or die, fear clutches at your heart. But since there was absolutely no hope for anyone who fell into that raging sea, fear ceased to exist. In fact, I felt strangely elated, buoyed up with an unearthly zest as if I could yell a challenge to the storm, defying it to take me. In the midst of all that fury, it was as if a bubble of calm had cocooned me and I could look around, quite dispassionately, and observe what was happening.

In that detached state of mind I noticed that the lightning seemed to be concentrated on a particularly turbulent part of the ocean. Bolt after bolt of harsh, white, light lanced out of the black sky and struck just one spot on the surging waters. And every time the lightning hit it, the surface of the sea lit up and seemed to keep glowing as if enflamed from below. But, because of the deceptive light, I couldn't tell how near or how far away it was and then, to my dismay, I saw Barney Gun swing the wheel and head straight for that patch of lightning-blasted, churning water.

'What is Barney Gun doing?' I yelled to the Captain. 'Where's he going …'

He lowered his head and shouted into my ear, 'Into the Devil's armpit …' the wind was keening loudly now, snatching the words out of his mouth. 'There's a great wave approaching … Boil out of the ocean … Old Scratch's foul breath …'

'Why are we heading into it, Captain?'

'Only way … never … push you with his scaled hand … too late to run …'

The *Coromandel* bucked like a startled horse. Thunder crashed directly overhead and the sky blazed an eye-aching white. A blast of rain slashed down on us, driven by the banshee wind. It also bore something else: a hot, evil, stench that held us for a moment making my forehead break out in droplets of sweat. The masts and spars were now alive with that unholy fire, crackling and hissing.

And then a wave began to rise out of the sea to our right, our starboard bow as I had been taught to call it. It was black and curled and its rearing edge was trimmed with white like the claws of a giant cat, rising higher and higher into the lightning-torn sky. The Captain yelled something, swung one arm around a mast the other around me, pulling me close to his chest. Barney spun the wheel to the right and the head of the *Coromandel* came around and plunged, headlong into the roaring, rising, monster. I heard an agonised groan, like a spiked beast, and then the Coromandel began to rise and rise up the dark green side of the ominous, curling, wave. For a moment, for a horrible moment, I thought we were going to turn turtle dropping like beetles from a hollow log. But we kept our head and rose and rose up the gigantic wave till we were high above the boiling sea and, for an instant, a dark face formed in the cloud directly above us. Its mouth was opening in a grimace and lightning flashed from where its eyes would have been. A shaft lanced down and struck one of our spars with a terrible explosion: sail and spar came crashing down on to the deck. And then we were racing down the other side of the mountainous, black, wave and it was rushing away from us carrying the hot wind with it, and the ghastly stench of sulphur.

After that, as dramatically as it had come, the wind fell and there was only the rain and the strangely tortured sea with white horses prancing on the waves and a faint glimmer of light in the cloud scud above.

The Captain loosened his iron grip around me, put his lips to my ear, and shouted, 'You've seen it, Johnny. There are very few seamen who have seen it and lived to tell the tale. This is the second time it's come for me. No man has ever fought it thrice …'

'What was it?' I yelled back.

'The *Shaitan Toofan*. The Devil's Wind. They say it comes from the mouth of Hell itself!'

The thunder had ceased and I saw that the lightning was now hitting the sea far to our left, on our port quarter, and racing away fast. I felt eyes on me and turned around. Bosun Adam Stitch was standing behind and staring straight ahead. The uncertain, flickering, light touched the gaunt planes of his face making it look like a skull. His thin lips moved soundlessly and his fingers twitched and formed curious patterns, locking and interlocking as if they had an independent life of their own. I saw a movement out of the corner of my eye and turned forward again. Barney Gun had taken his right hand off the wheel and was crossing himself. His soaked clothes clung to his squat, muscular, body; his bald pate gleamed; his slitty blue eyes peered into the distant horizon where the clouds were shredded like a beggar woman's petticoat. Suddenly, for no apparent reason, I recalled what Bosun Adam Stitch had told me.

Barney Gun had been born to a Chinese washer-woman on board an Indiaman. His mother had died giving birth to him on the high seas in a furious storm. 'He is a child of a storm, John Lynsdale,' Stitch had said. 'There's no one his match to handle a ship in an angry sea. No one!' Then he had grinned humourlessly. 'They didn't know who his father was so they christened him after the barnacles, because he clung so tenaciously to life, and in the ship's log he was entered as "The Son of a Gun."'

'Don't stand there and brood, Master John!' the Captain boomed. 'Hurry down and get dry and warm.' I staggered away across the slippery, heaving, deck, clutching onto anything I could grab. As I plodded past the Scythe's cabin, the door opened and Joanna Scythe stood there, her hair streaming over her shoulders haloed by the light behind her. She wore a loose robe of the gossamer material they call 'Muslin' and the light shone through it outlining the curves of her body. My blood began to pound and I felt myself going weak in the knees. She leant out and her breasts surged forward, pressing against the thin fabric, her nipples thrusting like tight grapes. She smelt faintly, disturbingly, of some heavy, musky, perfume.

'Johnny,' her voice was hoarse. 'The Devil came to claim us. But I'll face him again to have what I want …'

I glanced over her shoulder. Her husband was sprawled on their bed, his mouth open slackly. An empty bottle, fallen from his limp hand, rolled back and forth across the carpeted deck. Joanna Scythe reached out and touched my face and her hand was as hot as the Devil's Wind. Then she stepped back and closed the door. The *Coromandel* hit a trough and I staggered, recovered, and fumbled open my door. As I did so, Canker's door closed slowly.

The sea calmed as suddenly at it had angered. One night the *Coromandel* was ploughing through rough waters, the next morning the sun was out, bright and shining in a blue sky and the sea was sparkling with tiny ripples. The damaged sails were spread on deck and the rope and sail-makers were at work in the sun. A school of dolphins gambolled in the sea, keeping just ahead of the ship, and Mrs Scythe helped her husband to step out and settled him in a wicker chair. He looked wan and weak, wrapped in a dun-coloured dressing gown, his spindly legs sticking out like matchsticks under his grey nightshirt. He hadn't shaved. The soldiers started trickling out, looking as woebegone as the Rev. Scythe. His wife saw them, pulled her cloak around her and went inside.

A shadow fell on the deck beside me and Canker-chan, looking crisp and cool in white, said, 'Look at the swallows swooping near the rigging, Johnny. Land is near.'

Chevrons of swift, black, birds dived and skimmed above us. Gregorio came out, spoke to the sergeant, and the man barked an order. The men assembled in three groups. Barney Gun joined them carrying a fiddle and a long, black, box. The sergeant raised his hand, Barney poised his bow over his violin. The sergeant dropped his hand and, in a clear tenor voice, began to sing. The men backed him in such superb harmony that they sounded like a great church organ with Barney's fiddle weaving through the music.

The first song was new to me. *The water is wide*, he sang, *I can't cross over*.

It was filled with nostalgia and it was hauntingly beautiful as it spoke of love and longing. All I could hear was the song, the creaking of the masts and sails, the soft swish of the *Coromandel's* bow wave as it sped through the sea.

Barney put aside his fiddle, opened the case he had carried up, and took out a curious instrument. A bunch of reed pipes rose out of a small air chamber connected to a large mouth-piece. Barney put the instrument to his lips, his fingers on the stops of the reeds, and nodded. I recognised their second song as *The Minstrel Boy* but the sergeant announced it as *The Moreen* and he added, 'We Celtic people, the original inhabitants of the islands, have a long history of resisting invasions by outsiders and because there are not many of us, even our children had to defend their ancestral lands. This is about a boy who had to go to the wars.' It was beautifully rendered but, most surprising of all, the curious instrument that Barney played sounded sometimes like an organ, sometimes like flutes, most often like the small-pipes a wandering musician used to play in the square in front of the Abbey in Bath. I referred to it in my mind as a 'bag pipe' because the air had first to be filled into the bag at the base of the reeds. Its music was particularly beautiful when Barney accompanied the Welsh soldiers as they sang *The Groves of Blarney* which I knew as *The Last Rose of Summer.* I saw Mrs Scythe wiping her eyes when she came on deck to retrieve her husband. She had, obviously, been listening to the choir from her cabin.

I asked Barney afterwards what the instrument was.

'It's a *sheng*, Master John. An old Chinese instrument,' he said. 'It was one of the few things left behind by my late mother. An old gentleman in Shanghai taught me how to play it when I was doing the India-China run for nigh on five years.' He grinned up at me. 'I can teach you, Master Johnny, if you would care to learn. I taught it to a Russian who said he's going to make it popular in Europe.' I thanked him and said I really have no time on this voyage, but perhaps if our paths crossed again I'd become his pupil.

The Welsh choir and Barney had entertained us for an hour and soon they had had virtually the whole ship on the upper deck, listening to them. Tensions drained away and everyone started to smile. It didn't change even when a Portuguese ship crossed us, in the distance, the huge crosses on its sails clearly visible. Suddenly, after it was all over, and Barney had packed away his *sheng* lovingly, I began to feel very tired and every bone and muscle ached.

'It's your body relaxing after the storm,' Canker said. 'You've been bracing your body against the movement of the ship. It's normal. Drink plenty of water, do yoga and go to sleep.'

I was asleep as soon as my head hit the pillow and when I woke, the ship bobbed gently at anchor and, through the window, I saw boatmen with straw hats sitting in skiffs offering exotic fruit and fresh fish and calling out in a language which sounded very much like Tamil but with a different intonation. Bare-bodied stevedores were loading cargo onto a large punt poled by two men. The barge, for it was obviously that, had the words 'The Goldsmith Company' painted on its side. I felt I should know something about that Company but my memory was still fogged with tiredness.

Canker-chan walked in accompanied by a young man in a white sarong and shirt worn outside his sarong. I had seen Canker in such a dress when he had relaxed in his room in Shawclose.

Canker said, 'Don't get up, Johnny. This is my nephew Kunhi Krishnan who will be accompanying us to Madras.'

'Where are we now?'

'We're in the Indian port of Tellicherry, famous for its pepper. We're landing some cargo and will be sailing out in two hours or so to catch the tide.'

The name sounded familiar but my mind was still groggy with sleep so I couldn't establish the connection. 'How many days to Madras?'

'Ten days, maybe fourteen. We have to sail to the southern tip of India, round the island of Ceylon, probably stop for a while in their port of Galle. And then tack up the east coast past the colonies of the Dutch, French and Danes. And only then will we sail into Madras. John …'

'Yes?' I said, and couldn't control a yawn. My eyelids were leaded with sleep and I could scarcely keep them open.

'It doesn't matter. Go back to sleep John. We'll talk about things tomorrow ...' They went out, locking the door softly behind them. Before I fell asleep again the words 'Goldsmith' and 'Tellicherry' kept buzzing around my brain. I knew that they were important and I should remember, but I couldn't. I was still very tired and could think of nothing but sleep.

I sat up with a start the next morning. I knew why Galle and Tellicherry had sounded so familiar. In St. Helena a trader's wife had recorded selling a layette of Galle lace to Lucia for her baby, *my* baby. And Lucia had married a rich man who had a business in Tellicherry; or rather, they had disembarked in Tellicherry. Her husband's name was Gabriel Goldsmith; his barge had been receiving cargo just under my window. If I had had my wits about me, I would have been able to meet Lucia; and, possibly, my son. I was certain he was a son. After the fury of our passion, the child couldn't possibly have been a daughter. For a wild moment I thought of rushing up to the Captain and asking him to turn the ship around and sail back to Tellicherry. But it was just a mad thought. What reason would I give him? And even if he did turn back, my grandfather would be furious and probably summon me back to Bath. No: I just cculdn't risk it. After I had sluiced cold water on myself in the bathroom, I felt less confused. I rang for Gregorio, had a substantial breakfast finishing off with a wonderful fruit called a mango, walked out and met Canker in his cabin.

It was a rather unhappy meeting though it started pleasantly.

Canker and Kunhi Krishnan were sitting cross-legged on the broad-bottom chairs, talking. Both rose as I entered, waved me to another chair and Canker asked me if I had rested. I said I had and asked him if he knew anyone named Gabriel Goldsmith. Canker's eyes went heavy-lidded and I knew that he had guessed the truth and was unwilling to share any information with me. But Kunhi Krishnan was eager to talk.

'Yes, Mr John, he is the leading trader in the north of Travancore-Cochin. His head-office and mansion is in Tellicherry. Till a late age he remained unmarried but recently he returned from England with a young bride. She gave birth to a child shortly after their return. Do you know him Mr John?'

Canker coughed warningly. But Kunhi Krishnan did not get the signal.

'I knew her in England. Did she have a boy or a girl?'

'Oh a son. Definitely a son. He was recently … er … christened? Is that the right word? He was named George Albert David Goldsmith. That's right: George Albert David.'

I kept my face impassive. It was her way of telling me that he was my son: she had had him baptised with three of my Christian names.

Canker cleared his throat and said, 'Kunhi Krishnan has come here for a purpose. He will be your bodyguard from now on. He has two hundred men waiting for you in Madras.'

'Bodyguard?'

'Yes, John-chan,' Kunhi Krishnan said gravely. He looked very much like Canker, his voice had the same gravelly quality. 'You will not see my men unless you have a need. But they will always be there. They are all Nair warriors, be assured.'

I looked at Canker-chan.

'It is as ordered by your grandfather. It has all been taken care of,' he said with finality.

I began to feel suffocated again. I told him that, while I respected my grandfather, I was not obliged to carry out his orders and, if necessary, I would leave Madras and make my own life elsewhere in India where neither he, nor anyone else, would be able to find me.

Canker-chan hissed through his teeth in dismay when he heard this. He was silent for a long while. Then he said, 'Very well, John-chan. If that is your wish. But know this, your enemies have a long hand and they are determined to destroy you. They will not rest till they have done so. India is not too far away for them.'

'I prefer to look after myself.'

'I have read your horoscope, Johnny. You will be involved in more than one battle in India.'

'Our fate does not lie in our stars, Canker-chan, but in ourselves.'

Canker smiled slightly. 'Is that your belief: that the movement of the stars do not affect human affairs?'

'Yes. That is my Christian … my Catholic … belief.'

'Then why does the Bible say that the three kings, the three wise men, followed the star of Christ from the east?'

I looked at him blankly. I didn't know what to say.

'Believe what you like, Johnny, but I know what I have read.'

'I want to be a trader. I don't want warriors.'

'Even traders must defend their goods. Otherwise why are all trading stations … the factories … fortified?'

'I do not need an army.'

'Not yet, but when you do they will be waiting and ready. And now we shall leave to take our mid-day meal.' Canker said, and he and Kunhi Krishnan bowed and left the room. It was the first time Canker had bowed to me and, suddenly, I felt very lonely.

Adam's Bridge

The Captain was at his boisterous best during breakfast.

The Rev. Scythe looked morose, Mrs Scythe made a great display of being solicitous about her husband: tucking his napkin into his collar, ladling out his oatmeal, making a soft-spoken enquiry about the next dish.

'Iddlis, madam,' boomed the Captain. 'Steamed rice dumplings. Easily digestible. A favourite of the coastal lands we're passing now. Best eaten with a little coconut chutney: the green paste in that dish. Excellent for a revolting stomach.'

'I don't think the Reverend will have any,' said Mrs Scythe in almost a whisper. 'He's not been feeling well of late. Nor, for that matter, have I …' She allowed her voice to trail away presumably expecting sympathy for her sad plight.

The Captain and I excused ourselves and left the Scythes to their meal.

Canker and Kunhi Krishnan were peering over a large map they had unrolled on a table. I wished them, and Canker came to the point immediately, speaking in Persian. I was being tested for having challenged him.

'Please look at this map of India, Johnny-chan. It shows you how many major ports are held by the British … mainly by the

Company … and how many by other nations.' The words *map, major ports, British* and *Company* were spoken in English.

Dotted all down the west coast of the great subcontinental wedge of India were ports under the control of European nations with the years in which they had been taken over:

> **Diu-Portuguese-1535; Goa-Portuguese-1510; Surat British-1618; Daman-Portuguese-1558; Bombay British-1661; Goa-Portuguese-1510; Bhatkal-Dutch-1637-British-1638; Mangalore-Portuguese-1565; Mahe-French-1725; Cochin-Dutch-1663; and Quilon-Dutch-1661.**

On the west coast alone there were eleven ports in the hands of European East India Companies of which only three were controlled by us. I was dismayed. I had thought that we had only the French to contend with.

Kunhi Krishnan added in Tamil, 'We're roughly here: opposite Cochin now. From here let your eyes travel down to the southern tip of India, curve around between India and the island of Ceylon … which is held by the Dutch … and up the east coast where Madras is.'

Ceylon hung like a pendant on the lobe of India. Kunhi Krishnan's finger rose slowly up the east coast washed by the deceptively named 'Bay of Bengal': it seemed much larger than the Mediterranean Sea. I read the names of the ports as Kunhi's finger touched them.

> **Nagapatnam-Dutch-1658; Karaikal-French-1738; Tranquebar-Danish-1616; Pondicherry French-1699; Sadras-Dutch-1670; Madras-British-1639.**

Then, moving up from Madras,

> **Masulipatam-Dutch-1606; Yanaon French-1725.**

And far up, where the wedge of India spread into the huge delta of the Ganges River ... which the Rev. Greenwood of Bath had described as a '*great, swampy, forested land full of snakes, crocodiles, man-eating tigers and fierce riverine pirates*' ... and along one of the distributaries of the Ganges called the Hooghly:

> **Calcutta-British-1690; Serampore-Danish-1616; Chandernagore-French-1637; Chinsura-Dutch-1625 and Bandel-Portuguese.**

It suddenly struck me that our great East India Company, source of all the power and riches of the Yale-Lynsdales, had only five major trading ports in India and a few minor ones not listed on this map. Our rivals had almost four times as many. It was a very sobering thought, particularly when I remembered that the Portuguese, French and Dutch were still our rivals in Europe and whatever happened there would have grave repercussions here.

As if reading my thoughts, Canker said, 'Please sit down, John-chan.' Both had decided to retain the Malayalam honorific of *chan* even when they changed languages.

I said, 'Thank you,' in Persian and, very gravely, the three of us sat down. It felt like a stylised charade but that, probably, was the courtly nature of the Persian tradition: so different from the Germanic uncouthness of the Hanoverians! I dragged my mind away from that hateful thought.

The *Coromandel* had begun to roll gently. 'We're catching the swell from the Indian Ocean,' said Canker in English. 'Tomorrow we'll be near the Land's End of India, where the Arabian Sea, the Indian Ocean, and the Bay of Bengal meet. It could be rough.'

There was a knock on the door and Gregorio entered. 'The Captain's compliments to Mr Lynsdale. He is with Barney Gun and Mr Stitch.'

'Now?' asked Canker.

'Yes, Mr Canker. Now.'

I was relieved to leave. I didn't like Canker and Kunhi lecturing me as if I was a schoolboy. I found the Captain, Stitch, and the Sergeant standing near Barney Gun who was at the wheel. The Captain came to the point immediately.

'The reason why I asked you out here is because tomorrow, a little after eight bells, we are going to enter some of the most dangerous waters of the Indian Ocean: Adam's Bridge. It's a 22-mile stretch of sea between India and Ceylon and it's dotted with shoals, sand banks and little islands. The currents are very tricky. But, to add to our problems, it's alive with fishing boats and they believe that those waters belong to them: they resent our passage. We'll need both Mr Canker's and Mr Kunhi's help. I've already spoken to them. You'll find it very interesting.'

I had a rather restless night dreaming about death coming for me across a stormy sea. I woke up in a sweat but that could have been because of the heat; it was even more than when we had crossed the equator on our way to the Cape of Good Hope.

I had breakfast alone. Gregorio said, 'According to Mrs Scythe, the Reverend had a bad night; he was groaning and moaning and tossing in his bed. And the codeine helped only for a short while, but she gave him a dose of laudanum and he's asleep now.'

I was out on the deck when we were lying off Adam's Bridge, waiting for high tide. Canker walked up to me and said, 'There is a legend that this was made by the monkey army of Sugreeva, their king, to help Lord Ram rescue his wife, Sita, from the clutches of the King of Ceylon.'

I was about to ask him if he believed in the legend but thought better of it. He would probably ask me if I believed that the world had been made in seven days or that Joshua had trumpeted down the walls of Jericho!

Just then Mrs Scythe came running up, wringing her hands. Her hair was dishevelled and she wore the bed-gown I had seen her in when she had touched my face off Kapstaad as it was called in the

Afrikaans language. But now it was crumpled and stained with sweat and had a sour, unwashed, smell. She fell on her knees before the Captain, clutched his hands in hers and cried, 'Captain! Captain! Save my husband! He's dying! He's dying. He's breathing hard but he won't wake up. Please get a doctor. He's dying …'

The Captain rushed down, followed by Stitch. A little later they came hurrying back and the Captain said, 'We can't wait for the tide. We'll have to cross the Bridge now. Hawksey on the Crow's Nest. Cartwright, relay. Finlay, port leadsman; Eliot, starboard leadsman. All other seamen man the sails. Mr Stitch, please take the for'ard con. Barney on the wheel. Mr Canker and Mr Kunhi would you please take those two megaphones, stand on the right and left of Mr Stitch, and warn off any fishermen who might come in our way. Mr John I would like you to watch everything very carefully and try to remember it all. The tide is low but we will have to make good speed through these treacherous waters if we wish to save the Reverend's life. We could run aground and we could endanger the fishing fleet. Either way I could be in trouble. May the Lord of the Seas be with us …'

Men ran helter-skelter across the deck, swarmed up the rigging. Hawksey, a tiny man, he couldn't have been more than five feet, if that, shinned up the main-mast, a megaphone strapped to his back. A lithe young man named Cartwright followed and stood half-way up, another megaphone on his back. Finlay and Eliot were our two carpenters. They had identical mutton chop whiskers, beetling brows and enormous hands. They carried yellow lines, graduated with red, yellow, blue, white and green leather markers indicating fathoms and half-fathoms ending in conical lead weights. Their job was to throw their lead-lines ahead of the ship then walk back till the lines were vertical because the lead had touched the bottom of the sea. And then they called out the depth of the water below us to the left, the port, and the right, the starboard side,

Slowly the sails began to unfurl, fill with wind, and we started to move. Ahead, the sea snarled over rocks, shoals, little islets. Fishing boats dotted the water. There was a constant sequence of calls. Finlay and Eliot swung their leads and sang out the depth. 'Deep-eleven!' 'Nine-three!' Hawksey called down from the Crow's nest high above us, Cartwright repeated his words: '*Clear dead ahead*! Clear dead ahead. *Shoal starboard quarter*. Shoal starboard quarter.' Stitch had extended his right and left arms. '*Clear port quarter*! Clear port quarter.' Stitch's left arm lowered. The Captain ordered, 'Port five.' Barney turned the wheel and the *Coromandel's* head shifted to the left heading straight towards a mess of fishing boats. 'Warn then off! Warn them off, Mr Canker!'

Canker put the megaphone to his lips. His voice sounded unreal. 'Take care,' he shouted in Tamil. One of the bare-bodied fishermen raised his fist. 'These are our waters,' he shouted, 'you take care!'

'We have a dying man on board. Do you want his blood on your hands?' Canker shouted back.

The fisherman who had shouted at us cupped his hands around his mouth and called out to the other boats. They began to paddle furiously, out of our way.

It took the rest of the day to make that passage through Adam's Bridge and I would never like to repeat it. Five times I was sure that we would run aground as we manoeuvred between rocks and sandbanks seemingly as close together as the beam, the width, of the ship. Five times we escaped by the skin of our teeth and the incredible seamanship of Captain Hamish McGregor. And all the while, sails were being reefed slightly, or, as slightly unfurled, using every breath of breeze to control our speed. It was prolonged, tense and harrowing.

When, eventually, we reached open waters, and the sails were unfurled and filled with the wind, everyone was dripping with sweat. The Captain went in to see Scythe and we waited, unsure if we would have to divert into the Danish port of Tranquebar for medical help.

The Captain returned, his face a mask of suppressed fury. He bashed his right fist into the palm of his hand and exploded, 'Would you believe it, gentlemen? Our dearly beloved Reverend Brandell Scythe vomited two pints of raw brandy and is now sleeping as soundly as a baby.' He breathed hard, his great chest rising and falling with the effort to control himself. 'It is a pity, a great pity, that the good old naval tradition of the Cat is frowned upon by the Company.' I learnt later that he was referring to the cruel, 9-stranded knotted and barbed whip known as the Cat-o'-Nine-Tails. He thought for a moment and then boomed, 'But before we trim our sails for Madras, let us maintain another hoary naval tradition. Mr Stitch,' he boomed, 'pipe *Splice the Mainbrace!*'

There was great jubilation as an extra large tot of rum was issued to all hands. And I sincerely hoped that the despicable Reverend Brandell Scythe was kept awake till the early hours of the morning.

The Scythes kept to themselves though the Captain refused to allow Gregorio to serve them their meals in their cabin. Mrs Scythe dutifully collected their food from the pantry and dined sequestered with her husband. The end of our long voyage was in sight.

On the 149th day after leaving England, the lookout on the crow's nest shouted, 'Land ahoy! The tallest mast in India. Madras dead ahead.'

The Captain stood beside me and said, 'Legend has it that that mast was erected by your ancestor, your revered great-grandfather, Governor Elihu Yale. This must be a very proud moment for you, Mr John.'

I saw the towering mast piercing through the rising mist: it was just a little after dawn. The low sun was behind us, touching the tops of the buildings, limning the fort wall, highlighting the lighthouse and the flag-mast. I felt a slight churning in my stomach: a bit like the excitement when Lucia first touched me. It was this, but it was something more. It was a feeling … more than a feeling … that I had been here before, that I would soon walk along roads and amid mansions that I was familiar with, that I remembered. It was a feeling of great, great, relief. At long last, I was coming home again. From that moment I knew I belonged here. And, from that moment, I have never felt a stranger in this land.

Then, on to the deck, came Mrs Scythe. But this was still another Mrs Scythe. The mousy little Mrs Scythe had gone; so had the flirtatious Joanna Scythe of Kapstaad; and the caring Mrs Scythe with an ailing husband. This was a *grande dame* in a blue dress with enormous panniers and a wide-brimmed straw hat which was being tugged by the wind. Beside her stood her husband in a coat, breeches, embroidered waistcoat and a three-cornered black hat. The Captain's jaw dropped open for an instant, and then he recovered, nodded at them, and put an eyeglass to his eye. I wondered how Mrs Scythe had negotiated the narrow companionway: her pannier stuck out at least four feet on either side.

The anchor rattled and the ship came to a dead stop, moving gently on a low, off-shore, swell. The Captain said, 'The mail boat's coming and there's an Ensign on board. To what do we owe this honour, I wonder.'

'He must have been sent to welcome us,' said Mrs Scythe in a strange imitation of a hoity-toity accent. 'After all, the Reverend Mr Scythe is the assistant pastor of this community!'

The main deck was alive with activity. The troops had poured out and were falling in line. A large wooden cage had been rigged to a block and tackle. 'For the passengers,' said the Captain, almost in a whisper. 'Not for you, of course!' A rope ladder was unravelled over the side and I heard the shrill tweet of the bosun's pipe and the strangely carrying, gentle, voice of Adam Stitch announcing, 'Prepare to receive the mail boat and an Ensign of the Honourable Company.'

Mrs Scythe preened herself, shook her pannier, and took a step forward, closer to the rope ladder.

An Ensign scrambled up the ladder and stood looking around. The sergeant barked ''Shun!' and saluted as the troops sprang to attention. The Ensign threw them a casual salute. He was dressed in the tight red jacket and white breeches of the Company's army, and had a sword strapped around his waist. He was about five foot nine, sturdily built, had a round face, a high forehead, a prominent nose, and lips that seemed to be permanently set in a half-smile of cynical contempt. But what really set him apart from everyone else on that crowded deck was the intense stillness of the man. He seemed to be standing in a circle of light like a great performer on an empty stage, holding the breathless attention of the audience. Only his eyes, heavy-lidded at the outer corners, moved. They darted around, not just seeing but assessing: coldly, swiftly, meticulously. They settled on the Captain, moved on. Touched Mrs Scythe, flicked to her husband. The cynical lips twitched in contempt. Shifted to Canker-chan and paused, taking in his white sarong-*mundu*, his immaculate white shirt worn outside the *mundu*, the thin gold chain around his collarless neck. The Ensign nodded very slightly. And then those eyes, neither blue nor grey but some colour in between with green lights glittering inside, turned on me. And lingered.

I felt as if my whole life was under intense scrutiny, and I began to resent that unblinking stare.

Mrs Scythe, in her absurd hips-exaggerating pannier, stepped forward, her gloved hand extended, and said, in her strange new accent, 'I am Mrs Scythe, Mrs Assistant Pastor Scythe. Pray, have you come to receive us?'

Those lips stretched in a sardonic smile, very briefly, and then the Ensign took her hand, clicked his heels and, bending over, raised her hand to his lips. 'If only I was so fortunate, madam.' His voice was oddly resonant, every word well-modulated as if he were trying to suppress a tell-tale accent. He dropped her hand and turned to me.

'Mr Yale-Lynsdale?' he asked. 'Mr John Yale-Lynsdale?'

I stepped forward. 'That's right. And whom do I have the pleasure of addressing?'

Something flashed in his eyes and then it was gone almost before I could perceive it. But it had alerted me.

'I had the privilege of making the acquaintance of your grandfather, sir. The great Bernard Yale-Lynsdale himself.' He held out his hand. 'Welcome to Madras.' Again there was that momentary flash in his eyes.

When I extended my hand, I was prepared. He gripped it firmly and began to squeeze, the cynical smile widening slightly on his lips, triumph now blazing in his eyes. But I had already stiffened my hand and, as I squeezed back, my index and second fingers and thumb searched for, and found, the pressure points. I pressed them slightly, saw the surprise on his face, but his hand kept squeezing. I pressed down hard, sent pain shrieking up his wrist and forearm, knotting his elbow, lancing up into his armpit.

His eyes glazed with pain and he said, 'Ah!' very softly.

I relaxed the pressure and stroked the counter pressure-points, easing the pain. There was a thin film of sweat on his upper lip.

I said, 'I didn't get your name.'

Those strange eyes regarded me for a moment, then they smiled and there was a warm, almost mischievous expression on his face.

He said, 'My name is Kline. Ensign Norbert Kline.'

Elihu Yale Sahib

From that very first encounter, I became wary of Kline.

He seemed to be as coldly self-possessed as a reptile; and like the chameleons I had read about in school, he could change his coat at will. He had tried to put me in my place with that handshake, and then, when he realised that it wasn't going to work, he became warm and affable.

Kline turned to the Captain, saluted, and said, 'We've met, Captain McGregor, when Director Bernard Yale-Lynsdale visited us.' He extended his hand to Canker, 'And you must be Comprador Shankaran Nair.' That was the first time I had heard Canker's correct name. 'Welcome to Madras, again, Comprador. When you have the time, today or tomorrow, I would like to consult you.'

Kline introduced himself to a rather crestfallen Joanna Scythe, and her husband. I stepped back and shook Captain McGregor's calloused hand. He was a wonderful man and I was going to miss him. He lowered his voice and whispered, 'Be careful of him, Johnny. If you let him have his head, he'll ride you to hell and back. But if you handle him well, you'll make a great team.' Then, raising his voice, he said, 'And may the very best of good fortune attend all your endeavours, Master John. We sail in a fortnight. We'll probably meet again before we leave.' He nodded, 'The boat's waiting and all those rascals in the catamarans, and the *mussulahs*, will not come near till the mail boat has cast off. Goodbye to both of you.'

Kline walked back to me. 'You and I have been billeted together. Now, if you and the Comprador will care to climb down into my boat, we'll be on our way.'

Kline was the last to clamber down and Mrs Scythe leant over the rail and called out: 'Any room in your boat for us, Ensign?'

'I'm afraid not madam. You'll need a broad *mussulah* boat to accommodate that beautiful skirt of yours. I look forward to seeing you ashore.' With that he stepped in and ordered, 'Cast off!'

Canker and I settled ourselves on a pile of mail bags, at the bottom of the boat, as we were rowed away. The *Coromandel* became smaller and smaller and the shoreline grew, fenced by a snarling line of white-capped breakers. I wondered how we would get through them; they seemed fierce and turbulent and I had noticed, with alarm, that the planks of the boat had not been nailed together but stitched I hoped that the shipwright-seamstresses had been skilled! Then, suddenly, the boatmen shouted, the boat spun around, bucked like a fractious horse and breasted the first of the breakers with a sickening lurch. Then the next. And the next, And the next. My stomach, and its contents, rose into my throat. There was the sour taste of bile in my mouth. I swallowed hard to keep it down. Then, to my great relief, I felt the swishing-grinding abrasion of the beach below us. Two of our boatmen leapt out and hauled the boat away from the bumping swell of the surf. Men in livery came running down the strand, carrying two chairs on poles. Canker leapt lightly ashore; we were carried off the boat by the boatmen and onto dry land, where the two palanquins were waiting.

Kline put his hand on my arm and held me back. 'The Pannier-lady's *mussulah* will be next. It should be interesting.'

It was. The boatmen did not know what to do with her: she certainly could not fit into a chair. So they lifted her off the boat and placed her on the back of a muscled giant who wore nothing more than a narrow strip of cloth about his loins. But Joanna Scythe screamed and struggled and refused to hang on to the naked shoulders of her porter. Her human steed stumbled, staggered, and then they both tumbled into the water with an almighty splash! Kline and I rushed forward, waded in, and helped her to her feet. Many of the cane stays of her pannier had broken, her blue dress was soaked and dirty, and her hair hung in dripping strands over her face. She was so furious that all she could say was, 'Well! Well! Well! ...' We helped her into a palanquin and sent her off, her mousy husband trotting, spaniel-like, behind.

Norbert Kline and I looked at each other and then we doubled over with laughter. Only Canker-chan's expression didn't change. He gazed after the retreating Scythes and said, 'Both of you could have made an enemy for life.' But I was too excited about Madras to worry about the future.

The Fort, at Madras, was a little British citadel at the edge of an exotic land. Kline said that the governor would see me in a day or so. I would not have to report to the adjutant-general's and town mayor's office. 'All those normal formalities have been taken care of.'

The governor had allotted us three spacious, high-ceilinged, rooms. My luggage had been placed neatly at one end of the common room which led to both the bed-rooms.

We were served *tiffin* by a liveried servant. There was fried fish and large chips made from a root vegetable like a potato, ham and potato salad drenched in sour cream, and chicken curry much spicier than the ones that occasionally had graced the Captain's table on the *Coromandel*. It was accompanied with a heaped plate of boiled rice, garnishes and pickles, and an unusual curry biscuit called a *pappadam*. Then there was a rich, brown, caramel custard. It was all washed down with copious draughts of a sweet, red, Portuguese wine.

I felt heavy and drowsy after this enormous meal but noticed that though Kline had urged me to take second helpings, he ate very frugally and drank with great moderation. I retired to bed, resolving never to over-indulge myself in future.

'Master! Master! It is almost sunset, master. I have brought one pot of tea for you, master. China tea. Also milk and sugar in silver tea service.'

I opened my eyes in the midst of this refrain spoken in an accented, persuasive, voice. I smelt the fragrance of cloves.

A man, about my age, was bending over me, smiling broadly. I rubbed the sleep from my eyes. He had a cocoa-coloured face, a pitted skin, and the most brilliant white teeth I have ever seen on any person. I sat back against the bed-head and took him in. He was dressed in immaculate grey trousers and a grey tunic buttoned up to his neck. He wore a white turban with a red band tied diagonally across it; and a broad, red, buckled, belt. Both on the red band and on the buckle of the belt were monograms in shining brass. It took me a while to decipher the letters on the monograms, so intricately had they been intertwined. When I did, I was pleasantly surprised: they were J.D.A.G.Y-L.–my initials.

I smiled back at him and asked. 'Who are you?'

He bowed slightly. 'Master does not remember? After long trip from England, it is natural.' He touched his chest with his right hand. 'I am Joseph, your servant appointed and outfitted by Shankaran Nair-sir. Myself served your *tiffin* which master had with Kline-sir. At that time I am not having turban-band and cummerbund,' he touched his belt, 'so, maybe, master, you could not recognise. Now I will always wear turban band and cummerbund. I am now making hot water and placing in tub in bathroom. When master is bathing I am laying out clothes. I am serving supper at half-past six of the clock.'

'Supper?' I asked, still feeling heavy with luncheon.

'Supper, this first day, I make according to advice of Shankaran Nair-sir since master was resting, much fatigued after long sea journey. So: first lentil soup with sippets, that is fried bread cubes; then baked pomfret, which is very good fish. fresh, fresh, then …'

'Stop! Stop Joseph. I've had enough!'

'Master is displeased?'

'No. I am full. I can't have another meal so soon.'

He seemed crestfallen. 'Master not having any supper?'

'All right, Joseph. Since you've made it. But I can't eat all that. Will Mr Nair or Ensign Kline be joining me for supper?'

'Kline-sir is on watch duty: his meal will be taken to guard room. He will return after gates are closed at 11:00 pm of the clock at night. Nair-sir will come at 6:00, that is in 55 minutes exactly. Does master want any help in bath?'

I must have looked surprised because Joseph explained, apologetically, 'Some masters need servants for bathing; some masters do self-bathing.'

'Yes,' I nodded, 'I do self-bathing.'

That was my introduction to life in the Fort. Clearly, in this little world, a dot in the vastness of ancient India, the white person was king. It didn't matter what you were back home: cutpurse, domestic, nobleman, ne'er-do-well, yes, even a disinherited son like me. All that mattered was that you were an employee of the Company, and white. I also learnt that my grandfather had much more authority in India than he had exercised in Bath.

When Canker came, just as eight bells sounded, he explained it to me and added, 'The governor owes his present position to your grandfather. He wants Bernard-chan's continued patronage.'

'Why?'

'Because life in the Fort is uncertain, Johnny.' He paused and the low sun softened the sharp planes of his face. 'Your new friend, Kline, is cynical and ambitious so, if he's agreed to be billeted with you then, obviously, he wants you to do something for him. Think about it and then decide. But do not accept anything that will make your name known far and wide. That will be dangerous. Let someone stand in front, let someone else's name be on the documents.'

I found all this very annoying. I had fled Bath because of the intrigues that seemed to surround me. And now, here was I, in a strange land, with strange people among whom I felt oddly at home, and yet I seemed to be surrounded by more intrigues. Canker must have sensed my irritation because he rose in that effortless, smooth, way of his, saying, 'You will find out soon enough. And if you want me, tell Joseph.' And then he was gone.

Joseph brought in two oil lamps and an earthenware bowl in which embers glowed. He threw some powder on the red coals. Clouds of fragrant smoke billowed out. 'For to keep away the mosquitoes, master. They come at sunset. I will open windows, presently, and tell *punkha* coolie to pull strongly so that you get more air.' He called out in Tamil, 'More breeze for master!' and the huge sail fan overhead flapped faster, cooling me. I watched, fascinated, as Joseph unfurled the mosquito net from above my bed and tucked its ends securely under my mattress. He checked the little bowls of water on which the legs of my bed stood as moats against predatory ants. He filled a brick-coloured goblet with water and stood it on a table under the *punkha*-fan. 'Water will have little-little taste of herbs,' he cautioned. 'don't mind. They make water clean. Master not get loose belly if you drink this water. Master Kline's servant tell me his master would like to meet you after breakfast, not tomorrow, but day next to tomorrow. How you say, master?'

'The day-after-tomorrow.'

'Thank you master. The day after. Say four bells of morning watch which is 10:00 am of the clock. It suits master?'

I nodded.

'Yes, master. Now I put here, on Master's desk, one book sent to Master by Bales-sir, Writer of the governor-sir. He says, maybe, tomorrow you may read it because it is about one great governor-sir named honourable Mr Yale. He is, maybe, some grandfather-like of Master?'

'He was my great-grandfather.'

'Ah! *Great*-grandfather. Master has *verrry* high family. Now, with Master's permission, I will leave … But often, often, I will look in and whenever Master awakes, I will be there. Good night, Master …' and he stepped out, closing the door softly behind him.

Once again I felt very tired and looked at my bed longingly. I couldn't understand why I felt so lax after my long siesta. But the leather-bound book lying on my desk caught my eye and I walked across and began to leaf through it idly. Its title, elaborately tooled in gold, read:

> **The Life and Achievements of**
> **His Excellency the Hon'ble Mr Elihu Yale**
> **Compiled by**
> **Haji Mustaq Mohammed Moosa Late Dubash to His Excellency**

My hand began to tremble. This was an incredible treasure. My tiredness vanished. I picked up *The Life and Achievements,* opened the heavy cover and attempted to read the first, vellum, page. And then I realised that it would not be an easy task. Both the script and the language were florid and ostentatious, more like a poetic court proclamation than a record. The English was difficult enough but the Persian called for all my concentration. It riveted my attention nevertheless, and I noticed that whenever the author wrote about the personal life of Great-Grandfather Yale, he used Persian. I brought both oil lamps to my desk, turned up their wicks, and settled down. Much of it was a repetition of the information Grandfather Lynsdale had given me during those long conversations in Shawclose. It spoke about Elihu Yale's days in England, America and Madras; his marriage and Governorship of Fort St. George, his association with Yale University, the birth and death of his only son.

And then I came to the most startling bit of information about the origin of our surname. The *Life and Achievements* went on to say, rather cautiously and in Persian:

> 'It is believed that a daughter, Martha, was born to the Yales in Madras in 1690 but because an Indian soothsayer had predicted her death if she should ever be exposed to the Indian sun, her birth was kept hidden. She was, secretly, entrusted to the care of a wet-nurse, a soldier's wife named Colleen O'Sullivan who had a daughter of the same age as Martha. The girl Martha grew up a sickly, over-protected, child who first saw the sun when she was nine years old on the Indiaman *Madras Trader*, sailing to England with her anxious parents, her nurse-maid and the nurse-maid's daughter. Colleen O'Sullivan's husband had died of over-indulgence in alcohol. It is not known what happened to Colleen O'Sullivan's daughter but she is not mentioned after her father died. In 1711, at the age of 21 Martha Yale married Bernard Lynsdale, was delivered of a daughter in 1713, and died giving birth to a still born son in 1715. After her death, the distraught Bernard Lynsdale changed his surname to Yale-Lynsdale to continue the name Yale. Elihu Yale, apparently, left a substantial part of his fortune to Bernard Lynsdale.'

I had been so engrossed in the narrative that I looked up with a start when I found that there was light in the sky and my eyes were gritty with tiredness. A cool breeze had begun to blow across the parade ground. Joseph came in, soft-footed as usual, gave me the light breakfast I asked for, and then I flopped into bed and fell asleep. And I slept all through the day and didn't wake till the next morning, feeling very fresh and very thirsty. I had a cold sluice bath, dressed and was surprised to find Kline waiting for me at breakfast. I had quite forgotten our appointment. But there he was, bright and smiling, looking out of the window as Joseph laid the dishes on the table. Joseph wished me a cheerful 'Good morning, sir.'

Kline turned around. 'Morning, Lynsdale. Or may I call you John, since we have been billeted together? Please call me "Norbert". I detest "Nobby", it makes me sound like a lump!'

I couldn't help but laugh at this but somewhere, at the back of my mind, there was uneasiness. I knew I had to be careful.

Kline made his sally between Joseph's excellent *rice-opper* pancakes and the dessert of hot vermicelli porridge called *payasam*, and said,

'This is excellent. Don't care much for vermicelli, myself, but the hot milk, raisins, cashewnuts and almonds, all sweetened with *jaggery*, are very sustaining.' He began to sip his *payasam* appreciatively.

I waited.

'Have you met the governor?' he asked.

'Not yet. I have an appointment with him today.'

'And have you met the Major? Major Stringer Lawrence?'

'No.'

'Could I ask you a personal question, John?'

I nodded.

'Have you come to India to make your fortune?'

I wasn't used to such direct questions; not from a man I had met only the day before.

'Yes,' I said. 'That's one of my reasons.'

'Good. Making a fortune as soon as possible is most important for me. But I have a problem …' he waited till Joseph left, though I could see him standing behind a carved wooden screen eavesdropping on our conversation. 'My problem, John, is that I don't have any influence over the governor.' He placed his cup carefully in its saucer, dabbed his lips with a napkin. After that his words came out in a rush. 'The governor wants to put you in charge of the commissariat. It's a very lucrative post because you will buy all the local supplies for the Fort. Will you accept it?'

My thoughts raced helter-skelter. I called out to Joseph and asked for more *payasam*. Kline was silent, regarding me intently. Joseph hurried in with a brimming bowl of porridge, and tripped. The bowl flew out of his hands splattering sticky, white, *payasam* over Kline and me. We sprang to our feet. Joseph was incoherent with apologies, dabbing a duster nervously on our soiled clothes, pleading. '*Ai-yoooo! Ai-yooo!*' he wailed, 'Joseph has done so wrong … Joseph dies of shame and sorrow. *Ai-yoo-yoo*!!'

Kline's face was sculpted in ice. Without raising his voice he snapped, 'Shut up!' and then he turned to me. 'We'd better change. I have an appointment with Merchant Hurlingham Walls in fifteen minutes. What time's your appointment with the governor?'

'Two hours from now.'

'I'll see you after that.' And he hurried into his room, calling out to his servant.

I was angry with Joseph for being so clumsy, but when he entered my room and closed the door behind him, he put his finger to his lips and tiptoed close to me. 'Please take time, dressing, master. Canker-sir is coming to meet you after Kline-sir leaves.' And then he joined his hands in apology. 'I am sorry for inconvenience, master. It was only way I could delay you …'

Canker and I had a long discussion, and then I read the documents he had prepared for me.

Two hours later I was with the governor's writer, Humphrey Dumbarton Bales. He looked like a large boiled egg crowned by a pale grey prune, but he smiled with infectious joviality as if the whole world was a great, big, joke. I learnt, later, that this was his normal manner which was why he was known as Humpty-Dumpty Bales. I thanked him for sending me the Yale book and he said, 'It was the least I could do.' He waddled out from behind his desk, knocked at a door bearing the arms of the Company, opened it and announced, 'Writer John David Albert George Yale-Lynsdale,' with all the bubbling flourish of a court jester masquerading as a herald.

I stepped into a huge, plush, room full of red velvet curtains, a Persian carpet, dark carved furniture, and an enormous ebony desk. Behind it, backed by a large painting of the Company's headquarters in Leadenhall Street, sat a little man with a bald head, ginger mutton-chop whiskers and tiny blue eyes that blinked at me. He reminded me of a hunted fox turning on its tormentors. I felt very sorry for Senior Merchant and Acting Governor Malachi Mossworth Redant, trader, sycophant and five times the acting governor thanks to his ability to fawn, untiringly, on my grandfather. I had learnt this, and much more, from Canker when he visited me after breakfast.

The governor stood up and extended his hand long before I had come within reach. I caught a faint, feral, smell but his voice was surprisingly modulated and cultured.

'I trust you have been taken care of, Mr Yale-Lynsdale. I believe, I do believe, that you have a letter for me from my worthy mentor.'

I handed over my grandfather's letter. He studied the writing and the seals on the enfolding ribbon with great delight like a child revelling in a birthday present and not willing to unwrap it. Eventually, he prised open the seal, very carefully, with an ivory paper knife, studied the contents of the letter, nodding and smiling. Then he picked up a magnifying glass from his desk and scrutinised the letter all over again, nodding and smiling even more.

'Good, good!' he whispered. He folded the letter, and sat back with a smug smile on his face. 'I have, of course … as indeed you must be aware Mr Yale-Lynsdale … received a copy of this letter brought by the frigate *Valiant*.' His smile widened, revealing sharp little teeth. I started to say something but he held up his claw-like hand and shook his head. 'Well, Mr Yale-Lynsdale, I have decided to appoint you in charge of the Commissariat immediately. How does that sound?'

'Very agreeable, sir.'

'Capital, capital. But there is a point. My mentor does not want me to give undue currency to your surname,' he let his voice trail away. Outside, on a feathery-leafed tree, a flock of crows cawed raucously and dived at a hawk. The governor nodded and smiled absent-mindedly at the birds. Then he turned to me 'Have you given this any thought?'

'Yes, sir.'

'Good, good. And in what name should we register your appointment?'

'Could you, sir, formally appoint Norbert Kline to the Stewardship of the Fort on condition that he deal exclusively with the John Company?'

The governor frowned. 'Kline? Norbert Kline? What does he know about trade and shipping? He's fit only for skirmishes in the field. And what is this … this "*John Company*" eh? Never heard of it!'

'It is a company that I intend, with your permission, sir, to register immediately. It will deal, exclusively, with the buying and selling of goods and services for the Fort. If you permit it, sir, I shall be the sole proprietor of the company and, if such an arrangement meets with your approval, sir, I shall donate 5 per cent of my profits to any charity that your lady, so renowned for her good works, would care to expend it on. Anonymously, of course. It is my grandfather's principle, sir, never to take a receipt for any monies that he may devote to charity.'

He looked at me for a moment, a strange expression on his face. 'We place our orders on Kline on condition that he places all those orders on the John Company. Is that the plan?'

'Yes, sir,' and I handed him the two contracts that Canker had prepared. I stood back wondering how he would react.

Major Stringer Lawrence

The governor's mouth dropped open in amazement as he read the two documents.

And then his body began to shake and a strange hissing-neighing sound emerged, tears streaming down his cheeks with mirth. When he stopped gasping with glee he extended his hand and shook mine again.

'I see, Mr Yale-Lynsdale …' he said, hoarsely, between deep breaths, 'that my mentor has not lost his touch. No, sir. And Mrs Redant will be delighted, absolutely delighted. No question of it at all. None at all …'

He signed the documents with a flourish, rang a bell, and handed them over to, Bales. Then he leant forward. 'And now I would like you to meet Major Stringer Lawrence. He has been busy training our peons to become soldiers. My worthy mentor has prevailed upon Leadenhall Street to sanction a handsome amount, a very handsome amount, for the outfitting and equipping of Lawrence's native army. You will, of course … that is to say, the John Company will, of course … handle all the transactions connected with this,' and he rubbed his hands with an oddly rasping sound, his little pigs' eyes blinking rapidly.

At that moment Bales entered and announced, 'Major Stringer Lawrence,' and both the governor and I rose.

I had expected a whipcord thin, bristly moustached, martinet of a military man. But apart from his oddly thin lips, Stringer Lawrence looked more like a well-fed Roman cardinal: a little jowly, a shade portly, patches of sweat dampening his crumpled uniform. In spite of his appearance, however, he was brisk and a man of few words.

He nodded at me and shook my hand with only the faintest of smiles on his lips. When the governor told him that the Company had sanctioned everything that was necessary for the outfitting of his troops, all he said was, 'About time!'

Governor Redant cleared his throat nervously. 'John Yale-Lynsdale is Director Bernard Yale-Lynsdale's grandson, Major.'

Stringer Lawrence turned his head, slowly, and examined me for a moment as if he expected to see the taint of trader on me. The only time he showed any emotion was when the governor announced that he intended to make Kline the Steward of the Fort, if he relinquished his commission. 'Norbert Kline's a good man,' Lawrence said in a clipped accent, 'A born soldier. A leader. But no trader. Why do you want to make him the Steward?'

The governor shuffled out from behind his desk, rubbing his hands nervously. 'Because,' he whispered, and then cleared his throat and repeated in a louder voice, 'because the future enterprises of the Fort are intimately involved with military endeavours. A military man will make the best Steward …' He coughed and swallowed and dropped his voice again. 'But he has to relinquish his commission …' he seemed to be at a loss for words, 'besides …' his voice faltered.

'Yes?' Lawrence prompted.

'Mr John Yale-Lynsdale will assist him. He's had considerable experience in trade and shipping.'

Lawrence looked at me again and again his thin lips twitched in a smile. He nodded his head slowly. 'Doubtless!' he said, not bothering to keep the cynicism out of his voice. 'Well … follow me, Lynsdale,' and he turned on his heel and marched out without another word. I nodded goodbye to the governor and hurried after Lawrence. He was the second person I'd have to handle with kid gloves.

Nevertheless, I couldn't help but admire the skill with which Stringer Lawrence drilled the native peons, Indo-Portuguese topasses, and a few Europeans, on the sun-battered parade ground. He mocked, cajoled, badgered and humoured that motley crew of stoop-shouldered shuffling individuals till, by lunch time, they were marching in a cadenced *left-right! left-right! left*! Another group, a week their senior, had already begun their arms training under a Welsh sergeant. To my surprise I recognised a few of Canker-chan's men who had been waiting for us when we disembarked on the beach. I recalled his words, 'When you want warriors, they will be ready.' I wondered how many of them had got themselves enrolled into Stringer Lawrence's makeshift army.

Quite suddenly, I felt light-headed and I staggered. Stringer Lawrence gripped me and led me into the shade. I must have fainted for a moment. When I opened my eyes, I was sitting in a cane chair in the porch of the Quarters and heard Joseph saying, 'I am servant of Yale-Lynsdale-sir, master.' He was bobbing his head at Stringer Lawrence. 'Sun too hot. I shall take Yale-Lynsdale-sir to his room. Thank you master.'

The touch of the sun did not last long. And Kline's high spirits helped. He was overjoyed at being made the Steward of the Fort. 'I'll get back my commission when the need arises, and it'll arise very soon,' he said confidently.

In the mess, that evening, Kline was brilliant. He was gracious to his seniors, swapped tales with his equals, and stood at least three rounds of drinks to his juniors. Before the evening ended, most of our mess-mates would have followed him to hell and back. He then made the proposal Canker had warned me about.

'John,' Kline said, as we were walking back to our rooms, 'You've been here three days, you've formed your own Company, met some of our denizens. What do you want to do next?'

'I want to get down to work, Norbert.' Then, because I didn't trust this affable Kline, I added, 'After all, our fortunes are interlinked, aren't they?'

For a moment he froze and those strange eyes bored into me. Then his face relaxed in a smile. 'I should have admitted it when we shook hands on the ship,' he said, 'but I'll say it now. I think we understand each other, John. I'm sure good fortune, very good fortune, will attend our endeavours.' Once again the odd cynical smile, so like his hero's, played around his lips. Then he bowed and left.

Norbert Kline would cooperate with me as long as he had to. But, if it was to his advantage, he'd as readily throw me to the wolves. I had to move fast.

I fell asleep to the welcome roar of rain pouring down.

The next thing I knew was a smiling Joseph proffering a steaming cup of tea. The wind had blown away the storm and the parade ground had been scrubbed clean. There was a crisp feel in the air. I told Joseph I'd have breakfast later, dressed hurriedly, and ran down the stairs to the veranda facing the drill square. There wasn't a soul in sight and a silvery light, the colour of mercury, illuminated the Fort. It was very, very, beautiful.

'Peaceful, isn't it?' Major Lawrence stepped out from behind one of the pillars. He clutched a large, pewter mug in his hand.

'Morning Major. Yes, it does look very serene.'

He cleared his throat, sipped his tea. 'Deceptive, Lynsdale. Very deceptive. The storm will come again and, this time, I hope it doesn't sweep us off our feet.'

'Do you feel it will swing round and hit us?'

'Not that storm, Lynsdale. We can handle those. No. The storm being brewed by Dupleix. We're sitting on a powder keg and some fool might strike a spark. …' he belched slightly and said, 'Excuse me …' and then he asked, 'Do you know anything about the political turmoil that is gnawing at the entrails of India?'

'I know something about the coastal rivalries of the European nations: us, the French, the Dutch, the Danes, the Portuguese …'

He held up his hand. 'The Dutch, the Danes and the Portuguese won't give us much trouble. The French are another matter.' He took another sip of his tea and was silent for a while. 'Do you know anything about European history, Lynsdale?' he asked.

'A little, but …'

He didn't really expect an answer because he cut in, 'India resembles Europe after the fall of the Roman Empire. The Mughal Empire, here, is weak and rotten at the core. It can't hold on to its territories. Former generals and governors have set themselves up as independent kings, fighting with each other, asking the European nations to help them in their battles for territory. And there are people who make a living, a very good living, recruiting European military men to train the rag-tag troops of these native princes.'

He shook his head in disgust as if he despised such middle-men.. Then he added, 'But if we stay away from it, the Froggies will have a field day and emerge as the masters of India. They're sharp, they're sly, full of intrigue and treachery. And we have to beat them at their game or march out.' He looked at me again. 'Do you know the layout of the Fort, Lynsdale?'

It seemed to be a sudden change of topic but, obviously, he was thinking of the next French attack.

'No. I haven't had the time to find out.'

'Make the time, young man. Make the time … Mani!' A boy of about twelve appeared, seemingly out of thin air. 'Bring the map of the Fort from my room. Give it to Yale-Lynsdale-sir.' Lawrence ordered. The boy raced away. 'He'd lay down his life for me. I'll tell you how we met, some time.' The boy materialised at my elbow, holding out a map. I took it from him, looked down for a moment. When I looked up again, he had gone. Lawrence noticed my startled expression and laughed softly. 'Mani does that very often. I'm sure he can vanish in the middle of an empty parade ground. He says he *thinks* himself invisible …' Lawrence shrugged. 'Well, I must be about my work, Lynsdale. Study the map and take a stroll.' He nodded and strode away to where his recruits were lining up.

I studied the map after breakfast and then began to walk around the Fort.

Streams of Indian merchants and middlemen, frightened by the threat of another French attack, kept pouring in from our smaller trading settlements up and down the coast. They came on horseback, in carriages, in plodding bullock carts laden with trading goods and furniture, baskets of live chickens, parrots in cages. Milch cows and buffaloes were tied to the carts, dogs trotted dutifully behind.

'Blimey!' exclaimed the burly Gunner Alfie Harris, breathing the local, gin-like, arrack all over me. 'It looks like a county fair, it does! You getting the lay of the land, are you, sir?'

I picked my way through the human and animal traffic and climbed to the battlements to get a better perspective of the Fort. It was built rather like an irregular pentagon with its long, eastern, base on the beach. Its southern fortifications, almost as long, were protected by the natural moat of the Cooum River. Our western and north-western walls rose from the Elambore stream. And the northern wall was strengthened by six block houses backed by thorn and cactus fences. Beyond these were the common lands and then the geometric grid of the Black Town with thousands of houses packed close together. The caravan of merchants and middlemen wound through the Fort and into Black Town.

Black Town, as I could see from my perch on the battlements, was not, really, a part of the Fort: it was beyond the Outer Walls. Between those grey ramparts and the Inner Walls was White Town where the Europeans lived. And though many of their houses had been re-occupied after the French withdrew from Madras … and some had lines of washing fluttering in the hot, Madras, wind …

none of the families had really settled down. The future was, still, far too uncertain. The Inner Walls enclosed 'The Castle': the parade ground, the barracks, the Quarters which were formally called the Writers' Building where Kline and I had our rooms, the Governor's Office and Mansion, and the all-important godowns or warehouses. In The Castle, our flag flew again from the tallest mast in India, but there was still tension in the air.

The wind shifted slightly and I heard the Welsh sergeant barking his orders at the marching recruits, The Major's commands were also carried up to me. He was supervising the reinforcement of the defences of the Fort. According to Kline, Senior Surgeon Mathew Poulson had warned Lawrence that he was endangering his health by driving himself so hard but Lawrence had growled, 'There is no time. They'll be on us at any moment.'

When I climbed down from the battlements I felt the fear and uncertainty that trembled in the air. But trade couldn't suffer. I knew that I had to set up my business immediately. My problem was that I was, virtually, a private trader, and the governor could not give me space in any of the Company's buildings.

Canker stepped into the breach. He said, 'You must meet Avram Hawkenian. He's an Armenian ship chandler and Agent. He is the only private trader permitted to live within The Castle. His ancestor helped the Company get this piece of land and they've been here ever since. Hawkenian and his family live in their mansion a little beyond the parade ground. His offices and godowns are on the ground floor facing the parade ground.' I had seen the mansion with its walled garden.

'Hawkenian is a great admirer of your grandfather. Perhaps he could let you have part of his premises. It's worth trying.'

It was: even though I thought it very unlikely that one trader would help a probable competitor.

Nevertheless, I took Canker at his word and sent a peon with a message to Hawkenian that I was coming. After some time, I walked across. He was a tall, slim, elderly man seemingly as cold and impassive as granite. His hair was grey, his eyes were grey, and he wore a long grey coat that touched his calves. Even his trousers and soft shoes were grey. Only his fine-boned face, with a complexion that seemed to glow with inner health, relieved the impression of cold inflexibility. I felt that he had been so battered by life that he had withdrawn into himself. But his greeting was strangely warm, though his lips scarcely moved. 'It is a great pleasure to meet you, Mr John,' he said. He spoke so softly that I had to strain to catch his words.

I got to the point immediately and told him that I was looking for somewhere to set up my office. He nodded his head slowly and said, 'Ah yes. Of course, of course. And I have heard that you are the grandson of my revered old friend, Director Bernard Yale-Lynsdale. That is correct?'

'Yes, sir. And also the great-grandson of Governor Elihu Yale.'

'So! You have a great lineage!'

'Thank you, sir.'

'Ah yes. Good, good,' he nodded again. 'Then all that is necessary is for you to see the accommodations and decide if they are suitable. I will take you around.'

I could hardly believe my good fortune. The accommodations, as he called them, were excellent. A large godown and a sorting shed with a spacious cargo door; and two attached rooms looking out on the parade ground. I couldn't have asked for anything better. 'The accommodation is excellent,' I said. 'May we talk about the rent?'

He held up his hand. 'In due course, Mr John. In due course.' He smiled slightly, as if to reassure me. 'Married?'

I said I wasn't. He smiled frostily again and said, 'We all know Mr Bernard. You are his grandson. Everyone admires Governor Elihu Yale and no one believes the stories they spread about him.' I made another mention about the rent.

'Rent,' he said, 'I must charge so that you remain independent of me. So … I shall take from you, Mr John, the grandson of my friend, the great-grandson of Governor Elihu Yale … an absolutely, non-negotiable sum of … one pagoda a year.' He raised his hand when he saw that I was about to protest at the absurdly paltry sum. 'Say no more, Mr John. It is non-negotiable and final. Say only if you will accept it or not …'

I bowed slightly and said, 'Thank you, sir. I will very willingly accept it.'

'Good, then that is settled. Please move in. And if I can be of any help, please ask …' He stood up. 'Now, if you will excuse me, I am an old man and I must eat a little, frequently, or else my constitution protests.' He inclined his head and walked out through the door at the back of the room that I had already decided to make into my office. I looked around, delighted, planning how I would arrange the furniture, where my employees would sit. I decided to move in immediately.

That, however, took a little longer than I thought it would. But, eventually everything was in place, my employees had been engaged, and a suitable board erected, proclaiming:

THE JOHN COMPANY
AGENTS BY APPOINTMENT TO
THE HON. EAST INDIA COMPANY

I was in business and it had almost seemed too easy. But, I still had a queasy feeling. Kline was ambitious and ruthless. With him as my associate, I would have to be very careful, very, very careful indeed.

Coja Petrus Uscan

The uneasy feeling persisted through the next day, but there was no time to worry.

Kline was delighted when I shared the profits with him every month. He was a strange person. He divided his spare time between the governor's library and Stringer Lawrence. He hated parties. Once he asked me, 'Have you been blooded?' I asked him what he meant but he only smiled and said, 'You'll find out. Everyone has to be blooded, John.'

After dinner, one day, Kline said, 'I've got the day off tomorrow and we're going to the mansion of Coja Petrus Uscan, and then have luncheon with him, no less.'

'Who's he?'

'He's the leader of all the Armenians and he's invited you. And me, of course. You're mixing with nobility, John. I really am very fortunate.'

As usual, however, I didn't know if he meant it or was being cynical.

The next morning Kline was waiting for me near a crimson, four-wheeled, cab. It had a white canopy trimmed with crimson. Even the smiling cabbie wore a crimson livery trimmed with white. The horse was a handsome grey stallion, muscled like a thoroughbred.

When we got in, Kline said, 'Let's go, Nathan,' and we set off.

We drove through the Fort, nodded to the Major watching his troops being drilled on the parade ground, and out through the other portal. Just outside, we turned through tall, wrought-iron, gates, along a drive bright with cannas being irrigated by men carrying leather sacks filled with water, and into the porch of a large, squat building with green louvered windows and awnings. More men with leather water-sacks, drenched curtains made of the absorbent roots of fragrant *khus* grass. A whole row of *punkha*-coolies tugged at ropes which pulled the huge cloth fans inside.

Whoever lived here lived very well indeed.

We were received by a turbaned servant, taken through a maze of dark, cool, anterooms, and into a pillared gallery surrounding a courtyard garden. A fountain plashed into a lily pond bright with shimmering fish: scarlet and silver, gold, black and sapphire-blue. Birds twittered and sang in the trees. High above, covering both floors of the courtyard, was a dome of glass in an iron framework. It was all so unexpected, so breathtaking, that I exclaimed,

'This is incredible, Norbert!'

'I am so glad that you appreciate my little retreat. I spend most of my waking hours here. It gives me the illusion that I am back in my beloved Julfa.'

We looked around and, at first, we didn't know where the voice was coming from. It was a deep, slow, voice with a slight lisp and a tendency to pronounce all the 's'es like zeds. *Zo* glad, *apprezhiate, zpend* and *illuzhon* rumbled out very clearly. Then we saw him. He was a man of average height but he gave the impression of being much taller and heavier, because of his extraordinary dress. He wore a large, maroon, silk turban completely covering his head and a maroon velvet coat with pearl buttons reaching down to his ankles. His feet were shod in soft, white, slippers and he leaned heavily on an ebony stick inlaid with silver. He was clean-shaven and, though he must have been almost seventy, his eyes, on two sides of his beak-like nose, sparkled and seemed to change colour between blue and green and brown peering out from the overhanging cliffs of his shaggy eyebrows. He walked slowly, deliberately, up to us and extended his right hand on which a single, huge, ruby glistened in a heavy gold ring.

'And now,' he said, 'we will sit down on these cane chairs … some people call them peacock chairs … and converse and sample my hospitality. I have heard a great deal about you, Mr Kline and am glad that we, at long last, are able to meet. And Mr Yale-Lynsdale, your grandfather had, more than once, done me the honour of gracing my home and it is, indeed, a pleasure for me to welcome his grandson before I close my eyes. And as for your great-grandfather, he was a shrewd businessman but a very honourable one. His word was his bond and that is an admirable quality in anyone but particularly a businessman.'

As if on cue, servants in maroon livery appeared. They brought in a large brass table and placed a number of dishes, decorated with an array of food, on it. 'My chef, Salim, once worked in the kitchens of the Ottoman's Topkapi Palace in Constantinople. He was the favourite of one of the sultan's younger daughters. Perhaps too much a favourite. I had to use all my persuasive powers to spirit him away before, as the saying goes, the axe fell.' He laughed softly but with great good humour.

It was a memorable afternoon. Coja Petrus Uscan, head of the rich and powerful Armenian community, was a Company Councillor. He spoke softly and wittily of his family who had traded with the East for many generations; of his years in Manila, handling that Spanish colony's trade with India; of how he escaped when the French conquered Madras, took shelter in the Danish colony of Tranquebar, and sent a caustic reply in verse to Dupleix when the French tried to persuade him to settle in their colony of Pondicherry.

'This is a land as deceptively simple as a chess-board,' he said nodding his turbaned head, 'but the moves of the warring pieces are infinitely complex and only a fool would dare to predict the outcome of the game.'

The food, served in silver dishes, was cut into bite-sized pieces and was replenished constantly: ortolans, plovers' eggs, crabs, lobsters, fresh-water prawns and fish, fowl and lamb cooked in a myriad ways. All served with a variety of vegetables washed down with the lightest fruit juices and sherbets. We finished with a whole range of puddings, which Kline referred to as 'sweets', and an array of fruit including grapes and blood-red pomegranates.

The light through the glass dome was golden with sunset when we rose to leave. The Coja saw us to the door and then apologised, 'My wife sends her regrets that she was not able to meet you but she has been unwell for a few days. Nothing serious, we have been assured. And my grandniece, who is like a daughter, for we have no children, is away visiting a school friend a little to the north of the town. They have so much to talk about and there is so little company for her here that she usually returns after sunset. Well … hasta la vista, gentlemen. And I do look forward to the pleasure of meeting you again.'

On the way back in the cab, Kline said, 'Obviously, he's taken a great fancy to you, John. Pity you didn't meet his grandniece, Ann Hawkenian. She has hair the colour of port wine and eyes like emeralds.'

He lapsed into a reverie. The cab stopped in front of our building and, as we were climbing the stairs, I asked, 'Are you interested, Norbert?'

'I was. Very. She remained polite and distant. But even if she warmed to me, now, I wouldn't pursue the matter. I couldn't marry her.'

'Why not?'

'She's Armenian. I'd ruin my career if I did not marry an Englishwoman. The Company doesn't admit it, but as the influence of the Church, the Anglican Church, increases, it becomes more bigoted and hidebound about mixed marriages.'

'And morganatic marriages, I suppose.'

'What's that? What did you say, John?'

'I said, "And mormonatic marriages",' I lied.

'Mormonatic? Never heard the word. Oh, you mean a harem sort of thing. There's plenty of that around!. No one objects to you cohabiting with the other races. It's just that you shouldn't marry them.'

I thought about that for a long time before I fell asleep. This was another one of distasteful conventions that governed the brittle society in Fort St. George. The most snobbish were the ones who had borne the brunt of snobbery at home: working class people like the Scythes and Kline. The blue bloods had treated them like dirt in England; now, in turn, they treated Armenians and Indians as their inferiors: good enough to use, but not good enough to be equals. I, very definitely, did not want to conform to their stupid prejudices. I wondered what they would do if they discovered that I was of royal blood. For a while I toyed with the idea of revealing it. But then I realised that it was a stupid, destructive, thought: it would draw the Saxe-Gotha assassins to me.

I decided to conform till I was on firmer ground. But I did catch myself thinking of Ann Hawkenian with hair the colour of port wine and eyes like emeralds. And then I wondered if I would ever meet Lucia and see my son. Obviously, obviously, I was still on very shaky ground …

Shaky or not, however, it suddenly dawned on me that I had made very little effort to get to know many of the 200 or so people who lived in the Fort.

The governor had permitted me to have my meals in my room … 'I realise you must be very busy, Mr Yale-Lynsdale. There's little point in you conforming to the Fort's routine. Time enough for that when you've got things going the way you want them to. Eh?'… and I had been so involved in supervising every aspect of the John Company that there had been little time for paying polite calls. But the matter was taken out of my hands. The Fort's routine intruded …

One morning Joseph came in unusually early. 'Morning master,' he called out cheerily. 'It is six-half o'clock. I bring tea then Master have prayers at eight.'

I was still a little groggy with sleep. A ford had been flooded by a cloudburst in the mountains and my trader's bullock-cart caravan had been delayed. I hadn't got my goods tallied and stacked till three thirty in the morning. 'What did you say, Joseph?' I asked.

'Prayer time at eight. Master must be ready. Joseph bring *chota hazri*: one banana, two biscuits, tea or coffee. Then, after Prayer Time, Joseph set out breakfast. Will Kline-sir be having …'

I cut him short. 'What did you say about prayers, Joseph?'

'Yes, master. Prayer Time at eight of the clock.'

I had to settle something once and for all. 'Joseph,' I said, 'I say my prayers when I like, not when someone tells me to. Is that understood?'

He seemed genuinely concerned. 'Then Master not go to Assembly Room to say prayer with Governor-sir, Councillor-sirs, and all other ladies and gentlemens. It is Special Assembly for Master and the Padre-sahib and his lady. Notices on all boards, Master.'

I shot out of bed. Kline had told me that Special Assemblies were held to make important announcements and to introduce newcomers. Everyone, including the wives, had to attend.

There were many more than 200 people in the Assembly Hall. Urns of tea and coffee, and plates of snacks, had been laid out on tables at the entrance-end of the hall. This was the first time I had seen a congregation of the residents of the Fort and I began to have qualms of conscience at not having met most of them in the weeks I had been here. It was a warm, humid, morning without a breath of breeze and the Assembly smelt of sweat, unwashed clothes and a clashing onslaught of perfumes.

I spotted Kline in the second row, right. He caught my eye and tapped the vacant seat next to him. When I slipped into it he leant over and whispered, 'This is when you meet the other denizens of our menagerie. Many of them would make the March Hare seem the acme of sanity. Beware especially of the female of the species. They're either revolting or ravenous.'

'They look rather well groomed and well fed to me.'

'John! John! You've got a lot to learn … Hush! Here comes the Supreme Potentate himself accompanied by his August Lady, the Potentatess …' It was all I could do to suppress my laughter as we rose to welcome Governor Mossworth Redant and his gaunt and gawky wife, Camilla known, inevitably, as 'The Camel.' Redant mounted the stage, looked around, cleared his throat. We bowed our heads when he said the prayer, sat when he read the lesson. And then he made the announcements.

'Today, we formally welcome into our midst, the Reverend Brandell Scythe and his charming wife, Mrs Joanna Scythe. The Scythes will jointly share the pastoral duties of Pastor Ian Williamson who, as you know, has been long indisposed and is eager to return to his beloved York where his wife and seven children await him. We have already bid him farewell at an earlier Special Assembly and now we, again, bid him god speed and may the Lord guide him and keep him for many years to come. We wish this in Jesus' name …'

There was a chorus of 'Amen!'

Governor Redant looked around the hall, caught my eye, and nodded slightly. He cleared his throat again and, in a slightly more ponderous tone, continued, 'In this hour of peril, we give a special welcome to the youngest official to join our ranks.' He waved a limp hand at me. 'Mr John David Albert George Yale-Lynsdale.' I turned and bowed to everyone. Joanna Scythe, sitting in the front row ahead of me, turned, looked into my eyes, and ran her tongue over her lips, slowly. Kline whispered, 'Sit down, John. What do you expect? An encore?' I turned away and sat down hurriedly. Redant continued, 'We shall make use of John's attainments in the most suitable manner possible and I have, in fact, informed him of the special role I expect him to play in sustaining and protecting our little community. The Lord, in His wisdom, knows that we can use all the strength we can muster.'

'Amen! Amen! Praise the Lord!' proclaimed Mrs Walls, her hands raised in the air.

The governor looked rather startled and hurriedly said, 'As that concludes the official business of this Assembly, we shall now disperse for the customary one-hour reception for our newcomers.' Chairs were pushed back, there was a shuffling of feet and a babble of conversation. 'John, prepare to be dissected …' said Kline, softly, and moved away as he saw Joanna Scythe make a beeline for me.

She looked very feminine in pink and blue and she placed her hand on my arm and said, 'Why have you been avoiding me, John?'

'How's the Reverend?'

'As usual. Deep in spiritual comfort. Would you like to drop over at six this evening?'

I was spared the embarrassment of an answer as Mrs Walls hurried up. 'Oh there you are, Mr Male-Crindale …'

'Yale-Lynsdale, madam. Y-A-L-E L-Y-N-S-D-A-L-E.'

'Ah yes, of course. How silly of me. But, as I was saying …'

I never did find out what she was saying because a large group detached itself from the Scythes and surrounded me, shaking my hand, tapping my shoulder, spouting welcoming phrases:

'Are you related to … Is this the latest fashion in London? … If you're an angler, I know some … Believe you faced a terrible storm. Was it very frightening? … … You must drop over an evening, Mr Yale-Lynsdale. Send across a peon with a message … Do you think you can spare some time to help me out. Some other ladies and I are working with the families of our soldiers. They really need all the help they can get … What does London think about the situation in France. Do you expect they'll attack us? …'

I was spared answering their inane questions because Kline strolled up, radiating charm, and said, 'Do excuse John, ladies and gentlemen. We have a little business to discuss.' They smiled, nodded, and dispersed: in the Fort 'business' took priority over everything else. Kline bent forward as if he was whispering something very confidential to me but all he said was, 'Don't let their attention go to your head, John. Their initial assessment is that you are over-confident, have an inflated opinion of yourself, and are arrogant. Those are three of the more favourable opinions I have heard about you.'

'But this is the first time I've met most of them!'

'Here, in this insular society, opinions are formed at first sight, on the speculations of others, on prejudice. It's a nest of vipers with no one else to sting but each other.'

I decided to be as outspoken as he had been. 'And do you, Norbert, honestly believe that I am over confident, have an inflated opinion of myself. Am I arrogant?'

Kline became very serious. 'John, you were born into a rich family, highly regarded by society. The way you speak and behave shows a self-confidence which can't be learnt: you have to be born to it. And, to those who don't have your background, it looks very much like arrogance.'

I left it at that. Obviously, the Fort held a lot of hidden currents swirling under its bland, grey surface. I couldn't sleep for a long time that night.

The Blooding

Things took a curious turn in the days following the Assembly. Tensions built up; rumours started circulating; Kline was brusque; Stringer Lawrence became more of a martinet, increasing the hours of drill; even Joseph seemed to feel it.

'Is there going to be fighting soon-soon, Master?' he asked me at breakfast one morning.

'No, I don't think so. Why do you ask?'

'In the bazaar they are saying that fighting is coming. So prices of everything is going up-up. Also they are saying that Chanda Sahib in Arcot and Mohammed Ali in Trichy, both are buying many-many provisions so, maybe, they are also thinking of making fight with each other.'

Chanda Sahib and Mohammed Ali were the puppet princes supported by the French and us for the control of the goods of the rich Carnatic lands of southern India. Under the Treaty of Aix-la-Chapelle we could not go to war against the French directly, so we had to keep each other in check through our proxies. But if puppets took it into their heads to fight each other, we'd be sucked into the war and our trade would suffer. Both were small-minded men obsessed with their own importance.

I asked Lawrence if the two princes would go to war.

'Quite possible. They're swollen headed and unpredictable. And that witch, Jacqueline Dupleix, knows how to twist their minds. She's itching for a fight with us through our puppets.'

'Jeanne. Her name's Jeanne Dupleix,' I corrected.

'Whatever!' he snapped. 'The Devil has many names …' and he started bellowing orders to his marching men. Obviously, his nerves were frayed.

The tension began to affect everyone in the Fort. The married Factors and Merchants became as prickly as hedgehogs. Their women had a brittle, wide-eyed harassed look. And when I went for a walk around the Fort one night, I heard raised voices from Councillor Ackroyd's bungalow, and the sound of breaking glass from the Bales' cottage. Most people in the Fort seemed to be as irritable as rats in a trap and they fed on each other's unspoken fears. I tried to keep my anxiety under control and not bark at Kunhi Krishnan and my other workers. In the strained atmosphere that surrounded us, that wasn't easy.

I tried to work harder to tire myself. I put in long hours in the governor's Library and in studying languages: a Muslim scholar improved my Persian, a Tamil Brahmin burnished my Tamil, and a charming couple, the da Gamas, instructed me in the intricacies of Portuguese and French.

After the da Gamas had been tutoring me for a month Canker remarked, 'According to our Captain Livre, you can understand spoken French well but your accent has a Pondicherry intonation. But Kline's *dubash,* Joachim Sardesai, who is from Goa, says you speak Portuguese with the accent and manner of a *fidalgo*, a nobleman. You have good teachers.'

I kept thinking of the young Mrs da Gama. 'The da Gamas are a pleasant couple,' I replied.

He nodded. 'So I have heard. It is good that you work and study so hard. It is difficult to keep waiting for Dupleix: it is easy to find the wrong diversions.'

But I didn't have to find them. They found me.

Three days after Christmas, in 1750, Joseph brought me an invitation from Factor 'Plummy' Grover, to a *nautch* party that evening. Plummy's *nautch* parties had quite a reputation, and I was curious.

All the native princes had troupes of these dancing girls but we had to get our entertainers from the Black Town. At dinner in the Mess, as the arrack had flowed before its ban, there had been a lot of talk about the dancing girls. They danced and dressed in the Mughal manner: blouses and wide skirts, pantaloons tight at the ankles below the skirts, and a veil covering their heads and the upper parts of their bodies. They were accompanied by two musicians, one playing a sort of fiddle, the other a drum. The singer was, often, a retired dancer, no longer attractive enough to have coins thrown at her feet as they were at those of the younger and more lissom dancers. Since no one knew the finer points of the dance, or understood the words of the song, the girls had to earn their keep in other ways too.

I felt I was reasonably well prepared when I got to Plummy's bungalow that evening.

As I had expected, the *nautch* party started in a fairly decorous manner. All of us sat around a semi-circular dance floor at one end of the room. Servants brought around drinks, morsels of chicken, kebabs and heaped plates of those delicious fried cashewnuts. The musicians tuned their instruments and the singer tried a few, screeching, nasal notes; then hawked and spat a stream of red betel juice into a spittoon. This went on for the best part of half an hour till there was a general murmuring from the audience and hoots for the *nautch* to begin. Plummy threw a handful of coins on the floor and the singer smiled like a black-toothed, red-mouthed, ogress. She nodded and the music took on a more spirited beat.

The first *nautch* girl swept onto the stage. She was slim and attractive and danced with demure grace. Gradually the tempo of the music quickened and two more girls ran onto the stage. Their skirts began to swirl out like fans, revealing their red pantaloons. There was a cheer and the servants hurried forward with more drinks. A shower of coins rained on the floor, swiftly raked in by the singer.

The tempo speeded up. The three girls had changed in a trice and now their veils no longer covered their heads but were draped over their shoulders and bosoms. They swayed to the music, their arms and hands moving in sinuous rhythm. The music got faster and the girls swirled around, their veils billowing out. Someone yelled 'Bravo!' and coins pattered at the dancers' feet. Suddenly the billowing veils floated away from the bodies of the dancers and there was a roar from the audience. Their breasts were naked. They extended their arms out and stood still; and then their shoulders began to move and the movement spread to their breasts. Slowly, they put their hands behind their backs and thrust their trembling breasts outward and upward, moving all the time.

Someone put a glass into my hand. It was chill and misted. I drank the pale green liquid thirstily. It was faintly aromatic, with a sweet, resinous, flavour.

An ensign named Wellesley reached out for one of the girls but Plummy pulled him back by the scruff of his neck.

I was feeling very light-headed. I thought it was because of the heat and the excitement, so I swallowed another mouthful of that green drink.

Once again the musicians had begun to speed up their tempo and the singer was wailing in a throaty, quavering, voice which I seemed to have heard before but I couldn't recall where. My head seemed filled with cotton but, oddly, I had begun to feel at peace with the world. I knew I could do anything I wanted to whenever I wanted to.

The bare-breasted dancers began to pirouette: slowly at first, then faster and faster and their full skirts swirled higher and higher. I heard regular clapping, in time with the drum beat, quicker and quicker and quicker and quicker. I joined in, my heart throbbing in time to the tympanic rhythm. I had difficulty in focussing my eyes but I made an effort and succeeded. The girls swiftly moving legs were bare, bereft of the red pantaloons they had worn when they had started their dance. Higher flew the skirts, and still higher, the clapping urging them on. Bare calves. Knees. Higher still. Thighs. The skirts flared out like mushrooms and we began to roar. We got brief, tantalising, glimpses of triangles of black hair as they whirled and whirled.

Then, with a crash of the drum, the music stopped.

The girls touched their waists and the skirts unfastened and flew away.

For an instant they stood stark naked, their magnificent golden bodies filmed with sweat, their breasts heaving. And then they ran out towards us.

One of the girls caught my hand and said, 'Come!'. I downed the last of my drink and let her lead me, running out of the door with this naked girl, into the night. My mind seemed to be suspended above my body, looking down at me running with the girl to a little tent pitched at the bottom of the garden. Dispassionately, I noticed that two other naked girls were leading Wellesley and Hartley to other tents.

The tent was dark except for a single red lantern hanging high on the tent-pole. There was a strong fragrance of jasmine and I saw that cushions and a mattress had been spread on the carpeted floor. And everything had been covered with fragrant, white, jasmine, blossoms.

She grabbed me without kindness, without subtlety only with urgency and savagery; and I responded like an animal just as harsh and hard and unforgiving. There were no kisses, no touches, only clasping and enfolding and squeezing and thrusting. And the smell of crushed jasmine and sweat and the musky animal aroma of pumping body fluids. I heard her cry and I recalled the sound now: the throaty, quavering, cry that I first heard torn from Lucia that night when the fireworks exploded in the sky and we loved each other again and again and again. The girl made that animal cry as I exploded and it mingled with my bellow of ecstasy. We entwined and merged again; and again we cried once, twice, a third time, a fourth and, very slowly as she moved on top of me, a fifth time, before we fell into an exhausted sleep.

I woke with dawn filtering in through the mesh window of the tent. She was dressed and was washing me, gently, with a soft towel which she kept wetting and wringing out in a brass bucket. Then she helped me dress and smiled and handed me a letter. She led me out into the chill, dew-wet, garden. She put two fingers to my lips, placed those fingers on her heart, and said one word, before she ran across the lawn and out of the gate. I opened the letter in my room. It said, '*Congratulations. You've been blooded – Plummy Grover.*' But the word that the girl had whispered to me still rang in my head filling me with pride.

She had called me a '*Maha-sher*,' a Great Lion. I felt very elated.

Thomas Didymus

I bathed after staggering home from Plummy's party. Then again before breakfast; then once more after. My body itched with constant scrubbing but that didn't ease my fear. I had awful thoughts about the French Itch and of my genitals rotting and falling off.

The clouds sat fat and black over Madras, and sweat oozed from every pore but still my skin felt chafed and dry. So did my mouth, but I put that down to the weird concoctions I had had at the party, particularly that strange green drink. All thoughts of a possible attack by the French had been overtaken by a more imminent danger. As soon as I could, I hurried across the parade ground and stepped into the Sick Bay. Dr Poulson was in the next room grinding powders with a pestle and mortar.

'What can I do for you, young man?' he looked at me under his bushy eyebrows.

I swallowed and blurted out, 'I want to be examined, Dr Poulson. I want to know if …' I stopped.

'If what?'

I tried but couldn't bring myself to say it.

He gazed at me for a moment, frowned slightly, and nodded. 'Were you at Plummy's party last night?'

'Yes sir.'

'And were you blooded?'

'Yes sir.'

'And you're feeling sore and think you've got the French pox.'

I nodded.

He sighed and shook his head slowly. 'You're sore because you over-exercised your genitals yesterday. And scrubbed them over and over again, today. No, you haven't picked up the French pox from those *nautch* girls. I examined them before they went to Plummy's party. I always do. They're clean. But you might have reacted to *thandai.*'

'*Thandai*, sir?'

'The green drink they gave you. It's ground hashish, mixed with cream, milk and spices. It loosens your mind, makes you believe that you're as strong as a bull. Some people get a rash after they drink it. Come on in, I'll have a look at you.'

He examined me with a coach lamp and a lens. Then he said, 'Put it away.' He scrubbed his hands. 'You've over-used your instrument, or the *nautch* girl has, though they're usually careful: they can't afford to damage their principal source of livelihood. Rest it for a day or two and it should be in fine fettle.'

But I wasn't. Suddenly I felt the need to re-discover the warmth of my faith. I was a Catholic, we had suffered for our faith. It had always been the sheet-anchor of our lives. But I had not been to a Catholic church ever since I had left Bath. I yearned to attend Mass, go to Confession and be cleansed, receive Communion. I thought about it a lot and then decided what I had to do.

I was taught French and Portuguese by the da Gamas. He was born in the Portuguese colony of Goa, she in the French colony of Pondicherry. They both lived in San Thome: a former Portuguese colony taken over by the Company. He was short and muscular with a café-au-lait complexion and filled with boundless, restless energy. She had a sun-bronzed Mediterranean complexion, was a little shorter than her husband, and when she smiled it started from her eyes, moved to her lips and then lit up her whole face.

When they had finished my hour of instruction I said, 'Can we walk out of the fort and onto the beach for a short while. I want to ask you something.' They seemed surprised but they agreed. I wanted the people in the Fort to notice that I was treating them like friends.

On the beach I asked them, 'Can I attend Mass in your church in San Thome?'

They looked up at me. 'Are you a Catholic, Mr Yale-Lynsdale?' she asked.

'Yes. I am.'

'But we have never seen you in church.'

'Hush, Clarissa,' he admonished. 'That's sir's personal business.'

'I was told, Clarissa, that as an officer of the Company, I would not be welcome in San Thome. And I don't know of any other Catholic church in Madras. I'm the only Catholic in the Mess.'

They exchanged glances. The he spoke rather haltingly, 'All Catholics … are … are welcome … to all Catholic services …'

'Avelino, be frank …' her voice was sharp. 'You know how some people feel about the English, especially those who come from the Fort.' She turned to me. 'It is true that some people, the older people, don't welcome the Company's officials ever since the Company took over San Thome. But we shall speak to the Vicar. Mass is at 7:30 am on Sunday. It you are there fifteen minutes earlier, we will introduce you to some of the senior parishioners. Perhaps you might like to try out your Portuguese. It would make them very happy …' and she laughed.

'Would you like us to come for you at 6:45? We have a light, trotting, bullock cart,' he said.

'No, thank you.' I smiled. 'I'll take a horse from the stables.'

'And then, after Mass will you have a typical Goan breakfast with our family?' she asked. 'We'll invite a scholar who knows a lot about San Thome. Otherwise there'll be just my mother-in-law, Avelino, our infant son Francis, and me.'

'I'd love to join you for breakfast. And now I have to go back to the office …'

I saw them mount their little, cushioned, bullock cart. Avelino clucked to his bullocks and they took off, trotting and jouncing happily. I wondered if I had done the right thing. But then, I hadn't attended Mass ever since we had sailed out of Portsmouth. Besides I wanted to meet people who were not part of the tight, inward-looking, circle of the Fort, even if it meant breaking a stupid, rigid, convention. If I didn't set my own rules now I'd become like the others: holed up in the Fort, tense, frustrated, seeing India and its people through the blinkers of trade; and then fleeing back to the cold and misty isles to brood about their days in the tropics, while nursing their gout by the fire. To hell with the Saxe-Gothas; to hell with the French. I would spread my wings and if the people in the Fort didn't like it, to hell with them.

That afternoon Canker came to me and said, 'John-chan, you were seen walking with those people from San Thome, the da Gamas.'

I looked up at him and said nothing.

After a while he continued, 'You know that the people in the Fort frown on that sort of behaviour.'

'Really? But they don't frown on adultery and orgies. In fact they encourage them,' I replied.

'John-chan, what are you trying to do? Are you trying to change your people? You know what the Tamils say about the English? "Clean outside, dirty inside." Even the *nautch* girls charge extra for a party in the Fort and they laugh when the doctor examines them before a performance. "He's protecting *them* from us! Why doesn't he protect *us* from them?" And everyone knows what goes on between the young men and the wives, here. But that is the way of the Fort. If you want to live here you have got to live by their rules. And one rule is that you can employ the people of San Thome, you might even use them in other ways … but you must never get friendly with them …'

I had had enough. 'In that case, Canker, I shall break the rule …'

He hissed through his teeth in dismay. 'In which case, Johnny-chan, be prepared to be treated like a crow with a white feather …'

I thanked him and said, 'I shall decide for myself.'

On Sunday morning I mounted my favourite grey gelding, Ashdown, and trotted to San Thome. The sea was rough and the coconut palms were being buffeted by the winds of the north-west monsoon. It also snarled in white-horses, spewed a fine spittle-spray on the road. All the black catamarans had been drawn up and covered by palm-thatch, lashed down with tough coir rope. Apart from a bullock-cart laden with green coconuts, and a temple-elephant carrying its lunch of palm-fronds, I had the glistening road to myself till I neared San Thome. Then, as the houses of the former Portuguese colony hemmed in the streets, I rode past mushrooming umbrellas as people strolled to church under the grey and cloud-roiling sky. Everyone wore black and the women carried black head-scarves. I dismounted at the gate, hitched Ashdown's reins to a lamp-post, and walked up to a small knot of people standing around a priest in a white cassock. A man detached himself from the crowd and bustled up to me. Only when he was close did I recognise Avelino da Gama in his formal attire.

'Mr Yale-Lynsdale,' he welcomed, 'I'd like you to meet Clarissa's cousin, Father Julio Mascarenhas. Father, this is Mr John Yale-Lynsdale …'

The priest had rugged features as if they had been chiselled, rather roughly, out of old teak. His thin lips stretched in a smile but the warmth did not reach his eyes which continued to examine me suspiciously.

'Have you come to look round the church. Senhor Lynsdale?' he asked in strongly accented English.

'I have come to attend Mass, Father,' I replied in Portuguese.

He looked up in surprise. 'You speak Portuguese?'

'A little, Father. I am still learning.'

A thin, stooped, scholarly looking man with an imperial beard spoke. 'I am Professor Anaceto Fernandes … I have a longer name but this will do for the present, Mr Yale-Lynsdale … and, as a member of the … how would you call it? … the Parish Council, if you will … may I ask if it is curiosity that causes you to attend Mass in our historic church?'

I looked at him for a moment without answering. Then I said, very slowly, 'I understand that this is a Catholic Church. In other parts of the world, Catholic churches are open to all people provided that their presence or conduct does not offend the congregation. Does a different custom prevail here? Or does your Parish Council administer an Admission Test to everyone who wants to enter?'

The professor's eyes narrowed and his thin lips twitched but the priest extended his hand to me, and this time his smile did light up his eyes. 'Ah, Mr Yale-Lynsdale,' he said in English, 'Our professor is very zealous … as of course he should be. But Avelino and Clarissa have spoken about you. Welcome to our church …' He had a warm, firm, handshake. Then it began to drizzle and the priest put his arm around my shoulders and led me into the church, followed by the others.

There was a palpable aura of piety inside that I had not found in any church in England. It enveloped me like a warm cloud of incense. Everyone in the congregation was either deeply in prayer or in the queue in front of the three screened confessionals. I asked Avelino, kneeling beside me, which of the confessionals had an English-speaking priest. He nodded to the second cubicle where a ruddy-faced priest with a full ginger beard was entering. He sat down and pulled the curtain behind him. The cubicle was now sequestered from the congregation. 'That's Father Adrian Gomes; his mother was English,' Avelino said.

Most non-Catholics are suspicious of Confession. They are unable to appreciate the relief that one can get by unburdening one's transgressions to an anonymous priest. He can't see you and you can't see him and, since everything is spoken in a whisper, he will be hard put to identify your voice even if he does know you. But that, really, is the whole point of it. Catholics believe that the priest is merely a channel to God, and that the penitent is asking forgiveness from God who gives it through the priest. It may sound like a lot of mumbo-jumbo to those who have not experienced it but it does lift the burden of guilt from a penitent's mind if one makes a clean breast of all that one has on one's conscience. I did, even though my litany of lusty sins was a fairly long one. The confessor asked only four questions:

'Are you married?'

'No, Father.'

'Did you commit adultery, that is did you lie with a married woman?'

'No, Father. I don't think that that *nautch* girl was married.'

'Are you a young man?'

'Yes, Father. I am 20.'

'Are you truly sorry for your sins?'

'Yes, Father,' I said, very sincerely. I had a brief, and guilty, vision of Lucia but I put it aside hurriedly. She was married now and I had no intention of being trapped by a frustrated wife.

'You are young, impatient. You want to do everything now because you do not know if you will get this opportunity again. So you throw caution to the winds. Remember, however, that everything comes from God: your nature, your youth, your opportunities, even temptation. Christ was tempted. But He listened to His conscience. When temptation comes, take a little time, a few short breaths only, to listen to your conscience. Then there will be fewer occasions for you to face the humility of kneeling in a Confessional. But if your need does get the better of your conscience, come back to the Confessional, surrender the burden of your guilt to God and walk away lighter, cleaner, stronger. For your penance you will say one Rosary remembering the Sorrowful Mysteries of the Agony of Jesus who suffered and died so that our sins may be forgiven. I now absolve you in the Name of the Father, the Son and the Holy Ghost. Go and sin no more.'

I really did emerge from the Confessional feeling lighter, cleaner, stronger just in time to join the queue for Communion. The consecrated Host melted on my tongue and I became one with my ancient faith again.

When Mass ended there were more than sixty people waiting outside to shake my hand. Clearly, my partaking of the sacred sacraments had convinced the congregation that I was a genuine, practising, Catholic and many were smiling, and nodding their approval when I spoke to them in my halting Portuguese. Avelino and Clarissa walked with me to their cottage across the road from the church. On the ground floor was their *Panjim Bakery.* A flight of stairs, inside, led up to their home: warm, cosy, a little cluttered with bric-a-brac and dominated by a large altar with its burning votive lamp. The house was rich with the aroma of baking bread, freshly churned butter and the yeasty tang of coconut sap. And hurrying out of the kitchen, from which the fragrances emanated, came a remarkable little woman. She couldn't have been more than 4' 10", dressed in rustling black with a striking head of silver hair and a chubby, pink, smiling face, like a porcelain doll, out of which two baby-blue eyes peeped, bright with mischief. Her voice had the fluting tones of a child.

'I'm Rosita da Gama, Senhor Yale-Lynsdale. I am honoured to welcome you to our home. You have met my two children. You will, presently, meet my grandson, Francis, after he has been made presentable by his maid. And behind you comes our resident intellectual, Professor Anaceto Fernandes … I see from the way he is nodding his head that you have already met in church. Good. Please sit down wherever you are comfortable.' She nodded, wiped her tiny hands on her lace-trimmed apron, and bustled into the kitchen, followed by Clarissa.

I turned around to find a broadly-grinning Avelino. 'As you can see, my wonderful mother takes care of everything.'

The professor settled himself on a sofa and patted the seat beside his. 'Senhor Yale-Lynsdale, if I may make so bold as to say it, our parishioners were very impressed by your command of Portuguese, your devotion at Mass and … not the least …' he chuckled nervously … 'because of the effective way in which you trimmed my wings.' He shook his head as I raised my hand in protest. 'Yes, you did, Senhor, as elegantly as a *fidalgo* would have done. And … I must confess … I deserved it. So …' he smiled at me revealing large, yellow, predatory, teeth, '… what would you have me tell you?'

'Everything, senhor. I am a Catholic from a country in which we are in a minority. I know little about the history of Catholicism in other lands. And virtually nothing about it in India …'

'Then, Mr Yale-Lynsdale … may I call you Mr Lynsdale because though many Portuguese also append their mother's surname onto their own, in conversation we call them only by their paternal surname … now, where was I?'

'I wanted you to tell me more about the Goans? Your people are Goans, aren't they, Professor?'

'Strictly speaking, no. Goans are the people of Goa. My people came from the Portuguese possession of Goa. But most of the others in San Thome claim descent from Tamils converted by St. Thomas, the Apostle of Christ. I prefer to call them Thoman Catholics. But, to get back to your question, you have … if I might be a little presumptuous in this matter … come to the right person, in the right time, and in the right place.' He coughed, then raised his hand, 'But I may warn you: it will take many visits to San Thome to get even a feel of Indian Christianity. It is much older, by far, than its infant sibling in your Misty Isles. Are you interested enough to spare the time, senhor?'

The women came bustling in along with a maid and a freshly scrubbed and powdered child. The child toddled up to each of us, including his father, and gravely shook hands and then, as dignifiedly, toddled away with his ayah. His grandmother beamed with pride and invited us to sit down at the breakfast table. There, over *sanas* dumplings, *pao com chourico* sausage-meat spread over lightly toasted rounds of bread, *ale belle* pancakes with coconut milk and molasses sauce, washed down with a delectable chilled almond drink called *orchata*: over all these exotic dishes we chalked out my visits to San Thome for the next fortnight.

But I didn't have much time to brood over it because, as soon as I returned to the Fort, Joseph said, 'The governor-sir wants to see you at ten of the clock sharp, tomorrow, sir. Mr Bales, himself, delivered this message.'

Bales would not meet my eye when I stepped into his office the next morning, so I felt that something had gone wrong. He opened the door to Redant's chamber and closed it behind me. Redant looked up from his desk but did not ask me to sit down. When I stood in front of him he said,

'Do you find San Thome interesting?'

I was prepared for that. 'Very interesting, sir.' I said. 'I've been doing some research into the history of Christianity in India … I'm trying to find out how the Apostle Thomas came to India in AD 52. That's the sort of information that Leadenhall Street might find useful when dealing with the Mughals. They tend to claim that the Crescent came to India long before the Cross so we are the interlopers …'

Redant looked bewildered but my argument must have sounded impressive because he mumbled, 'Quite so, quite so. Exactly. The Cross arrived before the Crescent. Well put. Very well put. Thank you John …'

I walked out but I knew that I had been treading on very thin ice. Nevertheless, the professor's views on Christianity were so convincing, though unorthodox, that I was drawn to our meetings with an almost fatal attraction even though they shook the very foundations of my faith.

Briefly, he hinted that the Apostle Thomas was the blood brother of Jesus Christ and they bore a physical resemblance to each other. 'That is why Thomas was called "Didymus" which means "The Twin." Jesus had sent his own brother to India because India was Christ's spiritual home: he had spent all his formative years here, studying under the great Buddhist masters in Kashmir which was a strongly Buddhist country then. This is where he had learnt his gentle philosophy of turning the other cheek, doing good to your enemies ... It was contrary to the "Eye for an Eye and Tooth for a Tooth" creed that prevailed in the motherland of Christ at that time. "Christianity is really a reformed Buddhism,"' Professor Anaceto Fernandes asserted. 'What is more, Mary, the mother of Christ should have been the head of the church after the death of her son. She was opposed by that fanatic, Paul, who had persecuted Christians before he had a change of heart. But the original message of Christ, which proclaims the great role of women as the vessels of life, has been preserved.' In the words of the professor which I recall with great clarity, 'Jesus, therefore, encouraged women to assume positions of pre-eminence in a remote monastery he established in the Himalayas. He hoped that, in course of time, this gentle Matriarchal order would prevail over the harsh Patriarchal one. At one time,' the professor stated, 'I understand that they called themselves the *Meri Magadhalis:* literally My Ladies from Magadh. Magadh was a powerful Buddhist kingdom in Eastern India but, apart from that, I cannot appreciate the significance of the name. I also do not know if the Order still exists.'

That was the last message I had from the professor. He returned to Goa a few days after writing that and died there under mysterious circumstances. I burnt that letter, the only one he had written to me, because his theories were too dangerous to be revealed. But though his written words have been incinerated, they have also been burnt into my mind. And I have this strange feeling, almost a conviction, that I shall be confronted with them again.

Ann Hawkenian

News of my visit to San Thome had, clearly, spread around the Fort.

Walking across to my office I met Kline striding along with his *dubash.* He seemed unusually cheery. 'Morning, John. You look very relaxed,' he remarked, and told his man to go on. When Sardesai was out of earshot, Kline said, 'Would you like to come with me to the Black Town tonight?' He raised his hand when he saw the expression on my face. 'No women, I assure you. They're free ranging and I wouldn't touch them till they've been vetted by old Poulson. No, definitely no women … But since you seem to have got a fair idea of San Thome … probably better than the rest of us put together … I thought you'd like to see how the other half of the Fort area lives. Game?'

There seemed to be a veiled threat in his reference to my visit to San Thome so I could hardly refuse his invitation to the Black Town. 'Game!' I said, not too enthusiastically.

'Good! I'll knock on your door an hour after sundown and we'll walk across.' He strode off jauntily.

'What does he want, Johnny?' Canker-chan asked. He had been standing at the door of our office.

'He wants to take me around Black Town this evening.'

Canker was about to say something when a gust of air puffed in and swung open the door between our office and the Hawkenian's garden. I got a glimpse of a young woman with dark red hair and a black riding cloak getting into a carriage. Then a servant shut the door from the other side.

'Who was that?' I asked Kunhi.

'Miss Hawkenian, Mr John. She has a school friend on the other side of Black Town. Often, she goes to see her.'

I wondered if she had eyes like emeralds and I felt my heart thudding. I snarled at myself silently. This was stupid. I had just had a fleeting glimpse of her. But then why did I feel as if I knew her … as if I had known her all my life. As if I had known her even earlier. In an earlier life? But I didn't believe in earlier lives. I was a Catholic, not a Hindu. But this cold, dispassionate logic refused to still the thudding of my heart and the conviction … Yes the conviction, the *certainty* … that I had known her. But, of course, I couldn't have … Then I was brought back to reality.

Canker entered and shut the door behind him. 'Kline is happy because Dupleix is moving again. The French governor is stirring up trouble between Chanda Sahib and Mohammed Ali. Norbert Kline smells war, Johnny-chan. He might tell you something this evening.'

But Kline was still unusually buoyant when we left our quarters at dusk. 'We have patrols moving around the Black Town, John,' he explained, 'but we're not too strict. There's a lot of gambling and drinking and sometimes things get out of hand. You won't find any women around: they'll have retired into their houses. In India, respectable women don't move about in the streets at night without an escort.' He waved a breezy salute to the sentry at the gate and we strolled through.

We passed the Coja's mansion, crossed the block houses and the cactus fence.

Kline asked, 'Have you made any progress with our resident beauty?'

My heart leapt again but I feigned ignorance. 'Resident beauty?' I repeated, 'Who's that?'

'Don't be naive, John. Her father's given you an office in their house. Obviously he has his eye on you. He's not given that privilege to anyone else!'

I laughed but it sounded strained to me. 'If you're referring to Hawkenian's daughter, I've glimpsed her getting into a carriage. That's all. As for why he gave me accommodation for my office, he said he knew my grandfather and admired my great-grandfather.'

Kline nodded. 'Ah well, that's half the battle won. Middle Easterners, like most darkies, are great on family alliances: that's what they call marriages by negotiations.'

The man was a prig, like most others in the Fort.

'Isn't that the custom among all noble families, regardless of the colour of their skins, Norbert? Even our royals do it all the time, don't they?' The conversation was getting quite risky but I couldn't let him make light of something so close to my heart.

He backed off saying, 'You have a point there, John,' and we were quiet for a long time after that.

The red gravel crunched under our feet as the road led us through stretches of rough pasture. These gave way to a few water-meadows that glistened in the moonlight and were cacophonous with a chorus of frogs grating and honking in at least three different ways. But the sound of the frogs receded as we approached the lights of the Black Town. As we got closer, however, I realised that the lights were not streaming out of the houses but were occasional lanterns hung on poles, throwing small puddles of yellow on the narrow streets. Most of the houses were in darkness with only the tiniest chinks of light emerging through the cracks in shuttered windows and doors.

But for all the dismal appearance of Black Town, it was loud with the sounds of revelry. Voices, most of them slurring-drunk, were raised in a hullabaloo of song, argument and bellowing laughter. A tavern door opened, spilling light on the street, and two men, with their arms around each other's shoulders, came staggering out. Another door gaped, and more drunken men lurched out. Kline and I held back to avoid them; and then we hurried on. It was like the Stews of London.

We had walked half-way down the street when we heard the first cry. We froze, not quite sure where it was coming from. And then it came again. Very clearly, a woman was screaming, 'Help! Help!' We dashed down an alley and into a street parallel to the one we had just left. Three tavern doors had opened, illuminating the scene.

A light, single-horse carriage was being led by a grey-haired man. In front of it, a woman in a long riding cloak stood, petrified with fear. And circling around her, like hunting wolves, three men crouched, their hands extended.

'Yum-yum, Billy-boy. That's a fine tarty bit of white meat!'

'Forget the meat, I want a juicy quim. And I'll wager there's a juicy one hidden behind all them widow's weeds.'

'Come, girly-girly. Give a man wot's not 'ad 'is rocks off for a fortnight: a good roll. You won't regret it, lovey … you never will …'

One of the men reached out for the woman and then yelped as she slashed at him with her parasol. The horse reared and the old groom yelled, 'Careful missy, careful … they is bad man.'

'How right you are, you old fart. How right you are …'

What I did next was triggered by long hours of practice with Canker in the *kalari* in Shawclose without my willing it.

My mind dove, deep inside itself past my self, 'The self lies in the front of the mind which is why you always put yourself first, but you must sink beneath your self, past your will, plunge far down where there is no reasoning. There is no time to reason, Johnny-chan.' Deeper, leaving the emotions behind, writhing like a nest of coiled serpents. 'Emotions choke reactions, John. Go beyond. To the back of your brain where the backbone thrusts like the stem of a flower. Don't think, don't feel. Let your nerves, your blood, your bones, your muscles, tendons feed on your ten senses ... taste, smell, sight, touch, hearing, balance, pressure, flow, tensions, awareness. LET GO!' Canker's teaching flared like a landscape on a dark night etched by a flash of lightning, in a white searing moment ...

I EXPLODED …

Leap! Legs pumping, crashing into flesh and bone … Spin … hand smash into windpipe … Pirouette … Elbow slam into diaphragm … Kick into a groin … Testicles crunching … Jump … Leg-lock … Fling him upwards, backwards … Stiffened fingers thrust into soft nostrils … Heel grind into throat …

'Easy Johnny … easy … it's over … I think they're dead … two are dead, one's gurgling …'

I swam out of a cold, white, pit. Kline was speaking to me, faint at first, then more distinctly. I was standing in a patchily lit street. Two men lay grotesquely crumpled at my feet, a third groaned, rattled liquidly, and then was still. Other men surrounded us. There was the thick taste of bile in my throat …

'Cor blimey, it's Mister … Yale-Lynsdale … and Mister Kline,' a burly moustached man peered into my face. 'That was some fight, Mr Lynsdale, sir. They 'ad knives, all three of them … I saw it myself …'

'Ay,' said another man. 'And Mr Lynsdale, sir, you were like a typhoon, you were, sir … Your movements, sir, they were blurred, like. They were so fast …'

"struth! I nivver seen anything loik it! They's dead, Burt, ain't they?'

There was the sharp toot of a whistle and the patrol came clomping up to be greeted by a babble of voices. They recognised us, saluted, and looked at our attackers. 'These scum were intent on attacking this lady from the Fort,' said Kline. 'Mr Lynsdale came to her rescue! I think they're dead now …'

'Does anyone know who they are?' the patrol leader asked.

'They're part of a press-ganged crew who jumped ship a week back,' said the man named Burt. 'They've been boasting that they were murderers; been making trouble in the Black Town ever since. Good riddance, I say ...'

I walked up to the girl. Her lips were parted and she was breathing heavily. Her magnificent breasts rose and fell under the black cloak. I looked over her shoulder and asked the groom in Tamil, 'What happened?'

'The horse lost one of its shoes, sir, so missy said she would walk. Then these men came. I could not leave the horse because he was showing the whites of his eyes and might have run over missy. You saved her! You saved my missy!'

More doors had opened and people were holding lanterns aloft. And, for the first time I saw her clearly. Her hair was the colour of port wine and her eyes were like emeralds. She said, 'Thank you very much. I'm ...'

'Ann Hawkenian ...' I finished. 'I know ...'

My heart was thudding so hard and so fast that I thought it would leap out of my chest. I also knew that I had fallen head over heels, irrevocably, in love.

Love is a terrible thing. It's a ravenous beast that devours you, day after day after day, demanding all your time, all your attention. Lust can be satisfied, set aside once you have possessed the object of your lust. Lust is like hunger: a full stomach can appease it. But love is a fatal sickness. It feeds on itself. The more you posses the object of your love, the more you want to encompass it. You can never have enough of love or of what you love. Everything you see and do, and taste and feel and hear, every experience you have, reminds you of the person you love.

And yet ... and yet I found that it wasn't just a spiritual thing. It wasn't enough for me to think of her the way one thinks of a flower, or of a great piece of music; or even for me to pour out the longing in my heart in emotional images the way poets do. It wasn't only mental or spiritual or emotional. It was also salaciously, coarsely, physical. I touched her once, escorting her back home, when she had stumbled on a brick lying on the road. But that one touch was enough to etch a memory that kept growing. Would her breasts feel as soft as her hand did. Softer, of course, much softer. Lucia's breasts had felt much softer than her hands.

The thought of Lucia spun the most lascivious images in my brain. Of her writhing and crying and clutching me with her arms, her thighs. Somewhere in my feverish recollections, Lucia's face and body changed to those of Ann. Her breasts filled my hands, her body sank under mine, we began to move …

The recurrent dreams of Ann built up in vividness till, one morning, days after I had met her, I woke in a bath of sweat an instant before I heard Joseph clattering the cups and saucers in the ante-room. I clutched myself and raced to the bathroom to stroke the terrible pressure out of me. I leant back against the door, breathing heavily …

I hadn't quite recovered even after breakfast and I was relieved to find that Kline had left early.

'Kline-sir very excited, master,' said Joseph, piling fried eggs and bacon on my plate. 'I think so that he has heard some happy news.'

'What news, Joseph?'

'No one knows about Kline-sir. He is very secret-secret …'

'Secretive?'

'Yes sir. Very secretive.'

But when I reached the John Company, Kunhi said, 'Mr Kline has been here twice. He said he'd be back at ten-half … er … half-past ten. There, he is coming, Mr John.'

Kline's face was flushed. 'Can I talk to you privately, John?'

I nodded to Kunhi; he went out, closing the door behind him. Kline refused to sit, 'There's exciting news,' he said, breathlessly. 'Dupleix's sending his little rat, Chanda Sahib, to besiege Mohammed Ali in Trichy. We've got to go to his aid because if Mohammed Ali is defeated, and possibly killed, Chanda Sahib will take over Carnatic and we'll be cut off from our main source of textiles. The French will walk in and Leadenhall Street will pull us out of Madras. It's diabolical; typical of that witch Jeanne Dupleix. You understand, now?'

I nodded. If that happened, Dupleix wouldn't even have to attack Madras: it would fall like a ripe plum into his lap!

But Kline hadn't finished. 'Here's a list of all the stuff we need to mount an expedition to Trichy. Get it as fast as you can. And you can raise the prices by another 15 per cent. We can't afford to delay and we can't afford to lose this battle. Hurry, John!'

Avram Hawkenian cleaned out one of his warehouses and rows of tailors sat on carpets, stitching sacks and bags and panniers for the pack animals. A little later, the bullock carts started rolling in, long lines of coolies offloaded the supplies, and the carts rumbled out again. We worked through most of the night, checking, weighing, measuring, packing, stacking it in the godowns. Kline came over once and, a little after midnight, the governor and Major Lawrence arrived.

'You look very tired, John.'

'We'll rest, sir, as soon as we've got through this.'

Two liveried servants appeared with silver tea services and chicken pieces in a flaky pastry. One of the servants said, 'Hawkenian sir ask sirs to accept these refreshments.'

The governor and Major Lawrence left when the second caravan of bullock carts creaked in. At three in the morning I called a halt. 'Take an hour off, everyone,' I ordered.

Canker offered, 'I'll wait. You rest, John-chan.'

I shook my head. 'I've got to stay. Everyone must know that I've stayed. Please go.'

When I was alone, I stretched out in a club chair, swinging out the leg rests and lying back. I fell into a dreamless sleep.

I woke with the uneasy feeling that someone was looking at me. I opened my eyes and saw her sitting just beyond the circle of light thrown by the oil lamp. I tried to rise but it's difficult to spring up from a reclining chair.

Ann said, 'You're very tired. Don't get up.'

The sound of her voice, the sight of her, made my yearning for Ann well up inside me again. She wore a pale green dress which enveloped her to her ankles. The oil lamp shot highlights from her shoulder-length hair. My passion for her made me feel sick in the pit of my stomach. I breathed deeply and got control of myself.

'What time is it?' I asked.

'It's a quarter after three. You've been asleep for fifteen minutes.' Her voice had a soft, deep, resonance with a faint lisp.

'Have you been watching over me all this time?'

'I couldn't sleep, Mr John. They say the French are coming. Is that why you're collecting all these stores?'

I stood up slowly, walked across to a straight-backed chair and sat down. 'No, I don't think they're coming here. They're probably planning to attack one of our friends.'

'Should I worry, Mr John?'

'John. Please call me John.'

'Should I worry, John?'

'No, you shouldn't.'

She looked down at her hands folded in her lap. She had tiny hands, almost chubby fingers with dimples where others had knuckles. She looked up and said, 'If you say so, I believe you. Thank you for saving me. I … I was so frightened, I forgot to thank you. My father was angry with me … John, I hear them returning …'

'May I come and see you sometime,' I asked.

She tilted her head to one side as if she was assessing me. 'You'll have to ask my father, John.' She stood up swiftly, 'I think … I think he will approve.'

I got to my feet as she reached the door which led from my office to their private wing. I heard voices and footsteps approaching. She turned around, 'I hope he approves, John…' then she was gone leaving a faint fragrance of sandalwood.

Canker-chan remarked, 'You must have rested, Johnny. You look quite refreshed.'

The next fortnight is a blur in my memory. Coja Petrus Uscan died and everyone who was anyone in the Fort attended the grand funeral. He had built the road up to Saint Thomas' Mount and so his funeral first wound its way up the hill and prayers were said in the church. His coffin was then taken down to its final resting place. His heart had been removed and was carried in a separate casket because it was to be sent for interment to Julfa. I saw Ann walking just behind the coffin, supporting Uscan's widow: They were both heavily veiled in black and I did not speak to her.

The next day Kunhi handed me a sealed envelope. In it was an unsigned note. It said,

'I am going away. I shall try to return as soon as I can.'

It carried the faint fragrance of sandalwood.

The Hawkenian's servants told us that she and her father had left for the Danish colony of Tranquebar.

I was hurt, at first, that she had not wished me goodbye in person.

But, when I thought about it, there was no way she could have: she was in mourning and I had not asked her father's permission to visit her. I might have brooded over Ann's absence If I had not been kept busy, for more than fourteen hours every day, equipping the expedition to Trichy … The governor, Lawrence and Kline came, thanked me, and said that the expedition would leave that evening. Lawrence wanted to encircle Chanda's besieging forces and force them to lift the siege without firing a shot or endangering the lives of any of our men.

But things didn't quite happen that way.

When our soldiers reached Trichy they found that though most of Chanda's troops had besieged the town, some had been grouped in small pockets further away, protected by the mansion-sized boulders and hillocks that dotted the countryside. If Springer Lawrence had moved his troops in to relieve the siege, Chanda Sahib would have pinned them between his own besieging forces and his re-grouped troops. Very cleverly, he had used our own strategy against us.

The messenger who came panting back to Fort St. George gasped, 'Mohammed Ali says, "I am desperate. Food is low and so is the morale of my men. If I am not relieved soon, many of my men will desert to the enemy. Yesterday we found a French agent offering big bribes to my soldiers to mutiny. We cut off his arms and legs and hung him in a cage from the walls of the Fort. He yelled so much that I got one of my men to shoot him. But the crows are still feasting and squabbling over his corpse in full sight of Chanda's army. Major Lawrence, sir, was very angry. He says this is no way to fight an honourable war. He is camping some distance away unable to attack, reluctant to retreat. That is all I have to say."'

The bedraggled messenger hung his head and muttered, 'I am very tired, very hungry …'

The governor called a meeting of the Council and I was asked to sit in as the governor's writer because Bales had gone with the expedition to handle the commissariat. It was a very tense meeting.

If Lawrence returned, the Carnatic would be lost to us. If he stayed near Trichy, Madras would be open to an attack by the French. Either way, Dupleix would triumph. Most Councillors felt that the brilliant Jeanne Dupleix had duped us. Aga Shawmier, who had taken Coja Petrus Uscan's place as the head of the Armenian community, disagreed. He dressed very much like the Coja except that he had a heavy, black, moustache and spoke with a stronger Persian accent.

'I think …' he said, '…I think that we are giving too much, altogether too much, credit to the trade ambitions of Joseph-Francois Dupleix and his lady, Jeanne. It is not as complex a strategy as some of us, perhaps, would like to believe. All they want is for their puppet to take over the southern territories of the Mughal Empire so that the weak emperor will be forced to declare Dupleix the Subedar, the Viceroy, of the Deccan. We are concerned about trade and wealth. The French are spurred by the acquisition of territory and power. Madame Jeanne has enough wealth for a woman who rose from squalor and poverty. She now seeks glory. She wants to be the Vicerene of India and her besotted husband will leap through a hoop at her command.'

'I don't think … we should … make such … personal … remarks … against Dupleix, his wife and the Mughal Emperor,' pleaded Merchant Walls.

'Why not, Mr Walls?' Aga Shawmier shot back. 'We all know that the Mughal Emperor is ineffective. Even his own vazir, his Prime Minister, joined his enemies last year to grab some of the crumbling Mughal Empire. Do you blame the French for helping their candidate? No, gentlemen, there is no intricate, trade-grabbing, plot hatched by the beautiful Jeanne. Personal ambition is all that gnaws at her soul. If Chanda Sahib loses, she'll find another puppet. I don't believe that the Fort is in any danger as yet.'

'As yet?' Redant repeated.

'Precisely, *As yet*. If Dupleix attacks us, directly, he will be breaking the Treaty of Aix la Chapelle. His government will be angry and they will recall him. That will put an end to Madame Jeanne's vaulting ambitions. But, if we don't succeed in foiling Chanda Sahib, then, shortly after Trichy falls to him, he will move against us. There is nothing in the Treaty that bars the native allies of the French from fighting the English. And then the French fleet will sail in and cut off our access to the sea thereby effectively bottling us in the Fort. It will all be over long before word can get out to Leadenhall Street. No, there is no immediate danger to the Fort. But it is on the horizon and will stay there, and come closer, unless we do something now.'

No one, however. knew what to do. And, after that meeting, trading in the Fort fell. The families in the White Town started packing. Kline lost his newfound affability and became surly again. Ann had left and I did not know when she would return. The ache for her only grew and grew … Had her father spirited her away because he didn't want her to marry out of their community, a non-Armenian? Who were the Armenians? I knew so little about them. Then, suddenly, a long-forgotten phrase my grandfather had used during one of our long evening sessions, came swimming unbidden into my mind. He was reminiscing about a spice deal he had lost in Alexandria. 'I was betrayed by my most trusted assistant. He was an Armenian. I learnt, then, never, never, to trust an Armenian. They are the Shylocks of the Middle East. The sharpest, most deceitful, traders in the world.' Why had I recalled that now, just when I had found Ann? It was an omen, a sign. It added to the oppressive feeling of despair hanging over everything and I felt sick in the pit of my stomach. I dragged myself back to my room. I told Joseph not to disturb me. I bathed, changed, and lay down … I felt my whole world collapsing around me.

Joseph knocked and entered, apologising. 'Sorry, master. I am telling ship's captain not to disturb you. I am telling him many times. But he is not listening. He insisting. He saying, "*It very, very, urgent. Must see Mr Yale-Lynsdale.*" He is Captain of *Konkan Trader*. He bring something from your honourable grandfather. I bring him in? Or I keep him out?'

I felt uneasy. 'Show him in, Joseph. I will be out in a few minutes.'

When I entered, a little man got to his feet. He had the face of a gnome: all wrinkles, a large nose, bald as an onion, and tiny eyes.

He sprang across the room and grabbed my hand, dropped it, sprang back, and sat. 'Brian O'Malley. Captain of the Frigate-Indiaman *Konkan Trader,* just in. To see Mr John Yale-Lynsdale. Mr Yale-Lynsdale?'

'Yes, Captain.'

'The grandson of Mr Bernard Yale-Lynsdale of Bath, Director of the Company?'

'Yes, Captain.'

'Very well …' the 'r' of 'very' went on and on and on. His Irish brogue was strong.

Captain O'Malley stood up. 'I am to inform you, Mr Yale-Lynsdale, that the day I sailed, five months ago, His Royal Highness Prince Frederick Louis, Prince of Wales, and the eldest son of His Majesty, George the Second of Great Britain, died. May his soul rest in peace!'

The March

I leant against a table and kept my face impassive.

My heart thudded against my chest and I felt the blood draining from my face. I heard myself saying, as if from a great distance, 'I'm sorry to hear that, Captain O'Malley. Is there anything more?'

'Yes, Mr Yale-Lynsdale. I was asked to give you this,' and he handed me a small, silver, box.

I thanked him, and laid it on a table.

'I am also to ask you if you have any verbal message for your grandfather.' He put a slight, but distinct, emphasis on *verbal*.

I nodded. 'Tell my grandfather that I have settled down and that I am following the instructions he gave to Mr Nair and to me. Please convey my warmest feelings to him and to my beloved mother.'

Captain O'Malley closed his eyes and moved his lips slightly, memorising my message. 'Anything else, Mr Yale-Lynsdale?'

'Nothing else, thank you, Captain.'

He bobbed his head, flashed a smile, and scurried away. I bolted the door behind him: I was free, free, free. I felt as light as a feather. I could have yelled and danced and got blind, roaring, drunk. The father who had disowned me, broken my mother's heart, spawned children through his royal whore … was dead. Leo 'Anver' was dead. And he had never … never, never, never … become king. As for the bastard he had spawned, the usurper who had stolen my rightful heritage, he might have the crown placed on his head, and live in palaces, and be fawned upon by poufs and prostitutes, but he would never know peace. All the horror and the agony and the tragedy that my father had wreaked on us, all of it would be visited a hundredfold on his royal bastard. Strange phrases kept flowing into my mind: '*The crown will be too heavy for him. He will lose his head, he will lose his head, he will lose his head* …' Beheaded? No, impossible! This wasn't the 17th century. Today, kings could not be decapitated the way Charles I had been. But the words kept repeating in my mind: *he will lose his head, he will lose his head, he will lose his head …*

I stopped because I realised that I had been talking to myself and only the loud chattering of hundreds of mynah birds had drowned the sound of my voice.

To steady myself, I picked up the little silver box and opened it. Inside was a gold locket with a griffon with ruby eyes engraved on it. A griffon, born of a lion and an eagle, Leo and Aquila. My hands were trembling when I opened it. Inside, facing each other, were miniature portraits of my father and my mother. The painter had captured the gentle delicacy of my mother's features, smiling softly, lovingly. Another artist had, obviously, created the other portrait: a very flattering one depicting him with all the weakness strengthened, giving him the appearance of a thinker, a man of considerable intellect. Protecting each of the portraits was a gold mesh, cleverly fashioned: like a rampant lion in the form of an *F* over my father's painting, and a *K* like an eagle with its wings spread over the portrait of my beautiful mother. The likenesses blurred as tears filmed my eyes and started coursing down my cheeks. I sat on my bed, biting my lips to stifle the sob in my throat. Triumph and agony fought for expression, racking me. And out of this torture, something began to happen.

I felt a heat starting from my loins and rising, slowly. I began to tingle as if a thousand tiny ants were biting me. And, as the heat travelled up my body, the tiny hairs on my skin began to stand on end. The rising heat seemed to pause at places in my body, filling them, engorging them like a streaming river filling lakes and flatlands in its course before moving on. My genitals were inflamed first, like a precursor of lust, then between my navel and my spine. The heat flowed upwards, filling my heart, making it glow and throb. Then the heat rose up my spine and spread into my throat as if it had been filled with scalding soup which, strangely, did not burn. Still higher the flowing heat rose and I felt as if my head was swelling and my ears bursting with an inner pressure. My senses swam. There was a silent phut! at the top of my head. My vision blurred and images began flashing inside. And, along with the images, came sensations, but they were like nothing I have ever experienced before. The pictures had a life of their own and I was not only seeing them but also experiencing them: I was an observer and participant at the same time. Fragmented, disconnected, unreal images at first. Women became beasts, battlements, balloons, spheres, triangles, rainbows, rivers, billowing smoke bursting into successions of colours trembling with shapes forming too rapidly to be perceived. Then they flickered, slowed, merged, became specific, crystal clear, clearer even than normal vision. A scroll unrolled before me, became a long, bright, road down which I was moving at great speed. But, in spite of the swiftness of my passage I saw people, events, places with great clarity and, suddenly, I knew exactly what my vision meant.

Then, as abruptly as it had come, it vanished.

I was lying in bed, breathing hard but surging with energy. I leapt out and rushed to Kline's door. I banged on it, calling out, 'Norbert! Norbert! I've got it! Norbert, open the door…!'

He stood there, his face suffused with rage. He looked at me and his anger cooled.

'What is it? What have you got?'

'Everything! I've seen everything. I know what we must do to rout Dupleix once and for all!'

He made me sit on his bed, gave me a glass of water, waited till I had calmed down. Then he listened to all I had to say. He questioned me over and over again. When he had finished, he said, 'It might work, John. It just might …'

I didn't tell him that it had to work. If it didn't, then the woman I had seen in my vision would rule Madras. She was slim, had long black hair, an olive skin and large luminous eyes. And she radiated cold, implacable power.

My memories of the weeks that followed are blurred. I feel as if I am standing on a high peak with the mist drifting up from the valleys. Sometimes it reveals one thing, sometimes another, but never can I see the whole landscape at one time. And even the bits I do see clearly are disconnected. Sometimes later events come first, then the ones that preceded them, then something that happened in between.

I remember Arcot Fort and the fifty-three long, dreary days we spent there with the rain of the north-east monsoon slashing down and the unending heat and dampness. Everything smelt of mould: our clothes, even the stone walls which burst out with clumps of mushrooms and evil-looking toadstools. I remember the scattered clouds of fireflies winking like tiny, living, stars; and the mosquitoes whining and homing in to every exposed inch of skin; and the endless *drip!-drip!-drip*! And boots and hands caked with clinging mud. The water from the three wells of the fort was brown and had to be churned with alum to clear it. It gave every swallow a salt-sweet taste. Snails left slimy tracks across the damp floors of our rooms and we had to move out of the driest chambers in the citadel so that the gunner could convert them into his powder stores.

We had brought the rain with us, marching from Madras when purple storm clouds massed over the sea and there was an ominous, oily, calm on the water. The little gnome, Captain Brian O'Malley, had looked into the sky, licked his finger, held it up to the wind and said, 'Ah sure, I'll be able to get there and back in time, gentlemen. But it'll be touch and go, touch and go! But, nevertheless, I will start loading only the day after tomorrow.'

'You can start loading tomorrow morning, Captain. If the sea remains calm, it should be completed in three days, otherwise you should be ready to sail within a week.'

'Thank you, sir. But I can start loading only the day-after-tomorrow. As you know … and you do know, being a good Catholic and all that … that tomorrow is a Feast of our Lady, the Blessed Mother of God. She is also Queen of the Sea. She would not like it if I started loading on that day as if I had no respect for her feast. It would be very unwise. Very, very unwise, indeed sir …'

It had taken Kline several hours to convince the Council about the wisdom of our scheme. He had wanted me to present it … 'Because it *is* your strategy'… but Canker had advised me not to take the credit. 'We don't want your name to figure prominently in any report sent to Leadenhall Street, Johnny …' Kline had been only too happy to claim it as his own but he had asked me to go along with him to the meeting.

The tide turned in our favour when Councillor Smithers cleared his throat and spoke, for the first time. 'Kline and Yale-Lynsdale are right. For Chanda Sahib it will be a matter of *izzat,* of honour, to recover Arcot. He cannot afford to let it remain in our hands.'

'I find that difficult to believe, sir,' argued Councillor Ackroyd. 'Surely the strategic value of capturing Madras will outweigh the *izzat* of recapturing Arcot.'

Smithers turned his watery eyes on Ackroyd and said, very slowly, 'Regardless of what you may or may not believe, Ackroyd, the fact is that the Indian princes place an almost medieval value on honour, much like the knights of yore did. They would sooner sacrifice themselves and their families, than their *izzat.* It is an admirable martial code that few other *professions* …' he emphasised the word, and paused before adding '… adhere to.'

Everyone in that room knew that Smithers spoke with the authority of his years in the Mughal court. There was much less discussion now. Then the governor asked us, 'You, obviously, expect to be besieged for a long time because with 150 trained soldiers and 300 sepoys and topasses you can't risk an open battle with Chanda Sahib's 8,000 men, possibly more …'

'Our sepoys and topasses have also been trained, sir. By Major Stringer Lawrence,' Kline interrupted. 'Yes, we must expect to be besieged for a long time.'

'Then how do you intend to move such a vast quantity, such an enormous quantity of arms, ammunition, stores and victuals, to Arcot?'

'John Yale-Lynsdale has a plan.'

Their eyes turned to me.

I said, 'I have already spoken to the Captain of the frigate-Indiaman *Konkan Trader.* He is ready to carry all our stores, and an advance commissariat party, by sea, to the mouth of the Palar River. They'll make camp a day's march from Arcot. Most of our troops will march from here to the Supply Encampment and then, together, to Arcot. We will move at night and in the early hours of the morning. We will take very few camp-followers, no women at all.'

'The men will be most unhappy.'

Kline intervened. 'The men want to be trained like a European army, not like a Mughal one. I shall inform them that no European army would risk taking women onto the field of battle.'

We decided to leave the loading of the *Konkan Trader* to Kunhi and the John Company. We had planned to leave at eight the next night but the heavens opened and it deluged. And then, as suddenly as it had come, the downpour stopped. We started after dawn, under a starlit sky. This was my first experience of a marching army, and I shall never forget it.

Ours was a small column, a shade over 500 men in all counting the attendants like the barbers, the washer-men, the personal servants, interpreters and the column's commissariat staff. Also a large assortment of carts of various types all referred as *bandies*. All vehicles, in Tamil, are called *vandis:* this had been transmogrified to *bandies*. Here were bullock carts and buffalo carts; horse-drawn gigs and carriages; teams of mules hauling our three guns; a tumbrel carrying squawking fowls in bamboo crates pulled by a beautiful old mare named Sundari; and a large flock of bleating sheep and goats herded by three indistinguishably dirty and aromatic boys named Mustafa, Maqbool and Matim. When this column was strung out along the palmyra-fringed, winding, roads with its torches and lanterns flaming and winking, it looked for all the world like a long, winding, line of glow-worms.

We crept along till dawn flared silver across the flat, green, fields. Then, to cries from the ranks behind to move faster, we set a brisker pace.

The Indian countryside is very beautiful, particularly at dawn when mist shimmers over the dew-sparkling fields. And then again at sunset when a saffron light touches everything: the thatched huts, patches of reedy water, herds of plodding cattle. I yearned to know this land, to embrace it, to be absorbed by it. Perhaps it is because I no longer have a land to call my own, because I was deprived of my birthright. Perhaps it is something else, something much greater, a remembrance of things past, of a life lived before this life as, I am sure, Canker and Kunhi believe.

Somewhere inside me a voice said, *'What are you doing here, then? Why are you marching to fight the people who belong to this land? To impose on them the will of foreigners?'* But that question had hardly been asked when another voice within replied, *'But if you were an Indian in your past life, how do you know that the British people around you were not Indians, too? Perhaps they also feel the urge to retrieve what had been snatched from them by other invaders another lifetime ago?'* Many waves of invaders had swept into the rich lands of India, century after century. The English were only the last. It was a treadmill argument: one could go round and round endlessly and not come up with an answer.

'Captain Kline-sir is coming,' Joseph's voice brought me back to the present. The column had stopped and the men were moving off the road. The rain clouds that had dampened the start of our march had given way to patches of blue flecked with white and it promised to be a pleasant day.

Kline rode up and said, 'You're very pensive, John. Are you uneasy about anything?'

'Yes,' I replied. 'If we want to take Arcot by surprise, why are we not concealing our movements? And why are we moving so slowly?'

He smiled. 'We don't want to take Arcot by surprise. We want Chanda Sahib to be told, by spy after spy, that we are moving very leisurely, with great confidence, towards his capital. Every spy will add to the report by his predecessor till Chanda Sahib is convinced that we have got enormous reinforcements to storm and capture Arcot. He will then be convinced that the only way he can redeem his honour will be to withdraw all his besieging forces from Trichy and come after us.' He cocked his head to one side and looked at me quizzically, 'That was your plan, wasn't it, John? Diversionary tactics, draw the thunder, force him to lift the siege of Trichy in order to safeguard Arcot?'

'Yes,' I admitted. 'That's what I saw.'

'Good. So we'll take five days to cover these fifty-six miles. By that time our force will have been exaggerated by his spies to at least four times its actual size. We should be at the Supply Encampment on the Palar River by noon tomorrow, if it doesn't rain. If the rain slows us down, we should reach it by sunset.'

It poured and we reached the Supply Encampment at sunset. That night Canker came to my tent. 'They know we are coming,' he said. 'I sent Sukumaran's men to Arcot village to find out.'

'Is it well defended?'

'No, but they have sent messages by pigeons to Chanda Sahib in Trichy so we must expect him soon.'

I said I'd tell Kline. I was very tired and my eyes were heavy. Canker walked up to my chair and bent his head so that his mouth was close to my ear. 'Tomorrow there will be plenty of looting: it is customary. There is something in Arcot that I must get for you.'

I didn't answer.

He sat on a cushion beside me. 'If I gave you a crown, Johnny, would you refuse it? Would you refuse to be king? Would you refuse to establish a dynasty? Would you refuse to fulfil the threat you made to your father when you were a child in Bath? Have you, so easily, forgotten the reason why you came out to India, Johnny?' No I hadn't, but Lucia had also played a part in my decision, though she didn't seem so important now … or did she? I wasn't so sure; in fact I wasn't sure about anything. I was very tired. But Canker didn't give up. 'You're thinking of your father, aren't you? Forget him. He is rotting in his grave Johnny. Do you think this plan to take Arcot came from him? It was given to you for a purpose: there is a higher plan for you. Don't throw it away by brooding on the past …'

I was asleep even before he had finished speaking.

Arcot

We took the fort the next morning.

The rain held off and there was only a token resistance from some of the old men left to guard Chanda Sahib's capital. They fired a few shots over our heads. We marched into the fort with our colours flying and our band playing: it had been almost too easy.

Once again the days that followed are a little misty in my memory but images, sometimes, float to the surface.

I ran down the corridors to the harem wing. There was no one inside but the rooms showed signs of a hasty retreat. Brass and silver spittoons had been overturned; betel-nut boxes lay scattered among cushions, divans, bolsters and musical instruments. In a large, inner room, lined with mirrors and huge paintings of copulating animals and humans in athletic combinations, incense still smoked from a censer hanging from the ceiling. The soldiers looked around with amazement then, remembering what they were here for, dispersed into the other rooms and I heard the sounds of boxes being thrown open and furniture being turned turtle.

Canker-chan came silently to my side. He drew up a chair, stood on it, lowered the counter-weighted censer. He tipped back the hinged and filigreed top with its smoking contents, and reached into the hollow space below. Very carefully he removed something wrapped in a cloth of gold. Just then I heard the men returning, laughing and singing. Canker hid his trophy inside his shirt and walked out. The men staggered in carrying their loot bundled into curtains. They were very happy.

I took nothing. Kline said he had taken 'a few trinkets', but later I learnt that he had been very selective about his booty.

We expelled Chanda Sahib's servants from the fort, sent back most of our pack animals and their handlers. We could get them back when we needed them. We did a quick survey of the fort, mustered the men, allocated billets and watches, took an inventory of our stores and ammunition, and surveyed the terrain outside the fort.

On one side of the fort ran the Palar River. On the other three sides were the fields of the village offering excellent lines of fire. There were many cannon mounted on the battlements with pyramidal piles of cannon balls near them.

'Load four of the cannon and fire them,' Kline ordered. 'North, south, east and west. I want to assess their range.'

'On three sides they'll fall on the lands of the villages, sir,' said the gunner.

'Fire, nevertheless. But don't set those haystacks alight. Sergeant de Vere, send out as many men as you can muster, along with *bandies*, and bring in all the fodder, firewood, food and boats you can gather. But don't touch the thatched huts, only the brick houses of the landlords. If anyone resists, beat them. If they still resist, bayonet them: don't waste ammunition. Also bring all the fuel and cooking oil you can lay your hands on. But, on no account, touch their women or their valuables: they are not the enemy. They'll be scared after we've fired those trial shots, eager to please. If you're not too rough, they'll be very grateful.'

After our foraging parties had brought in whatever they could, we had three days of sunshine with only occasional clouds, so we were able to dry everything. Then the monsoon settled in and we sat in the fort, and waited.

Four days later our sentries reported activity on the far side of the Palar. Troops were massing like ants on the other bank of the river. The Palar was a brown, engorged, flood of water, overflowing its banks and stretching for long distances over the fields it had inundated. The pathetic debris of villages flowed past: cocks and hens on a thatched roof; a family sitting helplessly on a bamboo raft with a little girl hugging a calf; a puppy on a wooden bed, crying piteously. I was standing at the River Gate, with the water swirling around the highest step, when the bed caught in an eddy and went spinning around, closer and closer to the step. The puppy looked at me and wagged its tail. Without thinking, I stepped into the water and reached out for the bed as it spun past. The current was vicious and it drove the edge of the bed against my knee, sending me reeling back. The puppy yelped and the next thing I knew was that a ball of wet fur was sitting on my chest and a warm, wet, tongue was licking my ear.

Just then there was a fusillade of shots from across the Palar and chips of brick scattered into me. I grabbed the pup and, crouching, ran into the River Gate.

Kline, who had observed the whole incident, remarked, 'That was a very stupid thing to do,' spun on his heel and stalked away. But the men cheered and some came forward to stroke the little animal. It was a liver-coloured and white pup with the limpid eyes of a true pi-dog. I named him Rushes because he reminded me of the many tales of babies being found in the rushes on the banks of rivers.

Chanda Sahib's forces made many attempts to launch boats but all their vessels were carried away by the Palar. They had to wait forty-eight hours, and then they started crossing: on rafts, skiffs, dugouts, broad cargo boats, anything they could find. Some of the craft collided and capsized, a few were washed downstream, a raft carrying guns rammed into three skiffs and many men were drowned. But still they came on. The great camp of Chanda Sahib mushroomed under our eyes. In the three days that it took his army to cross the river, his huge royal tent arose with its great fish standard and its horsetail plumes in imitation of the emblems of the Mughal army. Around his tent were the smaller tents of his favourite wives and concubines. After which there were conglomerations of senior and junior tents, then the serried rows of the tents of his soldiers and the long bamboo-and-thatch sheds of stables stretching all around us. The makeshift huts of the camp followers straggled around the outer edge. We were hemmed in by a vast tented city and the swollen river.

Canker said, 'They have settled in. He can't allow you to occupy his capital: it's a great insult.'

'Will he also attack Fort St. George?' I asked, seeking confirmation of Councillor Connaught Smither's opinion.

'No. That will be interpreted as a *be-izzati* act, a cowardly and dishonourable deed. He must have his whole army here so that they can see how he routs the British. Please speak to Captain Kline and have the answer to the herald, ready.'

'What answer?'

'Tomorrow morning, when everybody can see and hear what is happening, a herald will approach the walls of this fort. He will praise his master, be arrogant about the British, and call upon us to surrender, or be wiped out. He will threaten us with dire consequences claiming that our corpses will be eaten by dogs, pigs, and vultures … There will be no attack till that message has been delivered. We can rest tonight.' He looked out over the vast camp of Chanda Sahib. Fires were flickering alight and smoke rose in thin, wavering, plumes into the damp, grey, sky. Then he said, softly, 'I suggest that we tie our reply onto rockets, let them soar over the camp and then float down on umbrellas. I have procured these things from Trichur where they are very proficient in making such pyrotechnics, such fireworks.'

That night we were encircled by the campfires of our besiegers as ominous as the golden eyes of wolves, blinking and hungry for the kill. But though we stood on watch, alert for an unexpected attack, nothing happened. There was a brief alarm from the sentries above the Water Gate but it was only three huge logs being carried away by the flood. When my turn came to snatch a few moments of rest, Rushes looked up at me trustingly, wagged his tail, and then curled up and went to sleep at my feet. His presence was oddly, illogically, reassuring.

The next morning at half-past-nine, the army of Chanda Sahib lined up in battle array. Out of the front line rode three horsemen, two carrying lances with pennants, the centre one carrying a curved bronze horn. They rode forward; the herald blew a long, brassy, quavering blast; and read out his proclamation.

It gave all the titles of Chanda Sahib; embroidered on all his triumphs, real and imagined; and then informed us that we were in illegal possession of the fort and palace of the Nawab and that if we vacated it at once, leaving behind all our arms, our lives would be spared. But if we hesitated we would feel the wrath of the great Nawab and our eyes would be gouged out by vultures, our flesh eaten by pigs, and our bones gnawed by dogs. We would then, assuredly, be consigned to Hell to be eternally tortured by the legions of the Devil, a fate which we rightly deserved for daring to take possession of the property of the great Nawab.

This was exactly what Canker had predicted he would say: it was, probably, the accepted form of challenge. We did not have to change a word of our reply, scripted last night.

Before the herald and his escorts had returned to their camp, we fired five rockets. They howled as they curved into the air, exploded in puffs of red smoke. And from each of them, three umbrellas floated down, releasing a number of slips of white paper. They all carried our reply, some in English, others in French, most in the Arabic script. A very light breeze, combing and rustling the palmyras, scattered the message all over the camp of our besiegers and we saw soldiers and camp followers scurrying to retrieve them.

Our message said:

> We, the subjects of His Majesty George the Second, King of England, are holding this fort for its rightful owner, Mohammed Ali, Nawab of the Carnatic. Those who grovel under the feet of the eaters of frogs and snails doubtless know much about vultures, pigs and dogs, being of the same despicable breed.

It was deliberately provocative. Now, even if Chanda Sahib's French advisers wanted him to attack Madras, he wouldn't do so. His sense of *izzat* would demand that he punish us.

His response came within the hour.

'They've begun to move, sir,' a sentry reported. They were not marching in ranks, they were walking like a rabble, horses dragging their gun carriages behind them. Our musketeers manned the battlements, our gun crews were at the ready. Sergeant de Vere stood at one corner. Sergeant Goulding at another, gunners' mates holding flaming torches near the cannon.

'Wait for them to approach,' Kline said softly.

A shot from one of their musketeers hit our walls, followed by a ragged rattle of gunfire. We did not react. A French officer raised his sword and shouted an order. It was repeated in Arabic or Persian. Chanda's front ranks began to shout and run, firing as they came.

'Musketeers stand by. Choose your target.'

Their cannon were being lined up, trained on us. Our crews moved our cannon slightly.

'Cannon, fire!'

The noise was deafening as five of Arcot's guns thundered. Acrid smoke swept over us. Two of Chanda Sahib's cannon were hit, two more balls fell among his gun crews making them scatter. One of our balls arched high and landed close to Chanda Sahib's great tent, throwing up a cloud of earth. The fish standard tilted to one side.

Shots were peppering our walls and their musket fire was like an incessant rattle of kettle drums.

'Musketeers, fire!'

The first volley had the front rank of Chanda Sahib's army. Men screamed and fell. The second line of our musketeers fired from the embrasures, then the third, then the first had reloaded and fired again.

Our cannon were now trained down.

'Sergeants, fire at will.'

The first broadside, from our big guns, mowed them down like ninepins and the agonised bellows of men and horses, musket fire and the boom of our cannon, mixed with the acrid smell of gunpowder smoke, was a scene from Hell. One of our men screamed and fell beside me, clutching at an ugly wound on his head. I knelt to help him and his blood covered my hands. His breath rattled in his throat and his gaze became fixed. His breathing stopped.

The orderlies rushed forward with a bamboo pallet and carried him away, leaving a trail of blood on the battlements and down the stone steps to the court below. A ball came whistling over the battlements and crashed into the court, throwing the pallet-bearers back.

'Clear the court! Stand against the walls …'

The bronze horn of the herald sounded again and Chanda's army began to retreat.

It was a massacre after that. With no shots being fired by the enemy, we redeployed our forces. Three of our musketeers manned each embrasure: one sitting, one kneeling, one standing. Every time our cannon fired, they cut swathes of dead and dying in our besiegers' ranks. Another ball landed in Chanda Sahib's encampment, starting a fire. Hordes of disorganised men ran helter-skelter, throwing buckets of water everywhere.

Our buglers and drummers sounded, 'Cease Fire!' and our men cheered lustily. We had lost only one man. Their dead and dying were strewn all over the field.

When I returned to my billet, Rushes was scratching at the door, begging to be let out. I walked him into the yard. There was a thunderclap as loud as a cannon shot, and rain began to fall in fat, warm, drops. Rushes had done what he had to and scampered back in to the shelter of the gallery.

I saw Canker and Joseph standing in the shadows, in front of a huge pile of hay. Rushes sniffed at their feet, looked up, and wagged his tail. Canker reached down and patted him.

'Are you feeling all right, Johnny?'

'I think so. It's the first time I've seen a man killed.'

Canker clicked his tongue in sympathy. 'Devan was the only son of his widowed mother. She has two daughters to marry …' He looked down at Rushes and said something to Joseph. Both peered intently at the pup who responded by barking and jumping up in delight. Canker nodded and smiled slightly. 'Should I say something, Johnny, even if I know you won't believe me?'

I nodded.

'This dog has double eyes. He is able to see things that we don't.' He knelt and held Rushes' head in his left hand and, with his right forefinger, stroked the white patches, like eyebrows, above the pup's eyes. Then he patted him and stood up. Rushes snapped at a fly on his back and then spun in a frenzy, chasing his own tail. I smiled at Canker's remark and retired to my billet, Rushes running ahead of me.

When it was quiet in the fort, it was very quiet, but every day Chanda Sahib's army attacked us and, every day, we repulsed it. Their cannon were ineffective.

After the destruction of their big guns during the first attack, they kept them out of range. But since Arcot's mounted cannon had a longer range than their field guns, only the occasional ball reached our walls: more an annoyance than a danger.

And every day it rained, heavier and heavier as we got deeper and deeper into the monsoon. One night, in a sluicing thunderstorm, I heard a sentry shout a warning. There was a faint reply from the river. I ran up to the sentry and said, 'Hold your fire!' In a flash of lightning I saw a lone man in a dug-out and I ran down to the Water Gate. In another prolonged flash of lightning I recognised the paddler as Lawrence's messenger-boy, Mani. I helped him out of the bobbing boat as a sentry ran up holding a lantern. Mani gasped, 'Yale-Lynsdale sir, Yale-Lynsdale sir. You remember me? …'

He was wet and bedraggled. 'What news of Major Lawrence?' I asked.

'Sir, I have a message for Captain Kline, sir. Only him, sir; only him. The Major sir told me, "Give message only to Kline sir, alone." Can I see him, sir?'

I told the sentry to take him to Kline, and returned to my watch. I was curious but I didn't want to intrude so I didn't mention it to Kline the whole of the next day. At dinner, however, Kline addressed us. 'I had expected Major Lawrence to relieve us, but a messenger came through yesterday. He had paddled across the river at night in a dug-out and was almost shot by one of our sentries before he could identify himself to Mr Yale-Lynsdale. Anyway … Chanda Sahib's army is still besieging Trichy under the command of his son … or so I've been told. He's encircled the town with five thousand men. Chanda Sahib came here himself, with a few of his regular troops and some French advisers. Most of the people out there are levies: untrained, indisciplined, reluctant to fight. They'll probably sit and try to starve us into submission. How long can we hold out, John?'

'Two and a half months, if all goes well.'

But all didn't go well. In the second week of our siege we discovered that a choked gutter had flooded our ration store and mould had settled on many of our sacks. Kline called the men together and said that we'd have to cut down on our rations. There wasn't a murmur of discontent though some looked sullen.

Canker said, 'This is the most dangerous time: the waiting.'

The sergeants had the men march and counter-march, polish their buttons and every bit of metal in sight, and play a game called

Rounders. Once a week, at least, we watched the Nairs practising their *kalarippayat*: a demonstration that never failed to hold everyone's attention. I had wanted to join them but Canker had cautioned against it. 'Don't reveal all your skills, John. Always keep something secret, in reserve.' During the long, lonely, hours of my watch, thoughts of Ann kept me company. Sometimes the images were warm, unreal. Ann in my arms, passionate and demanding as Lucia had been. Often they were worrisome. In those dark moments I would take out her note to me, inhale the fragrance of sandalwood. Sometimes I would feel a surge of irrational anger: why hadn't she written a longer letter? It was at the end of the Morning Watch, when our garrison was stirring to life, that Joseph came up, carrying a small package. Sergeant de Vere had been put in charge of the commissariat–such as it was–and Joseph was assisting him.

'What is it, Joseph?' I asked rather irritably. I was tired and thoughts of Ann's safety kept gnawing at me.

'This, sir. I found in emergency ration pack.' He held out the package. 'On top it is written your name.'

He handed it over and hurried away because the breakfast queue had begun. The package was a little larger than my palm and about an inch thick. A strip of paper had been sewed onto the palm-root wrapping. It bore my name, and my heart began to thud as I recognised Ann's writing. Inside the net of palm root was a basket made of plaited, pale-green, palm leaf. Nestled within were twelve dates, each holding a white cashew nut. This was the sustaining fare that Arabs on long voyages, and plodding caravan routes, carried with them.

I was ecstatic. She had thought of me. I took off the paper on which she had written my name. And then I noticed that there was something on the back of it. Very meticulously, she had painted a pink rose bud. Below it, in tiny letters, she'd inscribed *Psalm 23.* I closed my eyes and heard the Rev. Greenwood intoning those words of reassurance and protection at the commencement of every class.

The Lord is my shepherd
I shall not want ...

I had forgotten much of it. But I did remember other bits:

Yea, though I walk through the valley of the shadow of death
I will fear no evil, for thou art with me,
Thy rod and thy staff comfort me.
Thou preparest a table before me in the presence of mine enemies;

I had misjudged Ann. Before she had been hurried away by her father, she had thought of me, found time to send this to me. Then like a jolt, another message came through. The pink rose. Why a pink rose? I recalled Lucia's words when she had asked me to carry a bouquet of roses.

> You English people have no romance. Do you not know the language of roses? A white rose for virginity, a pink rose for fidelity. A red rose for passion. I have asked you to hold a bouquet of red roses. You understand, don't you?

Ann had painted a pink rose for fidelity. In all the anguish of the siege, I suddenly felt elated. But when I looked around, the situation in the fort was still grim.

We had slaughtered and eaten all our fowls, most of our sheep and goats; the fodder was down to ten days stock. I was preoccupied when I took Rushes for his evening walk. I chose the unfamiliar, lower, rooms of the fort. They were dank and dark and few people came here. I wanted time to think about the future and Ann and … the Lord help me … Lucia, wherever she was. Rushes was delighted with the new smells in this labyrinth of galleries and tunnels, most of them green with moss, some dripping water. I was about to whistle to Rushes to turn back when I heard him whining and scratching.

Thinking that he had hurt himself, I hurried down a flight of slippery steps and saw him scrabbling at the base of a dead-end wall. Or rather, it looked like a wall but, when I got closer and examined it in a beam of light from a ventilation shaft, I found that it was an iron-studded wooden door made of heavy logs. Rust and moss had covered the iron and wood giving it the appearance of a stone wall.

Rushes was scratching at the base of the door, sniffing under it, looking back at me, and whining. I wanted to call out to him but something made me hold back. Tiptoeing up to the door I put my ear to its damp surface. At first there was nothing. Then, faintly, I heard a regular *thud!-thud!-thud*! After that, quite distinctly, came the sound of a human voice followed by the regular *thud!-thud!-thud*! again. I scooped Rushes into my arms and ran back.

'That's probably a subterranean passage,' said Canker. 'Most forts have secret, underground, escape routes.'

'I believe, sir, that they're placing a sap under the walls using the old rabbit hole,' opined Sergeant de Vere.

We got busy filling earthen *chatties*, urns, with a mixture of oil-soaked rags, gunpowder, sulphur and some other ingredients. Three crews manned one of the three field guns we had brought from Madras. Still others built a barrier of sandbags where the stone stairs, leading to the concealed door, began. Kline walked down to the door, put his ear to it, and then came tiptoeing back.

'They've stopped digging. They're very near.' He stepped over the wall of sandbags and the men hurriedly built it up around the protruding barrel of the gun ranged point-blank at the door.

Kline counted to ten then ordered, 'Fire!'

The explosions were deafening in that confined space. Plaster and bits of brick rained down on our heads. Through the space between the sandbags I saw that the door had caved in revealing a tunnel on the other side, dotted with oil lamps shrouded in clouds of dust. Our men, positioned above the ventilation shaft, lit the smoke-pots and hurled them in. There was a moment of silence, then we heard the rattle of gunfire from our battlements. We ran up to find our musketeers firing at dishevelled men fleeing out from behind a huge boulder at the base of our walls. The rock must have concealed the entrance they had cut into the secret tunnel. Thick, yellow, smoke engulfed them and spread over the field. Deliberately, our shooters picked out the sappers, one by one, keeling them over.

I don't know if that broke the will of Chanda Sahib, or if it was the drenching rains and the Palar River still in spate and rising every day. The edges of the flood waters lapped at the outer fringes of the camp and the field had turned into a mire.

The end came quite unexpectedly. Three days later the sky was blue and cloudless, the river began to recede, and it became so humid that the slightest exertion drenched us in sweat. We could feel the moisture being sucked out of the soaked ground like steam from an over-heated bath. Kline stood for long hours on the battlements gazing down at the camp of our enemy. At dinner, one evening, he said, 'They're preparing for a celebration, in their camp. Do you know what it is?' I said I didn't but I would find out. I spoke to Canker. The next morning Canker said, 'Balakrishan's men infiltrated into their camp and found out. They are celebrating the *Urs* of a Muslim holy man, a *pir*. They dance … only the men … till they fall exhausted. Then they prophesy. So they say. I have never seen it.'

I recalled something that my Persian teacher had told me. 'Won't they be very tired at mid-day, tomorrow. The celebrations normally end at noon, don't they?'

'Sometimes, perhaps. I'm not sure. There aren't many Mussalmans, many Moors, where I come from.'

Kline looked up from a book. 'It says here that the Moorish calendar is not the same as ours. Sharafat, my *syce*, says that he's a Sunni Moor so he does not know much about the Shias. But he thinks that the festivities will reach their peak tomorrow. Is that correct, Mr Shankaran Nair?'

Canker frowned, excused himself for a moment, then returned, saying, 'It is tomorrow.' He stood hesitantly for a moment before addressing me. 'It is customary to have a truce on the main day of the *Urs*.'

Kline stared at him, then at me, stood up and gazed for a long time through the window. Then he walked out of the room and I saw him pacing the battlements. I joined him after a while.

'What's the mood of the men, Johnny?'

'Restive. No one likes being penned in, Norbert, waiting for the other man to make the first move.'

There had been no exchange of fire since we had repulsed the invaders at the breach, but we had had to keep alert, ready to ward off an attack if it came. Everyone's nerves were as taut as drawn bowstrings, and the men snarled and snapped at each other at the least provocation.

Kline said, 'When Alexander cut the Gordian Knot he broke a custom, but he won an empire.'

The next day we broke the custom of truce at the *Urs*.

When the sun had baked the earth hard, our cannon started booming. We blasted the enemy camp with a long cannonade at first. Then we threw open our gates and our horsemen swept out, burning and slashing. Following them our musketeers and foot soldiers spread through the carnage, shooting everyone in sight. Chanda Sahib's troops were caught unprepared while resting, exhausted, after their festival, not expecting such a heinous desecration of such a sacred day. They fled in disarray, dropping their weapons, scrambling into over-laden boats. Chanda Sahib's bodyguards had formed a tight ring around him and his harem as they hurried in a shameless retreat towards the river. Kline ordered, 'Let them go. They'll carry the right message back to Dupleix and others who might think of opposing us …'

Our troops held back till the royal party had boarded their barges and then they started ransacking the camp, piling the arms and ammunition into our carts, herding the horses together, filling their saddle bags. The groans of the wounded rent the air and the people who attended to them carried no arms. They worked silently, efficiently, and very dedicatedly, wishing us as we rode past. The tents and stacks of fodder were still smouldering and smoking. The wounded animals had been shot and a group of *chamar*-tanners had already begun skinning the carcases. We disturbed two groups of vultures feasting and squabbling over the flayed animals. There was a stench of blood and, under the heat and the humidity, decomposition had set in. Clouds of flies and blue-bottles swarmed around. We held kerchiefs to our noses as we rode through the carnage.

The last battle of Arcot had lasted for a little more than an hour. It shattered Chanda Sahib's ambitions once and for all. And with it came the decline of the French power; and the ascendancy of British authority in India.

But the sights and sounds of that devastation, the cries of the wounded and dying, still haunt me. As, indeed, they must have haunted Kline, in spite of our decisive victory and the great jubilation that followed.

Aga Shawmier Sultan

We were given a hero's welcome when we returned to Madras but I had had my fill of war. Suddenly, something I had read in the *Life and Achievements* of my great grandfather, Elihu Yale, came back to me. The Company that had made the fortunes of the Yales and the Lynsdales had been given a royal charter by Elizabeth I on 31 December 1600. It was called *The Governor and Company of Merchants of London Trading into the East Indies*. By this charter it was given a monopoly of all English trade east of the Cape of Good Hope.

But Arcot had not been a trading venture.

That first night in Madras, I had a terrible dream. I saw the dead and dying in the field outside Arcot Fort. Heard their screams and groans, smelt their blood spreading like an evil rust across the soggy grass. I had stepped on something soft and then pulled back in revulsion. It was a man's hand sliced clean at the wrist. And then … horror of horrors … the corpses blurred and became those of the Scots and English scattered across the bloody field in Culloden.

We had fought the same war in a different land with different people.

Would another war break out in India when the Saxe-Gotha widow learnt that her Protestant's husband's Catholic son, his eldest son and rightful heir to the English throne, had survived? Had she killed my weak father to preserve the Hannover line of English kings? And if she had done that, would she kill Grandfather Lynsdale and my mother who were the only living witnesses to my royal ancestry?

I pulled myself up short. There was no point in such dark speculations.

When I reached my office, Kunhi said, 'Missy Ann has returned. She says she has a message for you from Tranquebar. She is a little tired now but she will be at home at six o'clock this evening.'

I went back to my room; sluiced myself down with cold water from the copper drum, and slept.

Flying ants, those virgin mating queens and drones, were rising from the hot earth in the sunset, when I walked to the office. Mrs Walls was taking her corgi for a walk and she smiled at me when I wished her.

'Good evening, Mr Hale-Landsail. I was so thrilled to hear of your brave exploits in Orcote … or whatever it's called. Mr Walls speaks so highly of you …' she perambulated on, a happy but vacuous grin on her face.

Sergeant de Vere touched his cap and said, 'The lads in the barracks keep talking about you, sir. They wonder why you haven't been commissioned, sir.'

I smiled and walked on.

Kunhi had just locked the office. 'Should I open it?' he asked.

I told him that wouldn't be necessary. He said, 'My uncle presents his compliments, John-chan. He says that when you are less busy he would like to speak to you in your room. You can leave a message with Joseph.'

Canker could wait. My John Company occupied premises behind the Hawkenian mansion. I walked around, Rushes trotting happily at my heels, tugged the bell-chord set in the high wall beside a gate. The gate swung open soundlessly. A truly gigantic man with enormous, black, handle-bar moustaches filled the gateway. He stood with his legs apart, cradling a thick staff bound with broad metal rings. His pockmarked face had an almost-purple sheen about it and his eyes were bloodshot. His forbidding appearance was heightened by his shimmering black livery emphasised by glittering chain mail on his shoulders, a broad red leather belt holding a curved knife in a scabbard, and knee-high scarlet boots polished to a mirror finish. He was the most awesome human I had ever seen.

He looked down at me for a moment and then rumbled, 'Yes, master?'

'John Yale-Lynsdale to meet Mr Avram Hawkenian. And can I bring in my dog?'

He regarded me for a moment and then growled, 'I am finding out.' He turned and I noticed that there was a sentry-box to one side of the gate. He tugged a cord inside it and spoke into the bell-like mouthpiece of a voice tube. Captain Hamish had installed a few of these devices in his ship and had told me what they were though I had never seen him use any. The Colossus returned and boomed, 'Servant will come; escort you to veranda. Please take dog,' and he stood aside from the gate. A liveried servant materialised and led us down the drive but I was too nervous, and a little awed, to notice much till Rushes and I reached the veranda. The servant said, 'Please sit. Dog welcome. Master will come now.'

The winged cane chairs were tempting and I began to relax gazing out at a beautiful garden. A corner of it was dominated by a huge, feathery-leafed, *gul mohur* tree under which a gazebo stood, covered in yellow, climbing, roses … Against one of the walls, festooned with green-and-white creepers, was a triple line of succulent-stemmed trees with scarlet, white, maroon, pink, coral and orchid flowers, heavily perfumed. Their scent combined with those of the bushes covered with tiny white blossoms, and that of the roses, filled the garden with an almost overpowering fragrance.

'Coja Petrus and I planned it as a garden of tranquillity, Mr John. He brought back many of these plants from the Philippines. We wanted this to be a place where one can escape from the cares of life.'

I swung around. Avram Hawkenian had appeared silently. He was still a study in grey, still as austere as a Trappist monk, still coldly observant though his faint smile was warm. I stood up and wished him. Rushes sat between my feet, looking up at him expectantly, a little wary. Even when Hawkenian asked me to sit down, Rushes sat close to me, still eyeing him. A servant brought out a fine porcelain service of aromatic coffee and tiny cubes of sweets enriched with coconut. I still felt rather tongue-tied.

After both of us had sipped our coffee, and Hawkenian had offered me the sweets, he said, 'You wished to see me about something, Mr John?'

I cleared my throat. 'Yes, sir. I ... I would like to ask your permission to call on your daughter.'

He nodded his head slowly and gazed out at the garden for a while, then turned to me. 'Are you a Protestant, Mr John?'

'I'm a Catholic.'

'And your father?'

'I lost him when I was very young.' He ceased being my legitimate father when he accepted that Saxe-Gotha woman.

'You have brothers, sisters, Mr John?'

'No.'

He offered me another cup. I declined. He poured out one for himself. 'I drink a lot of coffee. My doctor says I shouldn't, but I do so, nevertheless. Do you resent my questions?'

'No. But I wonder why you're asking them. All I want is your permission to call on your daughter.'

For the first time I saw emotion in his face. He drew in his breath sharply and a faint sheen of perspiration appeared on his forehead. His voice had an edge on it when he said, 'Mr John, in our community, when a young man seeks permission to call on a young woman he believes that he will, eventually, be able to ask for her hand in marriage. Am I being too presumptuous?'

I felt he was, and I resented it. It was time to clear the air. I said, 'Mr Hawkenian, I appreciate your concern for your daughter. You have asked me a lot of questions and I have answered them. You know a great deal about me. I know very little about you. I saw your daughter in distress and rescued her without knowing who she was, or her religion, or what her father did, or how many brothers and sisters she had. It wasn't relevant then; it's not relevant now.' I got to my feet. 'Thank you for your time, Mr Hawkenian. Please give my regards to your daughter and tell her that I came here to call on her. But, in the circumstance, I am unable to do so.' I bowed to him, said, 'Come on, Rushes,' and walked out. Just before the liveried Goliath closed the gate behind me I looked back. Hawkenian had gone.

I went back to my room and lay on my bed staring at the ceiling, emptied of all hope, all feeling. Rushes barked and put his front paws on my bed and looked at me as if he sympathised with my plight.

'Are you unwell?' Canker was standing at the door of my room, holding something.

I got up and poured myself a glass of water. It tasted of *khus*: Joseph believed that a mild decoction of the roots of this aromatic herb purified the water.

'Have you received the message that Miss Ann brought from Tranquebar?'

'No,' I said. 'I couldn't meet her. I met her father.'

Canker busied himself unwrapping the packet he had brought. 'I have no children of my own, Johnny, but if I had I would not have built a fence around them.' From a white, cloth bag he withdrew something covered in fine, red, fabric. It was the sort of cloth in which orthodox local traders wrapped their account books when they worshipped them every morning and evening. 'But then, we Nairs have quite a different attitude to our daughters than the ones held by most other people. We bring up our daughters to look after themselves and make their own decisions. Here … This is what I've got for you.'

He held it out to me in his right palm, his left hand touching the elbow of his right hand in the traditional gesture of gift-giving. It was a palm-sized dagger. Its six-inch long black blade was flame-shaped, razor-sharp, with brilliant flashes of colour coruscating within. Its handle was clear, golden-orange, amber. 'Hold it up to the light, Johnny, and see what is imprisoned in the amber.'

Against the window, sunlight filled the amber making it glow like rich honey. Deep inside was a curious creature. It looked, for all the world, like a tiny human with translucent wings holding aloft a sword in its right hand while standing on a black, writhing, serpent. Grandfather had, once, shown me a lump of Baltic amber and explained that it was fossil resin from prehistoric trees, petrified under the earth. Little insects, leaves, twigs and ancient pollen had been trapped in the resin when it had been fresh and tacky and they had now been entombed in this beautiful stone. 'But,' he had explained, 'superstitious people see all sorts of curious things trapped in amber as they see strange signs in tea leaves and the movement of the stars. That's all rubbish!' But what I saw now in the haft seemed quite uncanny.

'What does the thing in the hilt remind you of, John?'

It seemed familiar and then my mind made the connection with a woodcut in an old Catechism I had studied as a child. 'It's St. Michael and Satan as the Dragon,' I recalled.

'Right, Johnny,' Canker took the beautiful dagger from me and slid it into its tiny scabbard of steel covered with brocade. 'I had a new brocade belt made for it, but the buckle is original. You must wear it next to your skin, Johnny, for at least one week, night and day, once a year. You will notice that even in its scabbard, the back of the handle will lie in contact with your flesh. Then it will become yours and it will make you a monarch.'

'And who,' I asked, 'made this magical knife?'

Canker shook his head. 'You don't believe all this, Johnny? You think I'm making it up?'

I felt a twinge of remorse. 'I'm sorry,' I apologised. 'I didn't mean to be rude. I've had a hard day. Tell me more about the dagger.'

He still seemed pained because he spoke in short phrases. 'Legends. Myths. Fairy tales. Some say it was given to St. Joseph, to defend the Christ Child when they fled to Egypt to escape the Massacre of the Innocents. It was made by the Magi. Brought to India by Jesus when he came to study here.' That was odd. Canker continued with his tale of the dagger. 'It was gifted to Charlemagne and then owned by Tamerlane. Genghis Khan. Babur, the founder of the Mughal empire. Chanda Sahib's ancestor stole it from the last Great Mughal and the empire began to decline after that. Chanda Sahib did not believe in it, as you yourself don't believe. For over a year he has not worn it next to his skin but had hidden it in the bottom of that censer in his harem.'

It was very beautiful and it would be useful to carry in case the Saxe-Gothas attacked me. I lifted up my shirt and buckled the dagger around my waist. The amber handle snuggled into my skin and, after a second or two, I could not feel it. In some strange way it seemed to have become a part of me.

I was now wearing two charms: the fossil horned-whale's tooth on the third finger of my right hand, given to me by Megan Ryder in Guildford, and this magical dagger around my waist. If I acquired any more I could start telling fortunes like a gypsy!

But my heart still ached for Ann.

I thanked Canker and he must have sensed that I was in no mood to talk. He nodded and left. As there seemed no point in meeting Hawkenian again I busied myself in my work, worried about Kline.

After Arcot, Kline's attitude began to change. It was very subtle at first but when he took to calling me 'Yale-Lynsdale' rather than 'John', I realised that he was trying to distance himself from me. Just before Arcot he had been commissioned as a Captain and, therefore, he was my senior in rank. But there was more to it than that.

I was about to mention it to Canker when a messenger, in the blue and gold livery of Aga Shawmier, came to the door. He drew out a silver salver from a leather satchel, placed an envelope on it, bowed, and extended it to me.

The message inside, on heavy vellum, was simple:

My dear John Yale-Lynsdale,

It would give me and Avram Hawkenian great pleasure if you would consent to have tea with us at 4:30 pm this evening in the Hawkenian mansion. We have some matters of considerable import to discuss with you.

We urge you to excuse this very short notice but if it had not been absolutely necessary then such a solecism would never have been committed by

Your friend,
(if I might be so bold as to term myself thus)
Aga Shawmier Sultan

I didn't want to face Ann's rigid old father, but he had not invited me, the leader of the Armenian community had. I had no quarrel with him and it would be churlish to turn down his invitation especially as he had apologised for the short notice.

The watch-bell rang and I realised that I had only half-an-hour to have a hurried bath, change and keep the engagement.

They received me in a drawing room with windows looking out on the Hawkenian's beautiful Garden of Tranquillity. Avram Hawkenian seemed far more composed than he had been when I had last left him. He was sitting on one of the peacock chairs, the Aga on another. In front of them was a large, intricately carved, camphor-wood chest. I recognised it as the one that had stood in the drawing room under the portrait of Lucia by George Romney. A shiver of fear ran up my spine.

The two Armenians rose when I entered with Rushes. They welcomed me and asked me to sit. They made polite conversation while the coffee was being served. When we were alone, Shawmier cleared his throat.

'We have, Mr John, Mr John Yale-Lynsdale, two important matters to discuss with you. One matter devolves around news from London. The other, the second matter, devolves around news from Madras …' Hawkenian coughed. The Aga shot him a cold look, stared at him till Hawkenian dropped his eyes, then the Aga looked at me again. 'I know little about the consequences of the news from London, but the second bit of news, we hope … we both hope … will bring happiness to you, Mr John.' He paused. 'Which would you like to hear first, Mr John Yale-Lynsdale?'

Rushes whined slightly, and tucked himself between my feet. I reached down and stroked him. He wagged his tail diffidently, his gaze fixed on Shawmier. I felt a churning deep inside me, starting from my loins, rising slowly.

Hawkenian coughed again, but this time the Aga continued as if he had not heard him. 'Some time ago, Ann Hawkenian, went to Tranquebar. It is, if you remember, the colony of the Danes. When the late Coja escaped from the French, he sought shelter with the man who is now the governor of Tranquebar. The late Coja introduced Ann to the Danish family when they came to Madras and they took a great liking to her. So, when there was a danger of the French returning to Madras, recently, she went to Tranquebar.' He paused.

I nodded, but said nothing.

'The day before she left to return here,' he continued, 'a Danish trading ship sailed in from London. It carried this Chinese box; and this letter, addressed to you.' He pointed to the camphor-wood box and handed me an envelope addressed to:

John Yale-Lynsdale Esq.
In care of
His Excellency The Governor
Fort Dansborg
TRANQUEBAR

In the stylised handwriting of the President of the East India Company, the letter inside said:

Dear Mr Yale-Lynsdale.

I know not where you are in India but I have been informed by Mistress Maureen O'Sullivan that this address, in care of the Danes, will find its way safely to you.

Would that this, my first communication with the grandson of my old friend, Bernard Yale-Lynsdale, contained happier tidings. but, alas, it has fallen to my sad lot to pen this distressing missive.

Your grandfather, the great Bernard Yale-Lynsdale, and your mother, the gentle Katherine Yale-Lynsdale, have been killed by brigands who held up their coach on the road from Bath to London, three weeks ago. It was only after they were buried in the Catholic cemetery in Bath that Mistress Maureen O'Sullivan wrote to me. She is the heir and possessor of your late grandfather's property, Shawclose, in Bath. She is of the opinion that your grandfather and mother were on their way to sail on the Carnatic Trader to pay you a surprise visit. She also assures me that this chest was all that your grandfather left you.

If you should wish to dispute possession of the property please apprise me and I shall have the best legal brains that money can engage to fight your claim.

My sincere apologies again for being the messenger of such sorrowful news.

I remain,
Yours in shared grief,

I felt as if a mule had kicked me.

My heart raced and my vision blurred. I fought to retain control of my senses while the terrible news pounded at me. Somewhere inside me there was a great emptiness and I wanted to scream, venting my anger and distress, cursing my father and his vile family. I knew, I was absolutely certain, that the fiendish Saxe-Gothas had done this, particularly that poisonous witch Augusta. From deep in my loins I felt the stirring of that strange thing that they called the *kundalini*, the black fire, the black serpent. I knew that if it rose I would not be able to control it and I would say and do things that I could never retract or redeem. Not really conscious of what I was doing I began to breathe deeply, holding in my breath for as long as I could, imagining its strength as a great boulder suppressing that uncoiling force within me. It was not easy; but it was ecstatic, painful, triumphant all at the same time.

I don't know how long the tussle within me lasted but it felt as if I was teetering on the knife-edge of a cliff for a lifetime and that if I lost my sense of balance I would tumble into darkness, dishonour, and irredeemable disgrace. But it couldn't really have been very long and I didn't even close my eyes though they seemed to have blurred out of focus. I remember seeing the letter in my hand as an indistinct white patch and I had to concentrate to recognise it. I transferred it from my right hand to my left, picked up a glass of water from the table at my elbow, and sipped it till my senses stilled, leaving me with an enormous coldness inside as if my whole being had become a lump of ice.

Strangely, neither the Aga nor Ann's father seemed to feel that there was anything amiss because they were still looking at me with mild interest as if they expected me to reveal the contents of the letter. Part of me said that they had every right to know but a louder, more urgent, voice inside bellowed, '*Keep it to yourself. This is not the right time. Just tell them that the news is not good for you, personally, but don't, now, give the impression that it is serious, certainly not that it is tragic. Be strong and be cold: be very, very, cold and self-controlled.*'

I listened to the louder voice.

In an unemotional tone I said, holding my voice very steady, 'The news from the President of the Honourable Company is not good … for me, personally, that is. But I do not wish to discuss it.' I folded the letter very deliberately and put it in my pocket.

I paused to let my words sink in, and then said in a rather stilted way,

'I hope that the information you have, Aga Shawmier and Mr Hawkenian, puts us all in a happier frame of mind. What would you gentlemen like to reveal the news about Madras?'

The Camphor-wood Chest

The two old men looked at each other and then back at me. Shawmier spread his hands apart, helplessly. 'This is the chest your grandfather sent. Here is the key: it fell out of the envelope when Miss Ann handed it to me. There's a folded piece of paper attached to it.'

I unfolded the paper and recognised my grandfather's writing. It was unsigned and it said:

Remember the Polos

That made no sense to me so I tucked it away in my pocket and slipped the key into the intricate brass lock. I recalled that it was an unusual lock. I turned it to the left twice, the right once, and then pressed it in. The hasp clicked open. I pulled up the heavy lid.

A foul stench assailed me. I staggered back and Rushes barked, lunging at the chest. I whipped my kerchief to my nose and found that the two Armenians were also breathing through their kerchiefs.

'What is it?' I asked. It smelt of rotting corpses and I shuddered.

Hawkenian stepped forward. 'It's asafoetida …' he reached in and took out a sticky, resinous, lump: glistening black with ruby highlights. He held it to his nose, then handed it to Shawmier. The Aga bent his huge beak to it, took a long, deep, breath, then raised his head, 'It is the best Afghan asafoetida. And there's layer upon layer of it, Mr John. It's worth a fortune!'

'What's asafoetida?' I asked.

'It's the sap of a shrub,' said Shawmier. 'It's added to food as a digestive. Also many people believe that it gives them … er … strength. It's very popular with the princes and those who have large … er … seraglios.' He couldn't bring himself to say harems.

I handed the slip to Hawkenian. He read it, frowned, and gave it to his companion. The Aga scanned it, closed his eyes for a moment, swaying slightly like a Mussalman boy reading his scripture. Then he opened his eyes wide, leapt up, grabbed a large pair of scissors from a desk and approached the chest. He dived his hand in and piled layer after layer of the stinking resin, and the dried leaves that separated them, to one side of the chest. Then he pulled out a long robe from under the last layer of asafoetida. It was stained and sticky and, as he held it out, the stench increased.

'Please bolt the doors, and draw the curtains, Avram.'

He waited till the three doors had been secured, the heavy curtains pulled. A diffused light filtered in from the broad skylights. Rushes rose from my feet, bounded to the robe, wagged his tail furiously and let loose a frenzy of sharp, excited, barks.

'May I, Mr John?' the Aga asked, holding the robe in one hand and the scissors in the other. I didn't know what he wanted to do, but I nodded. Very carefully, Aga Shawmier cut open the seams of the robe and dusted it out. A stream of gold coins tinkled onto the floor. As it did from the next and the next and the next … there were guineas, crowns, half-crowns, sovereigns, mohurs, and many others that I could not recognise then but learnt, later, were doubloons, ducats and louis d'ors. When the last seam had been split, the last coins added to the pile, Shawmier whispered, 'Never … never in all my life … have I seen so much gold money …'

I asked the Aga, 'What made you split the seams?'

'I recalled that when Marco Polo returned from his long voyage, he cut open his travel-stained garments and a fortune in gold coins tumbled out. That was what your grandfather meant.' He went to his desk, rummaged around, and returned with a large, leather bag. He scooped the coins into it, pulled the drawstring tight, tied it, and placed it near my chair. Then, after making sure that there were no coins left in the clothes, he shut the lid of the box, locked it, handed me the key, and piled the clothes on top of it. Only then did he open the door and pull back the heavy curtains.

I should have felt elated but I was uneasy. Hawkenian and Shawmier seemed to be tense and, somehow, I was sure that it was not because of the gold or the asafoetida. It was something deeper, more personal. I turned to them and asked, 'What else do you want to tell me?'

The two Armenians exchanged glances again. Shawmier said, 'Avram tells me that you want to call on his daughter, Ann.'

I nodded.

'Do you still want to do so?'

I nodded again. Rushes whimpered at my feet; I reached down and stroked him.

'Will you take offence if I ask a presumptuous question?'

'That depends on the question, Aga.' Hawkenian's hands were trembling uncontrollably.

'If,' asked Shawmier, 'if the friendship between you and Ann develops, Mr John. And if it matures into a mutual regard and affection. And if, when it so matures, you would propose marriage to her. And if she accepts your proposal … then would you insist that Ann becomes a Catholic by converting to your faith before the marriage?'

I still felt drained of all emotion: I had received too many blows since I had stepped into this house. I was battered, drained of all patience, fed up with these probing questions as if my beautiful Ann was a commodity to be bought and sold to the highest bidder. I didn't care about their feelings, their traditions, their customs, conventions, the stupid rules that governed their lives. They weren't going to impose them on me.

'Yes,' I said, 'very definitely.' And to hell with their reactions. 'Ann would have to become a Catholic.'

'*Have* to?' Shawmier repeated. 'Or would you leave the choice to her?'

'She would *have* to, Aga. The Yale-Lynsdales are Catholics and we have suffered much for our faith.' Grandfather and mother had been murdered because they were Catholics. I felt a sob rise in my throat and suppressed it. 'So the question of my marrying a non-Catholic does not arise,' I said harshly. A little voice inside me kept saying '*You're going too far. You're demanding too much.*'

Both Shawmier and Hawkenian let the air out of their lungs and seemed to relax. Hawkenian's hands weren't trembling any more. I felt that that was the answer he wanted although I couldn't think of any reason why. Rushes snapped at his tail and went spinning around in a circle, almost knocking down a small table.

'Your dog is very happy, Mr John,' Hawkenian said.

I asked, 'When can I start calling on Ann?' My voice sounded oddly hollow.

Ann's father smiled. 'She should be back by tomorrow morning. She's been away nursing an ailing friend.'

Shawmier added, 'When Ann returns, Mr John, you might consider it seemly to first call on her in her house. That is, here. And after it has become common knowledge that you are friendly with the full consent of her father, and if both still wish to continue the friendship, then, perhaps, the two of you could be formally engaged. Only then would it be fitting for you to be seen out together. Does that sound agreeable?'

I nodded. 'It does.'

In spite of my anguish, I marvelled at the many variations on the courting theme in the small community of the Fort. The *nautch* girl had virtually raped me; Joanna Scythe had been openly coquettish; and now the Armenians wanted me to go though the entire formal routine of request, permission, meeting under supervision, engagement, and then walking out together. It was as if all these people lived in different worlds with their own distinct tribal customs!

'Good,' Hawkenian said, rising. 'I shall inform Ann of our understanding and I shall have your chest delivered to your office.'

I thanked them, shook hands, picked up the heavy leather bag, and walked out of the house, Rushes trotting at my feet. It was all I could do was to keep my emotions under check as I trudged across the parade ground and climbed the stairs.

The reaction hit me when I reached my room. I dismissed Joseph and said I was not hungry. I locked the door, sat on my bed and let myself go. My icy barriers shattered. I sobbed and sobbed and hugged myself like a child, rocking back and forth, crying softly, uncontrollably. I cried till all my anguish had been drained out of me leaving a great emptiness and the awful pictures in my mind.

Out of the misty darkness they had come, their faces muffled ... horses neighed and reared ... pistols blazed ... the screams of my mother and grandfather ... then silence except for the sounds of the killers galloping away into the night ... the drip, drip, drip of blood ... horses bolting ... bodies jouncing limply ... falling to the floor of the coach ... red stains spreading while the frightened horses, showing the whites of their eyes, froth on their mouths, thundered down the dark road.... Grandfather must have anticipated that such a thing might happen when he put that tag *Remember the Polos* on the key to the camphor-wood chest. He could have stayed in Shawclose and then they would have been safe. Or would they have been? Those Hanoverians were primitive, vicious, swines. They would have revelled in informing those two old people that they were marked for death, had probably planned to burn them alive in their mansion. But grandfather had seen through their plans, converted his wealth to gold coins, and then hidden it in the chest under layers of asafoetida certain that those ignorant Huns would not recognise this valuable spice. Even in their death they had foiled the Saxe-Gotha woman. The thought that I would never see them hit me again …

'Mummy! Grandfather! Why did you leave me? Why now? Why this way? …'

The grief came again and bludgeoned me to sleep. A flame emerged out of the distant dark, closer and closer; became my father; snuffed out. Two flames formed out of the darkness, became my mother and grandfather, their hands reached out to me; snuffed out. I heard my grandfather's voice echoing from a great distance: '*A trader's duty is to trade, survive and succeed; trade, survive and succeed; trade, survive succeed ... tradesurvivesucceed …*'

I sat bolt upright, wide awake, drenched with sweat. My body was racked with nausea and my stomach began to heave. When I returned from the bathroom and the spasms had ceased, I felt weak and drained but the attack seemed to have cleared my head. I lit all three oil lamps to dispel the darkness and sat by the window to collect my thoughts. Rushes jumped off his cot, ambled across, and licked my hand. Then he curled up at my feet and went to sleep.

I was sure that my father's people had murdered my mother and grandfather. In fact, I had killed them. If I had not been born, they would not have died; not this way. But now if I didn't live then their deaths would have been pointless. I not only had to live but I had to have heirs, I had to start a dynasty defying the Saxe-Gotha killers. I had to succeed. But could I succeed now? With the death of my grandfather, I would become just another insignificant writer. Worse, I would become the target of all the long-suppressed jealousies of the people around me. But that would happen only when the folk in the Fort knew of the death of Bernard Lynsdale. How many people knew? Did Hawkenian and Shawmier know?

I recalled the words that the two Armenians had used when they gave me the keys to the chest. They had not mentioned his death. And the President of the Company had penned the letter in his own hand, he had not dictated it to a writer. Presumably, he wanted to keep it a secret, too. I checked through the sailing schedules lying in a drawer in my dressing table. The next Company's ship was not due in for another three weeks.

I took stock of my situation. I was much richer than I ever dreamed I would be, and that excluded the gold coins. I would have to be careful about changing them or else a lot of awkward questions would be asked. The Armenians knew about the coins but they would not bruit it abroad because I was marrying into their community and they looked after their own interests very carefully.

In spite of my earned wealth I had many debts. I paid the *dalals* only after Kline paid me. I made a rough calculation. Kline owned me 40,000 pounds; of that I had to pay the *dalals* 25,000 pounds. The gold coins in the sack were worth at least twice that amount. But if I started selling them in Madras, I would draw attention to myself.

There was a knock on my door. I opened it to find Canker standing outside. 'I saw the lights blazing in your room though it is almost midnight. Anything wrong?'

I made him sit down, offered him a glass of lemonade and told him. He went completely immobile and though his eyes were open, they were fixed and his breathing became very deep and extremely slow, almost trance-like. Then the stillness left him and he questioned me for about an hour: about my feelings towards Ann, my opinion about the Fort and its inhabitants, if I ever intended to return to England, whether I believed that I could spend the rest of my life in India or had other plans; and, finally, if I was still driven by the desire to be king of my own land even though I did not know where that land was. 'Adults have every right to forget their childish dreams, John-chan.' He was silent for a long while when I said, 'I *will* be a king. I am as certain of that as I am that I am alive today.'

When he broke his silence he was very decisive. He said, 'I shall dispose of the asafoetida. There is a north-Indian trader, a man named Aggarwal, who has been trying to buy this commodity for the last five days. He needs it very urgently for the senior hakim, the doctor, in the court of the Mughal emperor. He will take all we have. Then the chest will be cleaned out with palm vinegar, rinsed with hot water, and left in the sun. The perfume of the camphor-wood will return. The clothes will be washed and distributed to the poor, as you have wished. Please sleep till nine this morning. I shall pass the word around that you have a bilious attack, it is common at this time of the year. Either Kunhi or I shall visit you at ten and let you know the situation at that time. Hide the bag of coins under Rushes' cot: Joseph does not touch it and no one else will approach. By tomorrow we should have found a safer place for it. Now drink plenty of water, Johnny-chan, and go back to sleep.'

Rushes sniffed at the bag tentatively, then wagged his tail and accepted it. He and I then went back to sleep. That dream came again.

I was now standing at the other end of the valley with the snow-covered mountains soaring in the distance and a plume of smoke rising from the highest peak. Far below the snowline there was a curious structure which I knew was a monastery though its architecture was like nothing I had ever seen before. But the people tilling the fields seemed normal. It was all still, very peaceful.

As he had promised, Canker told Joseph not to wake me till nine and I was settling down to a late breakfast when Kline breezed through. 'Believe you're a bit under the weather, Yale-Lynsdale.' I grunted in a non committal way: I was in no mood for a conversation. But Kline continued, 'Armenian fare is rather exotic. A bit rich for our tastes, don't you agree?' and he strode away. I decided not to rise to his bait.

But my mind was filled with Ann. I had to find out if she would marry me, and I had to find out now. The social foundations of the Fort were like shifting quicksands. It was writhing with intrigue; there were so many conflicting customs, conventions and traditions; there was so much uncertainty, particularly about what would happen when news of my grandfather's death became public knowledge … the future was an ugly tangled skein and I would be a fool to wait. If I did not act now, tomorrow might be too late. As if he had read my thoughts and approved, Rushes barked, put his front paws on my knees, and licked my hand with great affection. It was all I needed to firm my decision.

I bathed, wore my Sunday-best, picked up my ivory-headed walking stick, and headed out. I was striding across the parade ground, in the still morning air, when I heard one of the English soldiers ask, 'Oos the toff?'

Exclaimed his companion, 'Strike me pink, Alfie! That's Mister Yale-Lynsdale, it is. Must 'ave got some new London togs for his-self!'

I had just reached the Hawkenian's gate when Rushes came racing up, leaping all over me, his tail a blur of happiness. I patted him till he quietened down, brushed his dust off my breeches, adjusted my hat, and walked on.

I had to wait in the veranda for a good twenty minutes before Avram Hawkenian appeared. He looked at my flushed face and frowned. Then he said, 'Good morning Mr John.'

I doffed my hat, 'Good morning, sir. May I have the pleasure of talking to Ann?'

He hesitated for an instant, then said, 'Please sit down. I'll tell her you've come.'

I had to use all the self-control I could muster to keep sitting. She came carrying the gentle fragrance of roses and the perfume made a brief vision of my mother flash before my eyes, filming them. And then it was gone. Ann wore an old-gold gown which lit up her eyes, the morning sun shone in her hair, her skin glowed.

She said, 'John, you wished to see me?'

'I would like to walk with you in the garden. I wish to speak to you in private.'

She cocked her head to a side, smiled slightly. 'Very well, John Yale-Lynsdale. We'll walk.'

We walked to the gazebo under the *gul mohur* tree. It was still covered in yellow roses, heavily scented. The roses screened us from the house. I said, 'Please sit down, Ann.'

I knelt at her feet. 'Ann Hawkenian, will you marry me?'

Her hand flew up to her mouth. 'Johnny, I hardly know you!'

I said, 'I have known you all my life. I have got glimpses of you in other women but it was only when I saw you for the first time that I knew it was you I have been searching for. Can we get engaged next Sunday in Uscan's Church? Can we get married in the same church two Sundays later? Will you become a Catholic? I have the means to support a wife in comfort and the heart to love you to the end of my days. Will you say yes?'

She blushed and closed her eyes and two, clear, tears rolled down her cheeks. She looked at me and her eyes were like green pools overflowing.

'I cannot become a Catholic, Johnny.' I stood up slowly, my heart thudding in my chest. 'I cannot become a Catholic, Johnny, because I am a Catholic. Uncle Petrus was a devout Catholic and he had been instructing me for a whole year. I went to Tranquebar: they have a Catholic Church there. I was received into the Church.'

She looked at me with so much love that my heart thudded in my throat and I thought it would burst.

Then she said, very softly, 'Yes, Johnny, I will marry you!'

The Portrait

I cannot describe how the next hour passed.

All I know is that I have never been happier. Perhaps because of the pain and the emptiness that I felt at the loss of my mother and grandfather, I was able to fill my heart with Ann; wonderful Ann; beautiful Ann; Ann who would be my anchorage when the winds battered me.

When we broke the news to her father I saw his face light up for the first time. He kissed his daughter and shook my hand warmly. Then, in an unexpected burst of spontaneity, which took me quite unawares, he embraced me and kissed me on both cheeks. When Ann was seeing me off, in the veranda, I asked her, 'Both your father and the Aga seemed very relieved when I said that you must become a Catholic before we got married. Why was that?'

She smiled and frowned. 'Johnny, must you know everything about everything?'

'Yes, if it concerns you.'

She looked around to make sure we were alone, then she put her hand on my cheek, very tenderly. 'Because, Johnny, they knew that I had become a Roman Catholic and I felt very strongly about my faith. They felt that if you were indifferent about it … because, they felt that you had been brought up in a Protestant nation … then, later in our married life, it would become an irritant between us. That is if you were not firm in your faith. So when you were firm … the Aga said you were "dogmatic" … they were very happy.'

Something still nagged at me. 'What religion were you before you converted to Catholicism, Ann?'

She frowned. 'I wasn't *converted* to Catholicism, Johnny. Most Armenians in Madras, and that includes my father and the Aga, belong to the Catholic Armenian Church. It's a very young church which broke off from the more traditional, Armenian Orthodox Church. The first Patriarch was elected only in 1740: Abraham Artzivian, the Bishop of Allepo.'

The history of the church didn't interest me; but something else did. 'But if you were already a Catholic, why did you become a Roman Catholic?'

Her frown deepened. 'Because there are too many factions in the Armenian Catholic Church. They contradict each other about basic teachings. Both claim that they have the truth. How can there be two truths? The Roman Catholic Church is very certain about its teachings. We need certainty … I need certainty … on which to base our lives. My father and the Aga knew my views and so they were very happy when you, too, were dogmatic about your faith. Are *you* happy, now, Johnny?'

My wonderful Ann was not only beautiful. She was also strong-willed and clear thinking. 'Yes, Ann,' I said. 'I'm very happy,' and I kissed my finger and touched it to her lips.

I got an appointment with the new governor immediately. Shortly after the Arcot victory, someone in the Council had unearthed an old directive of the Board that said that the tenure of an Acting Governor could not extend beyond a certain stipulated period. According to gossip in the Mess, the meeting of the Council had been tense but, eventually, they had agreed to appoint an outsider, that is someone from outside the Fort. They had chosen the Senior Merchant of

Tellicherry, the unassuming Malcolm Unger Shem who was known, in the Company, as 'Mush'.

He looked much like his writer, Bales: short, tubby, with a head like a pink plum pudding, black raisin eyes, black eyebrows, not a hair on his head. Unlike Bales he had a full black beard and moustache. The speculation in the mess was that his beard grew out of his chest because he had no neck. His voice sounded as if it had been filtered through layers of suet. Most officials, and their wives, had not met him officially because he had spurned the usual Assuming Office Party and just slid into his job as unobtrusively as possible. We had, however, caught glimpses of him as he toddled across the parade ground. He wasn't very impressive from a distance, even less so close up.

He was sitting at his desk and writing with a brown, eagle's quill when I entered. He said, in a thick, treacly voice, 'Sit down. Mr Yale-Lynsdale,' without looking up. He finished his letter, sanded it, blew, and laid it neatly on a pile on his right. He then brushed down his lapels, leaned back and crossed his stubby fingers across his globular stomach.

'Well, Mr Yale-Lynsdale,' he burbled, 'What can I do for you?'

'I wish to get married, sir. Four weeks from today.'

His black eyebrows rose slowly. I watched them climbing over his gleaming, pink, forehead till they reached where his hairline would have been. They then began to descend creasing his brow with deep furrows.

'To whom?'

'Ann Hawkenian, sir. The only child of Avram Hawkenian.'

'Hmm …' he steepled his hands and gazed at me over them. There was a long silence broken only by the muffled whisper of the sea and the bells of a bullock cart.

'What will your grandfather say?'

'I don't think he will say anything at all, sir,' I replied truthfully. Obviously he was not aware of Grandfather's death. I breathed slowly and regularly to control my emotions.

The black eyebrows began to rise again, thought better of it, and came down. The frown lingered.

'Is the young lady … that is to say … have you got her into trouble?' asked the suety voice.

'No, sir.'

'Then why do you want to marry her?'

I stared into his tiny, black, eyes unblinkingly till he lowered them.

'Then, John Yale-Lynsdale,' he said unctuously,' I will be failing in my duty if I didn't tell you that many people in this garrison, this Fort, are likely to give you the cold shoulder. They do not and, if I might say so, the Company does not as a rule, view such marriages kindly. Are you aware of this?'

Once again I looked at him in silence. Then I said, 'I shall send you, and everyone else in the Fort, invitations, sir. I do hope you will be able to come.'

He smiled ruefully. 'Very likely.' He stood up and extended his hand across the table. 'And the very best of good fortune, young man.'

I stood up, shook his damp hand, and added, 'I shall also send an invitation to the Danish Governor of Tranquebar and his lady.'

'Oh, really! And will they come?'

'Yes, sir. And they will stay in the garden house of Aga Shawmier. His Excellency's wife is related to Madam Shawmier by marriage.'

'Oh, really! … I am sure you have much to do, young man. Good day!'

The governor was a discreet man. He did not tell anyone about my forthcoming marriage. Kline was taken by surprise when I asked him to be a witness to our engagement. He went very still for a long moment and then he smiled though the smile never reached his eyes. He said, 'Congratulations, John!'

I waited for him to say something more but when he didn't. I repeated, 'Will you be a witness to our engagement, Norbert?'

He grinned and thumped me on the shoulder. 'Of course! Of course, John!' And he strode away as if he had other pressing matters on hand. In fact, as Canker told me later, he made a bee-line for the governor's office to find out if I had got Mush's permission.

After that the news spread like wildfire. People met me and congratulated me; and whispered when Ann and I drove, in separate carriages, to the Church of Our Lady of Miracles, built by Petrus Uscan. Ann's father and Kline were our witnesses because, as Father Paul Tuscani had insisted, 'When two such great families come together, it is an 'istoric moment worthy of record.' I had no idea that Ann's was a 'great family' but I soon found out.

The day after our engagement we met her father and Aga Shawmier Sultan in the Hawkenian's drawing room. Shawmier came to the point immediately. 'If you have no objection Mr John, we intend to have a big wedding: five thousand at least to be fed.'

I thought I had misheard. 'How many?'

'Five thousand, at the very least.'

'But I …'

The Aga raised his hand interrupting me. 'Say no more, Mr John, till you have heard us.' He looked at Ann's father, saw him nodding slightly, and continued. 'You and this beautiful young lady wish to get married. That is a source of great joy to you and to us. But it is much more than the merging of two hearts. It is the reaffirmation of a great tradition that began with Avram's family, the family of your affianced, many generations ago. Do you know what I am talking about?'

I shook my head, 'No.'

'Ah!' the Aga looked at Ann's father. 'Perhaps you would like to tell him?'

Ann reached out and held my hand. Her father swallowed, took a deep breath, and said, 'Do you know who William Hawkins was?'

The name was vaguely familiar, but I couldn't quite place it.

'He might not know, Avram,' the Aga said. 'Tell him.'

Ann squeezed my hand and I wondered what was coming next.

Her father cleared his throat. 'More than 200 years ago, in 1603, an English adventurer named William Hawkins was sent by the Company to establish a factory in Surat. That's far up north on the west coast of India; we, in Madras, are down south, on the east coast. At that time Surat was a great port for the cotton trade. But it was dominated by the Portuguese who paid large bribes to the local agent of the Mughals. They were against Hawkins and did much to force him to leave India. But William Hawkins was a typical Elizabethan adventurer: swashbuckling and quite fearless. He defied the Portuguese and set off on the long overland voyage to the capital of the Mughals, in Agra.'

Ann's father stopped as a servant came in bringing coffee, brown sugar and sugary, Turkish sweets which melted in the mouth. He waited for the servant to leave and added, 'These Turkish sweets remind me: Hawkins spoke fluent Turkish, the common language of the Mussalmans in those days.' Ann put two spoonfuls of sugar into a tiny cup, stirred it and handed it to me. The coffee was hot and very sweet: just the way I liked it.

'You drink coffee like a Persian gentleman,' nodded the Aga approvingly. 'Continue Avram …'

I was wondering where all this was leading to but I didn't think it prudent to interrupt my father-in-law-to-be. Not just yet, that is, though this rambling tale was beginning to irk me. But it was far from over.

'After ten weeks, Hawkins' party reached the court of the Mughal Emperor,' Ann's father continued in his soft, dry-as-dust voice. 'There, for some reason which no one has been able to explain, he became an instant favourite of Emperor Jehangir. The monarch insisted that Hawkins stay on in Agra and even offered him a wife from the pick of the women in his capital. Hawkins declined, pretending that his religion prohibited him from marrying any but a Christian woman. Undaunted, the emperor said that he knew of such a person: an Armenian girl whose father had died in his service and who had, consequently, become a ward of his, the Emperor's, family.'

Ann's father sipped his coffee and, very carefully, placed the cup back on the table. There was great deliberation in his movements as if he wanted to delay things as long as possible. The Aga coughed. Ann's father nodded and said, 'The Armenian lady and Hawkins were married by Hawkins' servant who, according to Hawkins, was an unfrocked priest.'

I didn't see any need to pretend any longer, so I interrupted, saying with as much false cheer as I could muster, 'And they lived happily ever after …'

Ann's father went as still as a Trappist again, and then he smiled wanly 'No, they did not. William Hawkins fell a victim to court jealousies and intrigues and his erstwhile friend, Jehangir, ordered him back to Surat. That was in November 1611. Their first child, Thaddeus, was two months old at the time. His mother could not expose him to the hazards of a ten week overland journey. She left him in the care of her mother and, after a long voyage, returned to England. Her husband died, she married again, and her second husband … who had been Hawkins' companion in India … had her portrait painted and sent back to Surat …'

Hawkenian took a deep breath. 'Thaddeus Hawkins was my ancestor. We changed our name from Hawkins to Hawkenian.'

I was jolted awake, a little shaken. The two old men rose and Ann's father said, 'Please come with us.' They led us through three rooms and into a woman's bedroom. There was a four-poster bed in the centre, a dressing table with crystal and silver accessories, a wardrobe with two doors … one with a framed full-length mirror, the other of clear glass revealing bright, embroidered, gowns. This was, obviously, Ann's room because I got the faint fragrance of roses. But the most striking feature of the room was on the wall at the head of the bed. It was a huge portrait in a heavy gilt frame. It was signed Cornelius Johnson.

The portrait held my attention, magnetically. It showed an imperious-looking woman in a white gown encrusted with silver embroidery and pearls. She wore a round cap as richly embellished as her gown. From her head, a misty veil fell in a long trail and spread around her feet. The painter had caught sunlight pouring in through a long window to one side of her. It touched the folds of her gown, the silver and pearls, her deep red hair and her veil. And it gave a strange, piercing, quality to her green eyes which followed me wherever I moved.

I stood transfixed by it: the woman in the painting was my Ann.

The Aga whispered. 'A startling resemblance Mr John, is it not?' He paused to let his words sink in. 'If we believed in reincarnation …' His voice trailed away.

That evening when we were alone in the garden, Ann asked, 'Now that you know how the family began, Johnny, do you have any doubts?'

'Doubts? Doubts about what?'

'About my origins? William Hawkins and my ancestress might not have been married. Thaddeus Hawkins could have been illegitimate …'

'Is that why you squeezed my hand when your father was telling the story?'

She nodded and her eyes were brimming with tears. But she must have seen the wonder in my eyes because she placed her finger on my lips. 'Wait, Johnny, before you say anything. I have something else to tell you.' She dabbed a lace kerchief to wipe away the tears. 'There's more. My mother … I never knew her because she died when I was two … my mother belonged to the Jewish community and … neither the Armenians nor the Jews would give permission for them to be married according to the rites of either religion … so my mother and father were married … in a temple … a Gentoo … a Hindu temple. So …'

My head began to spin. Not because of what she had told me but I suddenly felt that I would have to tell her about my parentage. But I couldn't do that, not now, not before we were married. Then I recalled something that Father Paul had said in his brief sermon at our engagement. I hadn't paid much attention to it at the time … I don't normally pay much attention to sermons … but the words seemed to be very relevant now. I held Ann's hand, 'Even the Church says that the sacrament of marriage is performed between the husband and the wife … that's what Father Paul told us at our engagement. In a Catholic wedding the priest is only a witness. And so does it really matter whether, at your parents' marriage, the priest was a Catholic or a Hindu, Ann? It doesn't matter to me …'

She looked into my eyes for a long time then, again, she touched my face very tenderly. 'Thank you Johnny. I now know that I am marrying the only man in the world for me, regardless of what happened in the past.'

I pulled her into my arms and held her close against me. 'Ann, Ann … the past doesn't matter. Our lives together began from the day we met. Nothing that happened to us before that, or to our families, matters. We must not speak of such things again …' After I had said that, I felt embarrassed, as if I had been spouting lines from *Romeo and Juliet.* I was about to say something to take the sugary tone out of my words when there was a barking at the gate. And when Goliath opened it, a bundle of white and brown came rocketing in, streaked across the lawns, and threw itself on Ann. I snapped, 'Rushes!' Ann laughed as Rushes covered her face with long, excited, licks. She cuddled him in her arms and he looked at me and barked, his tail frenzied with delight.

'I think he loves me,' Ann said breathlessly.

'He does. Like master, like dog.' Honey sweetened my tongue again and I began to blush.

Ann bent and put Rushes down, her eyes fixed on me. She extended both her hands, brought my hands together, and cupped them in hers.

'Will you forgive me if I sound like a very forward woman?' I smiled and nodded, not trusting myself to speak.

'Johnny, I find it difficult to wait all those weeks.' She shook her head as I reached out for her. She held me back. 'But we must because it will make it that much more wonderful. But Johnny …'

'Yes?'

'Promise me that you will never try to meet me alone, after dark.'

'Why not, Ann?'

'Because I might not be able to hold myself back from you … There, you've made me say it. Oh Johnny!'

I touched her face. It was hot and flushed. 'I promise … I promise, my beautiful Ann.'

I left hurriedly after that, Rushes trotting at my feet. My heart pounded and I felt as if I was burning with a high fever. When Canker saw me sitting at my table he asked, 'Are you unwell, Johnny-chan?'

'No. No. I never felt better in all my life.'

He nodded slowly. 'Keep your wits about you, John. The next three weeks could be very difficult. They will never forgive you for marrying a rich, "country-born" … as they term it … woman. They have more caste prejudices than we do.'

I was too buoyed up to care, but, when I stepped into my room Joseph said, 'The governor says he will be working in his office till midnight and that you should meet him before you retire.'

My joy drained out of me. I changed into more formal clothes and walked across to the governor's office. I asked Bales what was the matter, he said he didn't know. 'He received a letter from Tellicherry and immediately sent that message to you. That's all I know. You'd better go in.'

The Hon. Mr Shem looked up as I entered. 'Ah Mr Yale-Lynsdale. I've just had a letter from my old friends. Very important friends, too.' He smiled. 'Mr Gabriel Goldsmith sends his best wishes. So does his lady. I believe that your grandfather was her guardian.' I got a sinking feeling in my stomach mixed with a strange, forbidden, elation. The governor rummaged around in a drawer and brought out a letter which he read carefully. 'You might like to send them an invitation to your wedding. Her Christian name is … let me see …' he peered at the letter and held it closer to the oil lamp on his desk. 'Yes, here it is … it's a very pretty Italian name … it's Lucia.'

The Bait

Lucia was coming to my wedding!

How had she learnt that I was in Madras? And why had she decided to come here, at this time? I felt … I didn't know what I felt. Elation that I would at last meet Lucia. Fear of what would happen when I did. Hatred that she was going to ruin my life, that she would tear Ann from me.

I went for a long walk around the Fort, along dark roads, past the bungalows of the officers … the Poulsons were entertaining. A sentry challenged me at the west gate then said, 'Good evening, sorr. Out for a constitutional, is it?' when I stepped into a circle of light. Three soldiers standing in front of their barracks guffawed loudly at a joke, straightened up when they recognised me. Then I was in the church compound. I made my way to the back and sat on a bench in the churchyard dotted with a few headstones. It was very still and the dead don't disturb me: they have other things to do. An owl swooped down silently, caught a squealing mouse, flew up on to a bare branch near a lamp-post and started, very fastidiously, to eat its prey holding it in the claws of one foot, swallowing chunks of meat with the finesse of a gourmet.

The people of the Fort would dismember me just as meticulously, if they got the opportunity, led by Mrs Lucia Goldsmith. Obviously she was coming here to slice me into tiny morsels. Or was she? I had not harmed her. *She* had seduced me. And if she had had my child, it wasn't my fault. Suddenly my mind was filled with visions of her moaning and writhing in bed while the crackers exploded in the night sky. Then her body changed to that of the *nautch* girl who had called me her Great Lion and Joanna Scythe breathing hot Madeira all over me.

'*Gluck*!'

I looked up. The owl seemed to be having a fit. It kept stretching its neck and opening its beak. And then it went, '*Gluck*!' again and spat out a blob which landed close to my feet, glistening in the circle of light. I peered at it. It was a lump of hair, claws and bones: all the indigestible parts of a little animal disgorged by the owl.

My stomach heaved and I felt bile rising in my throat. I rushed to the bushes at the far end of the yard, where it was dark, and retched, and retched and retched. I staggered to the church well. There was some water in the brass bucket. I gargled, washed my face and straightened up. When I walked out of the church compound I felt much better. Things had fallen into place. All those women, all those bodies, were in the past, the experiences of them had become as much a part of me as the bodies of little animals had become part of the owl. They had given me momentary pleasure but that was over. I had to clear my mind of the indigestible parts: the ones that were not needed any more.

I wasn't in quest of pleasure now, I was searching for the joy that only Ann could give me. As I walked back to my room I realised that there was no deep, dark conspiracy on Lucia's part. The Goldsmiths were good friends of Shem, and Lucia had probably mentioned that she had been my grandfather's ward in Bath. And since the name Yale-Lynsdale was not a common one, certainly not 'John Yale-Lynsdale', Shem must have said that I was getting married. That was the simplest and most logical explanation. If Lucia came to our wedding, I'd be glad to see her and meet her husband; if she didn't come, it really wouldn't matter.

Rushes jumped off his perch on the camphor-wood chest, greeted me, and then curled up on top of it again. I fell into a deep and untroubled sleep as soon as my head touched the pillow.

The next day, the Aga and Ann's father visited me in the John Company.

'It is our custom,' said the Aga, 'for the bride's family to take care of all the arrangements for a daughter's wedding. We have instructed a Portuguese-Jewish jeweller to send his chief goldsmith to you to fashion the wedding ring on the spot. The important invitations will be calligraphed, and the others printed so that they will look almost as good as the calligraphed ones. They will be delivered by messenger. Avram will, personally, leave for Tranquebar in two or three days to deliver the invitation to the governor, His Excellency Admiral Pieter Jacob van Rijn, and his wife, Lady Sarah. Is there anything else you can think of, Mr John?'

'Do we really have to invite five thousand guests?'

The Aga frowned, then he relaxed and chuckled slapping his thigh in delight. 'Five thousand guests!' he chortled, his whole body shaking with mirth '*Five Thousand* guests! Where ... where can we accommodate *Five Thousand guests*?' He shook his head. 'No. Mr John, you misunderstood. We shall *feed* five thousand people from all over Madras. Of all communities, of all religions. It is a local custom. So then many, many, people will know about the wedding and they will all bless you and Ann.' He chuckled again.

Avram Hawkenian added in an unemotional voice. 'We shall invite only five hundred for the reception and it will be held in the Aga's mansion.' He paused and looked at his companion who nodded, still smiling broadly. 'They call it The Great House on Charles Street with good reason.'

'Thank you very much,' I was embarrassed so I added, rather feebly, 'but must it be such an elaborate wedding?'

Avram Hawkenian spread his hands and shrugged his shoulders. 'I have only one daughter, only one child. Permit me this indulgence. And now, if you will excuse us, we have a lot to do.'

I think it was the preparations for the wedding that fanned the fires of jealousy.

After Assembly, one morning, I was hurrying past Joanna Scythe and had doffed my hat, when she called out, 'John!'

'Yes, Mrs Scythe.'

'Joanna,' she corrected.

'Yes, Joanna.'

'Is it true that you're getting married to the Hawkenian girl in a few weeks?'

'It's true. The invitation to you and the Reverend Scythe should be delivered in a few days.'

'Where will you and your bride live, then?'

'I'm trying to rent a garden house on the Cooum.' I wondered what she was driving at.

'They're very rich, I understand: the Armenians. Will you leave the Company?'

'Which company, Joanna?'

She stamped her foot impatiently and twirled her parasol. Her eyes narrowed. 'The East India Company, of course … Oh, I see. I could have been referring to your own John Company. Well … what are your plans?'

The woman was beginning to annoy me. 'Joanna, please tell me why you're so interested in my plans?'

She clenched her teeth and looked around. There was no one else on the road.

'Because I'm interested in you and everything you do. Because you're the only man who's ever interested me after my girlish infatuation with the Afrikaaner in Kapstaad. And then again, in Kapstaad, if that snake had not appeared, you would have been mine.'

I didn't know what to say, so I stepped back, touched my hat, and walked away.

A few days later, Kline's *dubash*, Joachim Sardesai, was brought into my office by Kunhi. 'He wishes to deliver a message from Mr Kline,' Kunhi said. I asked Sardesai to sit down but he said, 'Thank you, sir. Most kind. But I am too small a man to sit in your honour's presence.'

'Do you have a message for me?'

'Yes, sir. It is from Kline-sir. A business matter, sir.' He cleared his throat, closed his eyes and intoned his memorised message. 'Kline-sir presents his compliments to Yale-Lynsdale-sir and wishes to say that since the honourable Mr Yale-Lynsdale is planning to enter into holy wedlock therefore he may not wish to continue running the John Company. If this is his desire then Kline-sir wishes to ask him if he would consider selling the Company to Kline-sir on such suitable terms as he, Yale-Lynsdale-sir, and he, Kline-sir, may mutually agree upon. That is what I have to say.'

It was such a pompous message that I burst out laughing. The effect on Sardesai was comical. His protuberant eyes bulged and he breathed hard, his face glistening with sweat.

'Yale-Lynsdale-sir is insulted?' he asked hoarsely.

'Of course not. Of course I'm not insulted. I was laughing because Captain Kline made no mention of this when I had breakfast with him this morning.'

The *dubash* hung his head. 'It is, perhaps, not seemly sir, to talk such business things at breakfast. Maybe. Perhaps … ' he murmured.

I nodded. 'I see. I wasn't aware of this custom. Please tell Captain Kline that I shall speak to him later today. Thank you for delivering the message.'

When he had left, Canker came in and asked what had transpired. I told him.

'You took it too lightly, Johnny-chan. In this society no one takes business and trade lightly.'

It was so unexpected that I asked him, 'Do you think that I should seriously think of selling the John Company, and resigning from the East India Company?'

'Johnny you must think seriously of your future. Your marriage is like a large stone dropped into a small pond. It has caused waves and ripples and everyone has been affected. And when news of your grandfather's death is brought in by the next ship, the storm will be great. Think seriously of selling the John Company; and also of moving out of Madras.'

'Why? In the name of all that is holy, why?'

'Because there are jackals and vultures: unholy creatures. Now you're the tiger and the adjutant stork before whom all the lesser creatures cringe. But when they find out that you are no longer the king of the carcases, they will rush in.'

'Carcases? What carcases?'

He shook his head pityingly. 'You are like your grandfather: honest, honourable, upright. But, for the rest: they want to make India into a charnel house filled with carcases on which they can gorge. Squabbling to grab larger and still larger chunks of the bleeding cadavers. There is no place for you in this rapacious society after the power of Bernard Chan has gone.'

I had never known Canker to be so bitter. For the first time since I had decided to become a trader I had glimpsed how the people of India viewed the trading companies: the Portuguese, Dutch, British, French, perhaps the Danes. It was a horrifying picture. I stood up and put my hand on his arm, reassuring him.

'I shall speak to Kline, today,' I said.

But it was Kline who raised the topic when we were alone in our rooms, after dinner.

'John, did you find my offer amusing? So amusing, that you laughed?'

We were both sitting in our common lounge and dining room, sipping glasses of Port. I put down my glass, 'No, Norbert, I didn't find the offer amusing; only the pompous manner in which it was delivered by your *dubash*.'

Kline sat up straight. 'He delivered the message I had dictated to him.'

'Well, it was very pompous. Why didn't you speak to me, either here or in my office?'

He mumbled something but I wasn't sure I had heard correctly. I stood up, 'What did you say?'

He looked up at me and repeated it clearly and distinctly. 'I said "I don't visit the offices of Armenian cojas."'

I bounded across the room and stood over him, 'Stand up, Kline, and repeat that.' I was trembling with rage.

Still sitting, he lashed out with his foot and kicked me in the testicles. The pain was excruciating, lancing up through my groin and into my stomach. I doubled over and fell, groaning. I think I was unconscious for a moment. Then I heard Kline say, 'That is the way to treat pariah dogs ...'

I looked up, my eyes blurred with pain. Kline was still sitting in his chair, his legs crossed, sipping his Port and looking at me with a cynical smile on his lips. I leapt at him and hit him with my fist on the mouth. The force of my blow sent him flying backwards in his chair. I grabbed him by the collar, lifted him and hit him in the stomach and, as he doubled over, again on his jaw. He was flung backwards and when I threw myself on him he lashed out with both feet. The blow landed on my chest and the air whooshed out of my lungs leaving me gasping. Kline sprang to his feet like a cat, grabbed a heavy brass vase and swung it down on my head. But I had rolled aside and the momentum of his swing unbalanced him and he fell flat on his face. I grabbed his right arm, twisted it high behind his back, my fingers gripping his thumb. He cried out but I tightened my grip, straddling his lower back and pushing his arm higher and higher towards his neck.

'Stop! For God's sake stop!' he gasped.

'Do you yield, you cur?'

'Yes, my God. You'll break my arm. Yes, I take back those words. Oh God! The pain …'

I eased the pressure a little. 'And when you're about it, Norbert Kline, when will you pay me the money you owe the John Company, you miserable scum!'

'Soon … today, today. I swear. Today …'

I got up, flipped him on his back and slapped him hard, twice, across his face. His mouth was bleeding and there were tears streaming across his cheeks. He staggered to his feet, nursing his arm. I picked up his glass and threw the Port on his face.

It was only then that I heard the knocking on the door and the sharp yaps of Rushes. Joseph had taken him out for a walk and, when I opened the door, Joseph took one horrified look around the room and asked, 'What happened, Master? Master hurt?'

My groin still ached and there was pain in my chest, but Kline's face was a mess and the dripping, red, Port made it seem even worse than it was. 'Captain Kline over-balanced in his chair and fell over, Joseph.'

Strangely, Rushes didn't make a sound. He stood near me, his muzzle raised towards Kline and, slowly, the hairs on his neck and his back came erect. When Kline began to stagger to his room, Rushes' lips curled back from his teeth and he uttered a low growl. I thought he would attack Kline. I reached down and stroked him but it was only when Kline had closed the door behind him that my dog looked up at me and wagged his tail, tentatively.

Joseph straightened the chair, picked up the brass vase and placed it on the table. Still busying himself getting the room in order, he said, 'Many gentlemens standing down below, looking upwards, wondering why *thud-thud* noise on wooden floor. So I tell them John-sir and Kline-sir doing exercises. Any help I can give, sir?'

'No thank you, Joseph. I'll look after myself.' But I wasn't really sure that I could. Norbert Kline did not forgive and forget.

He studiously avoided me for the next twenty-four hours and then he breezed into my office and handed me the money. 'Do count it, John. I'm sure you'll find it in order.' His injuries had been attended to but there was still a thickening of his upper lip. 'And … I almost forgot … Mrs Scythe wanted to thank you for the regular contribution you make towards church charities. She says she's starting a crèche for the children of the workers in the godowns, the warehouses. If you'd like to continue making your generous donations, she'd be home this afternoon at the usual time, 3:30 pm.' He stood up. 'And thank you for the invitation to your wedding. Sorry I won't be there: got to go to Fort St. David on an inspection. But I'll be there in spirit …' and with a happy wave, he left.

His manner appeared to be altogether too light-hearted, but it seemed to be genuine enough. I counted the money, removed the amount I had agreed to give to Joanna Scythe, handed the rest over to Kunhi and walked across to the Scythe's bungalow. I had visited her once every ten days. Either her husband or her servant had always let me in. I, therefore, felt rather uneasy when the door swung open on my knock and she called out, 'Come in, John. You know where to find me.'

I hesitated.

She stepped out into the corridor and said, very softly, 'If you stand there, you expose yourself to grave danger, John. Believe me. Trust me. Come in and close the door behind you.'

I was even more disturbed when I saw her because she was wearing a light, white, gown. Sweat made it cling to her body revealing the swell of her breasts, her nipples, the curve of her stomach, the thrust of her thighs. I hesitated again, my pulse pounding in my throat.

'Step in, you fool!' her voice was hoarse and she grabbed my hand. I allowed her to lead me into the drawing room. The blinds were down but light filtered in through the *khus-khus chicks*. 'Sit down, John.' She pushed me into a chair and, in a swift move, threw off the shift she was wearing. She sat, naked and damp, on my lap, took my face in her hands. And gave me an open-mouthed kiss, her tongue probing; her hand reached down and fondled me. It was so unexpected, so lascivious, that I hardened and my tongue battled with hers. She took my hand and cupped it to her full breast, pressing my fingers around her nipple. I could think of nothing else but this woman and lust rising in me. I grabbed her shoulders and started pushing her onto the floor when she wriggled out of my grasp and leapt to her feet. She was breathing hard, her heavy breasts with their pink, engorged, nipples, rising and falling. She let me look at her for a moment, then she slipped into her robe, picked up two glasses of water, handed one to me and drained the other.

'Drink it quickly. Cool your ardour and answer my questions. Do you love Ann Hawkenian?'

I nodded, unable to speak.

'Do you think she can match the passion I am offering you?'

'Yes,' it came out in a squeak.

She looked at me for many heartbeats, then she sighed. 'I believe you. Now listen carefully. Kline hates you. He and my husband have set up a trap using me as a bait. They want to disgrace you so that you will be dismissed from the Company, the East India Company, and your wedding will be called off. Kline wants to take over your business which he says he will share with my husband and that stupid Brandell believes him. He wants to humiliate you.'

'Why? What have I done to him?' Our fight was not public knowledge and surely that would not have made him want to destroy me.

'I don't know why Kline detests you. Professional jealousy, possibly. But I really don't know. I do know why Brandell wants to destroy you.'

'Why?'

'In a moment of anger I told Brandell that we had fornicated in Kapstaad and then again in this house.'

'Why Joanna? Why did you lie about us?'

'Because I wanted to make him jealous. I hoped that, for once, his member would get hard and he would take me. Just once. But he was so hurt that he cringed away and, ever since then, he's moved into the guest room. He now entertains his catamites openly.'

I broke out in a cold sweat. I had never been so scared in my life. All Joanna had to do was to scream, tear her flimsy shift, and I would be convicted.

'Are Kline and your husband waiting outside?'

'Brandell is. Not Kline: he's too clever. He's sent Robert Holmes, his newfound friend. But Holmes has been told that we suspect that one of the servants is a burglar.'

I poured myself another glass of water and gulped it down.

'Are you going to betray me, Joanna?'

'Did you, even for a moment, lust after me, John? Even for a moment?'

'Yes,' I whispered. 'You know I did …'

'Yes, I know. I felt you. Will you make love to me … sometime, anytime … if I promise not to betray you?'

Thoughts and images and emotions rushed through me. If I didn't give in to her, if I didn't promise to deflower her, I would lose everything I held sacred: Ann, my honour, the prestige of the Yale-Lynsdales, the respect of all those who held me in high regard. All I had to do was to promise to give her a few moments of ecstasy which she would remember for as long as she lived. And what would one more woman matter after the others: just another body. It wasn't as if I was giving her my love, only my body. I felt myself stirring

But then, the image of Ann came before me: '*Johnny, I find it difficult to wait …*' and my passion was diverted to the woman I wanted more than anything else in the world.

'Sorry, Joanna,' I heard myself saying, 'I can't.'

I knew that I had sealed my fate. I braced myself for her scream. It never came. She looked at me sadly and said, 'John Yale-Lynsdale, you are a good man, an honourable man, and Ann is a very lucky woman. Would that I were in her place. But …' she shrugged. 'We make our beds and we sleep on them.' She sat, sipped a glass of water and shook her head. 'It would have been wonderful if we had bought your business. It would have given me independence. An uncle left me some money. I wanted to invest it in the John Company. Two of the young writers also want to leave the company and I had promised them that I would employ them. The spinster teacher has agreed to let me have some rooms in her bungalow. Oh well … that's another dream destroyed, John …'

Suddenly I saw her for what she was: an ordinary woman locked in a cruel marriage.

I said, 'I'll sell you my business, Joanna.'

She shrieked with delight and clapped her hands. There was a pounding of feet on the garden path, the door was flung open, and Brandell Scythe and Robert Holmes burst in. 'Caught you, you filthy adulterer!' Scythe shouted.

Holmes seemed bemused.

Joanna rose very slowly. 'What did you say, Brandell?'

'This man raped you, Joanna,' he was the picture of injured innocence. 'You raped the wife of a man of the cloth, you sacrilegious cad!'

'Control yourself, Brandell,' Joanna's voice was cold. 'Do sit down Mr Holmes and allow my husband to stop foaming at the mouth. Would you like a glass of water, Brandell?'

Scythe subsided into a chair, his mouth slack. 'What is this man doing here?'

'Exactly what he has been doing about three times a month ever since he joined the Honourable Company: making his donations for church charities. Here it is …' and she picked up the envelope I had left on the table.

Holmes shuffled his feet. 'I am … I am most sincerely sorry for breaking in like this, Mrs Scythe …'

Scythe spluttered, 'Wait a minute. Wait a minute. How do I know that the two of you have not been …'

'Fornicating, Brandell?'

'How dare you use such a low word, woman!'

'It's a Biblical word, Brandell. Or have you forgotten your Bible?'

'All right. Have it your own way, you Scarlet Woman!'

Joanna turned to Robert Holmes. 'Mr Holmes, I am ready to be examined by Dr Poulson. He will certify that I am still a virgin. No man has ever known me, even after all my years of marriage to this … this creature. In fact, as my father, a solicitor, told me, consummation is necessary for a marriage to exist. This … this pederast in a dog collar, had not been able to consummate our marriage. Isn't that right, Brandell?'

Brandell Scythe seemed to deflate. He slumped, as flaccid as an empty balloon. Richard Holmes fidgeted with his hat in his hand and said, 'Er … if I may … I … er …'

'Do leave, Mr Holmes,' Joanna said. 'And do convey my good wishes to Captain Kline. Tell him that I overheard the conversation he had with Brandell: he'll know what I am referring to. Thank you for your donation, John. I shall call on you in your office with the papers. Good day, gentlemen.'

As we closed the garden gate behind us, Holmes breathed a sigh of relief. 'By gad! What a mess that might have been!' He turned to me. 'Norbert Kline was misled by that priest. Scythe said he wanted help to catch a thief red-handed.'

'A thief!' I repeated. 'In the Fort? In the middle of the afternoon? Really?' Holmes looked at me, his head cocked to one side. And then I added, 'Do tell Norbert that I delivered the donation to Mrs Scythe at half-past three this afternoon, as he had asked me to do.' I nodded and left him standing there with a strange look on his face.

I felt reluctant, at first, to relate the incident to Ann. But then I realised that it was more than likely that the story would get back to her anyway, suitably distorted to show me in the worst possible light! I gave her a brief account of it, leaving out the bit about Joanna Scythe's attempt to seduce me. Even so, Ann went quite pale.

'Why would Kline want to do that to you?'

'I think he rather likes you and is jealous because you chose me. He also wants to take over the John Company.'

'He wouldn't dare. Not as long as your grandfather is a Director.'

I looked at my feet, mustering my thoughts. 'Ann, my grandfather and mother are dead. They were killed by brigands on their way to London. They were coming out to India with that camphor-wood chest.'

Her eyes widened with horror then she buried her face in my shoulder. 'Johnny … my poor, poor, Johnny …'

I consoled her as best I could. 'I don't think anyone in Madras has learnt about it as yet, Ann. Please keep it to yourself.'

'Must I keep it from my father and Uncle Aga?'

'Yes, please. They'll know soon enough, when the next Indiaman brings letters from Leadenhall Street. Meanwhile we must behave as if nothing has happened. Are you strong enough, Ann?'

'Yes … yes I am …'

I felt that the Fort was suffocating me. And once its mean-minded denizens learnt that my grandfather was dead, they'd close ranks against me, egged on by Kline. I'm sure he had expressed the opinion of some of the people in the Fort when he called me an Armenian coja. Besides, even Canker had advised me to move out. I had made enough money to support a wife and family for the rest of my life but I couldn't see myself vegetating in some Indian village. So what could I do? I had some experience in trade but that had all been strictly within the fold of the Company. Would the *dalals* even give me a second look if I didn't have the Company to back me? In fact, if Kline had his way, he'd soon have me branded a pariah, an outcast. But then, could I afford to pull up my roots from Madras even if I had all the money in the world? And should I start on a new career just after I got married? Would it be fair to Ann? I'd have to ask her. But, before I did that, I would have to decide what I wanted to do. The decision, however, was taken out of my hands, in a manner of speaking.

Joseph came in and said, 'There is one gentleman who wishes to meet you, sir. He says he is from Calcutta.'

I was surprised. I didn't know anyone from that town. 'He has come on the *Bengal Trader* ship arriving one hour ago. He has come only to meet you: only for that self-same purpose. You will see him sir. Or I will ask him to go and come back tomorrow morning?'

For some odd reason, I did not want Kline to see this unknown visitor, and Kline was on duty. I said, 'Please ask him to come up. Did he give you his name?'

Joseph struck his forehead in remorse. 'Yes, sir, yes, sir. He say his name is …'

'Count Viktor Pavlovitch, owner and captain of the *Dnieper.* May I come in, sir?'

I looked up at the man standing at the door. He was tall and slim, with the gaunt features and sideburns of an aristocrat, immaculately dressed in a black coat, a high black hat, white breeches, a heavily embroidered waistcoat with a stock and a black solitaire tie. His thin lips had a faint, quizzical smile. I rose and said, 'Please do come in and sit down, Count. What can I do for you?'

'Thank you, sir,' He stepped in, placed his hat very carefully on a side table and sat with a certain prim precision as if he were posing for a portrait. He smiled, nodded and said, in an accent which had only the faintest trace of Russian harshness in it, 'I represent the Free Traders Association of Bengal. We have learnt of your great victory at Arcot.'

He paused as if waiting for a reply, his head tilted quizzically to one side.

'Our company was commanded by Captain Norbert Kline, Count.'

'Ah! So I have heard,' He cleared his throat politely holding a white silk handkerchief to his thin lips. 'Nevertheless, as I said, we have learnt of your great victory at Arcot.'

I saw no reason to contradict him a second time. I waited.

'We are, Mr Yale-Lynsdale, well equipped for the conduct of open warfare but …' he didn't finish his sentence.

I nodded and waited.

'But we find ourselves at a loss to combat an enemy who filters through the trees, launches skirmishes at night, bleeds us by constant harrowing …'

I still didn't reply.

He sighed. 'We have not your expertise or that of your Nair warriors …'

I waited for him to get to the point.

'We need you to come to the riverine swamps of the Sunderbans, along with your famed warriors, and rid us of the Hooghly Pirates, Mr John Yale-Lynsdale.'

Convergence

I felt a little light-headed.

Things were moving too fast … To calm myself I looked out of the window. An Indiaman was sailing into the anchorage, flying the Company's flag. Her guns boomed out saluting the Fort, puffs of smoke appearing from her gun-ports a little before the sound reached me. Soon, the battery in the Fort would reply.

I went cold.

This was the long-awaited ship from London. And it would carry news of my grandfather's death.

Joseph placed a hot cup of coffee on the teapoy near my chair, another on the little table beside my guest. The aroma of the fresh brew snapped me back to the present … Rushes jumped off his bed, stretched, walked across, licked my hand and curled up at my feet.

'That's very interesting, Count Pavlovitch. I'd like to have more details.'

'Certainly, Mr Yale-Lynsdale.' He sipped his coffee, touched his lips with his handkerchief, nodded. 'If you should accept this offer, sir, we shall make all arrangements for your conveyance and that of your troops to the … er … site. We shall pay their salaries, provide their victuals and supplies, and make a settlement for … er … any physical damages sustained during this operation which should not take more than a fortnight, and also recompense you handsomely for your time and effort.'

It was clearly a well-prepared offer but it left a bad taste in my mouth: it made me sound like a Janissary, a subservient mercenary.

The elegant Russian held up his hand. 'Sir, forgive me if I have sounded indelicate.' He coughed, putting his handkerchief to his lips. It was punctuation to his offer before he resumed. 'We know that you are a man of considerable acumen and an honest trader. These qualities, if you will permit me to say so, run in your family. The compensation will be entirely of your choosing and may not even involve a monetary transaction. If, for instance, you wish to settle in Calcutta … and we have reason to believe that, before long, most of the Honourable Company's trade will be out of Calcutta … if, then, you so wish, we shall present you with a suitable mansion on the banks of the river, and all the assistance you may require to become a Free Trader under the aegis of Fort William.'

Relief and anxiety conflicted in me. The count's proposal seemed to be a gift from heaven. I heard the guns in the Fort replying to the Indiaman's salute. Soon the mail-boat would bring news of my grandfather's death. I didn't have much time but I didn't want to rush into this, not without Ann's consent. I wrote a hurried note to her and sent it across by Joseph. It was not quite proper to call on an unmarried lady after sunset but this couldn't wait.

I took the precaution of going to the John Company, and then using the interconnecting door to enter the Hawkenian's private wing. She was waiting for me in their drawing room and her father was busy at his desk in his office beyond. He rose, nodded to me, and went back to work. He was, obviously, chaperoning us. Ann looked radiant. I told her everything. She was silent for a long while, gazing down at the table with its huge silver bowl of roses. The she raised her head and those beautiful emerald eyes looked into mine, 'Johnny. I'd like both of us to discuss this with my friends. They live outside the Fort and I had gone to see them when you rescued me in the Black Town. I trust the Gordons and I treat them as my family. Do you agree?'

I didn't want to share my problems with outsiders. But Ann trusted the Gordons. We agreed to set out early the next morning.

Ann drove her gig and I rode Ashdown, trotting beside her, bowing to the rigid conventions of these hidebound people. The Black Town was a different place in the morning. There were housewives and young girls in the streets, fisherfolk with their wares spread on palm mats, vegetable and coconut vendors, and open-fronted shops, fairly crowded. All the taverns were shut, there were no drunks or rowdies on the streets and even the huts with the tell-tale red lights hanging outside had their doors closed.

The town thinned out, gave way to wetlands and then, just before the dunes appeared, a red-gravel path wound up to a curious, rambling, mansion on a long ridge of high ground. The central section was double-storeyed and its two wings were roofed with red tiles. Stretching out from the two wings were long, low, thatched huts walled with bamboo slats. An iron fence surrounded the property. A sentry stood at the roofed gate. Across the gable of the roof was a board proclaiming THE GORDON BOATYARD surmounted by a blue shield bearing three boar's heads below a sailing boat.

I asked Ann, 'Isn't his name "Adie"? And isn't he the Commodore of the Aga's coastal fleet?'

'He is. But the Adies are a sept, a branch, of the Gordon clan. And the boatyard was set up and run by his son-in-law, Andrew Gordon. Andrew was an apprentice in a Glasgow shipyard.'

The gateman recognised Ann, saluted, and let us through.

As we rode up to the mansion, a burly man with a weather-beaten face, boots and a leather apron trudged down the steps and boomed, 'Ann, welcome. I was sailing when you last visited Allison. Ah, and this is the lucky young fellow,' and he looked up at me with a half-smile on his lips as if he was assessing me, as he probably was. I leapt off Ashdown and shook his hand. It was huge and calloused. 'Name's

Adie, Jock Adie. The seafarers call me Commodore. And this is my son-in-law, Andrew Gordon …' Andrew had run down from one of the sheds. He was stocky and well muscled and had a shock of carrot-red curls on his head. There was a smear of black smut on his cheek and he had such a strong Glaswegian accent that I had difficulty in understanding him at first. In a few moments I learnt that he was infectiously cheerful and bubbled with good humour as if there was a cask of cider fizzing inside him!

A groom led away the gig and Ashdown, Jock Adie put his massive arm gently around Ann's shoulders and said to me, 'And now we'll meet Ann's twin, my daughter Allison …'

'How is she, Uncle Jock?' Ann asked.

'Much better than she was; much, much better. And she's accepted her loss … our loss. For what the Lord sends, the Lord can take away …'

Beyond the porch was a flight of stairs leading to a pillared hall with a balcony running all around the first floor. Then the dining room with a large black table and black cane-bottom chairs. Adie threw open huge, carved, double-doors at the far end and a sea breeze hit us: chill, fresh and slightly damp. Before us the ground swept down to the beach where white-capped waves rolled in and the Bay of Bengal heaved, gently, to the blue horizon.

From the thatched sheds, on either side of the mansion, came the sounds of sawing, hammering and chanting as bare-bodied men put their backs to a capstan and hauled a wooden, coastal, ship down a slipway to a small bay protected by a breakwater.

'And this …' said Commodore Adie, drawing my attention away from the scene of all this activity, 'Is Ann's twin, Allison. Or rather, that's the way they've behaved: like inseparable twins.'

Allison had been sitting, curled up, in a deep cane chair. It must have been made for her father because it enveloped her. If she was, indeed, Ann's spiritual twin, she was certainly very different, physically. Ann was tall, slim and with deep red hair. Allison could not have been more than five feet with a figure that would become buxom after the second or third child but was grape-tight now. And she had the most delicate features: a small and beautifully sculpted nose, large and expressive brown eyes, and soft brown hair that the wind blew like a cloud around her face. In spite of the loss of her new-born child, she radiated warmth. I was quite enchanted. In fact, I felt an instant attraction to the whole family and it must have shown because the Commodore bellowed,

'What a fine young man, Ann's collared …'

'Oh Daddy! He's been trying to find a match for Ann ever since we were school girls. Please don't mind him. I'm Allison, John. May I call you John? Ann calls me Alli but that makes me sound a bit like a Moor. I'd like you to call me Allison.' Her voice had an unusually deep timbre in it but strands of laughter ran all the way through.

'Would you like to see our boatyard, John? It's by far the best in the east coast even though I say so myself?'

I said, 'I'd be delighted, Andrew.'

The Gordon Boatyard was an eye-opener for me. They made everything needed to construct a sturdy coastal cargo ship. 'From the keel to the crow's nest, and from stem to stern,' as Andrew put it. They sawed and planed great logs into masts, spars, ribs, decks, bulkheads. In hot, clanging, forges they created anchors, cleats, bollards, even long iron nails. High in the loft sail-makers transformed canvas into the billowing wind-catchers that powered these craft.

'All my skilled workers are from Malabar: they've been building Arab dhows there for generations.' I wondered why some of the workers nodded to me and then I recognised them as Canker's yeoman warriors. This is where some of them worked when they weren't fighting. 'They're brilliant people and they're as proud as any Scotsman ever was. Rightly so. And they're great boat-builders. Come over here.' He led me to another shed, pulled aside the bamboo mats screening it, and we stepped in. When my eyes got accustomed to the half-light I saw five long, slim boats of an unusual design.

'These are their traditional war canoes built for their south-western coastal lands which, they say, is threaded with tiny canals, rivers and estuaries. Their princes wage water-wars there and my Malabari boat builders keep fighting fit, practising on these boats whenever we have a slack period. My father-in-law has dug a special, winding, canal for them. They're a fit, restless, intelligent people and if you don't keep them occupied …' he shrugged. 'As the old saying goes, *The Devil finds work for idle hands to do.*'

A bell clanged urgently.

'Ah! That's the commodore summoning us to lunch. Let's go.'

When we reached the house, Ann stepped out of the family group and said, 'John and I have come to ask your opinion about something: something very serious. Tell them, John.'

I was still a little reluctant but the family was so warm and they loved Ann. I began to speak, hesitantly at first, and then with increasing confidence. When I had finished there was silence broken only by the sounds from the workshops, the mewing of seagulls and the surf breaking on the beach.

Then Jock Adie spoke. His voice was soft but it was edged with an intensity that was compelling. 'They're a low bunch of Sassenachs, the dregs of English society who've been booted around by the Romans, Normans and Saxons for so long that they have no self-pride left. They've now put a demented German on the throne. That's why when they come here they want to lord it over the Indians who were civilised when they were sharing their hovels with pigs!' His face was red with fury, beaded with sweat.

Allison reached out her hand and touched him. He looked at her, shook his head and the anger seemed to drain away as suddenly as it had come. He turned to me, smiling grimly, 'Leave this accursed place John, and take Ann with you. We'll miss her, and we'll miss you too. Though we have just met, we seem to have known you all our lives. And if you should, ever, anywhere, need our help we'll be there. Now let's have lunch. I'm hungry!'

We had just finished lunch when a tall, scholarly-looking man hurried up the steps carrying a sheaf of papers. His white shirt and sarong were crisp and immaculately clean. He smiled and nodded at us, the light catching the three white horizontal lines on his forehead.

'Ah!' boomed Jock Adie, 'The good Mr Siva Sundaram has arrived with my daily burden of woe. Siva this is Mr John Yale-Lynsdale.'

Sundaram inclined his head with great dignity and said, 'Mr Yale-Lynsdale, I am honoured to meet you. Your exemplary defence of Arcot has been bruited abroad, and if I might say so, you have the stature and bearing of your grandfather, the great Mr Bernard Yale-Lynsdale.' His voice was deep and resonant and he had a very cultured accent, enunciating every word. Jock Adie must have seen the surprise on my face. He laughed and said, 'Siva speaks better English than anyone in the Fort, much better than I do certainly.'

He stood up and said, 'Andrew and I must get back to work, Allison must rest for a while. If the two of you would like a little time to yourselves, we've rigged up a lean-to down on the beach. We, all of us, escape to it whenever we want to be alone. If you care to use it we'll summon you for tea.'

We walked down to the beach in silence. The lean-to was made of bamboo and palm thatch, open on its seaward side, screened from the house. A slatted bamboo wall divided the single room into two. In the inner section was a large bed strung with soft, cotton, rope. A bamboo door opened into a cubicle with a field toilet, a wash-hand stand, two brass buckets filled with water. It was a secure, compact, little retreat. We sat on the two cane chairs outside the room. On a low table between the chairs, was a carafe of coconut water and a lidded brass dish holding candied ginger and wedges of fresh coconut.

We were silent for a long while. The tide was out, leaving a glistening stretch dotted with busy avocets, curlews and terns. It was very peaceful but my mind was brimming with urgency to say what I had to though I didn't know how to start.

Ann solved it for me.

She said, so softly that I almost didn't hear it over the signing of the sea and the wind. 'Why don't you tell me what you want to, Johnny?'

I turned to her surprised. She was looking at me with those amazing green eyes of hers, and then she turned away. It was as if she had opened a floodgate.

'Ann …' I blurted out, 'You felt that your past, your family, had many dark secrets. We, the Lynsdales, have many more. I have many more. And some of the secrets could threaten the life of my wife and family. So you must know all this now even though I should have told you much earlier.' I took a deep breath. 'My father was the late Frederick. Prince of Wales …'

I told her everything. About the assassination attempts, the strange messenger from Europe, Lucia …

'But you don't know if you did, really, make her pregnant. Her child was born long after her marriage. Don't crucify yourself, Johnny.'

I told her about the strange Mrs Scythe, and my Blooding. She smiled at me and said, 'That's flattering …'

'What's flattering, Ann?'

'It's flattering that so many women have wanted you, and you've chosen me.'

'Do you want me Ann?'

'Oh yes, very much, Now more than ever. Let's go in, Johnny.'

We went into the inner room. She turned to me and held me and her lips were on mine, gentle at first and then open and ravenous, her tongue seeking mine with a hunger that could not be denied. I reached for her breasts and she began to moan, breathing hard …

And then she pushed me away. 'Not now. I want you Johnny. I want you so badly … but not now. Not here. Not like this …' I stepped away, turned and went out. I poured myself a glass of coconut water, sipped it and it cooled me. She joined me after a short while. She looked calm and self-possessed and there were drops of water starring her hair. She took the glass from my hand, turned it and sipped from where my lips had touched it.

'I see Andrew coming for us. Have you read *The Perfumed Garden*?'

'No.'

'Or *Kama Sutra*?'

'No.'

'I have. They are books of instructions for couples.'

I grinned and said, 'Theoretical Knowledge, Ann.'

She turned those amazing eyes on me again. 'Oh really? What I did just now: was that theoretical knowledge? You have a lot to learn, Johnny; and I am a very eager teacher … Hello Andrew. Has Alli woken from her siesta?'

I certainly had. In one afternoon Ann had shown me how trivial my concerns had been. And how much there was to know about the woman I was going to marry.

Pre-nuptials

Jock Adie was waiting for us when we reached the mansion. He held my elbow and took me aside. 'I've been thinking about that offer the Russian made you. And the more I think of it the more I like it.'

He paused as if he was mustering his thoughts. The tide was coming in, covering the shimmering flats. The wading birds had gone and white gulls squawked and dived and bobbed on the waves.

Jock said, 'I have three, sturdy, coastal ships of my own. One is my yacht. It's got two comfortable cabins and we use it for family cruises when we get bored of the land. You, Ann and I will be on the yacht. The other two ships will carry the Nair warriors including the ones who work for me. Towed alongside their two vessels will be those Nair war canoes. The yacht carries three cannon, small ones but lethal all the same.'

I held up my hand. 'Where do we get the other arms and ammunition from?'

'From the Russian Count. If he is what he claims to be, he'll be able to lay his hands on all that we need. Sundaram's brother runs a guest-house and he can find out where the count is staying. Leave all that to me. I'm eager for a good fight.' He grinned broadly, his face florid and eager in the light reflected off the sea. 'Good plan, eh? We'll catch those Ahom pirates with their pants down. They won't know what hit them when the Nairs come slithering through the backwaters and pounce on them.'

Jock's accent had become so strong that I had to strain to understand all he had said. 'Ahom pirates?' I asked. 'Aren't we after the Hooghly pirates?'

'Och yes, we are! But they aren't local people, you understand. They claim to be the remnants of the old army of an ancient race who once migrated into north-eastern India from China. They held the Mughals and British at bay and ruled their land far longer than the Moors and the Sassenachs combined.' He shrugged his powerful shoulders, 'That's as may be. My personal feeling is that they're nothing but a bunch of criminals.'

'I thought they were people from the delta tribes: the great mangrove forests.'

'Not at all! They're not people from the Sunderbans at all. They're outsiders and they're resented by the locals who are fishermen and honey-collectors. They'll guide us. Some of them sell their produce to a middle-man named Aggarwal.'

The name rang a bell. Canker had sold the asafoetida to him. This seemed to be falling into place. I said I'd discuss it with Canker.

Jock beamed broadly. 'Do that, Johnny; do that. There's not a brighter mind with a more devious brain than the one the Comprador has. Certainly, ask him what he thinks of our plan. Now let's get back to the family.' Then he stopped. 'That Russian Count. I've dealt with him. But, at that time, he said he was an Ottoman Pasha. He's more than a representative of the Free Traders. He's a sort of Martial Contractor …' He saw the quizzical look on my face. 'Yes, yes. With all the 500 or more local rulers in India, anxious to have their rabble trained by Europeans, there's plenty of scope for skilled middlemen to bring the rajas and the mercenaries together. They're fishing in rich waters in troubled India!'

We walked on and joined Ann, Allison and Andrew. I noticed that there were jars of golden honey along with bannocks, steamed iddlis and dosa.

The sun was fairly low in the sky when I turned to Andrew and asked, 'Will you be my best man?'

There was a moment of silence then Andrew said something that I could not understand. Allison laughed when she saw the puzzled look on my face. 'Andrew was born and brought up in the Highlands but he gets very Glaswegian when he's taken unawares. He said he'd be very honoured to.'

'Yer don't need to interpret it, lass. John heard me.'

'Yes,' laughed Allison undaunted, 'but he dinna unnerstan' yer.'

We laughed and after that the conversation got more and more hilarious until my sides were aching. When we left them, the sunset was splashing brilliant colours across the sky, lighting up the clouds with smears of reds, pinks and yellows. We reached the Hawkenian mansion just as the servants had begun to light the lamps and Ann's father tried not to look relieved that we had returned before her curfew. I thanked her and said that this had been the most relaxing and enjoyable day I had had in a long time. She smiled and said, 'They like you very much, too, Johnny. Allison's father said that you were a clean, upright, honest man who would never let me down …'

I was overjoyed.

Then Ann said, 'Have you noticed, John the Company's flag is flying at half-mast.'

I knew why and steeled myself for the inevitable. Joseph was fidgeting with anxiety and he almost collapsed with relief when he saw me. 'Sir, sir … Governor sir and Council waiting long-long time to meet you. Go now, pleeese … soon, soon.'

They must have been waiting for some time. The air was thick and almost suffocating with tobacco-smoke. The governor rumbled, 'Ah, there you are Yale-Lynsdale. Sit down my man. I have grave news to impart to you!' He cleared his throat, gulped down half a glass of Port.

Then he said, 'We have received very grave news from London. Very sad and grave news.' He cleared his throat again. 'It is my distressing duty to inform you, young man, of the death of your greatly revered grandfather, Mr Bernard Yale-Lynsdale and that of your gracious mother. May their souls rest in peace.' He then got up solemnly, reached across the table and shook my hand; and one by one, so did all the Council Members. The Aga was the last.

When that was over the governor addressed me again. 'Does this sad news result in any change in your plans, John Yale-Lynsdale?'

I was prepared for that 'How and when did my grandfather and mother die, Sir?'

'Er … many months ago, a few days before the ship sailed from London. As to how it happened, the details are not clear but … but I understand … I gather that it was a road accident, a mishap on the road from Bath to London … so I gather.'

'In that case, sir, the period of mourning is over and, recalling what my grandfather always maintained, life and trade must go on. There will be no change in my plans, sir, except that shortly after my marriage I shall resign from the Honourable Company and move to another place with my wife. With your permission, sir, and the acquiescence of this honourable Council, I shall have my resignation on your desk tomorrow morning.'

I stood up, bowed to them, and left.

When I reached our quarters, and Joseph was serving me supper, he said, 'Kline-sir gone. Transfer to Tellicherry with all baggages. No one, now, in his room. Mr Bales, he take over Steward of Fort. Cadet Wellesley now is reliever of Mr Bales for time being. They say you having verrrrry big wedding. Is true, sir?'

I nodded. Kline must have done something to warrant his sudden transfer. Later, Canker informed me that Kline had had an argument with the governor demanding that I should be dismissed from the Company for disgracing the name of Yale and Lynsdale by deciding to marry an Armenian. Bales had overheard this and had informed the Aga and he and three Councillors voted against Kline's argument. The rest abstained. 'The governor and three of the Council members are deeply in debt to the Aga for helping them when their private trade incurred a terrible loss. The Chinese burnt their cargoes of opium,' Canker explained. 'Your grandfather had banned trading in opium by anyone in the Company.'

I told Canker about the count's proposal. He closed his eyes for a moment, then said, 'Let me think about it. Now, John-chan, concern yourself about the wedding.'

There wasn't really much for me to do. The Aga and Ann's father were handling everything with quiet efficiency. There was a flurry when the invitations went out. There was speculation when the carpenters and decorators came to assess the space available. I was told that Ann and I could not see each other for one week before the wedding. 'It is our custom,' her father said with finality.

One evening, when I was signing the documents to sell the John Company to Joanna Scythe she said, 'That morning when you were away from the Fort, a messenger came from Kline offering to buy the John Company to save me from getting into trouble. It was a veiled threat. I told him that my father had been an assistant pastor in Shropshire and he knew about Kline's marriage.'

I frowned. 'What marriage?'

'Kline was married by proxy to Peggy Claymore. He has not got the approval of the Company for this marriage and so he could be dismissed dishonourably if the Directors find out.'

I had neither the time nor the desire to enquire into this but Joanna seemed very confident that Kline would not bother her again. She also told me that her husband had left her, and her two young assistants, who had joined the John Company, '… keep me very busy … much busier than Brandell ever did.' She smiled after that and looked like a contented cat who had just licked all the cream and was purring for more.

I had very little to do now. I helped Joseph make the down-payment for a coffee stall in the Fort. It had been run by old Ramu for years but his three sons had become messengers in the Company so they were not interested in continuing their father's business.

Finally, Canker said, 'Tomorrow, just after breakfast, Kunhi and I will go to The Gordon Boatyard. You come a little later. There, along with Gordon, Adie and the count we will work on the strategy for the attack on the Hooghly Pirates.'

We were there for the whole day, poured over charts of the Sunderbans and the Hooghly, and listened to Jock Adie. His flat-bottom, fish-tank, barges carried live catches of the famed *hilsa* fish from the Sunderbans to the eager markets of Calcutta. 'The pirates never touch us so we'll use that immunity.' We trimmed and shaped out original plans. Canker added, 'I have spoken to our men. Fifty-five are willing to join you.' The count listened to our discussions intently, asked questions, made notes and at the end of it, said exactly how much he thought it would cost, added a percentage, and told us how much he would pay. It was a fair figure with a separate amount for 'damages', as he called it, 'For any injuries to persons and property and a compensation for lives lost, which I sincerely hope will not happen.' When I saw him off to his carriage he said, 'Mr Yale-Lynsdale, the disparate strands of rope may be strong, but when they are entwined together in a hawser, the strength of the whole is much more than the individual strength of its parts. That, as I saw for myself today, is your ability, your great talent.'

I felt strangely happy about that but then, when I reached the Fort and Canker and Kunhi visited me my elation left me.

Canker said, 'Kunhi and I must return to our home. There is a family dispute we must settle. We will stay till you leave. And we will come to the church for your wedding but we cannot stay for the reception.'

That hurt. Canker had been a father to me. He was always there when I needed him and now, when I was venturing into a new life he was leaving me. He seemed to sense what I felt. He put his hand on my shoulder and said, 'Johnny, you do not need me anymore. Even your Bible says that.'

I didn't know what he meant.

He smiled very gently. 'The first book of the Bible, the one they call *Genesis,* describes that wonderful moment when Adam sets eyes on Eve. It says …' and he began to use the deep, cadenced, intonation he reserved for sacred Sanskrit verses. '*Therefore shall a man leave his father and his mother and shall cleave unto his wife and they shall be one flesh.*' For the first time I felt the love that this wonderful man had for me. He said, very softly, 'Johnny, she will be very good for you. She will guide you, comfort you and be your pillar of strength whenever you need it.'

He seemed so certain of himself when I felt so adrift that I wanted to hurt him. I asked, 'How do you know all this Canker. You've never met her.'

He shook his head slightly. 'We obtained the date and time of birth from the official records of her church and the Fort. Her horoscope and yours have been cast by two very learned astrologers.'

'I don't believe in astrologers, Canker.'

'No? But you do believe in the Magi visiting Avatar Jesus because they saw his birth proclaimed in the heavens. The Bible says that, Johnny.'

I had heard that argument before. 'So what does the horoscope say will happen to me today?'

'Horoscopes give the highlights of your life. How you react to those critical events is where your will takes you.' He nodded to himself, 'It says that soon … very soon … you will come to one such critical point. When that happens, remember Johnny that I can no longer help you because my involvement with you has almost faded away. Another person has entered your life and an older one is trying to be assertive. The choice between the new and the old is yours to make. That's all I have to, say, Johnny-chan.'

He joined his hands in the traditional *namaskaram,* and left.

It struck me then that as people grew older, they probably felt it necessary to go back to their roots and find comfort in the reassuring superstitions of their childhood.

I now think I was wrong.

That afternoon, a messenger from the governor's office, brought a letter addressed to me. It said:

> *Dear John Yale-Lynsdale:*
>
> *'My wife and I would like you to join us for dinner this evening to meet old friends of ours who have come down for your wedding. Gabriel and Lucia Goldsmith are staying with us.*
>
> *We look forward to seeing you at six-thirty, today, in the Governor's Guest House. Informal.*
>
> *In haste*
> *Malcolm Unger Shem*

I had a sinking feeling in the pit of my stomach,

The street lamps had been lit when I walked, hesitantly at first and then with a more determined stride to the governor's mansion. I announced myself to the guard at the gate who rang a bell to summon a servant. I wrote my name in the Visitor's Book, and he asked me to follow him.

Wellesley, who was still acting as the governor's Secretary, led me to the drawing room and announced, 'Mr John Yale-Lynsdale,' and stepped aside. There were four people in the room: two men and two women. The governor waddled forward, clasped my hand in a damp and flabby grip and burbled, 'John Yale-Lynsdale, so glad you could come, so glad you could come, so glad you could come …' his voice trailed away as if it was receding into the distance. 'I'd like you to meet an old friend of ours, Gabriel Goldsmith …'

He was a tall, heavily built, stooping figure of a man with an enormous mop of silver hair, a hooked nose, and piercing black eyes that held me in a gimlet gaze before a ham-like hand was thrust at me. It was dry and cold.

The jelly-bean of a woman filling an overstuffed chair fluted, in surprisingly dulcet tones, 'Do come over, my *dear* boy and meet the *charming* Lucia. But then you two have *met* earlier. Isn't that *too, too, delightful.* Don't you think it's *too, too delightful daahling.'*

Daahling's throaty response was lost in the great, black, herbage of his beard.

Then all of them faded from my vision as Lucia rose from her chair stepped forward and, putting her hands on my shoulders kissed me on both cheeks. As she did so, she whispered, '*You're still so macho, Gian,*' and stepped back leaving me enveloped in a cloud of exotic perfume and confusion.

Goldsmith, spoke in a hoarse voice and in a rather pontifical manner as if he brooked no contradiction. He was full of himself. He declared that he had started life as a navvy, then worked as a porter carrying fish in Billingsgate, moved on to become a stevedore in the docks.

'There I met this chinky-eyed person who, I learnt, was a prince of one of the many warring families of Nepal. He was a student in one of our posh schools: all airs and graces and lardy-dardy accents. He wanted something done. I did it. He paid well.' He laughed coarsely and looked around for approval.

Lucia was obviously embarrassed, her eyes downcast. She looked up and said, 'Gabby, I'm sure everyone but John has heard that story.' She turned to me. 'Apart from our traditional products from Tellicherry, we now also export the produce of the Himalayas … timber, furs, musk, fabrics, crafts, things like that … to England and Europe.' She looked at her husband. 'Gabby's a great trader.'

Goldsmith inhaled and seemed to bloat like an inflated balloon. The governor rumbled something about the weather and the conversation veered away from the self-important Gabriel Goldsmith.

After his third glass of grog, however, he called out, 'Lakshmi! Lakshmi! Where are you, you fat black bitch?'

'Coming Mr Goldsmith!'

'There she's said it again … calling me Mr Goldsmith instead of Master. Call me Master. You understand? Master!'

'Yes Mr Goldsmith!' A large woman dressed like a housemaid in England, appeared in the doorway holding the hand of a little flaxen-haired boy in a royal-blue velvet suit and black, buckled, shoes. He frowned at Goldsmith and then laughed as he ran into Lucia's arms.

'Ah!' exclaimed Goldsmith, with sudden enthusiasm, 'That's David Albert George Goldsmith: three appropriately royal names for my son and heir and the fruit of my loins. What do you think of him Mr John Yale-Lynsdale?'

'Remarkable, Mr Goldsmith.'

'Remarkable, you say. What's remarkable? That he's the fruit of my loins or that he has three royal names?' He leant forward in his chair peering at me aggressively.

'That he bears such a remarkable resemblance to his father, even at this tender age.'

The old idiot seemed delighted. The child did not look like him in any way but he said, 'Oh well. Stands to reason. Well now run along child … and Lakshmi, don't call me Mr Goldsmith.'

'Yes, Mr Goldsmith. Come along Davy … that's a good boy.' The child left his mother's lap, and ran to his nanny. Goldsmith glared after them. Lucia said, very softly, 'Gabriel, please do control yourself!'

Jellybean bubbled, 'What a charming boy, how *absolutely charming!* More horse de over,' she asked, waving her hand over the silver bowls of nuts and other pre-dinner snacks. Lucia smiled at her pronunciation of hors d'oeuvre.

There was an awkward pause in the conversation. Lucia filled it by saying, 'For Davy's sake Gabriel's ventured into the Himalayas with a friend, Louis Major. We now spend spring and summer in the Himalayas and Louis looks after the business here, and then we come to

Tellicherry and Louis shifts to the Himalayas. He has a …' she paused and bit her lip, Goldsmith cleared his throat. 'Louis has a household in Tellicherry as well as in the mountains, so it's very convenient for him.' I understood. I think everyone did. Like the traditional caravanners, Louis Major probably had families in both places and wives from the local communities. 'And, of course, it's very good for Davy to be in the Himalayas in the spring and summer,' Lucia added hurriedly.

I nodded and said, 'Of course, of course,' and there was another awkward pause before dinner was announced.

Goldsmith seemed to have problems following the conversation. Or perhaps he liked to set the topic. When the fish was being served the governor announced that he had, personally, shot the wild duck that would come next on the table. Unexpectedly, Goldsmith proclaimed, 'Man has always been a hunter: for the table, for land and possessions. Even for his mate …' and he bared yellowing teeth in a vulpine grin at Lucia. She took it in her stride and said, very gently, 'Sometimes, of course, the tables are turned and the hunter becomes the hunted,' she smiled at everyone and her foot touched mine under the table and ran provocatively up my leg.

'What?' questioned Goldsmith cupping his hand to his ear. 'Oh Yes. Of course. There was the time when a native went after a Himalayan bear and the animal turned on him and killed him. One less native. They breed like flies, anyway!'

I detested this bigoted, uncouth, man but my mind spun with Lucia's salacious touch. I pulled my leg away and she raised an eyebrow. All my life I had been hunted by women: except now, except when I had sought out Ann.

After dinner, Goldsmith's glass slipped out of his hand and his head lolled on his chest. I took that as a signal that I could depart. I stood up, thanked my host and hostess, nodded to Lucia and her husband and left.

My clothes were drenched with sweat when I got back to my room, possibly because it was a warm and humid night. Possibly.

The Wedding

Even after bathing and asking the fan pullers to tug a little faster, I couldn't sleep. I kept thinking of what might happen. Would everything go off well? Would Kline still disrupt things? Would the mean-minded denizens of the Fort stay away? What would Lucia do? Would Ann be injured by the pirates? Would there be a sudden storm tomorrow? There were so many things that could go wrong. Then, from somewhere deep inside me, I heard Canker's voice across the years instructing me in one of the last yoga lessons he gave me before we sailed into Madras.

Worry is the gnawing of uncertainty. When the great storm hit us, were you very worried. No? Why not? Because you were certain that if you were washed overboard, or if the ship sank, you would die. That was certain. There was no doubt about it. There was no uncertainty, therefore, there was no worry.

Whenever worry tears at your mind, conjure up visions of certainty. Fill your mind with the most eagerly awaited things that can happen tomorrow. Things that are within your power. Something so simple as a book you want to read, food you want to eat, a friend you would like to meet. The more intense your desire the greater the effect.

Hold that image in your mind. Experience it with all your senses. See it. Touch it. Smell it. Taste it. Hear it. Then when it is as sensually real as you can make it, clasp it closely, to your chest and draw it into yourself. Sink with it, deeper and deeper and deeper into yourself, to the innermost, most secret recesses of your being, hold it there, breathing deeply, slowly, regularly till what you have visualised becomes you.

In that place, deep within your being, there is only certainty because what you feel in that place is you; and the one thing that you are absolutely sure about is your Self. And there your Self and your desire are One.

I thought of Ann. I conjured her up. The Sight of her. Her Taste, Feel, Smell. The Sound of her voice. I put them all together and drew them deeper and deeper and deeper within me till she and I were one in the deepest, most secret depths of myself …

I woke to the sound of gulls mewing and a cool breeze whispering through the casuarinas. I heard the watch bell ring. There was light in the sky. It must be 5:30. I felt completely relaxed and fresh. The most lascivious thoughts of Ann moved slowly, languidly, through my mind. I flavoured them, relished them. Soon, soon they would all come true.

TODAY WAS MY WEDDING DAY. TODAY ANN WOULD BE TRULY, WHOLLY, COMPLETELY, ETERNALLY, MINE. AND WE COULD DO WHAT WE LIKE, WHEN WE LIKED, AS OFTEN AS WE LIKED …

Briefly, fleetingly, worries tried to intrude but they were like distant, guttering, candles and they snuffed out when I turned my attention to them.

After that I walked in the clouds as if it was all a dream from which I didn't want to wake till Ann and I were alone and free to explore each other.

I remember that day in brief, startling clear, snatches the way flashes of lightning sear vivid images into the mind on a dark night. Or as sunlit peaks thrusting out of a cloud-quilted valley.

Joseph had scented my bath with a blend of musk, honey and camphor. He helped me dress in the coat, waistcoat and breeches I had brought out from Bath and never worn. It had had to be altered slightly and skilfully, by one of the Fort's tailors. I stood in front of the full-length mirror, put on my three-cornered Khevenhuller hat. Before I left Bath, most gentlemen had had theirs made of black beaver but Maureen O'Sullivan had chosen one of white Arctic Fox in the conspicuous style of Beau Nash.

I stood back from the mirror and looked at myself. At 6' 1", I was taller than most men in the Fort. My flaxen hair had darkened in the Indian sun, so had my skin. My eyes were a shade between grey and blue. The one feature I objected to was the slightly protuberant Hapsburg lip: a legacy of my late father. It gave me a decadent, self-indulgent look. I smiled: perhaps I was.

I turned around as Joseph entered the room. 'Jeweller Benjamin Braganza has come, sir. He says he has been waiting long-long time,' I realised, with a start, that I had forgotten something very important. 'Show him in, Joseph. Show him in.'

He was a stooped little man with a slight hunchback and folds under his right eye formed by years of peering through a loupe. He bobbed his head and whined, 'I have brought Miss Ann's wedding ring in accordance with the instructions given by her father, Mr Hawkenian. He said, "Make sure it is delivered only on the morning of the wedding, not before. That is our custom." Similarly, the wedding ring is of entwined tri-metal, namely gold for the body, silver for the mind, platinum for the spirit. Also I started work on it only after midnight so that it is quite virginal … as instructed.' He spoke in a tinny, nasal, tone and had a faint odour of smouldering embers as if he had been singed.

I took the little red-velvet box from him and opened it. The ring glistened gently, its three metals locked in tight embrace. I took it out. Ann's fingers were small so I had to hold it in the light streaming in through the window to read the engraving inside. It said *John,* then there was an open-ended twist, *Ann.* The twist was the symbol of *Eternity.*

I said, 'Mr Braganza, it is very beautiful. Thank you!'

He stepped forward, grabbed my hand, bent and kissed it. His voice was choked and his eyes were shining when he looked up at me and said, 'For many years I have waited for this opportunity. Your revered grandfather set me up in my business when every other person turned their backs on me. Today, I have in a small measure, paid back that debt.' He nodded at me and backed out of the room as if he was in the presence of royalty.

Joseph said, 'He very good man. I serve breakfast now. Is last breakfast I serve to master.'

I looked at him and my eyes moistened. He had cosseted me from the day I had landed in Madras and now we would go our separate ways. He had packed everything and moved it into the Great House on George Street where Ann and I would spend our first night as husband and wife. After I left for the church, he would take Rushes to our rooms, and then to the ships and we would sail out of his life.

I said, 'Sorry, Joseph. I cannot eat before I receive Communion.' I reached into the pocket of my coat and took out the letter I had sealed and addressed to *Joseph Xavier, Valet.* When I gave it to him he looked up at me, straightened and said, 'Thank you very much, Mr John Yale-Lynsdale sir. It has been my privilege to serve you and I, my wife and family will never, never, forget you.' I stared at him, amazed. He had said that in perfect English, without a trace of accent.

'Why Joseph? Why have you not spoken like this before?'

He smiled ruefully. 'The other people in the Fort are not like you, Mr Yale-Lynsdale. They expect us to speak and behave in a certain way. So we do so. All of us love you and respect you, sir. The marks of respect can be demanded, sir. So we pay the marks of respect. But respect … that must be earned. The first is an act; the second is real.'

I was still recovering from that when there was a knock on the door and Andrew Adie bustled in, every inch a highlander with his Gordon kilt, sporran. 'Sorry I'm a bit late, Johnny. But if we hurry we'll get you to the church in time!'

It was a lovely morning with fair-weather clouds loitering in a blue sky and a fresh breeze streaming off the sea. There was a spanking black liveried coach, with two white horses and everything decorated with festoons of golden marigolds. We set off at a brisk trot and Madras never looked more beautiful. People were still streaming into the church. They wished me and smiled and then I was walking down the aisle with my best-man at my side and kneeling at one of the two prie-dieux before the altar, rich with white roses and lilies. The church was filled with whispered conversations, rustling clothes and hand-fans, heavy with perfume. The small organ began to play and Andrew stepped out of the bench behind me and whispered, 'Get up, man. She's coming.'

I rose and turned around.

She had just entered the church: unbelievably beautiful. She was a vision in white on her father's arm. She was dressed exactly as her ancestress had been in the portrait and the sun, lancing in from the rose window high above, made her red hair glow like a fiery halo around her head. She was unreal, ethereal and so desirable that my stomach churned with longing and I must have staggered because Andrew grabbed my arm and said, 'Steady on lad! There's a long day ahead of you, Johnny!'

And then she was beside me, and her father and Andrew had stepped back, and we were kneeling side by side and the priests from Our Lady of Miracles church, Father Tuscani and Father Mascarenhas from San Thome were at the altar, summoning us. We stood in front of them with Ann's father, Andrew and Allison Adie in attendance and Father Tuscani with his strong Italian accent was saying,

'Dearly beloved, we are gathered here today to join these two young people in holy matrimony. If there is any among you who know of any impediment of consanguinity, affinity or spiritual relations to this union, speak now or eternally hold your peace.'

There was a moment of silence broken only by the squeak-rustle, squeak-rustle, of the punkha-fans above. This was the time for Kline to raise his voice, or the hateful Pastor Scythe or any of the others who knew that my powerful grandfather could no longer protect me. The hours ticked by slowly punctuated only by the squeak-rustle, squeak-rustle, squeak-rustle. But it must really have been only a minute or so.

Father Tuscani cleared his throat. 'Now, therefore, I ask you, John David Albert George Yale-Lynsdale, do you take this woman Ann Mary Elizabeth Hawkenian to be your lawful wedded wife, to have and to hold, to love and to cherish, in sickness and in health, till death do you part?'

My heart was thumping in my throat, my voice got caught. Andrew gripped my arm. I said, 'I do.'

The priest nodded. 'And do you, Ann Mary Elizabeth Hawkenian take John David Albert George Yale-Lynsdale as your lawful wedded husband, to have and to hold, to love and to cherish, in sickness and in health, till death do you part?'

'I do.'

Andrew stepped forward and handed the ring to Father Mascarenhas who blessed it, gave it to Father Tuscani who blessed it again, gave it to me. I caught Ann's left hand and slipped it onto the third finger. Allison raised the veil from Ann's face. Both priests said, 'You may exchange a kiss.'

As my lips touched hers there was a thunderous explosion followed by a fusillade of gun-shots. I flinched but Ann grabbed my shoulders and whispered, 'Crackers, Johnny. Only crackers. It wasn't my kiss!'

I almost burst out laughing in relief.

My memory is a series of disconnected images after that.

Confetti ... congratulations ... being blessed by an enormous elephant placing its massive trunk gently on our heads ... Joanna Scythe saying to Ann, 'Look after him, Ann. There are many here who would harm him, but also many who think he is very precious.' And Ann's reply, 'He **is** *very precious and I will not allow any harm to come to him.' ... the drive in the larger, white, coach with four horses to a strange and very beautiful temple where all the priests wore brilliant red robes and had long, lustrous, hair touching their shoulders. A clean-shaven priest welcomed* *us and said, 'It is auspicious that the first place of worship you visit outside your holy church is the Temple of Mahadevi the Great Mother. She is the source of all the energy of creation. It is why we wear red: the colour of the life-force.' Bare-chested men with long wind instruments and others with drums hanging from their necks preceded us blaring and thudding. Ann said, 'The wind instruments are* nadaswarams *the drums are* thavils *and their sounds are both auspicious and ward off evil.' The musicians and the priests led us down a long corridor. The priest explained, 'Each of the pillars in this corridor is carved with the many aspects of the Mahadevi. We are now going to the Dining Hall where five thousand people will be fed from the temple kitchen in the* annadana.*' It was enormous, its roof supported by more superbly carved pillars. People sat cross-legged on the glistening, granite floor. When we entered, stepping onto a platform just outside the entrance, the musicians went into a frenzy of drumming and blowing. And then stopped. Ann said, 'Do a namaste: they are our guests,' I joined my hands and bowed to them. A man rose and returned our salutation, and then teams of attendants ran in, placed washed banana leaves on the floor in front of each diner, others ladled rice, sambar, vegetables, papads, pickles and a sweet. Ann explained, 'Five hundred people are fed at one sitting. There will be ten sittings. All of them will remember us and bless us. Make another namaste and we'll leave.'*

When we were in the coach, she said, 'Those were the gentle people. We're going to face the wolves and jackals this evening.'

'But before that we'll have a few hours to ourselves, Ann.'

'I don't think so, Johnny. There's a late breakfast with the family, the Gordons and Adies, and the Danish Governor of Tranquebar, Admiral Pieter Jacob van Rijn and his wife Sarah: they're our house-guests and Aunt Sarah is a distant relative …'

I interrupted her. 'Isn't that a Dutch name?'

'Yes, Johnny. As the original surname of our family was English!' She laughed, 'We fell in love so fast that we'll get to know each other only after we're married. But that is the usual Indian way. And then, as we get to know each other better we'll fall deeper and deeper in love …' She was lost in thought for a moment gazing far, far, into the future. She shook her head and said, 'And then we're going to the boatyard to see the yacht which will be our home till we reach Calcutta. Then it'll be time for the reception. Only then will we be alone …'

Breakfast was an elaborate affair with both Armenian and local dishes. The Admiral was as charming as a French courtier and his wife was strikingly handsome. 'My ancestors were boyars from Russia, my husband's were Dutch sailors who helped establish the Danish East India Company.' This was the first time I had heard about this Dutch-Danish connection but then sailors had no respect for frontiers or else America would never have been discovered. Even people from land-locked Armenia had spread across the world. My father-in-law kissed me on both cheeks and said, 'There are many of our people in Calcutta. Ann and Allison were educated in a convent there so she knows it well and speaks Bengali, the local language. Our people will help you settle in … Perhaps, sometime, I will visit you: God willing. Also, I may tell you, I have made a small settlement on Ann. Not a dowry, John … not a dowry in the Hindu sense. A dower, as fathers often do. And, accompanying you, there will be two well-trained servants. Solomon and Martha are middle aged and childless and they are now engaged in moving your luggage to the yacht with the assistance of your man Joseph. God speed, my son. Now let us join the others.'

After breakfast we changed in separate rooms, which I thought was very prudish. Joseph came with Rushes and said he would look after him till we boarded the yacht. We made a hurried trip to the boatyard, were surprised how comfortable our accommodation on the yacht was. Rushed back, changed again, and Canker and Kunhi met us. Happiness and anguish tore at my heart and mind. How could I, so suddenly, say goodbye to this man who had been like a father to me, who had shaped my life, guided me, protected me, and was there whenever I needed him. My eyes filmed and a sob caught in my throat. Ann must have seen my anguish. She touched my cheek and I felt my strength returning. Canker reached out and placed his hand on her forehead, covering her hairline, 'He is very gentle, *mol,'* using the diminutive for a girl, 'it is his greatest strength, and his greatest weakness. His grandfather gave him to me. I now give him to you because you and he were born to be together, many, many lives ago.' He bowed and did a graceful *namaskaram* to her and, unexpectedly, he embraced me tightly. For the last time I breathed in the warm, dry, herbal fragrance of a *kalarippayat* guru. My sight blurred and I could hardly discern Kunhi's features as he clasped both my hands in his. Then they were gone. Ann touched the corners of my eyes with a tiny lace handkerchief and said, 'I am here, Johnny, and I love you very much.' I smiled, held up my head, offered her my arm, and we stepped out into the garden of the Great House.

It was magnificent. The garden had been covered in a huge tent, brightly illuminated. All the chairs and tables were occupied … As we appeared, the drummers of the Welsh Regiment beat a long roll. Everyone stood. The buglers sounded a brazen fanfare. When they put down their trumpets, and our guests sat down, we were led by Ensign Wellesley to the high table where the governor of Tranquebar and his wife were seated, along with the Councillors and their wives. In the centre was a four-tiered wedding cake studded with pink and white roses. We sat between the governor and his wife. Governor Shem shuffled in his seat, stood up. There was a hushed silence. He raised a rambling toast to us but most of his words were lost in the forest of his black beard though I did hear something about the '*… coming together of two great families*.' When the clapping was over, I replied, thanking the governor and then said what I had always intended to. I informed our guests that Ann and I were following a tradition set by her ancestor William Hawkins, emissary of Queen Elizabeth to the court of the Mughal Emperor Jehangir in 1603. There, Hawkins had married a ward of the Emperor, an Armenian girl. Ann's maiden name, Hawkenian, is the Armenian derivation of the English name

Hawkins. The wedding dress that Ann wore this morning was a copy of the one worn by her ancestress in the 17th century.

As I expected, there was a flutter and then applause led by Shem.

I think that that bit of English-Armenian history surprised people so much that, when Ann and I made the rounds of the tables all they would say was 'Wonderful,' 'Fascinating,' 'Incredible,' 'Amazing.' The only one who did not refer to what I had said was Lucia. She was sitting with her son and his nanny. 'Gabriel sends his apologies to both of you,' she explained. 'He has slight fever and Dr Poulson has advised him to stay in bed. But he insisted that Davy and I come.' She tilted her head and smiled but the smile didn't reach her eyes: they remained cold and calculating. She turned to Ann and said, 'John met Davy when we dined with the Shems.' She touched the little boy's head. 'Davy's our son, as you probably know, Ann. As John admitted when he first saw him, he is the image of his father. Don't you think so, Ann?'

It was a deliberately provocative remark. Ann's smile was cool and friendly. 'I wouldn't know Lucia. I've not met his father.'

Lucia took in her breath, and then covered her surprise with a cough. 'Excuse me!' she said, 'I find the atmosphere of Madras rather stifling.' Then she reached out and touched Ann's hand. 'You must come to the Himalayas in spring and summer, my dear. The air is so clear there that the perspectives one gets are very edifying.'

I stood up before the thrust-and-parry could become more vicious.

That night when, at long last, Ann and I were together and I saw the full wonder of her, her hair framing her face on the pillow, luring me, she said, 'She believes that David is your son, doesn't she?'

'I think so, Ann …' my voice was hoarse with longing …

'Then come to me, Johnny, and I'll make you forget your little Italian adventure …'

She did, and the whole night was filled with fireworks of our own making.

The Hooghly Pirates

There was an unusual, low, morning mist softening Madras when we left the Great House.

Aga Shawmier wished us goodbye, touched our cheeks and whispered a prayer. Ann's father embraced both of us and laid his hands on our heads in blessing. His eyes were red and swollen and his voice was hoarse. He said, 'I know you will look after my girl, John, as she will treasure you. Don't cry, Ann. You will find much happiness in your new life, and you will give each other much strength and comfort for many, many, years. Now, my wonderful children, go with God and each other.' The Fort was quiet and both Ensign Hartley and Gunner Harris threw us a salute and wished us 'God speed' as we drove out of the gate. The fish-wives and the vegetable vendors were just setting up their stalls in Black Town. Then gravel was crunching under the wheels of our coach as we approached the jetty of the Gordon Boatyard.

The Gordons and the Adies were waiting for us. So were Joanna Scythe and her two young assistants. As I stepped out of the coach, there was a flurry of barking and Rushes, trailing his leash, leapt into my arms. Joseph walked up and said, apologetically, 'Rushes knew you were coming, Mr Yale-Lynsdale. He's been impatient ever since he woke up.' Joanna Scythe was blooming. She introduced her young men and said, 'We're thinking of branching out into a guest-house if Joseph will do the catering from his kitchen.' Joseph grinned and nodded. Joanna kissed me on the cheek, kissed Ann and stroked Rushes. 'Mr Adie has made a kennel for Rushes just outside your cabin,' Joseph said. 'I've brought his bed mat and bowls. I'll take him over Mrs Yale-Lynsdale.' That was the first time I had heard Ann called by her married name and I felt a glow inside. Joseph introduced us to the soft-spoken and grizzled Solomon and his wife, Martha.

We boarded the yacht. Our cabin was on the aft upper deck with the staff cabin and kitchen behind. Across the well of the deck was Jock's cabin on the for'ard upper deck. The six-men crew were housed below and the wheel-house in front. I had thought that the yacht would be steered by a man handling a huge oar at the stern, as they did on river barges, not a wheel and rudder as in ocean-going ships. And then I realised that this was an ocean-going ship. To cover my embarrassment I checked the lashings on our canvas-covered luggage in the well-deck trying to look very seaman-like. Then I noticed the carefully concealed gun ports: the one in the wheel-house could be swivelled through 180 degrees, and there were two each port and starboard. They, too, were covered in canvas.

We waved our goodbyes, the gangway was pulled in, Jock took the wheel, barked orders. The sails unfurled and we drew away from the jetty. Our friends grew smaller and smaller and Madras dropped from sight.

I had a lump in my throat till Ann reached down and held my hand and all became right with the world.

Jock handed over the wheel to the helmsman and joined us for breakfast. 'We're sailing very slowly to give the warriors time to get the feel of the Sunderbans. It'll be more than a week, nearer ten days, before we reach them because the monsoon is against us. We'll tie ashore every night at friendly coastal villages. The action will start only after we reach Machlighat in the delta.' The delta of the twin rivers, the Ganges and the Brahmaputra, is the largest in the world, a giant D riven with distributaries like veins on a massive hand. It is called the Sunderbans, the Beautiful Forests, because of its mass of marshes and dense mangrove jungles …

Jock Adie left us to make entries in the special cartographic log he was maintaining.

The uncertainty of the future, of how the battle with the Hooghly Pirates would end, probably gave an edge to our honeymoon. We were ravenous for each other. Or perhaps that is usual: I don't know. We explored each other tenderly, roughly, quiescently as we lay entwined relaxing in each other till we became aroused again and started where we had left off.

I don't remember the names of the ports we touched even though we stepped ashore at every opportunity. The seas were getting quite rough, the showers and thunderstorms more frequent, and we needed the reassurance of terra firma. Solomon and Martha were very solicitous. Rushes was a little upset for the first two days but adjusted after that, barking and rushing at sea-birds whenever they intruded into his territory. Jock Adie was wonderful. He joined us for lunch and dinner, spent much of his time making notes and sketches of the shoreline, recording the depths of the off-shore waters, and using his spyglass very often.

'I know these coasts like the back of my hand,' he said, early in the voyage, 'but cartographer Jean-Baptiste has asked me to make observations of these, the most dangerous waters in India.'

'Are they difficult to navigate?' asked Ann.

'They are. But mainly because this coast, all the way up to Calcutta, is dotted with the trading settlements of five nations. They're all in fierce competition to get the wealth of the hinterland: ivory and precious stones, indigo, fabrics, spices, saltpetre, coconuts and rice, and much else besides. They're locked in an uneasy, a very suspicious, truce now but it won't last long: it'll snap and when it does, the sound will be heard all over the world!'

Ann would not be put off so easily. 'If that is so, Uncle Jock, why don't they all get together to wipe out the Hooghly Pirates. Don't they attack all ships?'

He smiled wryly. 'You don't understand the bitterness of the Companies' rivalry, Ann. They'd rather die than ask for help.'

Martha and Solomon were serving us lunch. I waited for them to withdraw. 'Then why should the count intervene?' I asked. 'Surely the Free Traders do not have more ships than all the East India Companies combined?'

Jock Adie nodded his head. 'Perhaps not more ships but certainly as much cargo.' We didn't understand. 'You see, virtually every employee of every company does his own free trading on the side. So, for that matter do the Directors of the Companies. They're all involved in this underhand game.' I felt a surge of guilt: had grandfather also been an illegal free trader? I put the thought aside because Jock Adie was continuing. 'The count has more authority than any of the Directors of the Companies: he represents the private interests of all European traders.'

The conversation stopped because the servants had returned with mango custard and it veered off into other subjects like the enormous profits to be made by selling opium to the Chinese.

That night, Ann brought out her copies of *Kama Sutra* and *The Perfumed Garden* and I was amazed at the wonderful variations of love making. Every night, after that, we tried one of their couplings, often getting hysterical with laughter as we saw ourselves in the huge mirror, glistening with the sweat of our passion. Then, thankfully, we invariably fell into a deep and refreshing sleep.

On most days, ships flying the Danish, French, Dutch and Portuguese flags passed us, though they were further out at sea. 'This is the return monsoon which takes the ships back to Europe,' Jock Adie explained. 'It was discovered by the Greeks. Then lost. Then rediscovered by the Arabs who kept it a secret because they wanted to monopolise the spice trade. But then they got too greedy and raised their prices so high that the Portuguese decided to send Vasco da Gama to find the ocean route to India. That broke the Arab monopoly in 1498.'

I had been taught that in Greenwood's Academy in Bath. I was learning, now, that it's very difficult to concentrate on anything else but our intimacy. I looked at Ann, and yearned for her. She must have sensed it. She pursed her lips, put the tip of her right forefinger into her mouth and sucked it. It seemed as if she was removing something from her lip but, to me, it was so overtly sexual that my stomach churned with desire and I felt myself hardening. I closed my eyes briefly and the images of us together moved through my mind. Ann and I were on our own voyage of discovery, taking advantage of the long nights when the yacht was berthed in those little fishing ports. Our insatiable hunger for each other, and our need to find new ways to assuage it, seemed to give us enormous appetites for food.

But the looming conflict would not go away.

One evening when we were enjoying a delectable dish of Bengal-style mustard fish and rice Jock said, 'Tomorrow our holiday will be over. We will reach the village of Machlighat. The count and your Nair water-warriors will be waiting for us. We'll tie up to the village jetty a little before sunset as usual. They'll board us at night from the starboard, that is, the seaward side. We've already discussed our strategies, we'll ask them for the latest news about the Ahom pirates … they're really Chinese and Malay Dayaks … and then we'll launch our campaign.'

'What has the count been doing?' Ann asked.

'He's passed the word to the traders, and their Company friends, to steer clear of the Hooghly for the next week so that we have a free hand. I have arranged for four warriors to take turns to guard you, Ann, while John is directing the fight. They are men who are extremely loyal to me. They will protect you with their lives.'

Ann looked at him for a long moment and then she said, very slowly, very deliberately, 'John will need every man. I do not want anyone to guard me.'

Jock Adie turned to me, frowning. I looked at Ann. For the first time I saw an expression that I would learn to recognise. It was neither stubbornness nor determination. It was a cold, icy-cold confidence that, for some strange reason, sent a shiver through me. I have never seen that look in any man or woman.

She asked, 'Uncle Jock, have those pirates killed people?'

He nodded. 'Their leader, a fiend who calls himself Bhooth, the ghost, claims that he never takes prisoners. He butchers men, women and even little children, ruthlessly. He's cultivated an image that he is unforgiving and invincible. He is very determined and very skilled. I seriously advise you, Ann, to accept your guards.'

Ann shook her head. 'Thank you for being so protective, Uncle Jock. But I will not accept any guards.' She said it with such quiet finality that Jock Adie looked at me as if I should disagree.

I nodded and said, 'If that's the way she wants it, that's the way it will be,' I said it with a show of more determination than I felt.

The thought of the encounter that lay ahead, and the urgency it gave to us, made the hours speed by. Not another word was mentioned about it as we sailed into Machlighat at sunset, and tied up to the bamboo jetty. The mangrove forests of the Sunderbans stood on their outré stilt roots and backed away into the distance, surrounding the little fishing village. Cormorants and herons flew in on silent wings and settled squawking in the trees. Then they were silent and there was only the slap-lap of the water against the yacht. So far I had not seen a single human in the village. Two fat grey cats feasted on a pile of discarded fish. The sun set, night fell. Almost magically lights came on in the thatched and tiled huts. Mosquitoes began to whine around us till Martha and Samson lit smoke pots filled with aromatic herbs. The mosquitoes fled before the billows of smoke.

I neither heard nor saw the Nair warriors approach. One moment we were alone on the yacht, the next Rushes was barking and the yacht was filled with lithe men dressed in green. Suddenly, drums began to throb in the village, increasing in tempo, a campfire flared to life, and women appeared dancing around it, encircled by men sitting on the ground. Someone, standing at my elbow, said, 'The drums and the dance will draw watching eyes away from us.' It was the count. He was also dressed in baggy green. He bowed to me. Raised Ann's hand to his lips. Smiled at Jock Adie and said, 'Everything is prepared according to your plans, Mr John Yale-Lynsdale. May we now have a final revision?'

They had set up a table in the well-deck, lit by a single lantern. It illuminated a large map drawn by Jock Adie. It showed the Bay of Bengal and the morass of the Sunderbans like the florets of a sponge riven by tiny, sinuous, streams. 'This is the Meetha Nadi, the rightly named Sweet Stream,' Jock said. 'It is a clear, fresh-water rivulet rising in one of the springs in the Sunderbans. The pirates always camp on the bank of the Meetha, changing their location every two days.' He looked around to see if we understood.

'Where are the two fish-tank barges? The ones on which you and the Nairs came?' The warriors seemed surprised that Ann had asked the question.

'We have secreted them in a creek,' the count replied. 'The war canoes are also ready to venture into the morass. We would like to hear from you now, Mr Yale-Lynsdale.'

I went over my plan again, repeating it in Tamil for the Nairs who understood this Dravidian language.

We sailed out at dawn heading for Sagar Island at the mouth of the myriad-branched delta. The Hooghly was the broadest and the most navigable of the many distributaries of the river system. We entered the chocolate-brown flood very slowly, with two men swinging the lead-lines, calling out the depths constantly. A dense, green, wall of mangroves slid past eerie on their white, spider-leg stilt roots. Concealed in the gloom of this soggy wilderness were salt-water crocodiles and venomous snakes, pythons and the dreaded Bengal tigers who after generations of having to drink brackish water, had developed a taste for human blood. Or so the Honey-gatherers had assured us. These wiry people made a precarious living harvesting the great hives of wild bees hanging in the jungle, and fishing. They lived in small villages in clearings in the great morass, accepted the ravages of malaria, attacks by wild creatures and death itself as a toll taken by the forests to permit the rest to survive. They loved the fish-tank barges crewed by Jock Adie's men and feared and hated the Hooghly Pirates.

Our guide, Bishnu, from Machlighat had explained it. 'The pirates are not our people. They steal from us, kidnap our women because they do not bring their own; and when they have finished with them, they push them back to us, pregnant with their seed. We perform our defiled sisters' last rites, give them honey mixed with herbs and roots. Then they wander into the forests, fall into a deep sleep from which they never wake. We never find their remains: the forest consumes them.' When he had stared at me, the yellow lantern light had flickered in his eyes giving him a feral look. 'No one has ever had the courage to do what you are going to do. We have performed a puja to Vanadevi, the goddess of the forest, sacrificed a pig and now we are dancing in her honour. I will guide your warriors, but be careful of Bhooth. He is an evil creature. He does not look human. They say he can be killed only by the great goddess, Kali Ma: beautiful, implacable, her hair unfastened around her, naked and inflamed. But no one has seen this fearful Goddess of Destruction.' He had shrugged his bare shoulders. 'Maybe her spirit is with you …'

It had begun to rain as we sailed slowly up the river to a bend that the Dutch navigators had called Murderers' Point. This was just one of the many semi-permanent obstructions thrown up by the river. When they appeared above the surface they were soon covered in tall grass which farmers harvested for fodder and thatch. They called these the *diara* which, when cleared and cultivated, yielded a rich harvest. But the Murderers' Point had never, in living memory, raised its head above the surface. It was a viciously shifting sand-bar which always lurked below the surface, like a monstrous reptile, waiting to trap unwary ships. We dropped anchor and raised a distress flag, pretending to have run aground. I was tense. Mud banks, glistening like the skin of submarine predators, stretched on both sides of the narrow channel. I spotted two enormous salt-water crocodiles basking, the late evening sun shimmering on their armoured hide. Jock Adie called me up to his wheel-house, put his spy-glass to my eye. 'That plume of smoke is from the pirate's village. They're not attempting to conceal themselves. There's not another ship around. They think we're sitting ducks. Good.'

'I hope our plan works,' I said.

'It had better,' Adie said grimly. 'But they won't attack tonight. They wouldn't want to risk being devoured by those crocs in the darkness. My men are on watch but you two keep your pistols loaded and ready. That Bhooth is the Devil incarnate; a blood-thirsty monster if there ever was one.'

We didn't make love that night; we couldn't. Ann pulled my head to her bosom and when I felt her breathing deeply and regularly I, too, fell into a fitful sleep. Just before I dropped off I removed the legendary dagger that Canker had retrieved from the incense burner in Arcot and laid it beside the bed. It was a futile gesture, steeped in superstition, but it was reassuring just the same.

I woke when a mist-softened light began to filter into our cabin.

It had been a hot and humid night, and our clothes were drenched with sweat. Mosquitoes had feasted on us and our garments were speckled with blood where we had swotted their engorged bodies. There was a scratching at the door, Rushes whimpered and then Jock Adie's voice said softly, 'Something's about to happen. A man's approaching in a boat.'

We pulled gowns over ourselves hurriedly and stepped out.

The crew were standing in pairs behind the for'ard and river-facing guns but they hadn't uncovered them or raised the gun-port hatches. All of them had pistols in their hands. Jock Adie held a megaphone. Martha and Samson, also carrying pistols, came and stood behind Ann, Rushes was at her feet, his muzzle raised. I asked

Ann to wait near our cabin and strode across to Jock Adie. He said, in a low voice, 'Something's gone wrong, Johnny. The Nairs are late.'

The lone man in the dug-out paddled up to the yacht. He was bare-bodied. He stood up and said, 'Ahoy, English *kapitan.* Your ship stuck in sand-bar, yes?'

Adie shouted back, 'Yes. We're waiting for the tide to float us out.'

The man spread his arms wide. 'No tide, six hour. Bad-bad place.'

'Why?'

'You new, *kapitan*. This sand-bar Murderers' Point. Hooghly Pirate, they come. Kill everyone. Do bad things to missy.'

'Who are you, then?'

'Honey-collector, fishermens. My people are there … see? See?' he turned around and pointed. Men were trickling out of the forest. Some were carrying ropes and bamboo ladders. 'You pay. We pull out ship. You go. Right?'

'They're no more fishermen than I'm a blue-bummed baboon.' Jock Adie said softly. 'Those bloody Nairs are late,' then loudly, to the man in the boat. 'How much will it cost me?'

'Ha! We must see. I call my men,' He turned and waved. There was a flurry of activity. Men poured out of the woods like ants. They carried dugouts and launching them into the river, scrambled aboard and started to paddle towards us. Jock Adie growled, 'Not yet, not yet. Damn those sodding Nairs …'

The pirate boats were coming closer and closer and I could see the grins of anticipation on their faces. They had the broad features of Dayaks and southern Chinese. I recalled Bishnu's words, '*The Pirates are not our people. They steal from us, kidnap our women because they do not bring their own; and when they have finished with them, they push them back to us, pregnant with their seed.*' I looked at Ann, standing straight and proud, pistols in her hands, She would defend herself as long as she could. But how long would that be?

The stretch of river between us and the shore now seemed alive with the pirates' boats, laden to the gunnels with grinning, bare-bodied men. There were just too many of them like those Army Ants of the Amazon that overwhelm and kill everything in their path. Ann would be buried under the weight of their naked bodies as they ravaged her repeatedly.

Men in the lead boats were standing, holding their grappling hooks, ready to swing them onto our ship and scramble aboard.

'*Where's the bloody count and the bloody Nairs*?' Jock Adie shouted, '*Stand by to fire*!'

Just then there was a fusillade of shots from the shore. Or rather, they sounded like shots coming from the forest on the right of the clearing where the men had emerged from the forest. The pirates in the boats shouted and looked back. Those still ashore yelled. There were more explosions from the forest. The men in the boats leapt into the water and waded ashore carrying guns and long knives over their heads. They must have hidden them in the boats.

Jock Adie bellowed, 'Extend your cannon!' Our crewmen raised the hatches, pushed the guns out through the ports, touched flames to the powder. Both port guns boomed, the yacht rocked, acrid gunpowder smoke swept over us and two huge craters of mud appeared in the midst of the running pirates. There was another crackle of explosions from the forest on the right. The pirates, taken completely unawares, fled in a panic, away from the explosions, running into the protection of the forest on the left. And straight into the Nairs who had emerged out of the dense green wall of the mangroves. Our warriors wielded swords and spears and shields, and leapt and lunged, with the lethal grace of *kalarippayat* fighters. I saw the metallic flash of the deadly *urumi*: the flexible 'belt-sword' that reaches out like the lethal silver tongue of a dragon. The screams of the dying pirates carried clearly across the water. A small group of them threw down their weapons and stood, their arms raised in surrender.

The Nairs had turned the tide swiftly, decisively. The pirates had never been attacked from the forests and they'd been taken completely by surprise. Those who did not lie dying or wounded, threw down their arms and stood with the hands raised. Some knelt looking up at their attackers piteously.

I wondered what we would do with these prisoners, how we would attend to the wounded pirates? The decision was taken out of my hands.

Ann said, 'Can I have the megaphone, Uncle Jock?!' There was such an edge of command in her voice that he handed it over, looking at her in amazement. She raised the funnel to her mouth and, in a ringing voice, commanded in Tamil, 'Take no prisoners! Kill them all! They're murderers with the blood of innocent men, women and children on their hands!' She saw the Nairs looking at her, hesitating. 'Kill them! Kill them now!' Then she seemed to repeat it all in a language with which I was not familiar. I learnt later that it was Bengali, understood by the pirates.

More of the pirates fell to their knees, pleading, but the Nairs' swords and spears rose and fell, despatching them, coldly, efficiently. Their screams and bellows of pain battered into us. Then it subsided into groans, gurgles and silence. The count appeared, came to the edge of the river bank and called out, 'The Bhooth has escaped. Be careful. We'll set fire to their village. We'll sail in here tomorrow morning and, if you need it, we'll give you a tow. Our Nairs must rest now.' He and our warriors vanished into the jungles heading for their canoes, leaving the mud bank glistening and stained with the blood of the pirates, littered with their corpses.

Ten minutes later there was a series of explosions and a pillar of smoke rose as the village of the Hooghly Pirates was set ablaze.

Jock Adie was very pensive as the crew began to clean the cannon, haul them in and cover them. 'Why are you worried Uncle Jock?' Ann asked.

'We've won the battle, not the war. Bhooth has escaped and he'll go back to the border lands and assemble another gang of cut-throats. But for another six months the Hooghly will be safe.' He shrugged his shoulders then turned to me. 'That was a brilliant move, Johnny, to send a small party with firecrackers to the right and scare those bandits into believing they were being attacked from there. And they never expected the Nairs to manoeuvre their war canoes through the narrow backwaters of the Sunderbans, and ambush them while we fired our cannon to panic them further.' Then he shook his head. 'But it was touch and go, touch and go. Another five minutes and the first of those cut-throats would have boarded us, scaled their scrambling nets, and that would have been the end.' He looked at Ann pensively but said nothing about her cold, ruthless, order to massacre the prisoners. He just had a wry smile on his face, nodded, and said, 'I'll tell the crew to rest now, they have to take two-hour shifts tonight to make sure that the Bhooth doesn't sneak in.'

'Is that possible, Uncle?' Ann asked.

'Judging by his reputation, anything is possible!'

Something nagged inside me. When we were alone I asked Ann. 'Why did you order the prisoners killed?'

She had been stroking Rushes with great tenderness. She put him down and turned to me. There was a very calm, almost a cold, expression on her face. 'Johnny, Jesus said, "*For all they that take the sword shall perish with the sword.*" The pirates were an abscess that had to be cauterised to prevent the poison from spreading. We did that.' Her reasoning was as cold as that of a surgeon. I couldn't dispute it, but it disturbed me a little. She picked up Rushes and continued stroking him and cooing softly, reassuringly. The firing of our guns had made him shiver uncontrollably but he had not cowered, standing near Ann protectively, his fur bristling. I was very proud of him. He looked up at her, licked her hand and wagged his tail.

I was just beginning to know the woman I had married and the complex currents that stirred within her. I wondered if she found me as difficult to understand; and then gave up that pointless train of thought.

The rest of the day was an anti-climax. Nothing happened. I saw the salt-water crocodiles waddle ashore and begin to tear at the corpses, shooing away the vultures and crows. Some of the cadavers were dragged by the massive reptiles into the water and probably hidden in underwater hollows to be devoured later, if the tortoises didn't get to them. The rivers of the Sunderbans have a very efficient sanitation system.

We were exhausted after the tensions of the day and even Rushes curled up in his kennel and did not wake for his lunch.

The servants lit the smoke-pots since there was no need to have a clear view of our surroundings and we slept early.

I woke to find soft lips on mine and a warm, naked, body moving over me.

'Are you awake, Johnny?'

'I am now.'

'Yes you are. I can feel you. I want you, Johnny. All that blood and savagery excited me. Are you excited?'

'Yes.'

'Then don't move. I will … Like this. And this … this … … this …'

She engulfed me and throbbed around me and filled my hands with her breasts and raised herself and held me at the knife edge of ecstasy. Then she gasped and exploded and so did I.

We were both breathing hard, oiled with sweat and our body fluids when Rushes growled, barked and yelped. In the half-light of a monsoon moon a grotesque monster looked down at me: a ghostly white apparition, with white hair. He lunged down at us. Ann uncoupled herself from me, slid off the bed in a single motion, grabbed something, and lunged. The ogre screamed and clutched at his eye as blood spouted, covering his face. Ann lunged again and the ogre's other eye exploded in blood and he bellowed. His blood spouted onto us. I grabbed the pistol from my bedside table and put a bullet through his head. He fell, blood gushing out of him. Convulsed once and then lay lifeless on the ground.

The door burst open and the crew and the servants were clustered around Jock Adie holding the lantern aloft.

Ann was standing, covered in blood, her red hair a weird halo around her face, her tongue licking her lips where the attacker's blood had drenched her face and body, the dagger in her hand, her foot on the corpse. And she was stark naked.

The men held their arms in front of their eyes and fell to their feet. Jock Adie gasped, 'God in Heaven! What have I seen?!'

I threw a gown around Ann as they dragged the corpse of Bhooth out of our cabin and Martha and Samson hurriedly cleaned up as I pulled Ann into the bathroom and shut the door. Ann fell sobbing on my shoulder. I was stunned … Bishnu's words flashed into my mind. '*They say he can be killed only by Kali Ma, but who has seen the Great Goddess of Destruction*?' Perhaps no one had, but the Bhooth had not been the only eldritch being in our cabin that night.

We looked at his unsightly corpse before they shrouded him. He had been an albino with pale skin, blooded orbs where Ann had gouged out his eyes, and white hair. His features were flat and mongoloid. We wrapped him in a cotton sheet and buried him in the mud flats. Then we waited till the incoming tide brought the other two barges, with the count and the warriors, and they helped to free us from the clutches of the Murderers' Point. But before we left I saw three crocodiles drag themselves to the Bhooth's shallow grave and then, presumably, the Sunderbans absorbed him into their system.

Our attacker had tried to stab Rushes and had managed to nick his ear. Ann nursed him tenderly crooning, 'Thank you Rushes for warning us. You saved both our lives.'

I asked her how she had found the dagger in the dark and she said, 'It glowed with an amber radiance. A shaft of the moonlight had touched it.' Possibly.

We were given a grand welcome in Calcutta. But then, for all the jubilation, the Hooghly continued to haunt us.

The Himalayan Offer

The Hooghly had created Calcutta.

Or rather, it had created the low-lying, swampy ground on which Calcutta had grown. Here, Job Charnock of the Company had chosen a stretch of the river bank dotted with a few villages of fishermen, farmers, weavers and falconers. He had seen the trading potential of its fertile hinterland and of the river that linked it to the sea and the wide world beyond. Charnock's vision had blossomed into reality. In spite of a devastating storm and raids by the belligerent Maratha armies from western India, Calcutta had grown from three thatched villages to a Company town bustling with business. It even had a theatre in a place called Lalbazaar.

We loved Calcutta, at first.

After we had got over the initial wave of visitors congratulating us, we started settling down in this new city. Unlike Madras, Calcutta had virtually no history of its own, no old culture or traditions to temper its brashness. It was a town created by merchants for merchants: as bright and shiny as a new pair of scales. We felt we couldn't have asked for a better start to our new life as Free Traders.

True to his word, the count had done us proud. He had given us a spacious mansion, fully furnished down to the crockery, cutlery and linen, and servants. Our grounds stretched down to the banks of the river. Ann was in her element, setting up house, meeting her former schoolmates from the Young Women's Academy of Our Lady of Walshingham. The Armenians of Calcutta had invited the Anglo-Catholic Brown Sisters from Norfolk to set up this school. It had been so successful that the male order of Brown Brothers had been invited to open a similar school for young men.

'What's an Anglo-Catholic?' I asked Ann.

She had looked at me with an eyebrow raised. 'It's a sect of the Church of England that is Catholic in every way except that it does not recognise the authority of Rome.' When she saw me frowning, she added, 'The best school in Madras was in San Thome and it was Portuguese-oriented. Walshingham, as we call our school, taught in English, was run by English sisters and was supported by our Armenians. Allison and I were sent here as boarders: it's still a boarding school. All of us lived together as one big family, and we are still as warm and friendly as we were when we were schoolgirls.' I was happy that Ann had been able to find her feet in Calcutta so quickly.

I got on with the business of trying to establish a slot for myself. Selling opium to China seemed to be the fastest route to wealth but my grandfather had called it, 'A vicious business that robs humans of their senses,' and so I shunned it. There seemed to be interesting prospects in indigo: a fabric dye made from a local shrub. Saral Sengupta, the husband of one of Ann's Bengali friends, Madhu, had told me that his tenants cultivated the shrub and its purple dye had been popular in Europe since the time of the Greeks. The Senguptas invited us down to their estate, 'Everyone at home would love to meet both of you.'

But we never got around to meeting them because the party, and its aftermath, intervened.

We had had a whole stream of visitors dropping over to congratulate us on our victory over the pirates and so we decided to throw a party. Ann was particularly delighted. She invited her friends and former schoolmates, most of the important Armenian families, and the senior Company officials and traders. Jock Adie had stayed on to scout the timber market for his shipyard and had been persuaded to postpone his departure till the party was over, even though he seemed unusually reluctant. That bothered me a bit: it seemed very unlike him.

I had skimmed through the list of guests to make sure that none of the important Company officials had been left out. One couple had been particularly warm: the Philbert-Wrights were both second-generation Company folk. The angular, blonde Hermione had described themselves as, 'Sort of Brahmins of the Company: almost twice-born!' Adrian had added, in his pleasantly adenoidal voice, 'In England even if your bloodlines are right but your accent is wrong, you're rejected. Both of us have the right tonal quality.'

In contrast to the Philbert-Wrights was the brittle Karl von Erfurt. His harsh Germanic accent made my hackles rise. He was slim and pale, with faded blue eyes, platinum hair that curled over the nape of his neck, and a sabre scar on his cheek. Even when he congratulated me he couldn't keep the superiority out of his voice. 'It, *voz*, Mr Yale-Lynsdale, an *eggspegted vicdory* over ze naked natives. Ja?' I didn't ask him who had *expected* such a *victory*. I was tempted to strike his name off Ann's list but that would have made my prejudice too obvious.

Two evenings before the party, Jock took my elbow and steered me to the *chabootra.* Most of the mansions had these open, plastered, platforms as a sort of outdoor drawing room for the cool of the evening. When we had settled into our cane chairs, with lemon sherbets in our glasses, Jock asked,

'Who made out your guest list, John?'

I was surprised. 'Ann did, Why?'

Jock sipped his drink and gazed silently at the river. It was glowing with dusk and the last ferry from the far bank was being rowed in. We could hear the creak-splash of it oars.

Jock said, 'Tomorrow you will receive a note of regret from the Secretary to the Governor. His Excellency, as he likes to be known, has decreed that newcomers shall enter their names in the Visitors Book maintained at the gate of his Mansion. They will then, in course of time, be formally invited to the Mansion, if they are suitable. Only after visiting the Mansion could they then dare to invite Their Excellencies. But, of course, you don't know all this and so you'll receive a formal MRU, *Much Regret Unable.*' He sipped his drink again, then added, 'This place is stiff with the starch and snobbishness of little men in high places. There's more protocol here than in his Germanic Majesty's court!'

I still didn't know what he was driving at but I didn't say anything, waiting for him to continue. He slapped at a buzzing mosquito then said, 'Ah well, my worst fears may not be realised. Let's go in John,' stood up, finished his sherbet in a gulp, and then strode into the house without an explanation.

I was a little peeved at his conduct so I didn't mention it to Ann.

When the note of regret came from the Mansion, I told Ann what Jock had said. She shrugged, smiled and hurried away because the oil lamps had arrived. We had outlined the driveway with oil-lamps and, that night, the house was ablaze with chandeliers glistening off the silver and crystal. Ann looked radiant in a black and gold gown made from heavy hand-woven silk. We stood just inside the carved teak doors of the drawing room and welcomed our guests as their coaches drew up in the porch. Halfway through the reception line I noticed that Ann had lost her warmth and had become distantly formal.

Between guests I whispered, 'What's wrong, my love?'

'Your countrymen,' she whispered between gritted teeth. 'Haven't you noticed?'

I hadn't, and then it began to dawn on me. Not one of the English guests had brought his wife! And then the stupid excuses began to roll out.

'Maggie sends her apologies: the children y'know!' 'Althea is distraught at missing the party, but she had a splitting headache.' 'Jenny picked up a hacking cough and didn't want to pass it on, actually.' And on and on and on. They then stood in a tight group, drinking and mumbling to themselves, freezing into silence whenever anyone tried to break in. Worst of all, they all left before dinner.

Ann acted swiftly. She had the table seating rearranged so that when we trooped into the Dining Room it seemed as if the Company officials had never been invited for dinner. All except the Philbert-Wrights who had not joined the English exodus. When the rather indiscreet Bulbul Basu asked loudly, 'Why did the officers leave?' Ann smiled and said, 'The reception was the formal part: dinner is for our friends!' Adrian Philbert-Wright almost choked on his fish, even though baked crab au gratin was his favourite dish.

Ann's sally broke the ice and the party went very well after that. We asked Hermione and Adrian to stay back. When the servants had left and we were sitting in the small Breakfast Room, Ann asked, 'Why did they do it?'

Jock rumbled, 'Because they wanted to embarrass you.'

'Why?'

Adrian cleared his throat and sipped his brandy before replying, 'You see, my dear, you don't fit into their established order of things. Your lineage is impeccable: none of them can match it. And you, John, with the bloodlines of two great Company families, are very near royalty from their point of view.' If only they knew the truth, I thought. 'But you are a Free Trader and Free Traders are not Company.'

I had controlled myself all through the evening. Now I asked, 'Have they done this very often?'

Hermione answered. 'It was created by that Hun, Karl von Erfurt. He calls it *The Freeze* and it's meant to show people that they will not be accepted.' She turned to Ann, 'But don't worry Ann. The Company does not control all the trade in Calcutta. And you have the Free Traders on your side.'

She was right. As the count had proved, the Free Traders were a powerful force and we didn't have to conform to anyone's self-serving rules. We could live and trade in our own terms in this traders' town although it soon became clear that Calcutta's social life was, increasingly, in the hands of the Company.

Not that Ann or I missed being in the rather stilted circle of the English. Ann had volunteered to look after the youngest children in her old school. I felt that there was a great future being an indigo trader and, perhaps, even setting up my own indigo plantation. I had taken my Armenian friends into confidence when, one evening, on the *chabootra*, Jakob Arrakiel said, 'John, may I speak frankly?'

'Certainly Jakob. I welcome that.' There were just the two of us, sipping coffee.

He cleared his throat and looked at the river as if marshalling his thoughts. Then he turned to me. 'It would be unwise, John, to make any long-term plans at present.'

Jakob was known for his sagacity even though he was not the oldest of the Armenian traders.

'Why not Jakob?'

He looked at me as if assessing the impact of what he was about to say. Then, very deliberately and very softly so that his voice would not carry into the house, he said, 'You know, John, that the Company's hold on Calcutta is very precarious. This territory is part of the Mughal Empire but the Great Mughal, the Emperor, is far away in the north. Bengal, where we are, is administered by the Nawab of Murshidabad, up-river from here. The Company pays for the Nawab's patronage and also allows itself to be taxed by some of his nobles. It's been a profitable relationship but it could change.'

He closed his eyes and shook his head at his thoughts. I waited for him to continue. He sipped his coffee again, cleared his throat.

'The Nawab is an old man and has no male heir. He has designated his grandson as his successor. That is unfortunate, very unfortunate.'

He looked at me for a long time, then he nodded to himself. 'His grandson, Murza Muhammad, also known as Siraj-ud-daulah, is a dissolute, self-willed, tyrant. He believes that we are depriving him of what is rightfully his. We have no doubt that, at the very first opportunity, he will attack Calcutta and try to usurp it.' He closed his eyes for a moment, then continued, 'And Johnny, he will succeed. He has a vast army: foot soldiers, cavalry, elephants, cannon …' He let his voice trail away.

I didn't know what to say. He had painted a horrible picture, as if Calcutta was sitting on quicksands, poised to sink at the whim of a despot.

Jakob Arrakiel reached across and touched my arm reassuringly. 'It won't happen today, John, or tomorrow. But the old Nawab is very infirm. And so, Johnny, please do not make heavy investments in the future. Be prepared, as we are, to leave at short notice. This is a very perilous time in a very unsafe part of the land.'

I was shaken. I let the air out of my lungs, slowly. Suddenly my whole life had become uncertain again and I had no one to advise me. I missed Canker. What would I tell Ann? Where could we go? Just as I had collected my thoughts that night, and Ann and I were alone, she told me something that turned my anxiety to rage.

She said, 'This afternoon, just when their ayahs had come and my little ones were leaving, I had an unexpected visitor. Herr Karl von Erfurt walked over, smiling his icy smile. He said, "*Guten morgen, Frau Yale-Lynsdale. You are teaching zem ze nursery rhymes, no?*" I said I was. He nodded as if he approved. Then he continued … and I'll not imitate his accent …. "Nursery rhymes are, often, satirical verses expressing the sentiments of the common people which they cannot articulate openly." He spoke every word, making an effort to pronounce them clearly and distinctly. Then he said, "You will, I am sure teach these little ones:

Rock a-bye baby, on the tree top,
When the wind blows, the cradle will rock.

When the bough bends, the cradle will fall.
Down will come baby, cradle and all.

It is a charming bit of nonsense, is it not? Or don't you think so, Mrs Yale-Lynsdale? I wonder what Herr Lynsdale thinks of it?"'

My heart began to race: they had found me. The long arm of the Hanoverians had reached out across the ocean and the years and found me. Their spite had sent me out of England, small minded prejudices had alienated us from Madras; now both Ann and I would be targeted in Calcutta. I sat down and expressed my fears to Ann, my rage growing as I spoke.

'They are vicious, Ann. They murdered my mother and grandfather.'

She touched my hand, 'What do you want to do, Johnny?'

'Fight. I'm tired of running away. I want to stay and fight them, even though the whole colony is under threat.' I told her what Jakob Arrakiel had said.

Ann listened to me without saying a word. There was the same calm, cold, expression on her face that she had had when she justified ordering the Nairs to slaughter the pirates. And, once again, it disturbed me. At that time, however, I didn't realise how deeply it had disturbed her too.

Jock Adie had left us just after the party so I had no one to turn to. After the conversation with Arrakiel I had stopped planning to establish my own business. Time hung heavy on my hands and Ann was preoccupied, withdrawn and moody.

One morning when she did not join me at breakfast, and I saw her looking at the river, I asked, 'What's worrying you, my love?'

When she turned to me her beautiful green eyes were filled with tears. 'I wonder Johnny … I often wonder … what happened to the corpses of the pirates I had killed?'

I put my arms around her and said, 'They've been …' I recalled the phrase used by Bishnu the Honey-gatherer, '… absorbed by the forest, the Sunderbans.'

'But Johnny, some of them must have had wives and children back home. What has happened to them?' she bit her lip.

'Why do you bother about them, Ann?' I really couldn't appreciate her concern for people she had never even seen or who might not exist.

'Because I'm a woman. Because women are nest-builders as men are hunters. Because we're driven by love as men are driven by ambition. Because that is the way we are and not all the education and training and fads can change that. I feel very hurt when I think of the wives and children, the homes, that I may have destroyed.'

I didn't know what to say. She seemed to be driven by a fierce inner turmoil that could not be eased. She continued, in a hoarse voice, 'And perhaps, one day, when the great tidal bore wave surges down the river, I will see one of the corpses floating by, bloated and putrid … perhaps even the Bhooth … raising a decayed hand at me in accusation.' She shook her head, and shivered. 'Johnny, Johnny … let's get away from this place. I … I can't settle down; I'm not at peace. And I can't face the Hooghly and the poisonous people of the Company. Please …'

For all my love for Ann, we couldn't leave. She seemed to realise that because, after that outburst she calmed down and we didn't mention it again. I spoke to Saral again and he said that they had two cottages on their estate and we could move in any time we wanted to. I kept that offer from Ann because she seemed to have enough on her mind and I was busy studying the complexities of the indigo trade.

Then, one morning, just as the boatmen started shouting their warning that the bore wave had begun to rush up the Hooghly, Ann screamed. I dropped my quill and rushed to the veranda. She was standing, her arm raised, pointing at the Hooghly, shivering. uncontrollably. Her eyes were wide open in fear and she mumbled, 'He's there! He's come! He's there in the river …'

Rushes came rocketing out of the house. He stared at the river, went stiff, the hairs on his back stood erect, a low growl issued from his throat.

I saw what they were looking at. I said, 'It's only a bleached tree-trunk, with two roots and two branches, Ann. It's been carried by the bore.'

Her shivering subsided, but her body was bathed in a cold sweat. I realised that Ann was reliving the time she'd commanded the Nairs to kill the pirates; and the horror that followed afterwards when the Bhooth attacked us. In the days that followed, I wondered if our Bengali servants had seen her distress and gossiped about it.

Or was it just a coincidence when, a few days later, Samson announced, 'Count Viktor Pavlovitch wishes to meet you, sir. I have shown him into the veranda.'

The count had left a little before the party saying that he had some work to attend to. Now he had reappeared, as elegant and diplomatic as ever. He said, 'I hope, Mr Yale-Lynsdale I am not being presumptuous but may I ask if you and Madame are entirely happy with your circumstances in Calcutta?'

I didn't think it was any of his business but I said, 'Yes, Count. Thank you.'

He coughed politely and raised his handkerchief to his lips, then smiled and said, 'I am affected by the humid air of Bengal, excuse me.' He tucked away his handkerchief. 'Is there anything, anything at all, that we can provide you and your charming lady? Any comfort, or provisions, or servants … anything at all?'

'No, Count. But it's kind of you to ask …'

He stood up, and so did I, as Ann entered the veranda. He bowed to her, waited till she had sat, then we both resumed our seats. A beautiful, four cabin, budgerow sailed past, flying the flag of one of the private traders. The count waved and a man in the boat waved back. 'That's Louis Major. He's in business with Goldsmith and is on his way to the Himalayas. They have a unique partnership. He spends autumn and winter, as he refers to those months, in the Himalayas, when Goldsmith takes over the southern business. Then, after six months they return. Major's now going up the Ganges to the holy town of Haridwar from where he will board a coach, then a horse and finally a palanquin. It's a strange arrangement, but it seems to work.'

Ann asked. 'He seems to be travelling alone. Does he have a family, Count?'

Pavlovitch coughed politely. 'Yes, madame. He does.' He coughed again 'Two families, I believe.' Then he asked, 'Have you ever been to the Himalayas, Madame? They are more beautiful than the Swiss Alps, I assure you. Which brings me to the real purpose of my visit …' He paused, then said, 'Mr and Mrs Yale-Lynsdale, I have received another offer for your intervention. Are you interested?'

I was about to say 'No!' but Ann raised her hand. 'What is it?'

The count nodded. 'It is a very unusual request.' He cleared his throat. 'There is a small kingdom in the Himalayas called Ranastan. The ruler, the Rana, is plagued by the inhabitants of a valley on the Indian border of his domain which has been a thorn in the side of his family for many generations. If you can relieve him of this irritation, you can have the valley as your own.'

'But then,' said Ann, 'how does he know that we, too, will not be a thorn in his side?' Her voice was cold, precise.

'Madame, this valley is ruled by a religious sisterhood. It is an insult to the Ranas to be defied by women, nuns you might say.'

'Who are these women, these nuns as you call them?' I asked.

'Mr Yale-Lynsdale you have probably never heard of them. They are neither Buddhist, nor Hindu, nor Christian. They call themselves …' he took out a slip of paper from his pocket, looked at it and said, 'the *Meri Magadhalis*.'

The name sounded strangely familiar but I was in no mood to fight women and I said so.

He shook his head. 'Ah, no, Mr Yale-Lynsdale. It involves nothing so violent as war.' He shook his head again. 'No, not at all. The Rana wants to appoint you, that is both of you, as his special Ambassadors to negotiate with the nuns to leave that valley.'

I laughed: it sounded so absurd. 'And what makes the Raja …'

'The Rana …' the Count corrected politely.

'And what makes the Rana think that we would be able to persuade the nuns to leave and hand over their valley to us?'

The count sniffed then smiled. He was obviously embarrassed at what he was about to say. 'The Royal Astrologer and also … also an ancient prophesy. They believe strongly in those things in those remote mountains.'

I thought that was absolute rubbish and was about to say so, when Ann smiled at the count and asked, 'Will you excuse us for a few minutes?'

'Certainly, Madame.' He rose, bowed, and walked to the far end of the veranda, out of earshot.

Ann touched my arm. 'Johnny, didn't you tell your father that you would have a kingdom of your own?'

'Yes, I did.'

'Lucia has challenged me to meet her in the Himalayas. You told your father that you would have a kingdom before he did. And, Johnny, I cannot live looking at the river that might have destroyed both our lives, even though it's very beautiful. And I don't like the Company in Calcutta with its mean-minded prejudices. To say nothing of the Hanoverians and the impending attack by the Nawab. The count's offer seems to have been sent by God.'

I didn't think the Almighty had anything to do with it but when the elegant Russian joined us again I asked, 'What is your proposal, Count?'

He handed me a thick sheet of hand-made paper. I opened it with Ann looking over my shoulder. It bore a heavily embossed coat of arms with two gold dragons as supporters, and the quartered shield holding a trident, a hand-drum, a hooded serpent and a humped bull. I recognised them as the emblems of Lord Siva, the Destroyer of the Hindu Trinity. Intriguingly, however, it was crowned by a conch, the emblem of Lord Vishnu, Preserver of the Trinity. The motto was in the ancient Sanskrit but I managed to decipher it as ***Great Lord of the Mountains.***

Below it, in stylised Roman Script were the words:

From the Throne of His Himalayan Highness
Druk Rana Harihara XV Supreme Pontiff and Protector of
RANASTAN

To the Honourable Mr John Yale-Lynsdale and Madame Ann Lynsdale
Greetings:

As it has come to my attention that your presence in my kingdom has been foretold in our sacred scriptures and confirmed by my court astrologers, I am pleased to offer you the rank of Ambassadors Extraordinary to the Court of Ranastan in the expectation that you will persuade the religious order known as the Meri Magadhalis to vacate the valley known as the Shakti Doon watered by the Nag and Nagina Rivers and under the gaze of the sacred mountain Dhum Ketu.

Should you accept this offer, and should you persuade the Sisterhood to vacate the Valley, then I and my family and all possible descendants hereby renounce all and every title to the said valley in your favour as long as the Sun and Moon are in the sky.

My messenger to convey this commission and this offer is Count Viktor Pavlovitch and he is authorised to make all arrangements, in all comfort and every convenience, to transport you to the Kingdom of Ranastan from where you will be given a royal escort with all ceremonial to convey you to Shakti Doon and, in the unlikely contingency that you wish to return, to convey you back to any place in India in such aforesaid comfort and convenience.

Yours in Eager Anticipation of your Acquiescence
Druk Rana Harihara XV

I looked at the count smiling broadly, 'Is this a joke?'

He shook his head. 'No. It is a genuine proposal.'

'But really, Count, why should these women hand over their kingdom to us?'

'Because it has been foretold that a man with golden hair and a woman with red hair, from the Land of the Dravids are the rightful successors to their domain.' He thought a moment. 'The prophesy also gives other details which you and Madame fulfil.'

Ann asked, 'Such as?'

He smiled and shook his head. 'I am not permitted to tell you because you will be asked by the Prioress if anyone has given any details except the shade of your hair. If such other details have been revealed to you they will disqualify you.'

Something worried me. There was something I should have remembered but it was hovering at the edge of my recollection. I read the *Commission* from the Rana again and, suddenly, I recalled it.

'Have you been to this ...' I looked at the letter again '... this Shakti Doon, Count?'

'Yes, Mr Yale-Lynsdale, I have.'

'Tell me: does it have thermal springs?'

'It does.'

'Is the valley moated by a deep gorge. And beyond the gorge do thousand-foot high cliffs rise from which huge birds fly, quartering the sky?'

He frowned and was silent for a while, his eyes downcast, deep in thought. Then he said, 'Yes, there are high cliffs in which Lammergeyers nest. Have you been there, sir?'

My heart was beating fast. 'Is it a fact that snow never falls in the valley though it settles on the glaciers that rise to a strange, smoking mountain? And that the farmers in the valley have black water buffaloes and grow crops of rice, wheat, barley. And fruit: apples, pears, plums, peaches, apricots; and grapes trailed on trellises behind every home.' My voice was speeding up with an excitement I could not control. The count and Ann were staring at me.

The count sprang to his feet. 'Mr Yale Lynsdale, you *have* been there!'

I had just one more question. 'Is the entrance to the valley concealed by a grove of wild alder?'

The count dabbed his forehead with his silk handkerchief. His voice quavered when he answered. 'The entrance to the valley is through a very narrow, river-wrought, defile. It is almost a cave with a river gushing at the bottom of it. It lies behind a wood of wild alder.' He took a deep breath and then, in a hoarse voice, said, 'It is known as the *Sangali La*.'

I looked up at Ann. She had a strange look of elation, almost of triumph, and her face seemed to be glowing with an inner light.

I answered his question. 'No, Count Viktor, I have not been there but …' I turned to Ann 'if you agree, my love, we shall accept the Rana's offer and discover this valley for ourselves.' Her emerald eyes were bright with unshed tears. She nodded.

When he had left and I had time to myself, I began to have second thoughts about us having accepted this strange proposal. It sounded so unreal. Besides, things had fallen into place too adroitly: Ann's sudden fear of a floating branch; the arrival of the count with his proposal which so closely matched the repetitive dream I had described to Ann; the fact that, once again, we could put the threat of the Hanoverians behind us.

In the early hours of the morning I was woken by the chuckle of a nightjar. The little owl must have been sitting on a tree just outside our bedroom, I felt that Ann, too, was awake because her breathing did not have the deep rhythm of sleep.

'Ann?' I called, softly.

'Yes.'

The question formed in my mind even before I was aware of it. 'Tell me, truthfully, did that floating branch really scare you so badly?'

'Truthfully? No it didn't.'

'And did you have anything to do with the appearance of the count, and his proposal, at that time?'

There was no sleep in her voice when she replied. 'Truthfully? The count's proposal is real. Tell me, truthfully, Johnny, do you really feel that we should stay on in Calcutta? Is that what your manly pride demands?'

Was it my pride alone that demanded we should not leave Calcutta? I wasn't sure.

'And Johnny, are those memories of the valley your own, or did we create them and then, because they were so attractive, you made them your own?'

I said, 'I don't know what you mean.'

'I mean what Jesus meant, Johnny. He said, "*If you have faith even as small as a grain of mustard seed and you say to a mountain 'Go there!' it will go. Nothing is impossible.*" Don't you see? You with your black fire, and I because I love you beyond reason, have created our own reality, somewhere in the high Himalayas. Or, perhaps, of all the possible realities that there can be, this is the one that has appeared to us when we need it most.' She must have seen the bewildered look on my face, because she stroked my hair and said, 'Very often, women have to find the reality beyond truth. They have to create the memories and dreams of those they love.' She pulled me into her arms and whispered 'Come, my wonderful husband, let's build new memories; let's dream together.'

And so, together, we began our journey into a dream.

CODA

Caution. Don't start reading this if you have a tired or lazy mind. It might overburden you. It's a trip to the fringes of modern thought: a little beyond orthodox science but not quite as far as fantasy. Should you find the going too tough, abandon it. It is not part of the narrative though it does add to its immediacy. We start by repeating some questions we have been asked about ***The Lynsdale Raj.***

Did John and Ann find their dream valley in the Himalayas, and live happily ever after? What happened to Lucia and her love child? How did the great revolutions that swept the subcontinent in the next three centuries affect the fortunes of the Lynsdales and the Lynsdale Raj? Why have we called It *The Lynsdale Raj* in spite of the fact that it ends before John and Ann reach their dream valley?

We'll answer the last question first because it's the easiest.

It's called *The Lynsdale Raj* because John's dream of a wonderful kingdom in the mountains keeps driving him all through his life. It is responsible for much of what he does: his voyage to India, his determination to know as much as he can about the country, his feeling that he belongs to this land, even his decision to marry the India-born Ann in spite of the inevitable ostracism by his fellow Brits. John Lynsdale's dream moulds and governs his life. It is his Raj.

That, however, is as far as we can go.

We can't answer the other questions just yet. Since no one we know has lived 'Happily ever after' we can presume that John and Ann did not. In all likelihood, however, they came as close to it as possible, given the strange nature of the valley and the hint dropped in the title of the pass that led to it. But right now, we can't be sure. The problem is that once characters have been created they take on a life of their own, in their separate reality. This is where our reasoning becomes a little abstruse, a bit complex.

Scientists say that a new reality is created whenever we make a decision. All decisions can be broken down into two alternatives, which is what a computer programmer does. If you come to a fork in a road, you have to decide whether you will take the right fork or the left. Regardless of your choice, however, at that point two realities are created. In one reality you have taken the right fork, in the other you've gone left. Now there are two of you: one in the right reality and the other in the left. Under this theory, there are countless realities being created every moment.

This thought is mind-boggling. But another one is simpler and far more attractive.

The other theory is that if you want something really badly, you can have it. You can transport yourself into the reality where such a thing exists. It is like a person seeing a piece of land, visualising his dream house on it, and then building it. This is, probably, how miracles happen. Everyone present, including the miracle-worker, wants the miracle so badly that they move themselves into the reality where it happens. Creativity is the urge to give a nudge to reality and then describe what that impetus has done. It's like kicking a stone downhill and gazing, awestruck, at the avalanche it creates! So if John and Ann really wanted their dream valley, they would move into the reality where they have willed it to exist. But then, if Lucia also wanted John to acknowledge their son badly enough she, too, would move into the reality where that happens.

We won't wander further into that field because the concept of interlocking and interacting realities is far too convoluted.

We shall stick to the idea that we have not created John and Ann and Lucia and *The Lynsdale Raj.* We have merely wished that they existed and the creative process started. On a visit to Malaya's Sarawak we learnt about the Brookes: the, so-called, White Rajas. Their dynasty was started by an East India Company officer who brought law and order to a wild and chaotic region filled with warring tribes. We asked ourselves, then, 'Could such a thing have happened in India?' That's when the idea of the Lynsdales was born and, as a natural process of that seed-thought, the book took root in our minds, grew as we survived a furious storm at sea, experienced the joys and abrasions of life in a sequestered naval community, travelled to Bath, London, Cape Town, Madras and Calcutta before Madras and Calcutta acquired their new, politically correct, names. Then, when we were gravid with the book, and its time had come, we delivered it.

There are, consequently, two distinct aspects of creativity. The first is when people move into the reality of their choice, and live in it, as John and Ann did. The other is the artistic phase, the onlookers' segment featuring those people who merely observe such new realities as outsiders looking in: as we have done.

But Einstein said that the very process of looking at reality, changes it: the observer becomes part of the observed. That, we believe, is the true nature of the feedback of creativity. Observation tests reality. Comparatively few realities wished into existence by mankind are stable and so they collapse at the first gust of logic. Those that remain, however, tend to grow and take on a life of their own. Such created realities have leitmotifs like recurring dreams, portraits, red hair and the allure of small hands. They are neither coincidences nor deja vu but glimpses of the scaffolding around which these realities stabilise. When they do, and have become self-perpetuating, they come knocking at the doors of perception of their creator, demanding admission. As a famous sculptor reputedly said about his masterpiece, 'I saw it locked up in the stone and so I merely chipped away to set it free!'

When that happens, we shall invite you to join us again.

Hugh & Colleen Gantzer